THE SEEKER'S COMPASS

A NOVEL BY

JOHN DARR

BOOK TWO

Copyright © 2016 John Darr Books

All rights reserved.

ISBN-13: 978-0-9909740-9-3

I would like to dedicate this second novel of the
series to all my friends who listened to my questions,
read early drafts, and provided creative solutions.

Table of Contents

THE SEEKER'S COMPASS

CHAPTER ONE
GRIM GUARDS

Trevor Deriba's First Death happened at age fifteen. Now he was one of the UnDead, serving as a low-level courier in the Afterworld. He began to wonder if he would experience Second Death soon. The Grim Guards were storming his rebel hideout, no doubt, with orders to kill him and his visitor.

Sitting across from Trevor, the Alliance representative, a mortal who made the dangerous journey to the Afterworld, glared at him in obvious distrust.

As a leader among the rebels, Trevor managed to earn their respect despite his appearance, which was that of a kid. Whatever your age and the way you looked at your First Death was the way you remained in the Afterworld.

However, the mortal didn't seem to understand that point. The twitchy man winced at the sudden shouts and booms of distant fighting. "Are we safe?"

"No," the third member of the meeting said. He was an older rebel, a Spire Guardian from the Central Archives. "The Grim Guards are working their way here." Rankled at the mortal's attitude, he made a show of respectfully waiting for Trevor's orders.

Trevor gave his mentor a curt nod. "We should go. Lead the way."

The Guardian moved in the quick, fluid steps of a trained fighter, gripping the Alliance man by the arm and hustling him to the door.

The Alliance visitor regained some of his earlier arrogance as he yanked his arm free and whirled on Trevor. "How did they know about our meeting?"

"It wasn't me," Trevor hissed in annoyance. "Someone on your side sold us out to the Grim Reaper."

"But… but…" The man's sputtering was cut short when the Guardian opened the door to reveal a squad of grim-faced rebels. They snapped to attention. Each had their blades activated. Trevor slipped past his visitor and into the corridor, allowing the Guardian and his men to form a protective circle around him.

A sudden shout of pain echoed through the hallways. It abruptly ended. An eerie silence settled on the base.

"Where are we going?" the Alliance man asked with a shaky and too loud voice.

All the rebels glared at him.

Trevor sighed and said in a hushed tone, "We're headed to the portal chamber to send you back." Secretly, however, he began to fear they wouldn't make it that far.

His doubts were proven out when his group rounded a corner to find two Reapers, a man and a woman, blocking the hallway. They wore the signature, flowing blood-red robes of the Grim Reaper's inner circle: the Kin.

Both had the same dark features and curly, black hair. Trevor recognized them from the Alliance's intel. Fabian and Thera Rasmussen. Siblings. And deadly adversaries, if the blood on their blades were any indication. The doorway to the portal chamber was just beyond the Reapers.

Trevor had never seen a real Reaper in person. As an archivist and courier, he didn't associate with such beings who roamed the mortal realm, reaping souls. And the Reapers, in turn, showed open disdain for the work of the archivists. They shared a mutual distrust that went back eons.

Naturally, there were exceptions, but most rebels from the Grim Reaper's side chose to fall back to the mortal realm. Only within the human-Fallen Alliance did rebels from both groups work together in true harmony. That made this failed meeting all the sadder for Trevor.

Thera tilted her narrow chin upward. When she spoke, her smug voice vibrated the walls. "Heretics and a mortal." Her lip twisted in disgust as she added, "Pathetic."

"Prepare to die," Fabian announced as he brandished his Reaper's blades.

Trevor activated his blades. Like all the others', his were gleaming, double-sided, fifteen-inch weapons with flowing Angel script covering every surface.

When Trevor prepared to defend himself, the Guardian pressed his arm down. "You have to get out."

"I want to stay and fight."

The man gave his shaggy, red head one violent shake. "You're more important than any of us. You heard the Elder."

Trevor realized, for the first time, his friends expected him to cross to the mortal world to escape. He deactivated his blades and huddled with the Alliance visitor. The Guardian faced the Reapers, holding up his own blades, and shouting a challenge. The others in his group joined in as they rushed forward.

The Reapers were fierce, enhancing the use of their own blades with spells. Thera sliced a rebel across the abdomen. He screamed as the hot flames consumed his body in seconds. Fabian plunged his blade through the heart of a second rebel whose body was also instantly consumed by white-hot flames.

But the remaining rebels fought on with conviction and eventually forced the siblings back, clearing the way for Trevor and the Alliance man to reach the door.

"Go!" Trevor's mentor shouted.

At that moment, darkness and cold swept through the corridor as three tall figures in black robes rounded the far corner. Everyone, including the Reapers, froze. The Grim Guards approached the melee.

Their bone-white skull masks hid their faces, except for the glowing-red eye slits. They carried seven-foot long, wooden poles with jet-black scythes on the ends. The edges of the weapons glowed a sickly, green color.

One Grim Guard already had his weapon in motion, sending it whirling through the air. The weapon slipped in and out of sight, making it hard to follow. That's why Trevor and the other rebels were totally unprepared when the scythe reappeared right in front of the startled Alliance man, severing his head with a clean swipe.

Since he was a mortal in the Afterworld, his body didn't erupt into white-hot flames. Instead, it, and the now free head, dropped onto the polished floor amid an expanding pool of blood collecting at Trevor's feet. The attack was so swift, he never had a chance to react.

The Grim Guard summoned its scythe back to his hand. The blood that stained the weapon's blade sizzled, sickening Trevor.

The lead Guardian gripped Trevor's forearm and pointed at the door. "Go, now. Deliverer's speed to you, my young friend."

"May the Deliverer quicken your steps," Trevor replied. His hands shook, but he managed to type in the code before the door whooshed open. His anger boiled when his mentor shoved him into the portal room. One final glance as the door closed showed something that would stay with Trevor for a long time: his mentor placing protective wards over the opening.

His body ached with the knowledge that his friends would die in their efforts to protect him. *It wasn't fair*, he fumed, but he kept quiet. He had to stick to the hasty plan.

The portal dominated the center of the space. A few feet away stood the dialing pedestal. It had a simple stone base that flared at the bottom and a circular, flat surface on top. The Angel script symbols were etched into the surface.

He rushed to the pedestal and pressed the combination for the mortal realm. Several matching symbols on the portal flared, casting an eerie glow. A small hole appeared at the very center and expanded outwards to the edges. The opening reached its full size, revealing a well-lit, cavernous room on the other side.

A horrible screech came from the door, and Trevor spared a fleeting glance. A scythe sliced through the right side of the door, followed by a second one on the left. The metal continued to emit the ear-splitting screeches as both scythes cut, moving toward each other.

Using a small, watch-like device on his wrist, Trevor beamed his courier code through the portal just as the door behind him was ripped away. Corridor light flooded the room. The Grim Guards had to stoop to enter, but they were quick. Both charged Trevor, their lethal scythes already slicing through the air in order to decapitate as well as disembowel him.

Trevor dived through the portal and into the mortal world. He rolled to his feet inside a subterranean chamber. Against the far wall was an observation room and guard station. At the center of the space was the portal. Thick, plexiglass walls were erected around this precious device.

The only way out of the enclosure was the open doorway where the two guards stood. Their mortal guns were raised because of his unorthodox entry.

Before they could question him, Trevor felt the hair rising on the back of his neck.

"Look out!" He shot forward between the guards just as he heard the distinct sound of a scythe choosing through the air.

The guards began firing on the Grim Reaper's minions instead of heeding his warning. The scythe sliced through the abdomen of one guard, cutting the unfortunate man in half. His fellow guard blanched at the sight as he fumbled before hitting the button that sealed the inner chamber.

As soon as the door swung close, the Grim Guards went into a frenzy, plowing into the glass partition repeatedly. More security rushed into the outer room, weapons drawn and ready, but all were unsure what to do.

When cracks began appearing in the plexiglass, an electrical current was sent through the enclosed chamber. It was a practiced precaution used to dissipate magical and supernatural energy. In response, the Grim Guards released unearthly screeches of anger, freezing everyone in the basement.

Trevor had been warned, but it took him a few horrible moments to force his immobile muscles into action. He inched around the guards and toward the exit. The electrical discharges began to work, forcing the Grim Guards toward the portal's opening. Eventually, with one last, bone chilling howl, they soared back through to the Afterworld.

Relieved, Trevor slipped out of the nearest door. He ducked into an alcove and shed his Afterworld robes. Underneath, he wore a stolen guard's uniform.

With his job as courier, he managed to prepare rather well for this worst case scenario. He used a stolen security key card to open a maintenance hatch. Metal rungs were bolted to the inner wall of the narrow passageway. Making sure no one spotted him, Trevor clambered inside and started his long climb.

Several nerve-wracking minutes later, he pushed open the exit grate and thankfully inhaled the rich, hot air of the mortal world. It was night here. *Good*, he thought. That would help in his escape. In the distance, the alarms still blared from the unremarkable building that hid the portal.

A shudder hit Trevor. *Grim Guards. Gods below!* Even worse, his alias as a courier was blown. His former master would know he had defected and certainly hunt him down. He calmed his racing thoughts as he summoned all of his courage.

But he couldn't prevent the pang of regret that overcame him. *Was his mentor even alive? Would he ever see the Elder again?* He shook his head, striving to push aside the distracting thoughts in order to focus on his current situation. He couldn't go to the Alliance. They had a mole in their midst.

No, he needed another way back home. Trevor unhooked an amulet from the chain around his neck and broke it open. Inside was a small, slightly curved, rectangular piece of metal. He pressed it to his temple, where it remained. With a tap on the device's notch, he activated it, washing the side of his head in a soft glow while transmitting mission information directly into his mind.

What it revealed shocked Trevor. His way back to the Afterworld was located in a small town in Georgia, several states away. Trevor detached the device and dropped it onto the ground where it sparked and turned to slag within seconds.

He moved away from the facility and soon reached a lonely stretch of highway. Keeping to the high grass and scrubs, Trevor plodded along on a path parallel to the road. The going was rough, but his mind stayed focused on replaying the final, shocking information downloaded from the device.

It was about a boy, who, at age thirteen, had put on a Protector's Ring and fought the Grim Reaper. *Unbelievable!* Of course, every rebel was aware of the Elder's prophecies, which stoked the fires of rebellion against the evil Rulers of the Afterworld.

But to have a thirteen-year-old… Trevor stopped himself. People often doubted him because of his age. He wouldn't do the same to someone else. *Still, the kid must be something special.*

With that encouraging thought in mind, Trevor set out to find this amazing boy.

CHAPTER TWO
HORUS

Jonah Blackstone didn't feel special at the moment. It wasn't his fault he couldn't activate a magical shield bracelet. He wasn't a mage or a wizard. He was a half-Reaper, darn it!

Or rather, he couldn't activate the bracelet on command. Instead, he'd triggered it by accident, creating a protective bubble around himself. The natural sounds were dulled and his view of the trees became blurred and wavy.

He glanced at the connected polished pieces of darkened wood that made up the bracelet, thinking. He had activated it by accident. No one else had to know that. Not even his best friend, Mike Littleton, and his cousin, Robert Hightower, who were both watching Robert's twin sister Lynn and their best friend Wick work with him.

They'd come to this barren field on the outskirts of Mount Vernon so he could practice his abilities, a subject Lynn had grown adamant about over the last week.

She was two years older than Jonah, lanky, and sported long, thin braids that fell just below the shoulders of her ever-present sports-themed t-shirt. Today, Jonah's cousin had a baseball bat slung over her left shoulder while tossing a baseball in her right hand.

Wick, the maker of the magical bracelet, stood beside Lynn in his trademark fatigue pants, muscle shirt, and unlaced combat boots despite the early summer temperatures.

He shook his head, causing his short dreads to wobble. "Drop the shield."

"What are you talking about?" Jonah hoped his voice sounded innocent, but doubted he succeeded.

"Don't try it, Padawan. As a budding mage, I can see the distortions. You're supposed to activate the shield before the baseball hits you."

"Duh!" Jonah waved his arms, his voice coming out close behind the magical barrier that surrounded him. "That's what I did."

Lynn let the heavy end of the bat drop to the ground in frustration. "That's not what he meant, and you know it."

Jonah scowled, concentrated, and deactivated the shield. Releasing the magic was easier than summoning it, particularly because he knew how badly it hurt when one of Lynn's line drives hit him. That was more distraction than he needed.

He pointed at the pile of baseballs, thinking it a little unfair. "Why use baseballs?"

"Motivation." Lynn readied herself, bat raised and ball ready to toss and hit.

Wick offered him an encouraging nod. "Remember what you've learned, young one. Magic is using controlled thoughts to produce a result. Don't try to activate the shield. Just see it already around you."

Lynn let out an exasperated breath. "Enough with the Yoda."

"That was Obi-Wan." Wick pulled a mock hurt expression.

"Whatever." Lynn didn't wait any longer. She tossed the ball up, reared back with the bat, and hit it.

The baseball streaked through the air and right for Jonah's chest. He had less than a second to try and activate the shield. Of course, it didn't work. At the last minute, he contorted his body so the ball whizzed by his abdomen.

"You're supposed to activate the shield." Wick sounded disappointed.

Mike's oatmeal complexion twisted into a frown, but Robert doubled over in laughter. Normally Lynn would punch her twin brother to stop him from being silly, but today she allowed it. Jonah suspected she meant for Robert's laughter to embarrass him, and it worked. His face warmed.

Lynn smacked two more balls in rapid fire succession at Jonah.

Caught by surprise, Jonah didn't have time to even focus his mind. He phased, allowing the balls to pass through where he'd been standing. The process had been so sudden that he didn't even visualize a destination. That's how phasing, his power to move from one place to another in the blink of an eye, worked.

He would envision his destination, someplace he'd either visited or seen at least once. And with a mental nudge, the ripples would play along his body and he would phase. Marcus, his godfather, explained that when he phased, Jonah passed through the Afterworld, the domain of the Undead, for a split second before reappearing at his destination.

Real Reapers used the power to travel around the world, reaping souls. Fallen Reapers like Marcus retained the power when they returned to the mortal realm. The key was having a destination. Only this time, Jonah didn't have one and when the world burst into existence around him, Jonah stood in the same spot.

Wick let out a whoop of approval. "That was wikid cool! Do it again."

"Wick!" Lynn shoved him. "He's supposed to be learning to activate the shield, not phase on one spot."

Despite her objection, Jonah noted that Lynn looked impressed. The problem was Jonah didn't know if he could repeat the unique phase either. It had been sudden, instinct. Maybe Lynn had a point and he needed more practice.

It also occurred to Jonah that the mental nudge to phase was an act of will he had learn to do on command. So why couldn't he activate the shield bracelet the same way?

He dropped his hands to his side, accepting the inevitable, and shook his arms as if releasing pent-up energy. Sweat beaded his forehead from the late June sun. "Okay. I'm ready."

"It's about time." Lynn frowned, tossed the next ball into the air, and hit it straight at Jonah.

He stood his ground and sent the act of will into the bracelet. To his surprise, he felt the tingle along his arms as the shield activated. As soon as the ball impacted the barrier, it collapsed with a pop and the ball continued forward to thump harmlessly against Jonah's chest.

Before he could congratulate himself on at least a partial success, a second baseball smacked him in the sternum. Jonah collapsed to the ground, clutching his mid-section.

Mike was at his side in a second, kneeling down and shaking Jonah's shoulder. "Are you alright?"

"No." Jonah raised his voice. "Lynn broke something."

"Your rib?"

Jonah peaked behind Mike. "Well, no. But don't tell Lynn, okay?" He winked at his buddy.

Mike frowned and shoved the side of Jonah's head. "I thought you were really hurt."

Lynn stood over Jonah. "Don't worry, Mike. I can fix that." She pressed her bat into Jonah's chest.

"Lynn." He struggled, but she had the advantage. Jonah held up the bracelet. "Activate. Activate!"

"Too late." Wick stepped into view with Robert right behind.

"Pathetic." Lynn removed the bat. "You're supposed to be learning to use your powers, Jonah."

"I practice my phasing."

"Not good enough."

Jonah pushed himself up on his elbows. "You sound like Marcus."

Wick and Robert backed away, giving Lynn space to hit him.

She arched an eyebrow at Jonah. "Your godfather's right. Maybe I should call him."

"No, don't do that. I'll get better."

Lynn shook her head. "I don't know. You act like you want to be normal, and you know that's not possible."

Mike leapt to his feet. "What's wrong with being normal?" His outburst surprised everyone.

Lynn blinked once, and the irritation sharpening her edges flashed away. She reached for Mike, who wore a pained reaction, but he whirled and stalked away.

Jonah rolled to his feet to follow his buddy. When Robert blocked him, Jonah turned on his cousin. "Let me go."

Robert held on. "Give him some space, little cousin." He glanced at Lynn. "What gives? You do sound a bit like Marcus." He raised his hands. "Just sayin'." When Lynn didn't punch him, Robert leaned closer. "You sensed something's gonna happen?"

Lynn looked off over the field, avoiding their gazes. "Not really, but it's been quiet over the school year. I don't think that's gonna last much longer; that's all."

"Yeah, right." Robert rubbed his chin while frowning at his sister.

A loud horn interrupted the conversation as Wick's brother pulled his blue pickup to the edge of the field.

Lynn moved off to collect the baseballs. Robert hesitated until Wick pulled him toward their bags.

Jonah was torn between seeing what was up with Mike and helping Lynn gather the scattered baseballs. He decided on the latter. By the time they finished and reached the pickup, Wick had hopped inside the truck with his brother. Mike reclined in the truck's bed, head down, looking low of spirit. Robert was across from him talking to Wick through the cab's little rear window.

After tossing the bag of balls in the back, Lynn climbed in and began toying with her Reaper blades, activating and deactivating them with a familiar swish.

Jonah sat beside Mike. As they started home, he tapped Mike on the leg with the back of a fist. "What's wrong?"

Mike worked his jaw while staring at the dandelion clutched in his hands. "It's all of you."

Lynn glanced up at the remark. "What about us?"

"Everyone has a power, except me. I just work the database for the Summit blog."

Lynn nudged Mike's foot with her own. "That's a big help to us."

"She's right," Jonah added.

Mike shook his head. "You're just trying to be nice. I can't do anything special, and you know it." Mike held up a hand to stop Jonah's protest. "Lynn can use real Reaper blades. Wick can do magic, and Robert helps him." Mike glanced at Jonah. "And then there's you."

Jonah didn't bother to argue because Mike made a good point. Wick's ability with magic had grown stronger. Lynn was superb with the Reaper blades, and she had a strong intuition about things, hence Robert's earlier questions. And Jonah suspected Robert had some abilities that he hadn't revealed yet.

The task of Summit database keeper belonged to Mike. Jonah truly didn't think of the job as busy work. Mike was a marvel at organizing things as well as remembering dates, topics, and subjects.

Plus, Jonah delighted in having his best friend a member of the club. Robert, Lynn, and Wick remained a close trio, leaving Jonah feeling like an outsider. As a result, he grew weary of tagging along behind them and wanted to form his own group of friends. Mike was a logical choice to include in his club.

Wick leaned through the cab's window. "Don't worry about it, Mike. Everyone has a Haru in them. You need to find your purpose, that's all."

The others nodded, but Jonah scrunched up his face. "Haru? You mean hero?"

"No," Mike answered. "He means Haru, or Horus. The source of all hero myths."

Wick gave Mike a thumbs up.

Jonah leaned his head against the side of the truck bed, allowing the wind to buffet his face. He had heard the Horus stories before. As always happened, odd moments like this reminded Jonah of the wealth of information his mom and dad had taught him.

"You think so?" Mike asked Wick.

"Yeah, I do."

"You're part of the Mount Vernon Social Club for a reason," Robert seconded.

Mike's slouched posture straightened. A wan smile touched his lips as he raised the dandelion. The wind whipped the puffy white seed heads away, leaving Mike holding the bare stem.

He tossed it over the side and then elbowed Jonah. "It was easy for you."

"What do you mean?"

Mike smiled. "You're the one who beat the Grim Reaper and wore a Protector's ring. You're already a hero, Jonah."

"No, I'm not." Jonah crossed his arms. Yeah, he had faced the Grim Reaper and saved his friend's lives, including his godfather's. But Jonah still hated to be the center of attention. And being a hero demanded that he become the focus for everyone, including his enemies.

He was so caught up in his own worries that he didn't notice Lynn's gaze shifting to the cars behind them until her body and expression tensed. "Lynn? What's wrong?"

She met Jonah's curious gaze. "We're being followed."

CHAPTER THREE
THE TAIL

Jonah was speechless, forcing Lynn to repeat herself. "I said we're being followed." She tilted her head to the side. "Three cars back."

"How can you tell?" Robert leaned forward to see around his sister.

Lynn pushed him. "Don't everyone look. Geesh. Whenever there's not a car between us, they fall back."

Wick brightened despite the seriousness of the situation. "Should we check? There's a stop light coming up after we reach the four-lane section."

Lynn nodded, pulled her cell phone out, and opened the photo app. She tossed the phone to Jonah. Sure enough, the traffic grew thicker as the group entered the city proper of Mount Vernon and the two lanes switched to four.

Wick, who had a better vantage considering he faced the rear, whispered to Jonah, "There's a semi truck in the lane beside the target car."

Jonah nodded, glanced behind at the semi, and fixed a mental image of the truck in his mind.

"Are you sure it's a good idea?" Mike interrupted.

"It'll be cool." Jonah crouched low, making sure his head wasn't visible to cars around them. As soon as the traffic slowed and stopped, Jonah began to rise from his crouch. Before his head would have come into view of other motorists, he disappeared.

Another thing about phasing is that any motion you start before the phase continues on the other side. So when Jonah reappeared next to the overheated grill of the semi, he also continued the movement of raising from his crouch.

The phase had been perfect. From this angle, he could see through the side back window of the dark government sedan following them. Jonah raised the phone and snapped two quick pictures of the man in the driver's seat.

The stranger spoke into a radio mic while scanning the area. A chill traveled down Jonah's spine at the same moment it occurred to him the man suspected he wasn't in the back of Wick's truck anymore.

Jonah phased just as the guy twisted in his direction, and reappeared right behind the car. He tried to snap a picture of the license plate but was too close and couldn't get the phone to focus.

He reared back, smacking into the bumper of the car behind.

Come on. Jonah's hands shook, but he snapped a photo of the plate just as the traffic moved. He phased and returned to the bed of the pickup. The sudden forward motion of the truck pitched him sideways.

Lynn reached out to steady him. "Did you get it?"

"Yeah." Jonah handed over the phone. "It's a government car."

Lynn showed Robert the image. "Can your girlfriend's dad tell us which agency?"

"Aw Lynn." Robert frowned and ran a hand over his picky afro "I'd have to listen to all his conspiracy theories."

"Hey Bobby," Wick interrupted, "think about the points you'll score with Jennifer. That outweighs the inconvenience." He leaned out the window to hi-five Robert.

"Cut it, you two." Lynn smirked at Jonah. "There're kids present."

Jonah scowled and crossed his arms.

Mike looked just as pissed. "I've dated and..." His oatmeal complexion darkened in embarrassment.

Wick hooted at that. Lynn gave Mike a shrewd once over.

Robert leaned forward to tap Mike's foot. "Good for you, Mike. That means Jonah's the only one not getting–"

Lynn elbowed her brother but spoke to Wick. "Have your brother take us to the teen center."

Jonah sat in silence as the others went on talking. His thoughts were on the government car, wondering why anyone would follow his group, and fearing all the possible answers.

*

The actual name for the teen center was the Cedar Hill Recreation Center, and it was a renovated old southern mansion that still sported the majestic white columns. If Jonah stood at the central glass doors and faced out, he'd have a commanding view of the hilly surrounding neighborhoods.

The vista didn't draw Jonah's attention as he and the others hopped out of the truck and headed inside. Their destination was the attic, where Lynn edited a teen blog and Robert maintained a website for the center.

Mike seemed much happier as he peppered Lynn with all kinds of insightful questions about upcoming blogs. Jonah listened to the conversation without comment as they mounted the curved central staircase from the atrium to the second floor.

The group halted in front of an old attic door. A black sign with white letters adorned the entrance and said *The Summit*. A second sign below that read *The Mount Vernon Social Club*.

Robert pulled out his key to unlock the door. Instead of opening it, he yanked his hand away from the handle, confused. "It's unlocked."

Wick reached past him to pull open the door and inspect the staircase. "The director comes in sometimes."

"Yeah," Robert admitted, "but she usually tells us ahead of time."

"One way to find out." Wick entered the narrow doorway and started up. Robert exchanged a glance with his sister before following.

Jonah went next, with Lynn and Mike behind him. Within seconds, he knew something was wrong because Robert and Wick had stopped at the top of the stairs that divided the attic into two areas.

Squeezing past Jonah to join her brother, Lynn asked, "What's wrong?"

Robert lowered his voice to a whisper. "Someone's in the attic."

Lynn slipped between him and Wick and up into the attic space. Everyone else followed. Robert was wrong, Jonah discovered. There were two people in the attic.

The first was a tall black guy in tan slacks and a royal blue jacket. He stood with his back to the kids, gazing out the large, multi-paned window. His jacket had *GBI* stylized on the back in big yellow letters.

Lynn positioned herself in front of the rest of the gang. "What are you doing in here?"

The agent turned. "I'm Special Agent Ramsey, of the Georgia Bureau of Investigation." He spoke in a clipped baritone voice as he withdrew a black leather wallet from his jacket and flipped it open to show off a light bronze badge. "We have questions for you."

Lynn examined the ID the longest before focusing on the second guy. He was shorter, olive-skinned, and dressed in a black sport coat, pants, and tie.

Ramsey flipped the wallet closed and motioned to the black-clad guy standing beside him. A small white skull pin glimmered on the man's lapel. "This is a consultant with the department."

The guy's eyes narrowed when he saw Jonah. The quick flare of milky brightness in the pupils was a sure sign of Wraith possession.

As if to underscore that, Jonah's Death Sense gave a painful twinge of warning.

CHAPTER FOUR
GBI

Agent Ramsey's lean mocha face reminded Jonah of a hawk. His steely light-brown eyes seemed to look through a person. Jonah didn't like this agent nor the consultant guy, who caused his Death Sense to throb.

The GBI agent smiled. "The director of this center let me into the office."

Robert yelped and hurried over to the computers with Mike in tow.

This area of the attic, called the Summit, included printers and desks where Jonah's cousins worked on the blog. Everyone watched as Robert checked his servers and Mike typed away at a keyboard. After a while, and a relieved look from Mike, Robert's hunched shoulders relaxed and he gave Lynn a slight nod.

Agent Ramsey took a few steps toward Robert and placed a hand on the computer monitor. "I understand you do a teen blog. That's a noble pastime for young people. But I guess you get that from your father."

"What do you know about our dad?" Lynn asked.

Agent Ramsey turned to her. "You're Lynn Hightower and this is your twin brother Robert. Your parents are James, a local newspaper publisher, and Imma, a hair stylist." Agent Ramsey focused on Wick, "You are–"

"I'm Wick," the young mage proclaimed.

Ramsey raised an eyebrow and said, "Mr. Jean-Baptiste." He continued on to Mike, who had slipped behind the old gun-metal grey editor's desk in the back corner. "You are Michael Littleton." The agent ended with a dramatic show of turning and looking at Jonah. "And you are Jonah Blackstone."

"Yeah, glad you know all our names," Jonah said. He didn't like the agent's strange way of making statements sound like questions, like the man was challenging them.

Ramsey continued to scrutinize Jonah until Lynn stepped between them, arms folded. "You didn't answer my question."

Agent Ramsey took a notepad and pen out of his pocket. "I'm looking into the events that happened here in Mount Vernon last summer. The Bureau believes they may be connected to other crimes around the state." He paused and consulted his pad. "Despite a large amount of damage in the center's atrium, the vandals ignored the other offices and burglarized your space."

"Yeah, and we took a week to clean up the mess," Robert said. He didn't move away from the computers.

Ramsey turned to him. "You replaced all your computer equipment in a short period. The center's director told me she didn't use insurance proceeds for that. How did you manage it on your own?"

"Our parents paid for it," Lynn answered.

The agent smiled. "That information is also easy to verify."

"It was a gift from my dad's old company," Jonah volunteered.

Lynn glared at him, but Jonah didn't think telling obvious lies to a GBI agent was a good idea.

"And the name of this company would be..." Agent Ramsey had his pen poised over his notepad.

"Monarch Associates. They're in Atlanta and Washington, D.C." Jonah didn't look at Lynn. As long as Ramsey focused on this, the agent wouldn't ask more dangerous questions.

"My godfather works for Monarch. When he heard about the damage, he helped. I guess he thought doing a news blog was a noble thing for teenagers to do."

Lynn gave Jonah a thumbs up gesture.

If Agent Ramsey took issue with the implied dig, he didn't show it. "Why would the vandals break into your office and trash it?" he continued. "Were you working on a story that was damaging or embarrassing to someone?"

"No," Robert answered.

"It's also curious the vandals destroyed your mother's sculpture." With his eyes, Agent Ramsey searched every corner of the attic as he walked to the window. He tapped the frame with his pen.

"The Recreation Center replaced the window and frame. It was an egress point. Also interesting, don't you think, considering it's on the third floor?"

No one bothered to answer as Agent Ramsey continued to look around. "The local police were too quick to rule it simple vandalism."

Jonah couldn't resist asking, "Why do you think it's more than that?"

"There are other things that happened in this town at the same time. People found dead."

The goon snorted at that remark, drawing a sharp glare from Agent Ramsey before he continued. "Others complained of being drugged. The owner of a bookstore went missing and her home was destroyed." He closed his notepad and put it in his pocket.

As much as Jonah feared a GBI agent investigating Deyanira's attack on the center, he didn't believe the agent. He stepped forward, ignoring Lynn's warning glance. "Why are you here?"

Agent Ramsey refocused on Jonah like a laser beam. "I told you-"

"If someone stole a ring," Jonah barked at the man, "go find them and leave us alone."

Ramsey's jaw muscles worked as he loomed over Jonah. "Have you seen any strangers lurking around town?"

"You mean besides you?" Robert asked. "No, we haven't."

The consultant roared, breaking his silence. "You're wasting time." He glared at Jonah. "Where's the courier, half-breed?"

Jonah had never heard the term *half-breed*, but the goon's tone left no doubt the name was derogatory.

Jonah met the fool's gaze. "No one was talking to you," he paused before ending with, "…Wraith."

The consultant dropped all pretenses of hiding. His eyes shifted to pale white again, with that unearthly glow. He pulled a scythe from a scabbard attached to his belt. Before Jonah could blink, the wraith hurled it.

Lynn's fast reflexes—and intuition, Jonah suspected—allowed her to activate a blade and knock the weapon away. The scythe embedded itself into the wall beside the attic window. Lynn positioned herself in front of Jonah, and Mike who had come around the computers to stand with them.

Light flared to their left as Wick ignited two balls of supernatural fire.

Robert cursed and called the consultant names while pointing at the scythe. He finished with, "You lost your freakin' mind!"

Agent Ramsey ignored the comment as he stared at Wick's supernatural fire and Lynn's Reaper blades with smug satisfaction.

If Jonah hadn't seen the moment of panic on Ramsey's face, he would have believed the man planned the attack to tip their hands.

Hurried footsteps sounded from the attic stairs. Two adults charged into the room, a Native-American woman and a tall blond man. Jonah recognized the woman. Her name was Mage Trueblood, and she was the wizard who'd helped them fight Deyanira. The other person, a tall, stocky white guy with a mop of blond hair, was unknown to Jonah.

Trueblood's long black hair was done in twin, elaborate braids that fell below her shoulders. She wore a pale grey tunic reminiscent of her heritage, but beneath were jeans and hiking boots. When the accomplished mage raised her hands, magical energy infused her voice with power. "What's going on?"

Ramsey raised an eyebrow and stood taller. "Who are you?"

"I'm a youth counselor, working with the center," Trueblood answered, not missing a beat. "I came to talk to the young man about his blog."

Ramsey glanced between Robert and Trueblood, his eyes narrowed. After a long pause, he slipped a hand inside his jacket. The butt of a standard-issue gun showed, but Ramsey's hand reached beneath that, ready to pull out a different weapon.

Jonah wondered if the man had his own blades.

There were more hurried footsteps and then a second GBI agent pushed his way into the attic. It was the guy from the government car, Jonah noted. He was as tall as agent Ramsey and his black hair was cut neat.

The new agent froze, his pale blue eyes taking in the tableau until Agent Ramsey called out to him, "Harris. Take this fool out of here."

Agent Harris grabbed the Wraith-possessed guy and hustled him out of the attic.

Ramsey held both hands away from his body. "I apologize for my associate."

"Leave," Trueblood ordered.

Anger flashed across Ramsey's face as he assessed the situation. Trueblood never relaxed her stance. Lynn held her blades ready. Wick's green balls of flame showed no signs of fading, and the big blond guy stood ready to launch into action.

The agent relaxed his own posture and his hand moved in a non-threatening way as he pulled a card from his pocket. He strode to the attic stairs and dropped the card on the railing. "I'll have more questions for all of you." With that, he descended the steps.

Robert waited for the click of the attic door closing before yelling, "That guy tried to kill Jonah!" He jabbed a finger at the scythe.

The big blond man yanked the weapon free. Chipped paint and plaster rained down on the floor. "I'll be. A grown man trying to cut up a bunch of kids." The guy stammered, "Sorry. No offense."

Jonah moved from behind Lynn to face the man. "Who are you?"

"Oh, don't mind my bad manners." He extended a beefy hand. "I'm Rexford Montgomery. Everyone calls me Rex," he announced in his booming Southern drawl. "I work with Marcus."

"You're a Fallen Reaper?"

"Yeah, buddy." Rex patted his barrel chest. Then he jumped liked he'd been shocked and offered to shake hands with the others.

"Are you okay?" Trueblood asked Jonah in a calm voice.

"Yeah." Jonah nodded and poked Lynn's arm. "Thanks."

Lynn shrugged and deactivated her blades.

After greeting Rex and Trueblood, Mike said, "We're lucky you showed up."

Rex laughed. "It wasn't luck, young man."

Trueblood frowned at him. "Marcus sent us to warn you about the GBI."

Robert, still agitated by the attack, waved his arms around in frustration. "You're a little late for that."

"Relax, Bobby." Wick made calming motions with his hands. "It's not their fault."

Trueblood nodded, but her expression remained serious. "We'll have a talk with the director about allowing people inside the attic. And we should develop better protection."

Wick brightened at that idea. "I want to help."

Trueblood inclined her head. "That can wait. What did the agent ask?"

"He wanted to know about a courier," Jonah answered.

Mike raised his hand. "Who's this courier and why are the GBI following us?"

Trueblood shifted her gaze to the window. Rex glanced down at his big feet, refusing to meet anyone's gaze.

Jonah knew the answer before the adults responded. "You can't tell us."

"Someone tried to kill Jonah," Lynn shouted, just like her brother had done moments before. "You're not gonna tell him why?"

Rex rubbed the side of his nose with a finger. "It's Alliance Council business."

"Jonah's godfather's on the council," Mike pointed out.

"Yeah," Robert said. "Where is he?"

Trueblood raised her hands and motioned for them to calm down. "Marcus is in an emergency Council meeting at this moment." She crossed her hands behind her back as she came to stand in front of Jonah. "He is asking for permission to tell you everything."

Jonah gulped. He never imagined his godfather would fight to tell him something. Marcus had always been the one to hold back information.

"You can't give us anything?" he urged the mage.

Trueblood exchanged a nervous glance with Rex. "We've lost all contact with our allies in the Afterworld because of a mole inside the Alliance."

Jonah nodded, wondering how much more the adults would reveal. Better to try, he reasoned and asked, "What about this courier guy?"

"He was our Afterworld contact," Trueblood said. "When the Grim Reaper's minions attacked, he fled into the mortal realm to escape."

Robert's jaw dropped. "Wow." He scratched his head. "We call them Grimnions, by the way."

Trueblood didn't bat an eye. Rex chuckled.

Lynn frowned, remaining serious. "They're using the GBI to find the courier?"

"And Wraith-possessed goons," Wick added.

Trueblood nodded. "These agents were corrupted into working for the Grim Reaper."

"Plus," Rex held up a finger to make his point, "we've suspected infiltration of law enforcement. This confirms it."

Jonah could see the unspoken reality on the adults' faces. "The GBI agents already know all about us and the supernatural world, don't they?"

"Yes, they do," Trueblood admitted.

After that, Mage Trueblood and Rex refused to reveal more about the Alliance and the courier. Jonah tried, but the serious mage grew impatient and went off to discuss attic precautions with Wick.

Rex ruffled his shaggy blond hair as he watched Jonah. "We told you, can't say anything else because we don't know anything else. Just wait for your godfather to get here."

Jonah decided he'd go crazy waiting for Marcus to arrive.

Mike, who had been watching Jonah, motioned toward the stairs. "Let's go downstairs and get something to eat or play games."

Jonah agreed, but his intention to clear his mind came to an abrupt end as they descended the main staircase.

Today, Brandon Warner, the Third, stood at the entrance to the east wing. The tall man in the dark grey suit beside the bully had to be Mr. Warner, Jonah decided. The man had the same arrogant look as his son, the chin tilted up, and a knowing frown on his light caramel face.

The sight that troubled Jonah the most was that Brandon's father talked with Agent Ramsey.

CHAPTER FIVE
REAPER'S GIFT

Jonah and Mike were stunned, watching as Mr. Warner, as if he owned the place, pointed out various features of the center to Agent Ramsey and an older gentleman wearing a black suit and shades.

Meanwhile, Brandon, looking bored with the conversation, scanned the atrium and spotted Jonah. He scowled and muttered something, drawing his father's attention. The older Warner's hazel eyes narrowed as he too focused on Jonah.

Within seconds, Agent Ramsey and the man in the shades paused in whatever they'd been saying to look in Jonah's direction. The combined scrutiny caused Jonah's Death Sense to throb.

Mike intervened and pulled him into the café. They found a table in the back corner and out of sight of Agent Ramsey.

Jonah peeked over his buddy's shoulder and toward the atrium. "Why's Brandon's dad talking to the GBI?"

"Hold that thought," Mike replied. He made his way to the food counter and bought them both a strawberry smoothie. He returned and plopped the smoothies on the table before answering Jonah's question.

"That guy in the black suit owns a security company," Mike explained. He took a big slurp of his smoothie. "My guess is they're talking about new security for this place. They upgraded nothing after the break-in last summer."

"I can see that, but why the GBI?"

"Well, it's obvious the security guy has contacts in law enforcement."

That made sense to Jonah, and he nodded. Brandon and his father moved out of the atrium and into the east wing. Only then did an obvious question occur to Jonah and he reached across the table to tap Mike's arm. "Hey. How did you find out this stuff?"

Mike lowered his smoothie and looked away. "Drew told me."

"Drew?" Jonah snorted. "He hangs around with that bully Brandon."

"Jonah." Mike shoved Jonah's hand and then stage-whispered, "You don't understand. Me and Drew grew up together."

"Wait." Jonah lowered his own voice as a group of kids walked by, chattering to each other. "Drew didn't always hang with Brandon?"

"He started that after Brandon's family moved here. Before then, well..." Mike shrugged and crushed his empty smoothie cup in his slender hands.

Jonah worried he had touched a sore spot with Mike. He began to apologize when his cell phone buzzed with a text message from Lynn. Marcus and Omar had arrived. "Time to get some answers." He showed the message to Mike.

*

"Jonah." Omar's deep African-accented greeting filled the attic space. He pulled Jonah into a one-armed hug while ruffling Jonah's picky hair with his other hand. "I swear you're taller each time I see you."

The muscular model-by-day, Alliance member in secret, released Jonah and treated Mike to a vigorous handshake.

Marcus stood beside his partner, watching with a speculative expression.

Jonah noted that his godfather wasn't wearing his usual suit and tie for work, nor did he wear the dressy casual look he and Omar wore for special occasions.

Today, Marcus wore his long Reaper coat, a knee-length black coat with a distinctive Mandarin collar. And on the left chest, the Alliance symbol had been branded into the leather.

Even more unusual, a smile tweaked the corners of his mouth. "Trueblood told me you persisted in finding out what's going on."

Jonah glanced at the mage and felt his face warm. "Sorry about that."

Trueblood graced him with a nod.

Jonah wondered if the mage would complain about him later in private as he turned to his godfather. "How'd the meeting go?"

"Well enough." Marcus stood tall and spoke to the others. "I need to talk with Jonah alone."

Wick, Robert, Mike, and Lynn all protested at the same time.

Marcus waved them silent. "The Council gave me permission to share details with Jonah." Marcus focused on Lynn and raised an eyebrow.

Her mutinous expression morphed at once into understanding. "You need us to clear out?"

"Lynn!" Robert protested.

"He can't tell us," Lynn explained and smiled at Marcus. "My guess is Jonah can tell anyone he likes."

Rex guffawed. "How'd you work that one, Marcus?"

Marcus arched an eyebrow. "I'm a lawyer. As long as Jonah is alone when we talk…"

"He's not bound by the same oath," Rex finished and laughed even louder.

"You never heard me say that," Marcus added with a smile. "And to address Lynn's first question, no, I don't want to inconvenience everyone else." Marcus placed a hand on Jonah's right elbow. "I know a secure place we can talk."

Jonah had a few seconds to prepare himself. The sensation of phasing, when it occurred this time, was harsher and the transition longer than normal.

When the world reappeared, a moment of pure disorientation hit Jonah. He was outside and, judging from the high-angle view of the surrounding suburbs, up in the air. Jonah glanced at his feet to confirm he stood on something solid, a rooftop.

Marcus released his hold and entered a landscaped section of the roof that featured a dome-covered, seven-column portico at the center. Low flames flickered in tapers attached to each column.

Jonah fought down his disorientation and asked, "Where are we?"

Marcus glanced back. "We're on top of the Monarch Associates Building in northern Atlanta."

HQ. "The phase took longer," Jonah observed.

"This building is protected by strong magical wards and spells." Marcus gestured around himself. "The entire roof is covered in a protective shield, but I have a talisman." He pulled a black beaded chain from his long coat. "Being a partner has its privileges."

Marcus turned and mounted the shallow marble steps to the portico. Jonah followed. When he reached the top and moved between the columns of the structure, the sounds of the outside world dropped away.

"Oh." Jonah's jaw dropped.

The portico had a seven-sided stone slab, at least five feet wide, positioned in the middle of the columns. Jonah focused on the large black box with a bright lime green bow someone had placed on the slab's cushion.

Marcus lifted the box and handed it to his godson. "Happy Birthday."

Jonah accepted the gift. "What's this?"

Marcus smiled. "Open it."

"Aren't you gonna tell me about the courier?" Jonah asked.

Marcus gestured to the box, and Jonah peeked inside to find a leather coat. His irritation evaporated, replaced with disbelief.

"Is it...?" He lifted the coat from the box and let the garment hang free. "It's a Reaper long coat!"

"Yes." Marcus' mouth twitched with amusement. "Omar and I decided it best to give this to you away from the others." When Jonah gave him a curious expression, Marcus added, "It's enchanted."

"To do what?"

"Put it on and you'll see." When Jonah hesitated, Marcus added, "I'll tell you about the courier."

That was all Jonah needed to hear. He slipped the coat on. His first impression was the coat was too long and he'd have to grow into it. But no sooner than he thought that, a sharp tingle traveled over his body and the coat adjusted itself.

The hem shortened until it hung just below Jonah's knees. The arms shrank, fitting more snugly, but not tight. And the cuffs retreated, revealing Jonah's hands.

"This is so cool!"

Marcus didn't bother to hide his genuine smile. "The enchantments do more than resize the coat. You'll be protected from a wide range of spells and attacks." He grew serious as he watched Jonah turning on the spot, admiring the coat. "You know about portals?"

"Yeah, Deyanira used one to cross over."

"Correct," Marcus said. "Portals allow us to cross between the mortal and Afterworld. But what you may not have known is two portals are required to make a crossing. One in the mortal world and a corresponding one in the Afterworld."

Jonah's jaw dropped. "They're like subway stations."

Marcus nodded. "Through a mutual agreement, the Grim Reaper and his people control the main portal here in the mortal world. Another Afterworld faction called the Archivists controls the Afterworld portal."

Jonah paused the tweaking of his coat. "Archivists? Are they record keepers?"

"Yes. They maintain data on every mortal who's ever lived. A segment act as a police force of the Afterworld. They're called Guardians."

"Okay," Jonah said, trying to imagine archivists and Guardians.

When his godfather moved, Jonah glimpsed something shiny under his long coat and held out his hand. "Can I hold your blades?"

Marcus arched an eyebrow, but after a moment, let out a breath and withdrew his blades. He retreated a few steps as Jonah activated the weapons and went through the standard defensive postures.

The new Reaper's coat was like a dream to Jonah. It didn't hinder him at all as he moved.

"Not bad," Marcus observed. "It's well you're keeping up your blade skills."

The compliment focused Jonah. He asked his next question while testing the weapons. "What about the courier?"

"The Rulers of the Afterworld use special archivists called couriers to send and receive information through the portal." Marcus gazed out over the northern part of the city. "We did the same thing with our Afterworld allies. An undercover courier delivered messages to us by way of a secret drop not far from the portal."

Jonah stopped performing practice swipes with Marcus's blades. He sensed the sadness from his godfather. "What happened?"

"Three days ago, the Alliance smuggled an agent into the Afterworld for a face-to-face meeting. Our contacts had their own portal, so we thought the mission would succeed. But the Grim Reaper's people were waiting."

Marcus turned to face Jonah. "We lost our Alliance agent. The courier had to flee into the mortal world to avoid being captured by the enemy."

Jonah lowered the blades to his sides. "The GBI Agents are looking for him."

"We were surprised to learn the Grim Reaper has agents in the GBI," Marcus admitted. "The courier's afraid to trust anyone and is in hiding."

"What'll happen if he's caught?"

Marcus took a deep breath. "He would be tortured for information and then executed." When Jonah winced, Marcus patted his arm. "I'm sorry to be so blunt, but you're old enough to understand about our enemies."

"But why would those GBI agents come after me?"

"I'm part of the Alliance and your godfather..."

"They think I know something." Jonah deactivated the blades and handed them to his godfather. He pulled his new long coat closed as if warding off a chill. "Thanks, for the birthday gift."

"You're welcome." Marcus put his blades away. "Jonah, if you see the courier, please tell me. It's vital we find him."

"Why wouldn't I tell you? I don't want him to be tortured." That was true, even though he'd never met the man.

"Of course you don't." Marcus perched on the edge of the padded seat. "I'm worried about the courier for another reason. When a being travels through a portal, the change they undergo is temporary. If he doesn't cross back, well, he'll die."

Jonah gulped as a pit formed in his stomach. "How long does he have?"

"We estimate less than a week."

Jonah toyed with the clasps on his long coat as his mind raced with the sad information. "What about the mole? This is all his fault."

Marcus met Jonah's gaze, which was easier now that he sat on the slab. "I can't reveal anything else about that subject." Marcus paused. "I'm sorry."

The apology rung true for Jonah, even without using a partial Reaper stare. He nodded, letting his godfather know that he understood and wouldn't pester for more details.

Marcus's tense expression relaxed as he collected the empty gift box.

Jonah watched his godfather, feeling anything but relaxed. An invisible weight settled on him, and it wasn't the Reaper coat. One way or another, Jonah told himself, his quiet summer was over.

CHAPTER SIX
STRANGE VISITOR

Jonah covered his eyes as he squinted into the blazing summer sun. Mike, who hated getting baked in the sun, didn't even seem to notice today. He was too shocked by Jonah's recounting of the previous evening's visitation and dream-walk.

They were riding their bikes through the neighborhoods and to the teen center.

Mike overcame his shocked silence. "Telling your godfather was a smart move. It would be bad if the courier was caught by the agents."

Jonah was glad Mike sounded just as worried about Trevor as he. While Jonah trusted his godfather to keep the boy's appearance from the Alliance mole, he doubted he could convince Trevor of that, if he ever saw the boy again. "What do I do now?" Jonah glanced at Mike. "Wait?"

"Oh." Mike went silent as they did a switchback pattern up the steepest hill. "Figure out the compass."

Jonah shook his head. "Working out the compass in front of Rex or Trueblood would cause too many questions."

"But your godfather wouldn't have sent them if he couldn't trust them." Mike paused before crossing the street in front of the teen center. "We can go to the library."

Jonah brightened at that idea until he checked his watch. "The library doesn't open for another hour."

"Well, how about Ping-Pong or pool until then?"

Jonah agreed. They locked their bikes in the racks, went inside and were in luck. Lorraine Hughes, Anthony Freeman, Rodney Elkins, and Stephanie Brown, all younger members of the Practice Club, had gathered to play Ping-Pong.

Anthony, still a type of show off, assumed the lead in organizing an impromptu tournament. Jonah didn't mind as he and Mike joined the others. He realized the group accepted him into their loose circle because of his friendship with Mike.

As usual, Jonah and Anthony were in a friendly competition, each having lost only one game and in a tie for the lead. As Jonah stepped to the table, ready to square off with Anthony, he didn't see Brandon and Antwan enter the room.

The bully hurried over and shoved Jonah to the side. "Out of the way, DC."

Antwan tried to shove Anthony aside, but the boy was prepared and stood his ground. At least three other beefy guys had followed Brandon into the room. By this time, other kids had wandered into the room to watch, but the Practice Club members, including Lorraine and Stephanie, were on alert and unafraid as they faced Brandon and his crew.

Jonah nodded with pride at the others as he glared at Brandon, who was still inches taller. "Wait your turn, jerk."

"Yeah," Mike added.

Brandon laughed. "What are you gonna do, Brianiac?"

Mike's face flushed, causing Jonah's anger to build. He smirked into Brandon's arrogant face. "I'll school you again, in front of a crowd."

Brandon's light brown complexion grew darker as he swelled with anger. Just when Jonah thought the idiot would throw the first punch, someone grabbed Brandon by the forearm.

Wick stood behind him. Today he had on dark blue custodian pants and a shirt. He worked part time in the summer with the custodians at the center as part of his summer community hours. "Wait for the next tournament, Brandon."

Brandon tried to knock Wick's hand away, but Wick was too fast for that and let go.

"Mind your own business and don't touch me again, freak."

Everyone froze, waiting to see how Wick would react. He stepped right up to Brandon, looming over the boy. No one had ever seen Wick fight, but Jonah suspected the young mage could break Brandon in two.

Wick stared down at the bully. "You know, there's a reason they call me Wick."

He whirled his hands, causing Brandon to cower and cover his head. But instead of hitting the boy, Wick produced purple flames in his palms. Jonah thought they were beautiful. Everyone else let out startled gasps.

Wick leaned into Brandon's scared face. "I'd watch your mouth." He whirled his hands over Brandon's head. The boy yelled and ran for the door, Antwan right behind him.

The rest of Brandon's group seemed unsure what to do with their leader heading for the door. Wick threw the flames at the boys, scattering them. The flames didn't burn anything, they just splattered into nothingness upon impact.

Even so, Brandon's crew sprinted for the doors as the room exploded in laughter.

When everyone continued to gawk at him, Wick opened a hand and revealed an ornate silver lighter. "Just a little trick."

Kids laughed. Anthony grunted and motioned for Jonah to play him in Ping-Pong.

Jonah wanted to talk to Wick. "I'll be there in a second. " He had a bad feeling about Brandon. When Anthony let the others play, Jonah whispered to Wick, "He'll tell."

"I don't care about Brandon and his dad."

"Wick," Jonah glanced around. "I don't mean his dad. I mean the GBI."

Wick's face went slack. "Good point, Padawan. I forgot about that." He ruffled his twist and gave Jonah a lopsided smile. "They already know about us. That reminds me." He steered Jonah off to the side of the room and away from the other kids. Wick had to beckon to Mike twice to get him away from an intense conversation with Stephanie, who kept gazing at Wick with interest.

When Mike finally came over, Wick said, "Tell Stephanie that I already have a girlfriend."

Mike's eyes widened. "How'd you know she asked about that?"

Wick didn't bother to answer. Instead, he reached in his pocket and pulled out two of his polished, octagonal tokens. "These are for you guys. One each."

Jonah and Mike took the small tokens, both boys wearing matching confused expressions.

Wick beamed at them. "I helped Trueblood come up with a warning system. These are talismans. If you enter the attic without one, all the others grow hot and warn us."

"Whoa," Mike breathed, examining the token. "You did that?"

"Well," Wick hedged. "Trueblood put the spell on them, but she let me place the ward on the attic door. Also, if you hold the token up to the door, it'll get warm to remind you that some unauthorized person has been inside."

"That's cool," Jonah said. "But shouldn't the ward keep someone out?"

"Trueblood wanted to do that, but Marcus disagreed." Wick frowned. "He says we can't lock out the director. Anyway, that's why I came in here. See you later."

Jonah turned and found Anthony waiting impatiently for him to finish the tournament. Mike, however, headed for the door with Lorraine, Rodney, and Stephanie.

Jonah called out to his buddy, "Where're you going?"

Mike glanced at the others. "We're headed down to the creek side."

"Oh, okay." Jonah returned to the Ping-Pong game. During his decisive match to win the tournament, he felt a sudden pinpoint spike of heat against his thigh. He lost his concentration and the tournament went to Anthony Freeman.

When Jonah reached in his pocket, he found the source of the heat. The talisman was hot to the touch.

Jonah hurried from the game room and upstairs to the second floor. He paused at the attic door and held up the talisman. Sure enough, it warmed in his hand. That scared Jonah now. Should he go in or call his cousins?

Deciding to be brave, Jonah opened the door and mounted the narrow staircase. By now, he knew which steps creaked and avoided them. He reached the top attic step and peeked over the railing.

The attic was quiet and empty. But Jonah's Death Sense stirred. Something was off. He took another moment to make sure someone wasn't hiding behind the desk or the sofa and then headed down stairs.

He had pulled out his phone to call Mike, but he stopped in mid-motion. Harris approached the front doors with two hulking men in tow.

Jonah hurried into the west wing before the agent spotted him and then ducked into the community room on his left. He jumped when his cell phone rang, echoing in the empty space. "Mike?"

"Yeah." Mike sounded concerned. "Did you get the alarm?"

"Yeah. I bet Ramsey broke into the attic." Jonah cracked the door open and peeked outside. After a group of kids passed, he leaned out far enough to see Ramsey had joined Harris and the two goons standing in the atrium. When the agent turned in his direction, Jonah ducked back inside and closed the door.

"What should we do?" Mike asked.

"Well, I'm sure Wick and the others know. They'll call Trueblood." Jonah backed away from the door and bumped into a nearby table. He sucked in a breath when he turned around because someone had draped a large *Happy Birthday Jonah* banner over a pile of party supplies. "Wow."

"What's wrong? Is it Ramsey?"

"I forgot it's my birthday."

Mike laughed. "You want me to come back there?"

"No. Let's go to the library. Now's a good time to figure out the compass and get away from Ramsey and his goons. You still at the creek?"

"Yeah, by the old bridge."

Jonah used an exit door in the back corner of the hall and hopped over the railing along the rear sidewalk. He pulled out his compass as he started along one of the well-worn paths.

His thoughts had turned to Trevor and how the compass would figure into all of this. The spike from his Death Sense interrupted his musings. Before he could fully turn around,

Brandon grappled with him and snatched the compass out of his hands.

"What's this, DC?"

"Give it back!" Jonah lunged for the device.

Brandon used his height advantage to hold the compass high with one hand and push Jonah back with the other.

"You want me to throw it in the woods?" Brandon reared back as if to make good on his threat.

"No." Jonah waved his hands in a pleading gesture until the obvious occurred to him. "Go ahead." He suspected he could sense wherever the compass might end up and retrieve it.

Brandon blinked at his change in attitude. Then a nasty smile played across the boy's face. "Maybe Agent Ramsey would like to see it?"

Jonah experienced a moment of panic as Brandon poked at the compass face.

The bully frowned after several moments of useless prodding. "What the heck? This ain't even real gold? This sucks."

"Then give it back."

"Nope. You want it too bad." Brandon smirked. "Yeah. I think I'll give it to Agent Ramsey."

Fury surged through Jonah as he thought about a way to get the compass. The problem was he couldn't use any of his abilities. Then again, he was dealing with Brandon. Jonah had beat him in a duel last Summer's End. All he had to do was surprise the boy. Without giving it another thought, Jonah charged, ramming into Brandon dead center and knocking the taller boy to the ground.

Brandon was so shocked that Jonah almost clawed the compass out of his hand. But the bully proved he could also do the unexpected and shouted, "Help!"

Jonah's Death Sense prickled a moment before Antwan grabbed him from behind. Jonah kicked and struggled at first, then chided himself and called on what he had learned in his self-defense sessions. He planted his feet, gripped Antwan's arms, and bent forward at the waist. Antwan tumbled over Jonah's lowered head, landing flat on his back with a loud *oomph*.

Brandon took advantage of the distraction and sprinted for the tennis courts with the compass in hand. Jonah charged after him. By the time he reached the courts, Brandon had circled around them and started for the front of the Center.

Oh no. Agent Ramsey. Jonah decided to cut through the open gates to the tennis courts. That's when his Death Sense spiked.

Antwan tried to tackle him, but Jonah let out a frustrated roar as he pivoted and landed two solid punches to the boy's chest. As soon as he did so, Jonah knew something was wrong. He had hit Antwan with too much power, more than he could deliver.

The bully grunted in pain, stumbled backward, and hit the bike rack. The next moment, Antwan's feet shot up into the air as his head fell toward the pavement. Jonah didn't think twice about it as he leapt forward. *I'm too far away.* But the world around Jonah blurred for a dizzying moment and then he was right on top of Antwan.

In fact, Jonah was moving so fast he threatened to overshoot the boy. Without any time to puzzle it out, he grabbed Antwan's ankle and phased.

CHAPTER SEVEN
BULLY'S GAMBIT

Jonah and Antwan smacked head-first into the creek water.

Antwan let out a startled cry, rolled over in the water, and scrambled away. At a safe distance, he raised a shaky finger to point at Jonah. "That's how you got away from the basement last summer. But… but…" He looked around with terrified eyes.

Jonah sat up in the water. "Antwan, listen to me…"

"You're a freak."

"Antwan…"

The frightened boy stood and wiped the water out of his eyes. His clothes sagged against his thin body, making him look pathetic as he shook in fright. Antwan pointed at Jonah again. "Is that why Agent Ramsey's interested in you?"

Jonah began to tremble with fear as he stood.

Antwan sloshed out of the water and onto the bank. "Stay away from me. I'm gonna tell everyone about you!"

"Don't. I can explain."

"Jonah, what's going on?" Mike stepped into view. He'd come from upstream, along the creek. Jonah was worried that the practice club members were with Mike, but his buddy seemed to be alone.

Antwan stared between the two boys. "I knew you were involved, Mike." He only made it two more steps before he ran straight into Rex, who had just appeared. Antwan saw his buddy Brandon lying on the ground behind the big Fallen Reaper and opened his mouth to scream.

Rex blurred into motion, clamped a hand over Antwan's mouth and whispered, "Be still. I won't hurt you. Your friend is asleep. That's all."

Antwan must not have believed that because he continued to struggle in Rex's iron grip. That's when a vortex appeared and Trueblood and Omar stepped through.

The Mage took in the scene, including Antwan squirming in Rex's grip. She stepped over to the duo and pressed the spread fingers of her right hand along the base of Antwan's thin neck. Jonah saw her lips move with a silent spell. Antwan's body went rigid and then he slumped, unconscious.

Rex let out a relieved breath. "Thanks, Eleanor." He laid Antwan on the ground beside Brandon.

Jonah scrambled onto the edge of the creek and pointed at the downed boys. "How did you know about Brandon and Antwan?"

Trueblood held up her talisman. "I got the warning and asked Omar and Rex to come with me. We had just arrived in the attic when Rex glanced out the window, saw the mishap on the back lawn, and followed you."

Jonah pointed at Antwan. "He's gonna tell people about me. He'll tell Brandon's dad." He sucked in a shaky breath. "I'm sorry I phased, but Antwan would have hurt himself. What could I do?"

Rex responded with a tolerant smile. "Not to worry, son. Omar's here. He'll fix everything. You just watch."

Jonah turned to Omar with a start. "You will?" Usually, his godfather's partner was always the first to greet him, but today, he stood there quietly, watching.

"Omar?" Jonah asked.

Finally he smiled. "Rex's right. I'll handle this."

"How?"

In answer, Trueblood knelt over Antwan and muttered under her breath. Antwan's eyes snapped open and he rolled to his feet with surprising energy. Rex gripped the boy by the arms when he stood and tried to run.

Omar positioned himself in front of Antwan. In contrast to how Antwan had reacted before, the boy seemed relieved to have a fellow African here.

"Relax, brother." Omar's deep African voice was surprisingly soothing. "I won't hurt you."

Antwan's Adam's apple bobbed up and down as he swallowed. "Who are you?"

"I'm gonna remove those memories." Despite Antwan's constant squirming, Omar never broke eye contact. "You don't want those memories. You should not be burdened with them. Let them go."

Antwan's struggling subsided a little.

"Yes. Let them go. That's it." Omar held a hand to the side of Antwan's head. A faint glow surrounded his outstretched fingers. "Yes. Let them go, Antwan."

Omar continued to encourage the boy to let go. As he said it once more, something strange came over Jonah. His own body stiffened and everything went dark.

The next moment, Jonah stood on a busy street in Paris. At first, he thought he had phased until he recognized this from a snatch of dream he'd had once. It hadn't been a dream-walk, either. It had been a normal dream, as far as that went.

Then he remembered the Pale Man with the black clothes, top hat, and a shiny cane. As he watched, the man appeared in the midst of the pedestrians. The people parted for him, like a ship's bow cutting through the water as he strode in measured steps toward an upscale Parisian restaurant.

The sudden urge to warn the people inside that restaurant became unbearable. In fact, he needed to warn a particular person about the Pale Man. *My dad?*

He tried to move at the same time a strong, deep African-accented voice spoke to him. "Let go, Jonah. Let go of the memory."

It was Omar's voice. Jonah resisted because he needed to be inside the restaurant. Again, Omar's disembodied voice called to him.

"No, Jonah. Let it go."

"Jonah please." His mom spoke now. Jonah responded to her, relaxed, and everything went dark again.

When he opened his eyes, he stared at the treetops high above. The sound of gurgling water came from somewhere nearby. He remembered that he was at the creek with Mike, Omar, Rex, and Trueblood.

Mike's face moved into his field of vision, twisted with worry.

Rex loomed into view next. "You alright, son?"

"Yeah." Jonah sat up, rubbing his forehead.

"You went limp," Mike said. "Rex had to keep you from cracking your head on a rock."

Jonah stood. He was a little unsteady, and Mike propped him up. Rex also hovered nearby, ready to help. Antwan and Brandon lay out on the higher ground, apparently asleep.

Omar stood beside Trueblood with a worried expression on his face.

"I'm okay, Omar." When that didn't soften Omar's expression, Jonah pointed at Antwan. "Did it work?"

Omar spread his arms. "I know my job."

Afraid he'd offended the man, Jonah fumbled for something else to ask as his mind shook off its sluggishness. "How long will the block last?"

"For a lifetime." Omar shifted his gaze from Jonah to Antwan. "That is, if another Memory Charmer doesn't open the wall."

Jonah latched onto that, thinking back to the night he had defeated the Grim Reaper and saved Marcus's life. Omar had been so grateful that he admitted to blocking off some of Jonah's memories and apologized for doing it.

Since that evening, Jonah had given the matter some thought. He liked Omar and he couldn't imagine being angry with his godfather's partner. But maybe the time had come to find out what was blocked. He suspected it had to do with the strange dream that also had the unsettling feeling of being real.

Jonah met Omar's gaze. "Can you unblock my memories?"

A pained look returned to Omar's face. "I'm afraid I can't make that decision. Our jobs often require suppressing memories and events that could expose our world to regular mortals. And at other times, we're called in to suppress traumatic experiences."

Jonah understood. Someone must have called Omar to wall off a traumatic event that had happened to him. Jonah heard his mom's voice in the dream. Could she have ordered the block? The thought of experiencing something bad enough that his mom sought out protection scared him.

Rex squeezed his shoulder. It was gentle considering the man's size. "He's not saying it can't be done, just that maybe you should hold off."

Jonah stared at the adults. "Does everyone know what happened to me?"

"Nah. We don't know what happened. Only your parents, Marcus, and…"

"Rex!" Omar raised his voice.

Rex shook his shaggy blond head. "He should know that much. You think so, too."

"Yes I do, but..." Omar sighed and turned to Jonah. "There's so much else happening right now. Let this rest for now. We can talk to Marcus about it after this mess with the courier is done."

Omar was so unlike Marcus because he didn't hide his emotions, like now, when Jonah could feel the other man's concern flowing off him. He wondered if Omar had been afraid all along that something would happen. *Like I might remember?*

Jonah met Omar's troubled gaze and nodded. "Alright. But I wanna know someday."

Rex cleared his throat and held out the compass. "I took this from Brandon."

Jonah stared at the device, shocked that he'd forgotten about it. "What about Antwan and Brandon?"

"We'll leave them here," Trueblood said. "The pretty boy didn't see anything, and Antwan is safely blocked. Agent Ramsey won't get anything out of either of them."

Mike snorted and poked Brandon's foot with his own.

Omar stroked his clean-shaven chin, watching Mike and Jonah. "Why were you two meeting down here?"

Mike blushed. "We were gonna go to the library and..." his voice trailed off.

Jonah never told Mike about his godfather and Omar's relationship, but it seemed his buddy had caught on to the jist of Omar's question. Jonah had a different worry. After what just happened, he didn't think he could face seeing his dad's handwriting, not right now.

Omar seemed to understand his feelings. "Take it easy today, Jonah. It's your birthday."

"Why don't you help the others get the hall ready?" Trueblood offered. "I think doing something normal would frustrate Agent Ramsey."

Jonah glanced at Brandon and Antwan once more and thought Trueblood had a good point.

CHAPTER EIGHT
MEMORY CHARMER

Jonah and Antwan smacked head-first into the creek water.

Antwan let out a startled cry, rolled over in the water, and scrambled away. At a safe distance, he raised a shaky finger to point at Jonah. "That's how you got away from the basement last summer. But… but…" He looked around with terrified eyes.

Jonah sat up in the water. "Antwan, listen to me…"

"You're a freak."

"Antwan…"

The frightened boy stood and wiped the water out of his eyes. His clothes sagged against his thin body, making him look pathetic as he shook in fright. Antwan pointed at Jonah again. "Is that why Agent Ramsey's interested in you?"

Jonah began to tremble with fear as he stood.

Antwan sloshed out of the water and onto the bank. "Stay away from me. I'm gonna tell everyone about you!"

"Don't. I can explain."

"Jonah, what's going on?" Mike stepped into view. He'd come from upstream, along the creek. Jonah was worried that the practice club members were with Mike, but his buddy seemed to be alone.

Antwan stared between the two boys. "I knew you were involved, Mike." He only made it two more steps before he ran straight into Rex, who had just appeared. Antwan saw his buddy Brandon lying on the ground behind the big Fallen Reaper and opened his mouth to scream.

Rex blurred into motion, clamped a hand over Antwan's mouth and whispered, "Be still. I won't hurt you. Your friend is asleep. That's all."

Antwan must not have believed that because he continued to struggle in Rex's iron grip. That's when a vortex appeared and Trueblood and Omar stepped through.

The Mage took in the scene, including Antwan squirming in Rex's grip. She stepped over to the duo and pressed the spread fingers of her right hand along the base of Antwan's thin neck. Jonah saw her lips move with a silent spell. Antwan's body went rigid and then he slumped, unconscious.

Rex let out a relieved breath. "Thanks, Eleanor." He laid Antwan on the ground beside Brandon.

Jonah scrambled onto the edge of the creek and pointed at the downed boys. "How did you know about Brandon and Antwan?"

Trueblood held up her talisman. "I got the warning and asked Omar and Rex to come with me. We had just arrived in the attic when Rex glanced out the window, saw the mishap on the back lawn, and followed you."

Jonah pointed at Antwan. "He's gonna tell people about me. He'll tell Brandon's dad." He sucked in a shaky breath. "I'm sorry I phased, but Antwan would have hurt himself. What could I do?"

Rex responded with a tolerant smile. "Not to worry, son. Omar's here. He'll fix everything. You just watch."

Jonah turned to Omar with a start. "You will?" Usually, his godfather's partner was always the first to greet him, but today, he stood there quietly, watching.

"Omar?" Jonah asked.

Finally he smiled. "Rex's right. I'll handle this."

"How?"

In answer, Trueblood knelt over Antwan and muttered under her breath. Antwan's eyes snapped open and he rolled to his feet with surprising energy. Rex gripped the boy by the arms when he stood and tried to run.

Omar positioned himself in front of Antwan. In contrast to how Antwan had reacted before, the boy seemed relieved to have a fellow African here.

"Relax, brother." Omar's deep African voice was surprisingly soothing. "I won't hurt you."

Antwan's Adam's apple bobbed up and down as he swallowed. "Who are you?"

"I'm gonna remove those memories." Despite Antwan's constant squirming, Omar never broke eye contact. "You don't want those memories. You should not be burdened with them. Let them go."

Antwan's struggling subsided a little.

"Yes. Let them go. That's it." Omar held a hand to the side of Antwan's head. A faint glow surrounded his outstretched fingers. "Yes. Let them go, Antwan."

Omar continued to encourage the boy to let go. As he said it once more, something strange came over Jonah. His own body stiffened and everything went dark.

The next moment, Jonah stood on a busy street in Paris. At first, he thought he had phased until he recognized this from a snatch of dream he'd had once. It hadn't been a dream-walk, either. It had been a normal dream, as far as that went.

Then he remembered the Pale Man with the black clothes, top hat, and a shiny cane. As he watched, the man appeared in the midst of the pedestrians. The people parted for him, like a ship's bow cutting through the water as he strode in measured steps toward an upscale Parisian restaurant.

The sudden urge to warn the people inside that restaurant became unbearable. In fact, he needed to warn a particular person about the Pale Man. *My dad?*

He tried to move at the same time a strong, deep African-accented voice spoke to him. "Let go, Jonah. Let go of the memory."

It was Omar's voice. Jonah resisted because he needed to be inside the restaurant. Again, Omar's disembodied voice called to him.

"No, Jonah. Let it go."

"Jonah please." His mom spoke now. Jonah responded to her, relaxed, and everything went dark again.

When he opened his eyes, he stared at the treetops high above. The sound of gurgling water came from somewhere nearby. He remembered that he was at the creek with Mike, Omar, Rex, and Trueblood.

Mike's face moved into his field of vision, twisted with worry.

Rex loomed into view next. "You alright, son?"

"Yeah." Jonah sat up, rubbing his forehead.

"You went limp," Mike said. "Rex had to keep you from cracking your head on a rock."

Jonah stood. He was a little unsteady, and Mike propped him up. Rex also hovered nearby, ready to help. Antwan and Brandon lay out on the higher ground, apparently asleep.

Omar stood beside Trueblood with a worried expression on his face.

"I'm okay, Omar." When that didn't soften Omar's expression, Jonah pointed at Antwan. "Did it work?"

Omar spread his arms. "I know my job."

Afraid he'd offended the man, Jonah fumbled for something else to ask as his mind shook off its sluggishness. "How long will the block last?"

"For a lifetime." Omar shifted his gaze from Jonah to Antwan. "That is, if another Memory Charmer doesn't open the wall."

Jonah latched onto that, thinking back to the night he had defeated the Grim Reaper and saved Marcus's life. Omar had been so grateful that he admitted to blocking off some of Jonah's memories and apologized for doing it.

Since that evening, Jonah had given the matter some thought. He liked Omar and he couldn't imagine being angry with his godfather's partner. But maybe the time had come to find out what was blocked. He suspected it had to do with the strange dream that also had the unsettling feeling of being real.

Jonah met Omar's gaze. "Can you unblock my memories?"

A pained look returned to Omar's face. "I'm afraid I can't make that decision. Our jobs often require suppressing memories and events that could expose our world to regular mortals. And at other times, we're called in to suppress traumatic experiences."

Jonah understood. Someone must have called Omar to wall off a traumatic event that had happened to him. Jonah heard his mom's voice in the dream. Could she have ordered the block? The thought of experiencing something bad enough that his mom sought out protection scared him.

Rex squeezed his shoulder. It was gentle considering the man's size. "He's not saying it can't be done, just that maybe you should hold off."

Jonah stared at the adults. "Does everyone know what happened to me?"

"Nah. We don't know what happened. Only your parents, Marcus, and…"

"Rex!" Omar raised his voice.

Rex shook his shaggy blond head. "He should know that much. You think so, too."

"Yes I do, but..." Omar sighed and turned to Jonah. "There's so much else happening right now. Let this rest for now. We can talk to Marcus about it after this mess with the courier is done."

Omar was so unlike Marcus because he didn't hide his emotions, like now, when Jonah could feel the other man's concern flowing off him. He wondered if Omar had been afraid all along that something would happen. *Like I might remember?*

Jonah met Omar's troubled gaze and nodded. "Alright. But I wanna know someday."

Rex cleared his throat and held out the compass. "I took this from Brandon."

Jonah stared at the device, shocked that he'd forgotten about it. "What about Antwan and Brandon?"

"We'll leave them here," Trueblood said. "The pretty boy didn't see anything, and Antwan is safely blocked. Agent Ramsey won't get anything out of either of them."

Mike snorted and poked Brandon's foot with his own.

Omar stroked his clean-shaven chin, watching Mike and Jonah. "Why were you two meeting down here?"

Mike blushed. "We were gonna go to the library and..." his voice trailed off.

Jonah never told Mike about his godfather and Omar's relationship, but it seemed his buddy had caught on to the jist of Omar's question. Jonah had a different worry. After what just happened, he didn't think he could face seeing his dad's handwriting, not right now.

Omar seemed to understand his feelings. "Take it easy today, Jonah. It's your birthday."

"Why don't you help the others get the hall ready?" Trueblood offered. "I think doing something normal would frustrate Agent Ramsey."

Jonah glanced at Brandon and Antwan once more and thought Trueblood had a good point.

CHAPTER NINE
MIKE'S SECRET

Wick stood in front of the large attic window, legs apart and right arm held up while Robert tossed empty soda cans at him. Every can hit an invisible barrier, that flared at the point of impact.

"Wow," Mike, who stood beside Jonah, breathed.

Jonah agreed as he and Mike clapped.

The noise caused Lynn to frown at them. "Will you guys give it a rest?"

"Sorry Lynn," Wick grinned at her. "Last-minute practice for Jonah's party." Wick planned to do a magic show and to dress like a traditional magician. The clothes hung from a hook on the south attic wall: a white dress shirt, black slacks, and black shoes.

Wick rubbed his hands together, smiling at Jonah. "That's only part of the act. Robert's gonna do his thing."

"Really?" Jonah had discovered his cousin was more than a computer wiz and a fantastic traditional artist. Robert could draw whatever someone concentrated on as long as he maintained eye contact with the person.

Wick hustled a startled Mike over to the old sofa and pushed him down on a cushion. Jonah followed, eager to see Mike's reaction to Robert's ability.

Robert retrieved his sketch pad from the computer desk, plopped into an armchair, and opened the pad as he focused on Mike.

Lynn came over and waved Jonah into the second armchair. "You'll want to see this." Once Jonah sat down, she perched on the arm of the chair, arms crossed and waiting.

Wick waltzed around and behind Robert's armchair like he was already on stage. "Now, Mike, I want you to clear your mind and concentrate on one thing. It doesn't matter what it is."

Mike's eyes narrowed with suspicion. "Why?"

"Robert's gonna sketch it."

Mike's jaw dropped, but he nodded after a minute. When his eyes went out of focus, Jonah suspected his friend had decided on something. A quiet scratching sound drew everyone's attention to Robert.

Jonah's cousin never lost eye contact with Mike, but his hand moved in quick, sure motions across the sketch pad's surface. A slight furrow and wrinkle to Robert's brow was the only other sign that he, too, concentrated.

After several minutes, Robert's hand stopped. He closed his eyes while leaning back in the armchair.

Wick peeked at the drawing and whistled. Then he tapped Robert's head and pointed at Mike. "Show him."

Robert held up a very accurate drawing of a single-prop airplane.

"That's amazing!" Mike took the drawing from Robert. "I was thinking about the plane they use for my flying lessons."

Jonah was equally shocked at Mike's revelation of the flying lessons and at Robert's talent. He wanted to ask his cousin about the ability when Mike dropped the sketch pad on the steamer trunk and stood.

"You read my mind?" He trembled slightly.

"No." Robert gestured for Mike to sit down. "I didn't read your mind. I can't see anything unless I draw it and even then, the thought has to be focused." He shrugged. "My power's weird that way. I won't know what I'm getting until I finish drawing."

"Whoa." Mike leaned forward staring at Robert, at a loss for words.

Jonah sympathized, remembering his first session.

Lynn leaned on her brother's shoulder. "We use it sometimes while interviewing people." She raised an eyebrow at Jonah and Mike. "Don't tell anyone."

The boys agreed at once.

"So," Wick said, giving Jonah a lopsided grin. "You okay with us doing the tricks? It's your party."

"Yeah, I'm fine." The reality of the party caught up to Jonah. He glanced at his feet.

"What's wrong now?" Wick asked.

Mike laughed. "He's afraid no one will show up."

"No," Jonah objected. "I'm scared a lot of kids will show up."

Robert shook his head. "I don't get it. What's wrong with people coming?"

"I've never had a real party before." The confession spilled out of Jonah. "And it's gonna be here in the teen center, where everyone can come."

Lynn gave him the once over. For a moment, Jonah feared she'd make fun of him. Instead, she nodded as if finally understanding something else about him.

"Don't worry," she said. "You'll know everyone there."

"But, what if something goes wrong? What if... what if the courier shows up?"

Lynn's eyes widened slightly before she caught herself. Jonah noticed anyway.

Robert snapped his sketchbook closed and stood. "I doubt he'd do that, little cousin."

"Yeah," Wick agreed. "Too risky."

Jonah didn't think so, and he wanted to know what Lynn sensed.

She met his gaze. "Everything will be fine." She gestured to her brother and Wick. "We have a party to prepare."

Jonah and Mike trailed behind the others to the atrium. As they reached the west side hall, Lynn whirled on them. "You two go and do something else."

"Why?" Jonah gaped at his cousin.

"I want the final decorations to be a surprise for you." She crossed her arms, barring their way into the side hall.

Mike pulled Jonah toward the front doors "Don't worry. I have to watch the store for my uncle. Jonah can come with me."

CHAPTER TEN
PARTY CRASHERS

The transformation of the teen center atrium amazed Jonah and took his mind off his trouble with Mike. Black and white balloons hung in long streamers from the ceiling. The *Happy Birthday* banner was attached high between two of the streamers.

Given the height of the central dome, Jonah imagined Wick had talked the custodians into mounting the balloons. A DJ spun the latest tunes from a low stage in the west wing entrance. On the opposite side of the atrium, another low stage had been set up for the birthday cake and Wick's show.

The café was open and serving catered food for the kids. Perhaps the thing that shocked Jonah most was the number of kids crowded into the Atrium talking, shouting, and dancing.

The music dimmed in volume, alerting the crowd. The DJ grabbed his mic and said, "Ladies and gentlemen, the birthday boy has arrived. Give it up for Jonah!"

Jonah's face reddened as everyone turned to clap and cheer for him. Danita, the leader of their reading group, materialized at Jonah's side and pulled him into the crowd of kids. It was bewildering. He knew a lot of kids from his practice group or from hanging out at the teen center. But many others had come on their own.

Except for the owner of the café, the only other adult was Mr. Varnadore, the middle school assistant principal. Although he was cool with the kids, Mr. Varnadore was a former football player and none of the guys gave him lip.

The man prowled the edges of the gathering, preventing kids from sneaking off into the darkened hallways and side rooms of the center. He paused to wave a greeting.

Jonah acknowledged it and then busied himself searching the crowd of faces, looking for the courier. Danita had other plans. She pulled Jonah into the middle of the crowd of kids to dance.

Just a year before, he would have never done this. He had confessed to Lynn that he wasn't a good dancer. She took pity on him and, without telling her brother or Wick, taught Jonah the latest moves. As with the blades, Jonah was a quick learner.

"You just need someone to challenge you, that's all," Lynn had said, looking impressed.

He thought about that now as he danced with Danita, who also surprised Jonah. He thought of her as even more of a nerd than he and Mike. She devoured books of all genres. That, the straight A's, and the thick glasses she used to wear landed her on the geek and nerd lists. But tonight, her trademark ponytails were gone, she wore her contacts, and she held her own for three songs.

Someone tapped Jonah's arm at the start of the fourth song. He spun around and found Mike standing behind him. Jonah smirked at his buddy. "You wanna dance?"

Mike looked stunned and uncertain for a moment. "Not with you." He cracked a smile as Danita pulled him toward her, then paused long enough to point past Jonah and toward the front doors. "You're not gonna like who just arrived."

Jonah's stomach knotted when he looked. Brandon, Antwan, Drew, and a beefy crew of four boys stood in the entrance. He began to get a bad feeling about this because all the boys wore black polo shirts with the teen center logo on the left chest.

"No way." Jonah slipped through the crowd. Lynn moved to the doorway from the direction of the café, but Jonah arrived first and confronted Brandon. "You're not invited."

"The center hired us as security tonight." Brandon puffed out his chest to show off the word *Security* under the teen center logo.

"No they didn't." Lynn reached the doors. "My parents didn't order any security. And they wouldn't have hired you."

Brandon crossed his arms, but Jonah noted he stepped closer to his crew. "The director assigned us tonight. Either we stay or the party's over." Brandon smiled and pointed to Mr. Varnadore. "Ask him."

"I will." Lynn pushed through the crowd and to the assistant principal. A moment later, she crossed her arms, her nostrils flaring with anger.

"Told you." Brandon smirked at Jonah and stood right in front of him. "You step out of line, freak, and we'll close you down." He leaned closer. "You never know who'll show up."

Brandon bumped into Jonah as he pressed into the crowd. His guys didn't bother to avoid elbowing people out of their way, creating a ruckus and drawing irritated glares from the other kids. It was clear to Jonah the bullies were trying to start a fight.

That wasn't Jonah's biggest worry. He waved Lynn closer. "He's looking for the courier."

Lynn made a hand signal to Rico. He nodded in return and within seconds, the oldest boys from the Practice Club stood in a loose circle around him. After a few whispered words, the guys spread out through the crowd in order to check Brandon's crew.

The burning in Jonah's stomach worsened. "This isn't gonna end well."

Perhaps Wick noticed the tension in the crowd because he stepped onto the stage. With a cue to the DJ, who changed up the song to a Reggae tune, Wick began dancing around the stage while calling out to the crowd.

As the kids focused on him, Wick began his magic act, pausing between each gag to dance and strut around. The crowd loved it. Jonah had to give the young mage credit. Wick could dance, and he had a smooth and funny way with the crowd.

Then Robert hopped on stage, and more than a few of the girls whistled and called out to him. Once he started into his routine, the kids began to clamor for him to draw their thoughts. Wick handled that, too, and actually goaded one of Brandon's goons into having his thought drawn.

Throughout the entire routine, Jonah clapped like wild with everyone else. About the time the music started again, Jonah caught Brandon and Antwan talking to each other while watching him. Making sure Mr. Varnadore faced the opposite direction, Jonah headed for the stairs to the second floor balcony.

Once there, he placed his hands on the railing and watched the crowd below. The bass of the popular song vibrated the metal.

There was something primal about the whole scene that penetrated to his very soul. The energy in the room was almost suffocating. As Jonah grew in touch with his Reaper side, he wondered if that was the reason he preferred smaller groups of people.

Jonah shook his head and started to scan the tops of heads below again until he sensed the person behind him and to the side. He froze, trying not to alert the individual. Whoever it was must have already been up here, lurking in the shadows.

Think, Jonah told himself. His Death Sense wasn't buzzing, so the person wasn't dangerous. At least that was a good sign.

Then a familiar voice said, "Why aren't you down there enjoying the party?"

Jonah turned. Trevor stood in the shadows, watching him. The courier moved forward, but not close enough to the balcony that people below would see him. "You don't like crowds, do you?"

"I..." Jonah had to adjust his thinking to the question and away from his fear for this boy. "How do you know?"

Trevor shrugged, looking like a normal kid. "I wondered if it was your nature."

Jonah glanced over the railing at the crowd again to hide his reaction to Trevor's comment. His Reaper side could touch the other kids' souls. He let himself slip into a Reaper stare. Brilliant hues and colors of fun and joy swirled around the kids' auras. The brightness of the young, vibrant souls nearly blinded him. So much energy and potential.

"I can sense every soul," Jonah admitted. "It's..."

"Suffocating?"

Jonah nodded, wondering at his willingness to be so open with this strange boy. He never told his cousins and friends about this side of his nature. "It's like the physical bodies and souls double the pressure on me and I just need to get away sometimes and breathe." He glanced at Trevor. "But I don't get it. I've been to theme parks with my cousins. This doesn't happen."

"Maybe it's like telepaths in your movies. They have to learn to block out the other thoughts. When you're at a park, your mind is on having fun." Trevor gestured over the railing. "Tonight, you're worried about other things."

"Yeah, I am. Like you getting caught."

Trevor held a finger to his lips. "Not so loud."

"It's not funny."

"I know. This was the only way to see you. My time's running out. Have you activated the compass?"

"No."

Trevor's eyes narrowed. "Why not?"

Jonah blinked at the sudden intensity in the boy's question. "It's a long story."

"You're not at all what I expected," Trevor said, disappointment clear in his tone.

"Tough," Jonah shot back. He bristled at the feeling the boy expected more from him.

Before either one could respond, Jonah's Death Sense spiked.

He turned toward the stairs, but no one was there. That's when the elevator to the far left of the second floor dinged. Jonah wanted to kick himself. The elevator was locked after hours, so Jonah had expected danger to come by way of the stairs. He should have known the director would have given Brandon a key to the elevator.

As the doors opened to reveal Brandon, two of his bogus security team sprinted up the stairs. A third had distracted Mr. Varnadore near the front of the atrium.

Brandon signaled to Drew and the remaining guy below, and that's when things got crazy. The boys began to shove and push people, creating a ruckus.

Jonah knew why. Brandon wanted to take the courier without anyone noticing. Jonah wasn't going to allow that, not without a fight. He couched, ready to face the bully.

Trevor turned in the opposite direction as Brandon's crew rushed them from behind. The first boy swung at Trevor, who grabbed him by the arm, pivoted, and slung him into the second boy.

Meanwhile, Jonah ducked Antwan's punch and took the bully's feet from under him. Antwan landed on his butt. Brandon was right on his heels, using his friend to cover his advance.

He would have caught Jonah if Trevor hadn't whirled around just in time. He blocked Brandon's precise punches and kicked the bully, sending him tumbling over the second floor railing.

For one horrid moment, Jonah feared Brandon would smash into the kids in the atrium below. That didn't happened because Trevor was at the railing in an instant and grabbed Brandon's hand. He heaved Brandon upward, showing more strength than Jonah would have expected. "Hold on to the railing," Trevor said through clenched teeth.

Once Brandon gripped the rail, Trevor let go and backed away. He motioned for Jonah to follow. "Come on." He dashed into the elevator.

As soon as Jonah entered, Trevor flashed the key he stole from Brandon, slipped it into place, and pressed the down button. The last thing Jonah saw was Antwan helping Brandon over the railing.

Jonah stared at Trevor as the doors closed. He was impressed the courier wasn't even breathing hard. "Where'd you learn to fight like that?"

"Long story," Trevor deadpanned.

The elevator reached ground level and the door opened onto pandemonium. The Practice Club boys were wrestling with Brandon's crew. A couple of the would-be security guards were already down, with their hands tied behind their backs. The balloon streamers had been torn loose. Loud pops went off like gunshots as people stepped on the balloons in their dash for the doors.

The DJ's table and equipment had been turned over. At least one speaker emitted loud squealing noises, causing Jonah to wince and cover his ears. The birthday cake had toppled over and smashed against the wall.

Robert and Mike helped kids through the doors. Flashes went off like crazy, and not from the strobes. Kids were taking pictures and recording videos. Jonah had little doubt that this fiasco would be all over the Internet within minutes.

Brandon and Antwan raced down the stairs, only to get swallowed up in the mess they had created. Jonah met Brandon's furious gaze for a moment before Trevor pulled him into the darkness of the west wing.

"We can't go out the front," Trevor breathed. "We need a place to phase out of here unseen."

Jonah had an idea. He cut in front of the boy and ducked into a side hall, headed for the nearest exit door. "We can head out back." He burst through the door and was in the process of vaulting over the back railing when Trevor grabbed his arm.

It was too late. Jonah's momentum took him over the railing, and Trevor with him. The boys sprawled on the darkened grass. At the same time, an unpleasant tingling sensation traveled over Jonah's entire body.

Only then did he notice that they were surrounded by at least six people, and all of their eyes glowed a pale white. Each also held a scythe, the edges glowing with a sickly green color in the dimness.

Trevor ignored them while pointing at the spikes stuck in the ground in a loose circle. Each emitted blinking lights.

"What's that?" Jonah asked.

Trevor frowned. "It's a nullifying circle. You won't be able to phase." Trevor's voice shook with anger as he stood and helped Jonah to his feet.

Jonah wanted to kick himself for falling into the trap. It was obvious now that Brandon's group had been meant to lure him out of the teen center. Away from the chaos and witnesses, these Wraith-possessed goons could capture Trevor using whatever powers they needed.

"Sorry," Jonah said.

"It wasn't your fault," Trevor answered. "I should have seen this."

The silence of the group unnerved Jonah. Why didn't they attack, he wondered.

Then one of the Grimnions held a phone up and spoke into it. "Tell the agents we have the courier."

CHAPTER ELEVEN
REUNION

The group of Wraith-possessed goons tightened their circle while taking menacing swipes with their scythes. At least four more stepped into view behind these.

Trevor snorted. "They're just trying to scare us."

"It's working," Jonah whispered. He had to admit he was impressed with Trevor. But Jonah thought he should point out the obvious. "Ah, we don't have any weapons and I can't phase us out of here."

Trevor turned his head slightly, allowing Jonah to see the smirk there. "What do you mean?" He pointed at the guy on his right, in the two o'clock position. "I'll use his weapon."

Jonah gulped, not knowing if Trevor was joking or dead serious. When the boy shifted his weight in preparation, Jonah decided Trevor wasn't joking. Calling on his own training, he relaxed into the ready stance and prepared himself to snap into sudden motion.

He had discovered another burgeoning power. He could be pretty fast. It was something Lynn had first noticed. Since then, Jonah had tried slipping into the ability, but it was hit and miss. Tonight, he was sure he could do it.

Copying Trevor's confident demeanor, Jonah chose an opponent.

Trevor bumped his elbow against Jonah's and whispered, "Now."

That was it. Jonah summoned all of his will and pushed himself. Just like with Antwan earlier that day, the outside world blurred for a fraction of a second. That was all he needed to get inside the goon's safety zone and strike. Even before the guy could adjust, Jonah delivered well-placed blows to the man's arm and wrist.

The scythe flew free. Jonah snatched it out of the air as his Death Sense spiked. He rolled away, back toward the center of the circle. When he came up, he saw Trevor also had a scythe, but his guy was on the ground.

Jonah knew he and Trevor had shocked their attackers. He sensed fear in the air as they charged. Jonah went into defensive mode, using the scythe to block the attacks of at least two guys and cut back in return.

Trevor grabbed the striking arm of his assailant and flipped the guy over. He cut the man across the chest with a practiced flourish. The goon's eyes sparked and the Wraith within died.

"Kill the boy," their leader shouted. "We only need the courier."

Jonah's inside went cold at that. With the element of surprise gone, he had to flail with all of his might to defend against the renewed determination of his attackers. And Trevor was busy with his own Grimnions and couldn't help.

After one of the goons nicked him on an arm, Jonah began to grow desperate. That's when something black and whirling appeared behind the enemies.

One attacker's eyes sparked from a cut Jonah didn't see delivered. A split second later, he was hauled up into the air and thrown several feet away. Another goon faltered in his attack as a Reaper's blade protruded from his chest. He crumbled to the ground, dead.

Jonah thought Marcus had arrived as he watched the long-coated figure rip up three of the blinking spikes in a blurred move, breaking the nullifying trap.

When their rescuer stopped and moved closer to retrieve his blade from the downed Grimnion, Jonah gasped. "Kevin?"

The young Fallen Reaper nodded without his usual smirk. "That's right, little man."

Rex and Trueblood had also appeared. The adult mage used a spell to stun another attacker. Rex wasn't so kind and cut yet another with his blade, killing the Wraith inside. The mortal lay on the ground, moaning. The rest retreated.

All of this happened in the span of minutes. Jonah's brain attempted to process the sudden change of fortune. He also wanted to ask Kevin a thousand questions, but the boy was all business, helping Rex lay the dead and injured in a line.

Once he was done, Kevin pulled up and destroyed the rest of the phase-blocking spikes. At once, a new group of people arrived and began to retrieve the fallen. Jonah had never seen this side of the hidden fight among the supernatural. It shocked him.

"It's a clean-up crew," Trevor whispered to him.

Trueblood must have heard because she detached herself from the work and pointed at Trevor.

Rex nodded and grabbed the boy with his big hands. Trevor struggled until Rex shook him like a rag doll. "Be still."

"Get him to the safe house, now," Trueblood ordered.

Rex nodded and phased them away.

"Wait!" Jonah shouted. "I wanna go."

"You can't," Kevin told him.

Jonah whirled on the older boy. "Why not?"

"Because you have to go back inside. This is your party. People will notice you missing." He hustled Jonah through the back entrance and into the west wing of the teen center.

Jonah stopped just short of the atrium, forcing the older boy to halt. But Jonah lost his train of thought because Kevin had shed his long Reaper's coat. He wore a nice black tee, fitted to his developed upper body, and a pair of jeans. The young Fallen Reaper could have walked in to the party like anyone else.

With that thought, Jonah realized that was exactly the point. The clean-up crew out back, Omar's memory charm earlier today, and Kevin losing the long coat; it was all about keeping what they did secret. "Ah," Jonah stammered, trying to recall his earlier questions, "where did you come from? Where have you been all school year?"

"Training." Kevin prodded Jonah in the back. "Keep moving."

"I thought you weren't working with Marcus anymore."

"I'm not. I had to go out on my own missions to complete my training." Kevin motioned toward the atrium and the commotion, but Jonah stood his ground. Kevin sighed. "I'm a full member of the Alliance now."

"Oh." Jonah allowed Kevin to steer him into the atrium.

The place was a mess, and then there was Brandon's crew sitting on the ground, hands still tied behind their backs. Rico and the other boys stood over the group.

While Lynn and Wick worked with the other kids in cleaning up the atrium and café, Robert helped the DJ, who complained in a loud voice about someone paying for his ruined speaker.

Lynn broke away and hurried over to Jonah. "Where were you?"

"Ah, upstairs." Jonah knew that sounded lame. He raised his eyebrows and glanced at Brandon.

Lynn nodded and motioned to Rico. "Let them go."

Rico didn't look happy about that, but he did it. Brandon shot to his feet and poked out his chest until Rico loomed over him.

The bully backed toward the front doors. Once he had space between himself and the Practice Club guys, his snobbish air returned. "You're all gonna get in trouble. You can't tie us up."

"You were causing a problem at the party," Lynn said. "People took plenty of pictures and video."

They were interrupted when flashing lights arrived outside the center. Jonah's heart sank. If someone had called the police, they would be in trouble.

Lynn motioned for the other kids to keep cleaning. She stood beside Jonah and waited. It wasn't the local cops. Agent Ramsey charged through the doors, looking wild.

"What happened?" he asked the group in general, but Brandon started talking.

Jonah stirred when Brandon accused Rico and his guys of attacking. Lynn gripped his hand and squeezed.

Once Brandon finished, looking smug, Ramsey turned to Jonah's group.

Lynn met the agent's angry gaze. "He's lying. We're cleaning up after they started a riot." She gazed down her nose at Brandon. "Besides, they look fine to me."

Ramsey squared his shoulders. "Where is he?"

"Who?" Lynn adopted a confused expression.

Ramsey's hand flicked toward his belt. "I'm searching for a fugitive."

Lynn made a grand show of gesturing around. "Well, he isn't here. Now, if you and Brandon want to help us clean up, start with the café."

Agent Ramsey vibrated with repressed anger. But what could he do, Jonah wondered. There were too many witnesses. He wanted to smile, but feared that would send the guy over the edge.

Ramsey lowered his voice to a whisper and hissed at Jonah and Lynn, "You two won't get away with this."

In response, Lynn reached over and took a broom from Mike and offered it to the agent. The look of fury on Ramsey's face was frightening to see up close.

Rico stood beside Lynn. He was as tall as Ramsey and returned the agent's glare, measure for measure. Lynn never flinched.

Mr. Varnadore entered the atrium. At his arrival, Agent Harris grabbed his partner's arm and pulled him toward the door.

Ramsey continued to glare at them all as he went outside. Harris motioned to Brandon and his crew to leave and followed them out.

Once they were all gone, Lynn let out a breath and leaned against Rico for support.

"What the hell was that about, nena?" Rico asked.

"Just a crazy GBI agent. That's all," she whispered.

Mr. Varnadore clapped his hands. "Let's get this place cleaned up."

Lynn took both Rico's hands in hers. "Come on. We'll be here all night." She pulled her boyfriend into the café.

Jonah glanced up at Kevin. "Where's Trevor?"

"Safe for tonight."

"Trevor? He was here?" Mike winced and lowered his voice. "That's what this was all about? Why didn't you tell me?"

"It all happened so fast. And now the Alliance took him," Jonah explained. "And Kevin won't tell me where."

Mike cornered the taller boy. "I want to see Trevor."

Kevin frowned. "You can see him tomorrow. Right now, both of you have to stay here." Rico caught Kevin's attention and waved him toward the stage.

Jonah tugged on Kevin's shirt before he could move away. "How long are you gonna stay?"

Kevin smiled for the first time that night. "You're my new assignment." He went to help Rico break down the stage before Jonah could ask any more questions.

The cleanup process went fine until the real police arrived. The assistant principal intercepted the officers with Wick's girlfriend, Lynn, and Danita in tow. It wasn't lost on Jonah that Mr. Varnadore kept the cops' focus on him and not the others.

The teen center director's arrival was the only thing to defuse the situation. She was a woman of medium height who wore her hair cut short but stylish. During the day, she sported large earrings, a lot of makeup, and dressed business professional. Tonight, she clutched at a wrinkled coat she had pulled over a printed t-shirt and rumpled jeans.

And she was livid, at Jonah's group and the police, who she succeeded in sending away. Even so, a squad car parked itself within obvious view of the front doors with lights flashing the whole time.

Lynn had a quick conversation with the director.

"We'll have it out in the morning," the director announced and stormed out the front door.

The head custodian had also arrived and assessed the damaged as he scratched his uncombed hair. "Don't worry about her. Just clean up everything best you can. I'll get the rest in the morning," he told Wick before stepping outside to pick up stray trash that had been left out there.

Meanwhile, Lorraine and Rodney had rescued what remained of the cake. Anthony stepped over to gaze at the partially smashed creation. Jonah expected the arrogant boy to make a snide remark.

Instead, Anthony surprised him and shrugged. "The bottom layer never touched the floor. I think it's still good." He turned to Jonah, waiting.

When everyone else also stared at him, Jonah nodded. Plates and forks were passed around and soon all the kids found spots to sit and eat his ruined cake. The tension seemed to leak out of the group and kids began to joke and laugh.

Wick moved to an overturned smaller table and yelped when he lifted it. "Jonah! Your presents."

With Rico's help, the older boys grabbed the presents that had toppled out of sight behind the stage. They dumped them at Jonah's feet.

One by one, he opened the gifts and showed his friends. The whole thing was a bit surreal considering everything that had happened, but Jonah enjoyed it. The final gift was a small bracelet made of polished wooden pieces. "Thanks, Wick."

"You're welcome, Padawan."

Jonah slipped it on his wrist, feeling the power stored inside. *My own shield bracelet.*

After that, people gobbled down the rest of the cake at an alarming rate. Someone suggested they take a piece outside to the custodian and Mr. Varnadore. The two men were still out front. At the last minute, Danita also suggested a slice for the police officer. Rico didn't care for that idea, even though Lynn agreed.

Kevin sat next to Jonah in a brooding silence, watching the others. When people began to toss their plates in the trash and leave, Jonah stood.

He watched Lorraine fold the cardboard cake box. He thought the ruined cake represented his first real party. Smashed but still okay.

When Kevin rose and gently bumped against him, Jonah sighed. "I'm never gonna live this down, am I?"

Kevin snorted and said, "Nope."

CHAPTER TWELVE
OUTCASTS

Jonah blinked the bright morning sunlight out of his eyes and tried to focus on the bedside clock. When his eyes cooperated, he groaned in surprise. It was half past nine in the morning. *Dang!*

He lay his head on the pillow, thinking about sleeping a little longer, when he heard Aunt Imma's raised voice. Jonah's drowsiness evaporated as he listened. Was his aunt yelling at someone?

He had his answer when both Robert and Lynn yelled in reply. Jonah sat bolt upright in bed and threw his covers off. Today was a weekday. Aunt Imma should be at work by now.

This wasn't a good sign. Well, the yelling made that obvious, Jonah guessed.

He slipped on a pair of basketball trunks and exited his room.

Aunt Imma's angry voice became crystal clear as she bellowed, "You should have told us about the fight."

Jonah stopped, hoping no one would notice him. But it was too late. Aunt Imma turned in his direction. She was dressed in her pastel shirt, black slacks, and black comfortable work shoes.

"Oh, Jonah." She cast an angry glance at Robert and Lynn, who both looked just as heated yet carefully defiant. "I don't blame you for last night," Aunt Imma continued. "I'm just disappointed your party was ruined."

Robert gave him a pleading look and Jonah gulped as he moved into the family room. "It wasn't their fault. Brandon and his gang crashed the party."

"See, Mom?" Robert said. "That's what we've been trying to tell you."

Aunt Imma placed her hands on her hips. "That's not what Brandon's father is saying, nor the director of the teen center."

"She's covering her..." Lynn stopped herself in a huff and stared out the sliding door to the backyard.

Jonah's worst fear was coming true. Brandon had lied and now his powerful dad was interfering. "It's true, Aunt Imma. Brandon did crash the party. Lynn and Robert helped the other kids."

"You don't understand, Jonah." Aunt Imma paused, collecting her thoughts. "With people like the Warners, it's best not to get into anything with them." Aunt Imma seemed stuck between wanting to yell and fearful of doing that to Jonah. "Couldn't you let them patrol the party?"

"No!" Robert and Lynn shouted in perfect unison.

It would have been funny to Jonah in any other situation. "They started the fights," he added. "They did it on purpose to cause trouble." As he recalled the events, his own anger began to leak out. "What was I supposed to do, tell everyone to go home just to keep them from ruining it? How was that fair to me? It was supposed to be my party."

Aunt Imma's eyes widened and she didn't seem to know what to say for several long moments. Eventually, she crossed to Jonah and gave him a hug. As much as Jonah wanted to be a big kid, the hugs always got to him.

He was glad when the front door opened and Aunt Imma released him.

But Jonah's relief changed as soon as he saw Uncle James' face. Not only wasn't his uncle at work when he should have been by this time, but Uncle James also looked worn out. The man's collar was open and his tie was loosened and flopping against his chest as he strode down the hall.

Jonah's insides burned because he could guess why.

"Well?" Aunt Imma asked as soon as her husband reached the family room.

Uncle James threw his wrinkled sports coat over the back of his favorite armchair, pulled his glasses off, and took out his handkerchief. Jonah knew that was his uncle's way of processing what to say.

"I had it out with the director," Uncle James began. "She wanted to side with Brandon's father."

Aunt Imma swelled with anger. "She never said anything about having security."

"I know, Imma." Uncle James put his glasses on and blinked around at the group. "Brandon's father threatened to file a police report."

Everyone shouted at the same time, forcing Uncle James to wave them silent. "Please."

Aunt Imma wouldn't be quieted. "I hope, James, that you told that woman you'll pull her free ads from your paper."

Jonah wanted to cheer for his aunt. It seemed she was finally on their side despite the earlier yelling.

"Yes, I did." Uncle James eyed Jonah. "I also reminded her that Jonah's godfather is our attorney. I gave her Mr. Armstrong's card to pass along to Brandon's father."

Aunt Imma blinked in surprise.

Robert whooped, "Way to go, Dad."

"Did that work?" Lynn asked.

"Well, judging by the change in her expression, I don't think any charges will be filed. It's one thing to mess with the locals, but Marcus' firm is worldwide."

That was the best news Jonah had heard, but his uncle's face remained solemn. Jonah opened himself to a partial Reaper stare and sensed the dread leaking off his uncle.

"That being said," Uncle James continued in a low voice, "I suggest you three stay clear of the teen center for a few days."

Lynn's arms dropped to the sides and she stared at her father. "Why? We didn't do anything."

"I know that, Lynn."

"Then why can't we go around the center, Dad?"

Uncle James closed his eyes. Jonah suspected he was counting to ten or something like that. His voice was measured when he continued. "The director's still angry, plus Brandon's father is working with the firm adding in the security cameras. So, I think it's best if we let things cool down."

"That's not fair." Robert sounded as bummed as his sister. "It's like we're outcasts from our own space!"

"Oh Robert, don't be so dramatic," Aunt Imma said.

"I'm not being dramatic, Mom." The veins on Robert's thin neck stood out as he yelled. "What about the website and blog?"

Uncle James' eyes gleamed as he said, "You can work on the blog from one of my offices. The teen center website will have to wait. In fact, without you doing updates, maybe they'll see how important you are." He offered Robert an encouraging smile.

Robert shook his head in dismay. "It still isn't right."

"Well, don't forget the break-in last summer," Uncle James added. "This makes two incidents in about a year."

Jonah was numb. In one night, their clubhouse was off limits. But Uncle James' comment about the break-in sparked something else in Jonah's mind. "It's those GBI agents."

Lynn nodded. "I bet Agent Ramsey is egging things on."

"That's another reason to stay away." Uncle James met Lynn's gaze. "Why don't you and Robert come with me today?"

Robert stormed off to his bedroom, looking defeated, but Lynn didn't move. "I have some things to do with Rico."

Aunt Imma made a disapproving sound under her breath and looked away. Jonah had discovered that his aunt didn't care for Rico. It was the tattoos that covered his arms. She thought that proof positive the boy was in a gang or something like that.

"Don't go near the teen center, Lynn." Uncle James' voice had a rare edge to it.

"I won't." Lynn stalked off to her room, leaving Jonah alone with his aunt and uncle.

When Uncle James turned to him, Jonah said, "I'm hanging out with Mike. We're going to the library."

"Good."

Aunt Imma grabbed her purse and kissed Mr. Hightower on the cheek. "I have to go. You sure it'll be okay?"

"Yes," he assured her.

Robert came out of his room, dressed to go. Uncle James called out to Aunt Imma, "Hold the door. We're coming."

"See you around, little cousin." Robert followed his dad and mom out of the house.

The buzz in Jonah's head from everything that had happened began to irritate him. It was as if every time he made plans, something else happened. Jonah retreated to his room and grabbed his clothes for the day.

By the time he finished with his shower, he was less bummed with the situation and ready to find Mike and hang out. As he walked down the hall to his room, shirtless, Jonah received an unpleasant surprise. Lynn, Mike, and Kevin sat talking in the kitchen.

Mike waved at him.

Kevin smirked and said, "Show off."

Jonah gazed at his bare chest, so much less developed than Kevin's, and hurried to pull on his shirt. "What's going on?" he asked, moving through the family room and into the kitchen.

"Marcus wants me to bring you to the safe house," Kevin said.

Lynn wore a defiant look on her face. "I've already told him I'm going."

"Me too," Mike chimed in.

"I thought you were meeting up with Rico?" Jonah thought to point out.

Lynn shrugged. "I was just saying that to bug Mom."

Jonah smiled at that, then he focused on the central question. "Is Trevor all right?"

"Yep." Kevin glanced at Jonah's bare feet. "You gonna put on some shoes?"

Jonah experienced that quick annoyance at Kevin's poking fun. At the same time, he liked sparring with the boy. "I thought I'd go barefoot." He raised his foot to wiggle his toes at Kevin.

Mike giggled while Lynn rose from her chair and shoved Jonah toward his bedroom. "Get real. You have one minute."

Jonah only needed half that time to grab his favorite pair of red sneakers and return to the kitchen. "We can't phase from in here," he said while slipping on his socks and then shoes.

"I didn't intend to." Kevin rose from the table and opened the back door. "Come on." He stepped outside and crossed the backyard to the shed.

"You also can't create vortices, either," Kevin added.

"Wow," Mike breathed. "That's cool."

"No it's not." Jonah said it before he could stop himself.

Kevin laughed. "You must have been trying to sneak out of your room at night."

"No." Jonah's face warmed, causing Mike to laugh. Jonah scowled at Kevin. "We can't phase in the daylight, either. Someone could see us."

"He knows that too, Jonah." Lynn unlocked the shed's door and stood back to let everyone else inside.

It occurred to Jonah that Lynn, Mike, and Kevin had talked things through while he showered. He stepped into the darkened shed. With the lawnmower, gardening tools, and all three bikes still chained inside, the fit was tight.

Lynn came in last and closed the door, leaving them in almost pitch black except for where sunlight leaked through gaps in the wall joints. With the door closed, the overpowering smell of grass cuttings, oil, and a faint whiff of gas from the gas can became more pronounced.

"Everyone hold onto me," Kevin said.

"You can handle three people?" Lynn sounded impressed.

"Of course he can. He's an alliance member now." Jonah let some of his irritation come through.

Even in the darkness, Lynn's aim was true as she smacked him across the back of the head. Mike stifled his giggles.

Jonah fumed. An awkward shuffling happened when Lynn and Mike fumbled to grip Kevin's hands. Jonah started to grab onto Kevin's arm when he remembered the last time they did this sort of thing.

Today, Kevin wore a light blue t-shirt and dark cargo pants without a belt. Jonah decided to slip a finger through a belt loop on the boy's pants. But when he tried, his aim was off and he poked Kevin in the hip.

"Excuse me," the older boy said, sounding amused. "That's not my hand."

"What?" Lynn asked.

"Nothing," Jonah said, glad that the darkness hid his embarrassed face. He succeeded in threading his finger through a loop on the second attempt. When Kevin shifted, Jonah wondered if the boy was smirking at him in the darkness.

A second later, the familiar ripples traveled over every inch of Jonah's body. Lynn didn't utter a sound, but Mike gasped. The sensation only lasted seconds. One moment, they were in the darkened shed. The next moment, muted light flared around them as they reappeared on a large, shaded patio.

A lush manicured yard and garden stretched out to their right. The smell of late summer plants filled the air. And on their left was a huge mansion.

"This is nice," Lynn gushed. "When you said safe house, I was thinking something smaller."

Kevin motioned for them to follow him to the upper landing and then to a back door. "We only called it a safe house because of the courier, but it's really a guest house."

He opened the back door and entered a large pantry and then a restaurant-grade kitchen. Rows of silver pots hung from hooks overhead. The stove contained numerous burners, some with bubbling pots on them.

The aroma of cooking sauces hit Jonah's nose and his mouth watered, reminding him he hadn't eaten breakfast. Plates were stacked to the side on a large wooden worktop. And beyond the kitchen and in a side nook was a round wooden table.

Trevor sat there, eating and talking to a stout woman whose hair was a bright cinnamon color. The courier dropped his fork when he saw Jonah and shot to his feet. That caused the woman to whirl around. She rose from the chair and, despite her size, moved rather quick to enfold Kevin in a bone-crushing hug.

"Kevin!" she mumbled into his chest because that's as far as her face reached.

Kevin returned the hug, wrapping his long arms around her. "Hey Mom."

Jonah's jaw dropped. He, Lynn, and Mike exchanged similar shocked expressions.

CHAPTER THIRTEEN
SAFE HOUSE

All Fallen Reapers had first lives. That's the period of time from their original birth to their moment of death as mortals. Once they became one of the Undead, if they rebelled and became mortal again, all contact with former families was forbidden. At least, that's the way Marcus explained it to Jonah.

In most cases, such as Jonah's godfather and his dad, they had been Reapers for decades and their immediate mortal family members were long gone. But Kevin was different. He confessed to Jonah last summer that he had only been a Reaper for a few years and still had a family and little brother alive and well.

For obvious reasons, Kevin could never show up on their doorstep and say, "Hi." And there was the fact that Kevin's family lived in Chicago and not Georgia. For all those reasons, Jonah was confused when Kevin called the woman…

"Mom?" Jonah repeated while gaping at the older boy.

He didn't get it for another basic reason. Not only was the woman's oatmeal complexion as light as Mike's, whereas

Kevin's skin was a deep chocolate, they also didn't favor each other at all.

The woman smiled at Jonah's confused expression. "I'm not really his mom." She held out a hand. "Hi, my name is Mabel," she said with a hint of a Creole accent. "You're Jonah." Mabel gently ran her hands down Jonah's cheeks. "My God, you were just a bundle in your parent's arms when I last saw you. Now, you're all grown and look so much like your father."

"You knew him?" Jonah asked.

"Of course. I took him in when he came back. He wasn't much older than Kevin is now. Well, in human years." She winked at Kevin.

"She runs a foster home in D.C. for special people," Kevin explained.

"And all the kids call me Mom," Mabel finished.

Jonah's eyes widened. "Kids? You mean Fallen Reapers?"

"Oh no, *mon cheri*. Most are mortals like your friend here." She graced Mike with a smile. "Except they have a talent like Omar, who can do memory charms." Mabel stroked her double chin, peering at Mike. "I'm sure you have a gift too."

Mike shrugged. "I don't think so."

Mabel chuckled. "Give it time, *mon cheri*. Give it time. Humans are capable of a lot of things. The Alliance tries to find and recruit them."

She took Lynn's right hand in her own. "I hear you have the Sight, like all the women in your family." Lynn nodded. "Jonah's mom, your aunt, was strong in it. Don't you be afraid to use the talent, girl." Mabel released Lynn's hand and gazed around at the group. "It's often young people about your ages who show up. Their powers and gifts suddenly come out and they tend to do something big. It's easy to find them at that point."

"They need a safe place away from their families," Kevin added. As he looked around the kitchen, Jonah thought the boy was remembering his time there. "The Alliance teaches them to deal with their abilities."

Mabel patted Kevin's bicep, like a true proud mother. "Kevin was so young-minded when he came back that he fit right in with the rest of the young people."

Kevin frowned. "Marcus said I needed someone watching over me."

Jonah thought his friend was a little embarrassed. So he decided to help and bring the talk back to Mabel. "Where's your house? Here in Atlanta?"

"Oh, no. I still live in Washington. I just come down from time to time." Mabel smiled at Kevin and Jonah. "I'm lucky I did. I have my chance to see you," she continued. "Your parents kept you away. And when they died, Marcus bundled you up and shipped you to Georgia. I know they made arrangements, but..." Mabel sniffled, and Trevor handed her a Kleenex. "Thank you. I'm so sorry about your parents, Jonah." She gave his hand a gentle squeeze. "At least now you're on the right track."

She touched Trevor's cheek. "Now there's a new one to help." She gently turned Trevor and prodded him toward the opposite door. "Move along. Marcus will want to talk to you."

True to Mabel's words, Marcus waited for the group in the large living room. He stood by a fireplace and nodded to Jonah as he entered. Overstuffed comfortable furniture filled the space. Trevor sat down on a tartan-colored love seat, and Mike hurried to sit beside him.

Kevin and Jonah took the large sofa opposite them while Lynn picked a high-backed armchair. Jonah thought the chair fit her like a regal queen when she lifted her chin, surveying the room. He averted his gaze before Lynn could catch him.

Mike peppered Trevor with questions. "Why didn't you tell me you were the courier? What's it like?" Mike took a breath. "What's your cover job?"

Trevor laughed. "I'm just a glorified record keeper, and a real courier."

The answer seemed to animate Mike even more. "But what's it like, keeping records on the other side? I do the records for our blog."

A shy smile transformed Trevor's face as he regarded Mike. "What's a blog?"

"Well, it's a series of chronological articles, like written records."

Jonah smiled as Mike explained. His buddy suddenly showed more enthusiasm for a job he had called lame two days ago.

"Do you use Seeker archive boxes?" Mike pressed.

"You know about those?" Trevor turned to face Mike, ready to ignore everyone else.

"We can talk about his job later." Marcus had finished his quiet conversation with Mabel and waited as everyone settled down. "We know about the party and the aftermath. The law firm made it clear that if Brandon's father tries to make an issue of it, we'd counter."

Jonah wanted to ask about the bodies behind the teen center but decided he really didn't want to know the details. He chose something safe to comment on. "I bet Brandon loved that."

"Well," Marcus hedged, "I can't speak for Brandon, but his father isn't a fool. It's more important they keep their true aim undercover. So we expect him to back down."

Jonah welcomed that news, but they still had another problem. "We can't go in to the teen center."

"I know." Marcus crossed to the second armchair and sat down. "This is Agent Hunter's doing. It's an old tactic. Apply pressure to draw out the target. He's shutting you off from the places you can call a refuge."

Marcus's blunt statement confirmed Jonah's hunch, but he had never thought of it in that way. Lynn's expression also worried him. She looked spooked. Jonah begin to think she'd sense this would happen all along.

"What do we do?" Mike asked.

Kevin rapped the coffee table with a knuckle. "We keep moving forward. Don't let the enemy win." He glanced at Marcus. "Right?"

"Yes. And to do that, you need information." Marcus gestured to Trevor. "It's time to share everything you told me last night."

Trevor sat forward, resting his elbows on his knees and clasping his hands together. The posture and worry lines on the boy's forehead exuded the air of someone who'd been through a lot. Even his short dreads seemed to droop under the invisible pressure.

At that moment, Trevor struck Jonah as older than he appeared. But the effect was gone within seconds, leaving Jonah puzzled.

Trevor stared at his hands while he began. "My job was to meet with the Alliance rep and smuggle him through the portal and to the other side. We thought a face-to-face meeting was the next step in moving our common cause forward."

"You mean fighting the Grim Reaper?" Mike interjected.

"He means the Rulers of the Afterworld." Marcus gestured to Trevor to continue.

"The Grim Reaper shares power with the supreme record keeper, the Grand Oracle," Trevor explained. "While your Alliance works on this side to stop the Grim Reaper's plans, my people have their own quiet rebellion against the Grand Oracle."

"You already know that someone inside the Alliance betrayed us and told both sides about the meeting," Marcus interjected to the group. "Now they're after Trevor."

Lynn asked the more probing question. "What do you know?"

Trevor met her determined gaze. "No one has ever seen our leader in person. We call him The Elder. As a safety measure, he transmits instructions and speeches in separate dispatches to one cell at a time."

Lynn's eyes widened and then she smiled. "You're the only one to ever see his face?"

"Yes. He's very high in Archivist administration. That's how he's able to help the dissidents."

"As you can imagine," Marcus added, "the Grand Oracle wants Trevor. With his knowledge, they could destroy the Afterworld rebels from the top."

Mike touched Trevor's arm. "But what about the Grim Reaper?"

Trevor shrugged. "He wants the leverage, I think. He'd use my information to end the power sharing arrangement. That's why I have to return. Not only am I running out of time, but the longer I stay, the greater the chance they'll catch me." He pointed at Jonah. "Ramsey will continue to come after you."

"Yeah, I know, but your cover is blown on the other side."

"I'll have to work directly with the Elder from now on." Trevor closed his eyes. "He can protect me."

Jonah was moved by the conviction in the boy's voice. "How can I help?"

"It's your compass."

Jonah pulled the compass from his pocket. He'd been planning to go with Mike to the library and try to figure it out.

Trevor stretched out his hand, and Jonah placed the compass on the boy's palm. "This is called a Seeker's compass." He held the device close to his face, examining the surface. "It's one of a kind, Jonah. Special."

"How will it help you get back?"

When Trevor hesitated, Jonah suspected the boy of filtering what he would reveal. He'd seen his godfather do it often enough.

Trevor glanced around. "This compass can open a back door to the Afterworld. I'll be able to cross over. But to do that," he looked at Jonah, "you have to uncover the true compass face."

Marcus stood. "Are you sure?"

"The Elder told me himself." Trevor handed the compass back to Jonah. "Only Jonah can do it."

"What happens when I open this true face?" Jonah glanced at the device and the normal face displayed at the moment. "Will it activate a vortex or something to the Afterworld?"

"No." Trevor sucked in a breath to continue. "Opening the doorway is a two-step process. First you have to find a Cognitive Enhancer. That's what the true compass face will reveal. A code or location where you can find it."

"Cognitive Enhancer?" Mike asked. "You mean a mind booster?"

Trevor gave him a wan smile. "I didn't name it, but mind booster is better."

Mike nodded. "And the second step?"

"There's a cavern with a special pedestal. If you set the compass inside the pedestal, you'll open a second set of special codes, each one a different location in the Afterworld. With the Enhancer, or mind booster, Jonah can decipher those codes, enter one into the compass, and open the doorway to that chosen location."

The implication staggered Jonah. At the moment, he didn't see a way to enter codes in the compass. He began to wonder what the true compass face would look like.

Lynn held up her hands. "Wait. In order to decipher the special codes, you need an Enhancer? But in order to find that device, you need a different code from the compass." She eyed Trevor. "Did I miss something?"

"No." Trevor seemed at a loss to explain further.

Jonah got it. "It's like our computers at the clubhouse, Lynn." He paused at the stab of pain at not being able to even go into their sanctuary. "We're the only ones who can log into the system and access the files."

Mike nodded and sat forward, excited. "Jonah's right. You can get into the system with a club password. That's like the first code when Jonah opens the true face of the compass. But to access your encrypted background files for stories, you need a second code, the encryption key."

Jonah snapped his fingers. "It's added protection to make sure the person using the compass is the right one."

Lynn frowned. "Sounds like a geek came up with this process."

Kevin snorted and clapped his hands. "Now that we figured that out, where's this Enhancer?" He looked ready to go right now.

Trevor pointed at the compass. "That initial code is locked inside."

Lynn stared at Jonah. "You need to figure out that riddle and open the compass, hero."

Jonah's annoyance flared. "I planned to do that twice already, but things keep happening."

"Well, you're in luck today. No interruptions. Get busy; we have a mission." Lynn pulled Jonah to his feet. "The County Library?"

With a graceful move, Marcus rose and blocked the doorway. "Given the importance of the compass, I think Jonah should figure it out here."

"But–" Jonah started.

"I'm afraid that's an order." Marcus arched an eyebrow.

Mike stood beside Jonah. "We can do it."

"I guess, but it would have been nice to use the library."

Kevin snorted. "There's a library here."

"Really?" Jonah thought the boy was joking.

Marcus moved aside and Kevin led the way down a wide hallway to a well-stocked library. Mike and Jonah moved into the large room of dark wood and earth tones. A huge table was situated in the center, with books of all kinds already placed on it. Some were opened. A few smaller tables were scattered around with study-type chairs beside them.

The room had the feel of the older college libraries Jonah had visited in Washington. Kevin's comment about this being a Guest House for young people made more sense.

Jonah turned to Marcus, who stood in the doorway. "The other kids use this?"

"Yes."

"Where is everyone?"

"They'll arrive next month for the summer session."

Jonah nodded.

Mike grinned. "It's like Xavier's school in the X-Men." He and Jonah laughed.

Kevin exchanged a glance with Lynn. "I see they haven't changed."

"Nope." Lynn thumped them on the heads. "Get busy, geek boys."

Jonah sat the compass on the center table and pulled the riddle from his other pocket. As the others headed for the doorway, Jonah called out to Kevin, "What are you gonna do?"

"I'm taking Lynn and Trevor down to the bat cave."

When Kevin grinned, Jonah wanted to punch him. The older boy knew the name would pique his and Mike's curiosity.

Mike beat Jonah to the next question. "What's the bat cave?"

Kevin lingered in the doorway. "That's the basement with the pool and Ping-Pong tables, the latest game consoles, big-screen TV, and all the movies you ever want to watch." He grinned. "Plus it has the best sofas and chairs, and a refrigerator full of sodas and snacks." He pointed at the compass. "Get to work."

CHAPTER FOURTEEN

THE RIDDLE

Jonah spent his first moments in the Guest House library thinking of all kinds of choice names for Kevin.

Mike pulled the thick curtains back to allow brilliant sunlight to stream through the massive window. "You think Kevin's telling the truth?"

Jonah blinked at the interruption to his pleasant thoughts of revenge. "Yeah."

Mike peered at Jonah as he returned to the table. "Why does he tease you?"

"Don't know." Jonah had to use two hands to pull out one of the heavy wooden chairs. He sat down.

Mike went around to the opposite side and pulled out the other chair. He had to hop on his knees in order to lean across the table. "Maybe you're like a brother he never had, or..."

Jonah hadn't intended to respond until Mike said that last bit. He paused, the riddle still unfolded. "Or?"

Mike met his gaze and then shrugged. "Maybe he likes you or something. I don't know."

Jonah thought his buddy tried to sound offhanded with the comment. But he caught the quick, nervous glance that Mike gave him.

The truth was, the idea didn't bother Jonah at all. He had wondered the same thing. Since Mike brought up the subject, Jonah figured it'd be safe to kick around the idea and ask about Trevor.

Mike tapped the riddle with a finger. "Hurry up and read it."

"But..."

"What?" Mike looked genuinely lost. "This is important. Trevor's waiting."

"I know that." Jonah tried to hide the irritation in his voice.

When Mike let out an impatient sigh, Jonah swallowed any comebacks and began to read the riddle out loud.

Who am I?

I always start at the beginning

But rarely end at the ending.

I am ruled by War and find comfort in Fire.

Freedom is my greatest desire.

Who am I?

I control the balance and tip the scales.

I'm driven by love and beauty's heroic tales.

My self-expression is done with style and flair

You'll find I repose in the air.

Who am I?

I am the bringer of old age and Time is my friend

Security is my cloak and on the earth I depend.

I'm extremely hard to open, my secrets reveal

Once naked and exposed I rarely conceal.

If you can answer these questions and unlock my true face

I will ever point you to the right and proper place.

Jonah's voice ended on a strong note. He was impressed with himself and relieved. Rereading the note hadn't made him lose it.

Mike took out his glasses and perched them on his thin nose. As soon as Jonah gave him the riddle, he settled into the mystery, his eyes darting back and forth as he read over the page several times.

The silence in the library stretched into minutes. Jonah grew impatient and tapped his fingers on the table. Mike ignored him, too engrossed in the riddle.

Jonah huffed and began spinning the compass on the table between them.

Mike broke off reading and leaned close. "Can I touch it?"

"Yeah."

Mike lifted the compass. "Wow. I never saw it up close until today. It looks normal except for the button on the side and this dial around the face. These are Zodiac symbols, Jonah."

"I figured out that much. I even tried turning the dial to my sign and pressing the button, but nothing happened."

"You had the right idea, but…" Mike paused, running his hand down the note while cupping the compass in the other. "I think you need three zodiac signs."

"Are you sure?"

"The riddle's divided into three sections, so I figure that means three signs, not one. That has to be it." Mike set the compass aside and used both hands to press the riddle flat. "Notice how each stanza mentions one of the four elements? Fire, air, earth, or water." Mike snapped his fingers. "We need an astrology book."

Without another word, Mike jumped out of his chair and began to search among the books. Jonah checked the shelf closest to him. The books covered all kinds of subjects, but most were on mythology, fairy creatures, folktales, and obscure histories.

Mike dropped two books on the table with loud thuds, drawing Jonah's attention.

When he saw the title of the book on top, Jonah smiled. "*Astrology and You?*"

Mike shrugged. "You have a better idea?"

Actually, Jonah thought Mike's idea was brilliant. He opened the book and found a section for Astrological Signs. "What should we start with?"

"Try fire."

"Okay." Jonah read down the list of zodiac signs. "I see three fire signs: Aries, Leo, and Sagittarius."

Mike gasped, "What are their characteristics?"

"That may take too long. What does the riddle say?"

"I always start at the beginning but rarely end at the end."

"Gee wiz, that could be anything."

"Well the second line says the symbol is ruled by war."

Jonah flipped the page. "Aries is ruled by Mars. That's the god of War. And it says that all Fire signs like freedom." He sat the book on the table. "Freedom is my greatest desire. That's what the last line of that first stanza says."

"The sign has to be Aries. It's the only sign to fit all the clues." Mike pulled out a sheet of paper and wrote *Aries* on it in a small, precise print.

The excitement begin to build inside Jonah as he lifted the book and read through the Aries characteristics. "Cool."

"What?" Mike tried to peer over the top of the book.

"Aries are quick to initiate new things but often don't follow through."

Mike laughed. "They are rarely at the end because they leave early. Your parents were interesting."

"Yeah, they were." Fresh pain spiked inside Jonah at the sad realization that his birthday would always bring pain because his parents had died the same day. Mike apologized, but Jonah tapped the riddle. "Let's keep going."

Now that they had the flow, figuring out the second sign, Libra, and third, Capricorn, was a snap. Afterward, Mike sat back in his chair, staring at the names of the three Zodiac symbols. "I wonder if we have to figure out the right order?"

Jonah shook his head. "My dad wouldn't make it that hard. He wanted me to be able to use it."

He rotated the dial to the first sign and pressed the button. He thought the compass vibrated in his hand, but couldn't be sure. When he rotated the dial to the second sign and pressed the button again, he was certain of it. He looked at Mike. "It's vibrating."

"You wanna keep going?"

Jonah nodded, turned the dial to the third sign, and pressed the button. The compass didn't exactly vibrate, but it hummed with power, growing warmer in his hand. The face began to waver and suddenly folded in on itself.

"Wow!" Mike said, then hurried around the table to peer over Jonah's shoulder.

A new, far more ornate face appeared on the compass, one made of a smooth, polished material. Its circular dials contained strange, yet beautiful, raised symbols.

Jonah pointed at the markings. "Those are the same symbols on Robert's archive box and Lynn's blades."

In addition to the double rows of symbols, the compass had two hands like an expensive clock. The longer hand resembled the engraved nib of an old-style fountain pen. The smaller hand looked like a short dagger. And at the very center of the face, a red button pulsed.

"Do you know what they mean?" Mike asked.

"We never figured them out."

"Maybe Trevor knows."

Jonah thought that a good possibility. He and Mike jumped when the longer clock-like hand jerked into motion on its own. When the hand stopped, the symbol directly above its pointed end began to glow a bright yellow.

The hand snapped into motion again. When it paused beneath another symbol, it too began to glow. The hand rotated again and again until six symbols in all glowed. The red button in the center of the compass's face switched to a pulsing green color.

Jonah moved his own finger over the compass face and the symbol directly beneath his finger glowed brighter. He paused, then brought his finger back to the edge of the dial. The symbol not only glowed brighter, but it also expanded. As his finger moved away, the symbol contracted to its original size.

"Cool!"

He wiggled his finger left, then right, watching as each symbol expanded and contracted. The fluid magnifying effect allowed him to easily see each symbol. That gave Jonah an idea and he moved his finger over the long hand of the compass, and it followed his movement.

He jerked a finger back and forth and the hand wavered, trying to follow the quick action. When he swiped a finger all the way around the compass, the long hand whirled around. Jonah laughed.

Mike shoved him. "Stop that."

"Sorry," Jonah said. "This is so cool."

"It's obvious you can change the combination of symbols. But we don't want to do that. Trevor said this was the code to the mind booster."

"Then what does the green button do?"

Mike hunched his shoulders. "Well, green usually means *go*."

Jonah considered that for a moment. "So you think it'll take me to the mind booster?"

"Yeah, I do. And that could be dangerous."

"Dangerous?" That had never occurred to Jonah, but considering it now, he didn't think it possible. "My parents meant for me to figure this out on my own and press the button. I'm sure they visited the place, which means it can't be dangerous."

Mike nodded. "I can see that."

"We should try the code." The recklessness nagged Jonah. He hated to wait after being pushed into doing something.

Mike tapped the table to get his attention. "Jonah..."

"You said this was important." Jonah pressed the green button, drawing a scathing look from Mike. His moment of rebellion was short lived. "Mike? I feel funny."

Mike slugged him in the arm. "Listen to me the next time, idiot."

"I'm serious. The compass is doing something to me."

Mike's mouth dropped open. "Oh. Well, let go of it!"

"I can't." Jonah's skin began tingling. "It feels like the times I phased. The compass is causing me to phase."

Mike started for the door. "I'll get Kevin."

"There's no time!" Jonah heard the fear in his own voice and hated it. The mocking voice in his head was ruthless and sounded a lot like Lynn. *Oh no, hero, you wanted to press the button. Now deal with it.*

Mike hurried back to Jonah's side and reached out.

"Don't touch me," Jonah said, realizing too late what his friend was doing.

Mike ignored the warning and slapped his hands over Jonah's hand and compass. "This may be stupid, but I'm going with you."

The air around them wobbled and distorted a second before a rippling sensation shot over Jonah's body. Mike let out a startled gasp. An instant later, the old library vanished.

CHAPTER FIFTEEN
PARENTS' HIDEAWAY

Jonah could usually shift his position while phasing, but the compass had thrown off his concentration. When the device transported the boys to a thickly wooded area, Jonah was still in a seated position.

"Oh no," he said and dropped to the hard ground, numbing his butt. Mike, who had been leaning over him, came down on top of him, crushing the air out of his lungs.

"Hey!" Jonah managed to scream.

Mike ignored Jonah's protests and scrambled for his glasses, which had clattered onto the leaf-covered ground. He succeeded in kneeing Jonah in the side.

"Get off me." Jonah heaved his friend off.

Mike whirled, his recovered glasses in one hand, and landed two punches to Jonah's chest with the other. "Don't you dare. This was your fault, not mine."

Jonah rolled away from his buddy. Mike didn't like to fight, but a year in the Practice Club had taught him to hit with power.

"You decided to come with me." Jonah climbed to his feet and winced. "And that hurt."

"Good." Mike dusted off his glasses, then folded them in angry motions. He shoved them in a pocket and began rubbing his arms. "Where are we?"

"Hold on." Jonah had already decided to try and sense how far they had traveled. Marcus said a Reaper could do it, and Jonah had been practicing.

Once he was sure Mike wouldn't hit him again, Jonah closed his eyes and thought of the library. With that firmly in mind, he visualized this new location, creating an imaginary line connecting both points. The answer that materialized in his head shocked him.

"Well?" Mike asked.

"We're still in Georgia," Jonah answered, "but we're over two hundred miles from Atlanta."

"Wow." Mike gave him an awed look

Jonah began to explore the immediate surroundings, noting that the ground below them was higher than the rest of the immediate area. He stomped his foot, feeling the unexpected hard surface beneath. That gave Jonah an idea. He knelt down and brushed away the leaves, not caring about the dry dirt getting under his fingernails.

Mike knelt beside him. "Jonah? What are you doing?"

"Help me."

Mike frowned but joined in and together, they quickly uncovered a circular piece of concrete with large bricks bordering the edge. One brick in particular was larger and different from the rest. Years of hard-packed dirt covered it, falling away in dry flakes as Jonah began clearing the surface. Soon, he uncovered six symbols embedded in the brick's rough surface.

When Jonah sat back, Mike leaned closer to peer at the brick. "Those are the same symbols from the compass. Have you ever seen this place before?"

"No, but my parents went so many places that I never knew about."

Jonah brushed away as much dirt as he could from the edge of the concrete platform to reveal a connected walkway. It seemed to go directly under a thick wall of rhododendron bushes that was beside them. That's when he noticed a line of bricks beneath the bushes.

He stood, examining the bushes for a second before digging his hands into them and pulling the branches apart. "Look! It's a stairway, and it leads up a hill."

Mike squeezed beside him, pulling more branches out of the way. He gasped and pointed. "That looks like a brick wall at the top."

"Yeah." Portions of a brick wall were visible through the thick bushes and trees. "I say we go up."

"Are you sure? Maybe we should just go back."

"What about the Enhancer? My dad wanted me to come here." Jonah tested the first step.

Mike hesitated. "Jonah, you can get us back, can't you?"

"Yep," Jonah lied, keeping his face turned away from Mike. The truth was, he wasn't sure. He'd phased Mike or one of his cousins short distances on the practice field. But this was two hundred miles. "Let's look around first, okay?"

Mike crossed his arms.

Jonah sighed. "Come on. Don't you want to find the Enhancer?"

Mike let out a breath. "Of course."

"Well, what's wrong?"

"Why hide it in the middle of the woods?"

Mike's question stumped Jonah until he remembered how his dad thought. "Don't be afraid of the new and unexpected."

"What?"

"It's what my dad always told me. Don't be afraid. I think it's part test." When Mike refused to move, Jonah grinned at him. "You were the one who said my parents were interesting."

"That was the riddle. I didn't mean anything like this."

Jonah's irritation flared as he gazed up the steps. "Fine. I'm going up. You can wait here for me."

Without another word, he slipped through the overgrown bushes and mounted the brick steps. Soon, he heard Mike huffing and following.

Trees were evenly spaced on either side of the staircase. He could appreciate that the whole effort would have been nice once, but it was obvious no one had trimmed these trees in a while. Errant branches hung at odd angles, including right over the staircase. Plus there were accumulations of dead leaves covering many of the steps. They were bone dry from the near drought this summer and crackled loudly underfoot.

Mike stepped on a moss-covered branch, causing it to snap. He kicked it away and frowned when Jonah paused to look back. "Why not hide it in plain sight? The Protector's Ring was in the teen center."

"I don't know," Jonah admitted. "But it would be something unexpected."

The more Jonah thought about it, the more excited he became. His parents had found the Protector's Ring. Why wouldn't they have the Mind Booster too? Maybe this stairway led to a hidden entrance to an ancient cave and the device.

Without realizing it, Jonah started to leap over the debris on the steps. But when he reached the top, he paused, confused. The stairs opened onto a flat, brick-paved courtyard. At the center of the space was a tree with extremely long branches twisting up into the air.

Mike made a disgusted sound. "They look like worms."

The tree trunk was covered in bark with a patchwork pattern of various greens. Jonah guessed the tree reached at least thirty feet into the air. The branches wavered slightly as if in a breeze.

Jonah leaned back to see the top. "It's different. I've never seen anything like it."

"Do you think it's magical?"

Jonah shrugged. "Too bad Wick isn't here. I'm sure he'd know." He walked slowly around the tree as the disappointment replaced the earlier excitement. The tree may look weird to him, but it seemed like just another tree. "Why would my parents want me to see this?"

Mike didn't respond. Instead, he continued around the courtyard. Besides the tree, old wooden benches had been placed on the north and south facing sides of the square space.

Jonah sat down on the nearer one. "I don't understand," he continued. "I thought I would find the Mind Booster. What's so important about this stupid tree? Why bring me here?"

Mike wrung his hands for a moment, then he knelt beside Jonah. "You thought this was a test. Maybe you're supposed to figure it out."

Jonah's irritation peaked. "There's nothing to figure out. My parents were archeologists, not park rangers."

Mike pointed at something behind Jonah. "Look! It's an arrow. Someone pressed the shape into the wood."

At first, Jonah thought the arrow pointed into the woods until he spotted another brick step covered with fallen branches.

He stood and moved toward the step while Mike ran around to the opposite bench and called out, "There's another arrow on this one."

"And there's a set of steps over here." Jonah beckoned to Mike. "Come on."

They found a smaller courtyard at the top of the second series of steps. An uneven brick-covered path led from the stairway straight to the far side, disappearing into the surrounding forest. A second path bisected this one, leading off into the trees. And a sculptured rhododendron bush in a large brick planter sat at the center of this courtyard.

The end of a gold-colored cylinder stuck out of the bush, near the top of the planter, and glimmered in the weak sunlight. Jonah ran over and gently pulled the cylinder free. It was tied with a bright green ribbon.

He glanced at Mike and raised an eyebrow. "Should I open it?"

Mike nodded.

Jonah slid the ribbon off and turned the cylinder over in his hands. It had a line down its longest length and two latches that were clearly locks. Could this cylinder have been coded for him? It was just like Robert's archive box, which Jonah's cousin had accidentally coded for himself when he dripped a bit of his own blood on the box. Not even Lynn could unlock it.

Did my parents use a bit of my own blood?

After a second of exploration, Jonah's finger touched a small knot. He took a breath, pressed the knot, and the latches retracted into hidden niches that sealed themselves.

Mike's mouth hung open. Jonah had expected the weird latches, but he didn't know what he'd find inside. He blinked in surprise when his trembling hand brushed the surface of a rolled piece of paper.

"I'll hold that." Mike took the cylinder.

"Thanks." Jonah lifted the paper free. It was heavy, expensive paper with subtle designs woven into its texture.

And it was exactly like the paper his dad had used for the compass riddle. Excitement ignited in Jonah's chest as he unrolled the paper, revealing a message in his dad's handwriting.

Jonah, if you're reading this note, you've learned to control your fear of the unexpected. I'm proud of you, son. You've also figured out the riddle and discovered another power. The compass engaged your phase ability. That's the ability to move from one place to another in the blink of an eye.

You must have a million questions, son, but don't worry. The compass was programmed to send me a signal. Your mother and I will arrive shortly and explain everything. You've known for some time that you're different from other kids. It's time you understood everything about yourself.

Jonah stopped reading because his eyesight blurred. He wiped his eyes with the back of his hand and sucked in a breath.

"They were going to tell me everything on my thirteenth birthday." Jonah lowered the note. "I already know I'm half Reaper. I know I have Death Sense. And I know I can phase."

He leaned against the brick planter, allowing the little branches to poke him in the back and not caring when one poked especially hard.

Mike sat beside him, their arms touching. "Jonah you're forgetting the compass was supposed to be your gift a year ago, before all those things happened. Think about it. If your parents hadn't died, this would have been a big deal. You would have figured out the compass on your own and come here alone."

Jonah blinked away the tears. "Maybe."

"It's true. Your mom and dad would have taught you about your powers."

Jonah nodded, remembering the phasing lessons Kevin and Marcus had given him. His father would have been the one training him, if he had lived. As sad as the thought made him, Jonah became aware of something else.

He stared into Mike's eyes. "I wouldn't have known you, or my cousins."

"You can't be sure about that. I believe your parents planned for you to meet your cousins anyway. Why else give Robert and Lynn those gifts?" Mike glanced down at the note in Jonah's hand. "Can I see it?"

When Jonah didn't respond, Mike slipped the paper out of his slack grip. "You didn't finish it." He rolled out the note, found where Jonah had stopped, and began reading.

There's a whole world out there you've only just begun to sense. You've come of age and it's time to take your place in it. We show you this hideaway. It is our favorite place to get away, to think, or to meditate. We share it with you, son. Welcome to our world.

Mike's voice quivered on the last sentence. He stared at his own hands as he rolled up the note and slipped it in the cylinder. Eventually, Mike raised his head, looking around the courtyard. "Jonah, they never mentioned any code. I don't think the Enhancer is here."

"I know. Trevor was right. My parents didn't know about the mind booster or the back door to the Afterworld."

The frustration burned inside of Jonah. He yanked the compass out of his pocket and held it tightly in his hand. He wanted to hurl it into the woods, for all the good it did him now.

Mike gripped his hand. "Jonah, what if the other code is still in there?"

Jonah gaped at his friend, ashamed he'd been too angry to even think of that possibility. He open his hand, palm upward. Mike touched the compass with a forefinger. Unlike the last time when nothing happened, there was an audible pop and a flash of light raced across the device's surface.

"Ow!" Mike yanked his finger away.

"You alright?"

Mike shook his hand. "Yeah."

The compass began to vibrate as the long hand whirled around and stopped six times, in quick succession, setting six new symbols aglow. The center button pulsed with a green light. Jonah couldn't believe his eyes.

Mike sounded sure when he said, "It must have been on a time delay. Don't you think so?"

Jonah nodded for his friend but didn't think the code was on a time delay. The compass had reacted to Mike's touch. Jonah wondered that his friend didn't make the connection.

Like before, the device buzzed and pulled on Jonah's phasing ability. With the knowledge of how it operated, Jonah knew better than to press the green button.

Mike touched the compass again in a tentative manner. When he didn't receive a shock, he tried to place his whole hand over the device. Jonah drew it away, afraid his friend would activate it.

Mike frowned at him. "Why can't I touch it?"

"I…" Jonah was stumped for an answer until an idea occurred to him. " I think I should close it."

"Can you do that?"

Jonah didn't know. "Maybe if I reverse the Zodiac symbols?" He tried, rotating each into place and pressing the notch. To his relief, the normal compass face folded into view. He showed Mike. "Let's get back and show everyone." He hoped his voice didn't betray any of his suspicion about Mike's ability to control the compass.

If Mike had any doubts or suspicions of his own, he didn't show it. Instead, he smiled. "Things are never boring around you, huh?"

"Who wants boring?" Jonah asked. He motioned Mike to grab a belt loop. Then, summoning his courage, he phased them to Atlanta.

CHAPTER SIXTEEN
FIRST CODE

Marcus, Lynn, Trevor, Kevin, and Mabel had crowded into the library during their absence. All wore varying frantic looks that dissolved into expressions of relief when Jonah and Mike returned.

Marcus stalked over to the boys, breathing heavily. "Where have you two been?"

Jonah held up the compass. "We figured it out."

Marcus covered his face with a hand and breathed between his fingers. "You weren't supposed to activate the compass."

"Sorry..."

"Mr. Armstrong," Mike chimed in, "we didn't think it would hurt to–"

"That's right, you didn't think," Marcus snapped, then collected himself.

Kevin crossed his arms, frowning at Jonah. "You could have run into trouble."

"The code was from my parents," Jonah said. "They wouldn't give me something dangerous."

Marcus seemed ready to explode again. "Jonah…"

"It took me to their hideaway."

"Hideaway?" Lynn scrunched up her face.

Trevor pushed to the front. "You mean it didn't take you to the Enhancer?"

"No." Jonah exchanged a glance with Mike.

"Was the Enhancer there or not?" Kevin asked. Jonah noted that the Fallen Reaper had edged between him and Trevor and watched the boy with a guarded expression.

"No," Mike answered. "But we have the real code. We can go and get the Enhancer."

Jonah quickly opened the compass's true face and showed them the waiting code. Every eye scanned the device. It was strange to see each person take a different amount of time to come to the same conclusion.

"It was on a time delay," Mike continued.

"Way to go, geek boys," Lynn congratulated them.

Jonah turned to Marcus, who had been quiet ever since hearing of the hideaway. Judging from the look on his godfather's face, Jonah suspected Marcus knew about the place. He wanted to ask questions, but didn't think now was the time. They had a mission to plan.

Marcus gave him a slight chin nod. "At least you showed enough judgment to return here instead of pressing the button again."

"Well," Jonah's face warmed, "yeah. We aren't that stupid."

Kevin snorted. Lynn crossed her arms, a skeptical expression on her face.

Trevor was the only one intent on the compass. Jonah began to sense a strange urgency in the boy. Of course, he reasoned, that could have to do with the fact that Trevor's time was running out.

When Trevor reached for the device, Kevin blocked the attempt. "Not so fast."

Trevor blinked at him, but not in surprise. Jonah had stood next to the boy at the teen center and seen him prepare to fight. Trevor had that same look in his eyes now and his body had tensed.

Kevin wasn't a slouch either, Jonah soon realized. The Fallen Reaper balled his hands into fists. "Calm down or else," he warned Trevor.

Lynn had also moved closer to Mike and Jonah. The tension in the room was palpable for several moments.

Trevor raised his hands as he took a few steps backward. "We have the code and know what to do. Let's get the Enhancer."

Marcus cleared his throat, drawing everyone's attention. "I don't relish the idea of traveling blindly to an unknown location."

"Why not?" Trevor countered. "We know what's there."

"Well, not really," Mike said.

Trevor frowned at him. "I'm running out of time, Mike."

Mike's eyes widened. "I know that."

Kevin cracked his knuckles and glared at Trevor. "We have to decide who's going."

"Well, I am, of course." Trevor tapped his own chest.

Marcus shook his head. "No, you're not. You're too important to risk. You stay here and that's final."

Trevor pressed his hands flat against the top of the large table. He fumed in silence.

"I've called Trueblood," Marcus went on. "She'll be here soon." He motioned to Kevin. "I think you should go, to watch over Jonah."

Kevin nodded.

"Maybe I should stay and keep Trevor company," Mike offered.

"We'll do that," Robert announced as he and Wick entered the library. Trueblood stepped into view behind them.

"What are you doing here?" Lynn asked her twin brother.

"Are you kidding?" Robert grinned. "Trueblood told us what's happening. We couldn't miss out."

Lynn asked, "What about Mom and Dad?"

Robert's grin widened. "We got that covered." He pointed at Jonah. "Although I think you should call and tell them you and Mike are cool. Say you're staying at the library or something." He glanced around the room. "That's not a total lie."

Wick sidled up to Trevor and slipped an arm around the boy's shoulders. "So, you're the courier?"

"Yeah. Who are you?"

Wick wasn't bothered by Trevor's surly tone. "My name's Wick."

Robert arched an eyebrow like his sister always did. "He's a mage."

Trevor lost some of his combative stance.

Wick steered the boy toward the door. "You can show us this bat cave."

Jonah caught Robert's arm when his cousin turned to leave the room. "That's why you want to stay behind."

"Not true, little cousin." Robert tapped his own forehead with a slender finger. "We want to pick Trevor's brain for details about the Afterworld. We're working on an upgrade to the video game."

"I thought you had to finish the game before you started upgrades," Lynn jeered.

Robert ignored the comment as he joined Trevor and Wick.

Kevin threw up his arms in frustration. "Are we doing this or not?"

A pained expression crossed Marcus's face. "I wish we could send a scout."

"Jonah's the only one who can work the compass," Kevin answered.

Once again, Jonah wanted to say that wasn't true. He was sure the compass would respond to Mike. But again, he kept the thought to himself.

Marcus motioned the group to gather around Jonah.

A grin spread across Lynn's face before she wrapped her arms around his neck. "We all have to hold on to you."

"Lynn." Jonah squirmed under her embrace, but she wouldn't let go.

"I think holding hands would suffice," Marcus said. Jonah saw his godfather trying not to smile.

Lynn had mercy and released her hold on Jonah's neck. She grabbed his right hand and Kevin held her other hand. Mike, who stood on Jonah's left side, gripped his left wrist since Jonah held the compass in that hand. And last, Trueblood held Mike's free hand.

"This isn't gonna work, guys," Jonah said. "I need a free hand to press the button."

"Fine." Lynn released his right hand and wrapped an arm around his waist.

At the same time, a flash went off from the doorway as Robert snapped a picture with his phone. "You guys are so cute."

"I'm warning you, dear brother," Lynn breathed. "If I see that posted anywhere..."

Robert laughed.

"Wait," Kevin shouted. He activated his blades, which required he hook his left arm around Lynn's arm instead of holding her hand. "You have your blades, Lynn?"

Lynn activated her right one and held the second deactivated blade in her left hand. "Don't want to stab you by mistake, geek boy," she whispered to Jonah.

"This is the picture I need," Robert said, holding up his phone again.

"Jonah, hit it." Lynn ordered.

Jonah pressed the green button a split second before Robert could snap another picture.

*

Lynn and Kevin released their grips as soon as the group reappeared. They whirled, in unconscious unison, scanning the darkened surroundings, their blades ready. The weapons seemed to hum and emit light in the dim interior.

Likewise, Trueblood had released Mike and took up a protective position with both arms raised. Jonah sensed the crackle of magic about the mage as she too scanned the area.

They had arrived in a large alcove. Judging from the rough rock walls, Jonah figured the entire structure was underground. A smooth dome had been carved out of the raw stone high above their heads.

Mike stirred and pointed at the ground. "Jonah, those look like the symbols at the hideaway."

Jonah knelt. This platform was made of marble instead of concrete. Bricks bordered it, one larger than the rest. And that brick was just like the one at his parents' hideaway.

What amazed Jonah was that the symbols not only matched those of the code, but they continued to glow for several more seconds before fading.

Mike knelt and ran his fingers over the smooth stone. "Do you think every location has a stone like this and a platform?"

"Yeah, that's a good guess," Jonah agreed. "Two locations, two platforms." He rose to his feet.

"What do you think?" Kevin asked.

Jonah turned on the spot and pointed at the only doorway out of the alcove. "That way?"

Kevin nodded and assumed the front position. Trueblood waved everyone else to follow and then took up the rear.

Kevin reached the opening and peeked both ways. "Clear." He stepped into the corridor.

It was narrow and dark. The air was stale but not suffocating despite some decayed vegetation seeping through gaps in the stone. The dead plants also hung from the ceiling and walls like weird cobwebs. The sight caused Jonah's skin to crawl.

"Interesting," Trueblood said in a low voice. "There's a weak current of air."

Kevin nodded. "Either there's a opening nearby or..."

"Or what?" Mike asked.

"Someone's using this place," Lynn answered.

Kevin pointed to his left. "There're doors at the end of the tunnel."

As they proceeded down the eerie passageway, Jonah's Death Sense throbbed but not with anything imminent.

Kevin reached the doors and stopped to examine them. "These were repaired not too long ago. Look." He pointed at the hinges and latch.

The wood looked ancient to Jonah, but the latch was shiny and new.

"What does that say?" Mike pointed at the words pressed into the wood.

Jonah recognized the writing but not the actual words. It was an ancient African dialect, he was sure. One his parents had shown him.

Kevin prodded the door with a blade. "I say we go in."

At that moment, Jonah's Death Sense screamed. He jerked and turned around to warn Trueblood.

She was already in motion and produced a shield that blocked a thrown scythe. The owner of the weapon was a black-garbed, glowing-eyed Grimnion who charged in with another weapon.

Lynn leapt to help the mage when the doors behind them swung open and another Grimnion attacked from that side. Kevin blurred into motion, blocked the man's attempt to cut him open, and punched the goon hard in the face.

The Grimnion grunted and stumbled back a foot. When he charged again, Kevin went low, caught the weapon arm, and twisted the guy into the wall. He delivered two high-speed blows to the man's head. The Grimnion dropped to his knees. Kevin followed with a third blow that finally put the man down.

He turned to Jonah. "These Wraith-goons are hard to knock out."

Meanwhile, Lynn had charged the first Grimnion. While she presented the more dangerous target, Trueblood was able to get past the man's defenses with a well-placed spell. The guy dropped like a stone and didn't move. His scythe clattered on the stone floor.

Within seconds, it was over. Jonah appreciated the cover the others provided, but he also felt useless without his own blades.

Trueblood nudged her attacker with a foot before saying, "I think we should get inside and look around."

"What about them?" With her blades, Lynn motioned at the downed men.

In answer, Trueblood used a spell on the guy that Kevin had knocked out. "That should keep them out long enough for us to search what lies beyond."

"Security patrol, keeping watch," Kevin said. He readied himself and stepped through the open doors first. He stopped a short distance inside.

Jonah didn't understand until the taller boy moved aside and he could see the full room. It was an indoor amphitheater complete with tiered rows of circular seating all facing a large stage. And on that stage stood a gleaming portal.

"What's that doing here?" Kevin asked.

Mike moved around Jonah and his jaw dropped. "I thought the main portal was somewhere else?"

"This isn't the main portal." Jonah proceeded down the center aisle, not even conscious of Lynn, who dogged his steps. As he drew closer to the stage, he begin to notice that the amphitheater looked like a bomb had gone off inside. Scores of stone benches had been blackened in a radial pattern, originating from the stage.

In a flash of recollection, Jonah recognized this place and started for the steps.

Lynn grabbed his arm. "Where are you going, hero?"

"I've seen this place before, when I put on the Protector's Ring." He hurried up the steps. Lynn followed while the others spread out to search the space.

"The last person to wear the Protector's Ring was killed here." Jonah glanced down at the stage floor and at the obvious signs of the explosion.

"I thought you were the only one to put on the ring in over two thousand years?" Lynn's eyes widened. "You're telling me this damage is that old?"

"No. My dad found someone who could wear a Protector's ring, but not control it. Deyanira's people discovered the location and they were gonna kill him so he..." Jonah waved at the floor and Lynn hissed.

"Wow."

Now that he was close enough to the portal, he was sure of something else. "That's the one Deyanira had in her underground chamber, remember? It has the same scorch marks." Jonah's voice hitched because some of the marks were seared into the device's surface when his parents died.

Trueblood came to the edge of the stage. "If that's Deyanira's portal, we should finish our search and leave."

"Amen," Lynn called out while moving to examine the far edge of the stage.

Mike remained near the center of the amphitheater, gazing at the ceiling. Kevin stood nearby, splitting his attention between watching the door and Mike.

"Well?" Trueblood urged.

"Okay." Jonah had turned to leave the stage when a squat pedestal to the side of the portal drew his attention. He stepped toward the device just as his Death Sense spiked.

Trueblood shouted to him, "Don't move!"

It was too late. As Jonah's foot came down on a certain spot, magic surged and within a second, an almost-transparent bubble popped into existence around Jonah, trapping him.

CHAPTER SEVENTEEN
POWER OF THE SORCERESS

Jonah was pinned inside the bubble, unable to move as it lifted into the air and floated four feet above the stage. Lynn attempted to reach him but smacked into a separate barrier and tumbled backward over the lip of the stage. Kevin blurred into motion and zipped down the center aisle to catch Lynn before she hurt herself on the stone seats below.

Trueblood hurled spells at the outer barrier, her face a determined mask of concentration and worry. But her attacks couldn't penetrate the second magical ward that extended the entire edge and length of the stage.

Jonah's shock at the suddenness of the trap gave way to panic when he heard the low, evil laugh. A vortex had blossomed a few feet from his bubble and Deyanira exited, in her mortal guise as Neera.

The Reaper's brilliant red hair fell to her shoulders in curls. Deyanira wore all black, as usual, but this time the black was in the form of a long, elegant gown and high heels. Jonah wondered if the sorceress had been at a party. The notion of Deyanira loose in the mortal world attending social events scared Jonah.

Deyanira was a real Reaper and could only navigate the mortal world in her Neera personae, a human sorceress, by using a portal. Like Trevor, she had to cross back within a certain time period. But Jonah had no clue how long that might be.

The Reaper laughed again in a relaxed way and stepped to within an inch of Jonah's trap. At this close range, the sheen of the woman's lip gloss reflected the muted glow of the bubble. Deyanira's cheeks crinkled and her emerald green eyes sparkled with triumph. "Well, well, well. Look what I caught in my stasis bubble. Young Jonah Blackstone."

The sound of the sorceress's voice produced an involuntary shudder in Jonah. She regarded him for a moment before walking around the stasis bubble. Jonah experienced a moment of pure panic when she moved out of sight behind him and only relaxed when she came into view on his other side. The sorceress trailed a single finger along the bubble's surface, creating a dissipating trail of magic.

"I grow tired of catching you stealing my possessions." A wicked grin tweaked the corners of her mouth. "Aren't you turning into a tired cliché? A young boy of color resorting to crime because he doesn't have a father at home?" She cackled at the very idea.

Jonah's fury surged at the taunt. "I didn't come to steal anything."

"Really?" Deyanira motioned toward the portal. "You didn't come to take this?"

"We didn't even know it was here." As soon as the words left his mouth, Jonah knew he made a mistake.

As a real Reaper, Deyanira had the Reaper Stare and could tell if someone was lying or being truthful. Jonah had no doubt she subjected him to it now.

Deyanira's eyes narrowed. "You're telling the truth." The disappointment in her voice was mixed with growing suspicion. "Why are you here, young one?"

Jonah closed his eyes. "Just looking around."

"Now you are lying, Jonah Blackstone. I can't have that." Deyanira flicked her hand and lightning hit the stasis bubble.

Jonah couldn't stop himself from flinching in fear, but the frightening display coursed along the outside of the bubble without harming him. *She's toying with me.*

Kevin responded by beating on the outer ward with his bare hands. Trueblood waved him back and then shot an impressive volley of magic at the barrier, to no apparent effect.

Deyanira ignored them. Her focus was on Lynn. When she turned back to Jonah, an evil grin worked her mouth. "Remember what I did to your cousin?"

Remember? Jonah would never forget Lynn's heart-rending screams as Deyanira tortured her. He glared at the evil woman.

"Now it's your turn to suffer while she can't help you." Deyanira raised her hand toward the stasis bubble.

Jonah's terror spiked. He needed to stall her, but how? Behind the Reaper, Trueblood continued to subject the ward to various spells, as if studying the barrier. Jonah had an idea. "Trueblood's gonna make it through."

Deyanira lowered her outstretched hand. "She's a capable mage, but honey, I'm better. Now," she held her hand toward the bubble again. "Why are you here?"

"I told you, I don't–"

Deyanira touched a finger to the bubble and it reduced in size, enough to send a wave of agony through Jonah's shoulder, which had been caught at an awkward angle behind him when the trap was sprung. He let out a muffled cry of pain as the smaller bubble threatened to dislocate his shoulder.

"I told you no more lies." Deyanira stroked the bubble and the pressure relented a bit.

Jonah sucked in ragged breaths.

"I wonder," Deyanira mused, "if your healing ability will try to repair your shoulder while it's being pressed out of the socket." Deyanira tapped a finger on her bottom lip and adopted a ridiculous thinking pose. "It would be perpetual torture for you."

"You're crazy."

Deyanira touched the bubble, and it contracted for several excruciating seconds. She relented and frowned at Jonah. "Show some respect, child. And answer my question."

Jonah sucked in deep breaths, which was hard considering he couldn't fully expand his lungs. He was too confined and in pain. What could he do? He could phase, but when he tried, sigils appeared all over the bubble.

Deyanira laughed. "It's designed to prevent you from phasing to freedom." She touched the bubble again.

Jonah lost himself in screaming until the pressure eased. He gasped, thinking. *Stall her.* "We're... looking for something."

"Obvious." Deyanira reached for the bubble again.

"It's a device!" Jonah hurried to add.

"And?" Deyanira prompted. Her finger hovered less than an inch from the bubble's surface. "What is it? What does it do?"

"I don't know everything," Jonah lied. When Deyanira's eyes narrowed, he admitted, "It's called an Enhancer."

A thoughtful expression transformed Deyanira's face.

Jonah used the brief respite to try and adjust his position. Any twitch on his part sent waves of agony through his body and stole his breath away. But he did feel something, around his wrist. Wick's gift, the bracelet.

Jonah wondered if he could activate it. The bubble kept out magic, but the bracelet had its own power stored inside. Jonah closed his eyes and tried to concentrate on Wick's lesson, despite the pain.

"What are you doing?" Deyanira's voice sounded closer.

Jonah refused to open his eyes as he spoke. "Thinking."

"Of more lies?"

"No." Once again, Jonah prepared himself for the stasis bubble to contract and send him into fresh agony. That didn't happen. After a few confused moments, Jonah opened his eyes and recoiled. Deyanira stood right beside the bubble, gazing at him.

"I've heard of Enhancers," she said. "The Archivists used them to elevate the minds of chosen mortals for short periods of time. But the devices have been forbidden for centuries."

Jonah found it curious to watch Deyanira's mind working through the limited information she had. At least she wasn't torturing him for the moment. Taking advantage of that, he focused on the bracelet, sensing its stored power again. He didn't have to collect it, just release the energy.

"Why would the Alliance want an Enhancer?" Deyanira asked. "It's useless without something ancient to decipher. Where is the device?"

This is it, Jonah thought. She wanted an answer and would shrink the bubble when he couldn't give it. Jonah bared down, called on that inner will, and pushed it into the bracelet. The result was like being suffocated as the energy of the bracelet collided with the bubble and had nowhere to go.

Jonah feared he'd made a mistake and would kill himself until cracks begin to appear on the bubble.

Deyanira backed away. "Impossible!"

The next moment, her stasis bubble burst with a release of energy. Jonah had a split second before he dropped to the ground with an audible pop from his shoulder. White-hot pain lanced through his body and into his head and he screamed.

The bubble's explosion rammed into the outer shield, producing eddies and distortions across the surface. Trueblood succeeded in collapsing the damaged barrier with a well-placed spell. Deyanira, still reeling from the initial explosion, phased to the opposite side of the stage. Trueblood attacked anyway, keeping the dangerous sorceress at bay while Kevin, Lynn, and Mike rushed in to surround Jonah.

Kevin lifted him, causing Jonah to waver on the verge of fainting from the pain. "Sorry," Kevin said, "but we gotta leave."

Trueblood backpedaled to them so Kevin could grip the back of her tunic. Lynn understood and clamped a hand on Kevin's forearm, and Mike held onto her. A second later, ripples played across Jonah's body, making his injury ache more.

That pain was nothing compared to the agony he experienced when they smacked hard into something and the amphitheater appeared around them again. They tumbled to the stone floor in a painful huddle.

Kevin helped Jonah stand.

"What was that?" Lynn's voice sounded pained as she regained her feet.

"Sigils." Kevin growled and kicked open the doors. He supported Jonah under one arm as they hurried down the dismal corridor that looked even more foreboding than ever. Jonah realized why when the old dead vines trembled and begin to grow out of the cracks and crevasses at high speed.

"Look out!" Kevin activated a blade and sliced through vines that tried to wrap around his arms. "It's Deyanira."

Lynn's blades worked non-stop, fighting to keep herself and Mike free of the grasping vines. As they made their way toward the alcove, the passage ahead grew darker. The vines had grown into a dense knot to block their way.

Kevin glanced back at Trueblood, who kept their rear covered. "Trueblood!"

The mage turned, mouthed a silent spell, and shot the magical enchantment over their heads. When the spell hit the blockage, it turned a ghostly white.

Kevin moved in front of Jonah and ran headfirst into the mass. It shattered into a large puff of bone-dry vine fragments and choking dust. But they were through and rushed into the alcove.

More vines crawled out of the passage, but now they began to merge together. Jonah and the others were transfixed in horror as the mass took on the general shape of a four-legged creature. The bulbous head was made of an undulating mass of vines.

"Oh my God." Mike sounded terrified.

The vine creature reared up on its hind legs and prepared to launch itself at the group. Trueblood positioned herself in front of the creature. She raised a slender piece of dark wood, about fifteen inches long. Jonah gaped at her, never having seen the mage use a wand before. He didn't even know she had one.

"Help me, Ancestors. Show the evil one your power." The mage's long black hair became tinged with fire and her eyes glowed. "Caha-queene!" She waved her wand and a fiery shape shot out of the end. It grew in size, sprouting two wings and a head with a beak. The creature was a much larger version of the phoenix the mage had used in her magic show last summer.

The majestic phoenix let out an ear-piercing scream. It dove into the midst of the vine creature, flapping its huge wings and lighting the vines on fire. The magical creatures stumbled around, sending burning vine fragments all around the alcove.

Jonah and the others huddled close together as much from the heat of the phoenix's fire as from fear of being trampled. The phoenix proved stronger, and the vine creature's entire body erupted into flames. Its scream of agony hurt Jonah's ears. Both creatures flared like a bomb going off and then they were gone, leaving behind a trail of glowing embers.

"Not bad, Shaman." Deyanira had appeared at the alcove entrance and began firing a barrage of supernatural fire at them. "Not bad. Maybe you should join us."

Trueblood put up a shield just in time to stop the fire, but not the heat. It began to blister everyone's skin.

"She wasn't grandstanding," Trueblood said through clenched teeth, sweat beading her forehead. "I'm no match for her."

Jonah wanted to argue after seeing the mage produce the phoenix.

Kevin cursed under his breath. "No matter where I phase, she'll trace us."

"What about Alliance HQ?" Lynn suggested. "That way she'd be surrounded."

Kevin shook his head. "We need clearance first and don't have time."

Trueblood grunted and dropped to one knee. Her arms shook with the effort to push back Deyanira's onslaught.

Mike dug his hands in to Jonah's pocket. "Ow!" Jonah screamed.

"Sorry, but we need the compass." Mike freed it from Jonah's pocket and manipulated the dials.

Lynn's mouth dropped open. "I thought Jonah was the only one who could work it?"

Mike ignored the question until he finished. Then he grabbed Lynn's hand. She didn't argue as she gripped Kevin's forearm again.

Trueblood risked a glance at Mike and touched his arm. "You better go now!"

She released her shield at the same time Mike pressed the compass's activate button. The onrushing ball of supernatural flame disappeared as they vanished from the alcove and reappeared at the hideaway.

"We need to move," Kevin said while turning on the spot.

Mike reached into the bushes and pulled them open, revealing the stairs. Kevin squeezed through and ushered Jonah up to the first courtyard.

Lynn motioned Jonah to a nearby bench and huddled close, examining his arm. "The shoulder's out of the socket." She gripped his wrist with one hand and the side of his shoulder with the other. "Hold still."

"No!" Jonah protested. "I know how this works. You count to three but try it on..."

Lynn made a sudden motion and the next thing Jonah knew, his world dipped sideways and went dark.

CHAPTER EIGHTEEN
MEMORY WORK

Jonah awoke with a start. He lay on a bed in a darkened room with the only illumination slivers of brilliant sunlight that leaked around the edges of dark curtains. The faint scent of jasmine tickled his nose. Jonah groaned and turned over. That's when he saw Kevin, sitting crossed-legged on the floor.

The Young Fallen Reaper was shirtless, arms resting on his knees, palms upward. And he faced a small burning scented candle. It was a classic meditation setup.

What drew Jonah's attention was the graceful binding patterns spanning Kevin's muscular upper back. Jonah had seen him shirtless once, over a year ago in Marcus's condo. The older boy looked more muscled now.

Jonah swallowed, unsure what to do. He didn't want to disturb Kevin's ritual to restore energy. The binding patterns allowed Fallen Ones to retain some of their former powers, but they had to recharge at regular intervals.

Deep in the meditation, Kevin's back heaved up and down in a slow, regular rhythm. Jonah couldn't be sure, but the patterns looked black, meaning fully charged. That was good. He released a breath he didn't know he was holding.

"Stop checking me out, little man," Kevin said.

"I'm not checking you out," Jonah lied, his face warming. "I don't like that name. Remember?"

After several more breaths, Kevin hopped to his feet and blew out the candle. He took his time stretching his arms over his head and bending from side to side at the waist.

Jonah couldn't resist returning a taunt. "Show off."

Kevin's laugh was relaxed as he retrieved his black t-shirt from the chair. "You're just jealous." He didn't pull on the shirt. Instead, he playfully nudged Jonah's head and quipped, "About time you woke up. You've been asleep for over an hour."

"An hour?"

Kevin slumped in the chair and dropped the t-shirt over his lap. "Trueblood gave you something to keep you out. Your snoring messed with my concentration."

"Funny."

Kevin poked Jonah's good shoulder. "Remember, you heal faster when you sleep."

"I know." The reminder of his injury filled Jonah's mind with Deyanira's torture and he shuddered for a moment.

Kevin switched from the chair to sit on the bed beside Jonah. "You okay?"

"Yeah."

"Turn your side to me." When Jonah complied, Kevin took Jonah's right arm and touched the injured shoulder. He began to work the arm around.

Jonah sucked in a breath from the brief spike of pain and the forgotten warmth of Kevin's hands. He had discovered last summer that the boy had a higher than normal body temperature. But he didn't know if that were true for all Fallen Reapers.

Jonah let out an involuntary sigh and asked, "Why are you so hot?" When Kevin grinned, Jonah's face warmed. "You know what I mean."

The boy shrugged. "It's an effect of using the binding patterns. All Fallen Ones are like that."

Jonah marveled at the news, and the boy's gentle touch.

"How does it feel?" Kevin asked after a few minutes.

"Not bad." Kevin's manipulation did hurt some, but as he continued, the pain lessened.

"Deyanira's an evil witch," Kevin breathed, the anger radiating out with his exhale.

"Oh no." Jonah met Kevin's close gaze. "I told her about the Enhancer."

"Doesn't matter; it wasn't there anyway." Kevin continued to massage the shoulder. "Better?"

"Yeah," Jonah whispered. It was wonderful, in more ways than one. His aborted talk with Mike in the library popped into his head. Or maybe it was Kevin's closeness. Jonah's nervousness returned and he chickened out on asking the older boy the question he really wanted to ask.

The maddening thing was that Kevin watched and waited. Jonah wondered if the boy sensed he wanted to say something else. What would Mike do in this situation,

Jonah asked himself. The answer wasn't reassuring because Jonah didn't know. He'd never been interested in anyone before. What if he was wrong about Kevin?

After a moment, Kevin let out an impatient breath, stood, and pulled on his shirt. "Let's go," he said. "Everyone's waiting for us."

*

Jonah's first sight of the bat cave made him groan in envy and almost forget his embarrassed shyness a few moments before with Kevin.

The basement boasted all the name-brand game consoles, regulation-sized pool and Ping-Pong tables, a huge smart TV with cable, a legal bar, and separate movie room. And the spacious sitting area had two large sofas, scattered comfortable chairs, and a low coffee table complete with cup holders along the edges.

Amidst all these wonderful things, Jonah expected to see his friends and cousins playing video games, not in a heated conversation. When they noticed Kevin and Jonah, everyone went quiet.

Judging from the embarrassed expressions, Jonah suspected he'd been the topic of discussion. He experienced a sudden stab of fear. What if the others were talking about him and Kevin being absent, and speculating why?

Jonah glanced at Kevin, to find the boy looking at him with brows furrowed. Once again, Jonah suspected their connection allowed Kevin to sense his rollercoaster emotions without doing a true Reaper stare.

Lynn hopped from the sofa she shared with Mike and hurried to Jonah. "How's the shoulder?" She aimed the question at Kevin as she too begin to rotate Jonah's arm around like he was a doll.

"He's says it's fine." Kevin's eyebrows weren't drawn together anymore, but he continued to cast quick glances at Jonah.

Lynn finished her inspection and hustled Jonah to the space she'd vacated. Once he was seated, she squeezed between Robert and Wick on the opposite sofa.

Jonah was a little afraid to ask, but he needed to get it out in the open. "What's the argument about?"

Mike gave him a guilty look and didn't answer.

Lynn let out an exasperated breath. "Trevor thinks we should go back. Mike says it's not necessary."

Jonah gaped at the others. "Why not?" He elbowed Mike to get his buddy talking.

"I told them I saw an opened nook and it was empty," Mike explained. "I think someone took the Enhancer."

"Wick and I bet it was Deyanira," Robert added. Wick nodded in agreement.

"Trevor's saying we should go back and check to be sure." Mike cast a disappointed look at the boy. "I know what I saw."

Trevor turned in his chair to face away from Mike. Jonah couldn't believe his eyes.

Lynn gestured at the fuming boys. "That's where it stands. Do we go back like Trevor suggests–"

"No," Kevin interjected.

"Or," Lynn continued, "do we trust Mike?"

Every eye turned to Jonah and waited for his answer. He gulped, not really wanting to step into the middle of the fight but relieved they weren't talking about him and Kevin. "Well, I trust my buddy. If Mike saw the empty nook and thinks the Enhancer's gone, I believe him."

Mike was pleased, but Trevor frowned at Jonah's words.

"Besides, Deyanira doesn't have it," Jonah thought to add.

Trevor sat forward in his chair. "How do you know?"

"Because," Jonah paused, not sure how the next bit would go down with everyone, "Deyanira wanted to know why we were there. I told her about it."

Trevor hissed and covered his face with both hands as he slumped back.

Wick and Robert were stunned. Lynn tapped her bottom lip while staring off into space.

Kevin leaned on the back of the sofa, speaking right over Jonah's head. "As I told Jonah, that doesn't matter because I think Mike's right. It was gone."

"Where does that leave us?" Trevor blurted out. "We don't have the Enhancer and we don't have the next code."

Jonah patted his pockets, looking for the compass until Mike held it up. "You used it?"

Mike smiled and lowered the device to his own lap. "Yeah."

Trevor's eyes widened. "You can use the compass?" Mike nodded. Trevor stood, still marveling at Mike. "How did you know it would work?"

Mike's face reddened and he shrugged. "It just made sense."

"But you had to put in the code, dude." Wick looked impressed with Mike. "That was wikid cool."

"I think that's how we got away," Kevin explained. "Deyanira couldn't follow us when we used it."

Trueblood shook her head. "We can't be sure of that."

Marcus looked thoughtful. "We have to sense the person in order to follow. Maybe the compass obscured the scent." He met Kevin's gaze. "We'll have to test that theory, but that can wait." He turned to Mike. "Has the compass given another code?"

"No. I don't think it will." Mike cut a glance at Jonah before explaining. "The first code was a test. Jonah had to figure out how to activate the compass to access it." He looked around the room. "The next one will be somewhere at the location."

Mike sounded so sure and reasonable, no one bothered to argue with him.

Trevor banged his hand on the armrest. "Then we have to go back."

"I said no," Kevin growled. "It's too dangerous. Marcus will back me up."

"Did you see a code?" Trevor challenged the Fallen Reaper.

Kevin made a show of cracking his knuckles. Trevor didn't look intimidated and half-rose from his chair. Jonah didn't know whether to be impressed with the boy or not.

Mike stood and held up his hands to stop the boys. "Please. I think the answer was on the ceiling. It had a lot of design work."

"I guess you can remember all that in detail?" Trevor snapped at him.

The boy's harsh words caused Mike to redden again.

Jonah had enough. "Hey!" he snapped. "Be cool with my friend."

Lynn tapped the coffee table to get their attention. "Did you get a good look at the ceiling?" she asked Mike. When he nodded, Lynn gestured to Robert. "Do your thing."

Robert's confused look morphed into a knowing grin. "Yeah, right. I'll need some paper."

Wick, Lynn, and Robert jumped from the sofa and began to rummage through all the drawers in the basement. Wick found a ream of printer paper, pulled out a few sheets, and hurried back to the coffee table. By that time, Jonah understood their plan.

Kevin was at a loss.

Trevor, having seen the act at the party, scowled. "Magic tricks?"

"You know," Lynn crossed to Trevor and towered over the boy, "we can lock you in a room."

Trevor slumped back in his chair and remained quiet.

Meanwhile, Robert produced a pen and had it poised over the blank sheet of paper while staring at Mike.

Mike tore his troubled gaze from the brooding Trevor and sat forward. Focused now, he exuded a confidence Jonah had never seen in his buddy. Mike rested his slender hands on his lap as he returned Robert's gaze.

"Relax" Robert began, "and picture the ceiling of the amphitheater in your mind."

After a few quiet, yet tense moments, Robert's hand begin to move and the scratching sounds of his pen filled the quiet basement. Over the next half hour, Robert fast-sketched a rather detailed rendering of the amphitheater ceiling.

No one had to tell Trevor to keep quiet because the boy was amazed. Once Robert finished, everyone crowded close, scrutinizing the drawing. The drawing resembled a starry sky with repeated patterns of stars.

It was Robert who spotted the symbols. "Here, and here. Look, there's another one. They're worked into the design. Unless you knew about the symbols, you'd never notice them."

Mike sucked in a breath. "All of those are on the compass."

"Yeah," Jonah nodded, impressed that Mike had memorized the compass symbols. "Which order?"

"Go by the quadrants," Robert suggested. "Start in the North and work clockwise."

"Good call." Wick exchanged an excited glance with Robert. "This could go in the game. A player has to find the symbols in order to reach the next level."

Robert whooped and high-fived his friend. "Yeah, before the evil sorceress fries you."

Mike ignored the older boys as he entered the symbols into the compass. The green button activated and he raised it for all to see. "We got the code."

Clapping commenced as people congratulated each other, except Trevor, who sank into his chair again.

"What's wrong with you?" Jonah asked.

"We have the last code, but it's useless without the Enhancer. And we don't know where that's been taken."

"Or by whom," Mike added.

"Wow," Robert said. "You two are definitely the glass is half-full types."

Lynn threatened him with a knuckle punch.

"I think my parents took it," Jonah announced. He'd been mulling that over all along. They were the last ones to use the compass. His dad found a way to put in a code. Maybe they did know about the Enhancer and the back door into the Afterworld.

"Okay. Let's go with that," Lynn offered. "But where would they take it? You and Mike said it wasn't at the hideaway."

"We may have to search it to be sure," Trevor said. "Please tell me you're not gonna shoot that idea down." He glared at Kevin.

Lynn glanced at Trevor. "I hate to admit it, but he's right. Unless you can think of anywhere else, Jonah."

A final piece of the puzzle snapped into place in Jonah's mind. It was something that had been nagging him ever since they arrived at the alcove and discovered the circular platform identical to the one at his parents' hideaway.

Jonah had seen a third stone and brick platform in a dream-walk. He met everyone's expectant gaze and said, "I think I know where the Enhancer may be."

The moment of elation was quickly overshadowed by severe dread. The location from the dream-walk was also the location where his parents had died.

CHAPTER NINETEEN
DREAM REVISITED

❝This is it," Jonah said in a hushed voice. He stood facing the building from the fateful dream-walk. The crumbling stone façade had the same words carved into the face: Free Public Library. He, Lynn, and Kevin had appeared outside the abandoned brick building.

Lynn tapped his arm. "Jonah? What is it?"

Jonah ignored his cousin as the rush of memories roared through his head, more vivid than he would have expected.

His parents had appeared on this exact spot and he'd called to them, even though they couldn't hear him. At the time, Jonah didn't know how the dream-walks worked. He didn't know a lot of things back then, including that his parents would die here.

Kevin patted him on the back. "Are you okay? We can go back if you want to."

Jonah stared at the library and wiped the beads of sweat off his forehead. The day was still hot, in the low nineties. And the heat added to his sudden misgivings. Maybe coming here wasn't such a good idea, but they had a mission.

Jonah pushed aside his doubts and shook his head. "I'm okay."

Lynn examined a second drawing Robert had done before they left. "Looks just like it."

Jonah had asked Robert to pull details of this platform from the dream-walk memory. He'd been sure he noticed it and was relieved when Robert's drawing confirmed it.

The symbols on this platform's designation stone still glowed a bright yellow. Jonah knelt down to touch the stone. The symbols were hotter than the rest of the warm stones.

Lynn and Kevin stepped off the platform and moved toward the library, leaving Jonah behind. He finished his inspection of the stone and hurried to follow.

Kevin reached the building first and paused, frowning at the structure. "Are you sure we should go inside? It doesn't look like anyone's been there in ages."

Jonah slipped between him and Lynn. "Someone came here a year ago."

"How do you know that?" Kevin insisted.

"I just do." Jonah kept the real significance of the place to himself. "Come on."

Jonah ascended the cracked stone steps to the weather-beaten front doors. He pushed them open and crossed into the relative darkness. The old counters and railings of the main lobby were still in place. Everything looked just as it did in the dream-walk.

Kevin and Lynn lingered just inside the front doors, but Jonah continued on. He was on auto-pilot as he replayed his parents' movements in his mind. They had gone straight through this larger room to a back hallway, and Jonah did the same.

Lynn called after him, "Jonah, where are you going?"

"Follow me."

"Maybe I should go first," Kevin suggested, his long legs allowing him to easily catch up to Jonah. "In case there's danger."

"You don't know where to go. I do."

Kevin narrowed his eyes. "What aren't you telling us?"

Lynn nodded in agreement as they trailed behind. Jonah reached an open stairwell door, which his dad had kicked open in the dream. The splintered wood showed a large boot print. *This is the way.*

Kevin gripped the back of Jonah's shirt when he started forward. "Hold on."

"Let go!" Jonah whirled, trying to get free, but the Fallen Reaper refused to release him.

"It's my job to protect you. Unless you tell me what's going on, I'm taking you back to the safe house." Kevin shook Jonah to emphasize his point.

Jonah admitted to himself the Fallen Reaper could literally carry him back. He gave up squirming and said, "There's a basement. That's where we need to go."

"You think the Enhancer's down there?" Kevin peered into the gloom.

"Yeah."

Kevin crossed his muscular arms and didn't move. "Why?"

"That's where my parents came to meet the Elder."

"Hold on, hero." Lynn positioned herself in front of Jonah, blocking his path. "I thought Trevor was the only one to see the Elder's face?"

Jonah swallowed, his throat dry now. "The only one still alive."

Lynn's hand dropped to her side. "I'm sorry."

"So," Kevin said, looking around, "they came here and met the Elder?"

"No. He never showed up." Jonah knew if Kevin believed the half-truth, they could continue on. And he needed to know if he was right about this place.

Kevin sized him up with plain, human eyes before nodding. "Let me go first. You can follow me. Lynn's in back. Got it?"

Jonah relaxed and nodded. He and Lynn waited on the landing as Kevin activated his blades and descended the stairs. He let out a curse when he reached the bottom. Jonah knew why. The hallway had been musty and rat infested in the dream. Kevin muttered under his breath and one of the blades flared with light.

Lynn bumped against Jonah. "What's that sound?"

"Rats."

"I hate rats, Jonah." She didn't sound frightened as much as disgusted.

"It'll be okay," Kevin called up the stairs. He stomped around and Jonah heard the little patter of rat feet dwindle. The glow of his Reaper blade gave Kevin's dark skin an odd, ghostly look. "Better?"

Lynn peered into the dimness below. "Not really."

She nudged Jonah forward and they descended.

Kevin waited. "Where to now?"

Jonah followed his father's actions and stood in front of a blank section of the dingy wall. This level was dark, making Jonah glad for the light from Kevin's Reaper blade. It reflected off the light-colored walls, adding a soft haze of illumination.

He glanced at Kevin. "Can you move closer to the wall?" Kevin held the blade to Jonah's right. "Hold it up about here." Jonah pointed to a section.

Kevin adjusted the position of the blade and Jonah ran his hand over the spot. After a few seconds, his hand brushed over a slight impression in the old plaster. Jonah let his fingers trace the circular pattern of raised bumps. He pulled the compass out and held it against the spot, just like his dad did in the dream-walk.

Jonah began to feel a little foolish when nothing happened. What if it didn't work for him like it worked for his dad? Maybe he had to say a spell?

Kevin leaned over Jonah's shoulder, examining the wall. "Is something supposed to happen, little man?"

"Yeah," Jonah answered. "It's supposed to…"

A low rumble started underneath their feet, and the wall wavered. Jonah pulled the compass away just as a small opening appeared. The cinderblocks melted away, creating a hole. The opening grew and stabilized into a perfect circle large enough for a single person to step through.

Jonah was also relieved to see the faint glow of light that came from inside. What he didn't expect was the strong whiff of stale smoke, as if something had burned.

"What the …" Kevin coughed. "What happened down there?"

Jonah motioned to Kevin. "There are stairs leading down to a hidden chamber."

Kevin hesitated before stepping through the opening and starting down.

Lynn paused next to Jonah. "You saw this in a dream-walk about your parents, didn't you?"

Jonah nodded.

"That must have been over a year ago."

He swallowed. They were about to find out anyway. "I saw my parents here the night they died."

Even in the dimness of the hallway, Jonah could see the shocked expression on his cousin's face.

"Jonah…" Lynn shook her head. "That's what you meant by this place being personal."

"You two coming down?" Kevin called.

"Yeah, here we come." Lynn nudged Jonah. "Go on."

Kevin stood before two high metal doors, running his hand over the gold symbol spanning both: three interlocking circles with a pair of wings spread out above.

"This is the Alliance's symbol." He turned to Jonah. "What is this place?"

"You'll see." Jonah placed the compass in the depression at the center of the symbol. It rotated ninety degrees, followed by a loud click. When he removed the compass, the massive doors opened. The overpowering smell of burnt things rolled over them.

Jonah raised his hand to cough, reminded of the night his family home in Virginia had burned. He had smelled of soot and smoke for hours.

Lynn covered her nose. Kevin mumbled a curse under his breath and inched forward into the room.

A strange tightness developed in Jonah's chest and the dread increased as he entered the chamber. It was all the same, and so different, like walking in the nightmare version of the original dream.

The ceiling high above was scorched and blackened from the intense smoke and fire. The shelves that covered three walls used to be full of ancient books. Now, they were reduced to patches of blackened boards and piles of ashes.

The loss of all those ancient books staggered Jonah.

Kevin picked his way to the fourth wall to study the large stone base, also blackened by smoke damage.

He called to Jonah, "A portal used to be here."

"It's the one Deyanira took," Jonah answered.

Kevin whirled around. "You mean this is where she got it? How?"

Jonah scanned the ground. Dust, dirt, ashes, and other debris had accumulated over the past year. Pain gripped his heart when he saw the large scorch marks. His knees buckled and he knelt down, pressing his hands against the charred stone.

"Jonah!" Lynn rushed to him and wrapped an arm around his shoulders. "His parents were here, Kevin."

Jonah nodded, aware that he would cry soon. "Deyanira attacked them in this chamber and the Grim Reaper killed them here!" Jonah's shout reverberated through the space.

Kevin swore under his breath.

Lynn pressed her forehead against Jonah's, whispering to him. She gently rocked him until he stopped crying.

"Jonah," Kevin whispered in an urgent tone, "you should have told us about this place."

"Kevin, this is personal and painful," Lynn said. "I'm sure he didn't like talking about it."

"I get that, Lynn, but we've already crossed Deyanira in a place she fought Jonah's mom and dad."

Jonah felt the sudden tightening of Lynn's hold.

"Oh my God." Lynn released him and stood. She took out and activated her blades. "You're right. She probably had some kind of alarm set."

"I'm sorry," Jonah began as he regained his feet. When he opened his mouth to continue, Lynn patted his arm.

"We don't blame you, Jonah," Lynn said, "but we should leave."

"What about the Enhancer?"

Kevin turned his ear toward the opened entrance. He activated his own blades. "Too late. Someone's here." He sprinted for the door at the same time a whistling sound filled the air.

A whirling scythe flew through the open door and headed straight for Kevin. The boy simply phased, allowing the scythe to continued through empty air. Kevin reappeared inside the doorway in time to duck and tackled the Grimnion who tried to enter.

Kevin heaved the guy back through the door and into a second henchman just outside.

"Lynn!" Kevin shouted as he gripped the heavy doors and pushed them closed with a loud clang.

Lynn joined Kevin and they leaned against the doors, keeping them closed despite the heavy blows from the other side.

Kevin had extra-human strength as a Fallen Reaper, but Wraith-possessed mortals also had above average strength. Jonah cringed when the banging against the door became frenzied.

Pressing his back against the door, Kevin dug in his heels while shouting to Jonah, "Find the Enhancer!"

"Yeah, yeah." Jonah began a frantic search around the chamber.

"I think it's more than just two Grimnions," Lynn gritted through clinched teeth as the door bucked inward again.

"I'm worried Deyanira will show up," Kevin said. "Too bad the lock is only on one side."

Thoughts of Deyanira subjecting him to more pain galvanized Jonah. He spun on the spot, searching. If Deyanira and her gang never found the Enhancer, it had to be out of the way.

Almost out of pure frustration, he focused on the dust and soot-strewn floor. That's when he noticed the stonework. It actually made a pattern in the relatively clear patches he could see.

A muted shout came from the other side of the door at the same time it bucked. Lynn was thrown forward. Kevin shoved the door back into place, his muscles straining the entire time.

"Jonah, hurry up!"

"I am." He used his foot to smear away dirt from a large concentric design of circular rows of stone. Each layer got smaller and smaller.

He dropped to his knees and brushed away the dirt to reveal a soot-filled hole at the center of the chamber's floor. Jonah shoved his hands into the crevice and scooped out the mess. That done, he pressed the compass into the hole.

A second later, Jonah leapt backward. A round section of the floor sank at least a foot before sliding sideways into a new crevice. Jonah gawked at the octagonal space beneath and the crystal half-globe inside. A dull gold object floated around inside the globe. It was thin with a slight curve to it, and the edges contained intricate details as well as angel script.

Jonah lifted the half-globe out of its hiding place. "Cool!"

"You can be awed later," Lynn shouted.

Kevin caught Lynn's attention and used his chin to indicate a warped iron candle stand.

Lynn darted to the piece and brought it back. In between shoves of the door, Kevin pressed one end against the doorknob and gouged the other end of the stand into the stone floor.

"That won't hold for more than a second," Kevin grunted. He slipped his blade in a pocket as he bounded over to Jonah. Lynn was right behind him, but her blades were out and ready.

The attackers hit the door again. For a second, the stand held. But the next blow knocked it free and sent it flying through the air.

Kevin ducked under it as he slid through the ash and soot to grab Jonah's hand. Lynn dived and gripped Kevin's foot a second before the Fallen Reaper phased them away from the chamber.

CHAPTER TWENTY
COGNITIVE DISSONANCE

The hot water pummeled Jonah's shoulder, forcing a sigh of relief from his lips. The others would have to wait, he decided, taking his time in the shower as the water washed away aches as well as the grit. The moment of quiet bliss didn't last long before his mind began replaying events.

Visions of the scorch marks on the chamber floor popped into his head. Jonah sucked in a ragged breath, fighting back tears. At the same time, he had a strange thought. His parents had been buried in urns. Yet the chamber had been locked, so the Alliance couldn't have retrieved his parents' bodies…

Jonah shook his head, not finishing the morbid thought. Back then, he had been in shock over their deaths. The idea of empty urns never entered his mind, but as he accepted the reality, his anger at Deyanira and the Grim Reaper spiked. He smacked wet fists against the tiled wall of the shower several times.

All the memories of his parents played out, every emotion and feeling he'd been holding off and not facing over the past year. At times, he smiled while remembering his dad's laugh or his mom getting angry at both him and his dad.

And just as quick, the grief, pain, and loss would surface. Jonah didn't hold any of it inside, allowing his tears to mix with the shower water.

"I miss you." The words caught in Jonah's throat. He smacked his hands against the shower wall again.

Somewhere in all the mashup of emotions, he decided that next year, he'd place roses on the alcove bench at the hideaway. Jonah didn't think he was ready to visit the actual tomb in D.C.

The decision fortified his resolve to get on with their mission. He toweled off and slipped into the clothes Mabel had given him: a pair of tan pants and sky blue shirt with *Camp Monarch* on the upper left front. Jonah checked himself in the mirror, shrugged at the fit of the slightly over-sized clothes, and headed for the bat cave.

*

Kevin stood outside the basement entrance with Lynn. He had changed into a clean pair of dark jeans and a pale green shirt. Jonah suspected the Fallen Reaper had phased to wherever he stayed to fetch fresh clothes.

Lynn was dressed like Jonah, since she didn't have a change of clothes either.

She pulled him close before he could enter the basement. "Marcus is gone."

Jonah glanced through the doorway and noticed Omar was there in his godfather's place.

"Where's Marcus?"

Omar heard and motioned them into the room. "He's been called to Alliance HQ, Jonah."

"Why?" Jonah asked as he entered. "What's happened?"

"The Council knows about Trevor. Marcus is trying to head them off, but he fears they'll take the courier into custody." Omar patted the globe. "At least the Alliance doesn't know about the compass and the Enhancer. Before that changes, I think Trevor should explain it to us."

Mabel waved her hands in frustration. "They need to eat, Omar."

"I'm sorry, Mabel. They'll have to do it while Trevor talks."

Mabel made a disapproving sound as she beckoned Jonah, Lynn, and Kevin to a high-top bar in the kitchenette area. "Kevin and Lynn wouldn't touch a thing until you got here."

Jonah didn't know what to say, so he kept quiet. Once Mabel had them seated, the motherly woman placed three full plates of thick, real turkey sandwiches and potato salad in front of them. She added bottled water and a bowl of fruit to the feast.

Jonah began wolfing down his sandwiches but paused long enough to glance around the room. Robert and Wick stood beside Mage Trueblood. Rex hovered near Omar, who held the Enhancer globe.

Mike sat beside Trevor, compass in his hands, prodding the device.

Omar cleared his throat. "Trevor. We don't have a lot of time."

The courier rose from the couch. "We should use the compass and go to the cavern right now."

Rex chuckled. "That's not gonna happen, young man."

Omar favored the courier with a tolerant expression. "We've been over this before. Jonah and the others have to return home before they're missed."

Trevor's mouth opened and closed without words and his body spasmed.

Omar's immaculate eyebrows drew together in concern. "We can have a healer come and check you out."

"I don't want a healer poking me." Trevor drew in a deep breath to calm himself. "A healer can't stop what's happening."

Jonah wondered if that was the reason Trevor's mood seemed to shift. Maybe the effects of staying in the mortal world were starting to get to the boy. He did act more agitated and, Jonah noted, beads of sweat continually broke out on his forehead.

Omar patted the half globe. "Hurry."

"Please," Mike added.

Trevor glanced at Mike and placed his hands on either side of the half-globe, down near the base, and twisted the top with practiced ease.

There was a hiss of escaping air as Trevor lifted the globe free and then detached the Enhancer from its stand.

Jonah hopped off his stool and hurried closer to peek at the device. It was made out of the same strange metal as the compass. "So this is the Enhancer?" he asked.

"It's *an* Enhancer," Trevor corrected. "There are others. Most have been locked away by the Grand Oracle." The boy's voice was low and angry. "They are forbidden devices because Enhancers allowed a mortal to read angel script and the ancient texts for a short period of time."

"Awesome," Jonah breathed.

Mike also scanned the small device. "This is the only one not locked away?"

"We have a few others in our possession," Trevor confessed as he turned the device, showing Mike and Jonah all the angles. "It's another reason we're called heretics."

Mike's eyes widened.

Jonah sensed a punchline coming. "Why did the Elder want us to get this one? Why not use another?"

"This is the only one that can decipher the compass data." Trevor held out the device to Jonah. "It's meant for you."

Jonah thought this sounded like the Legend of the Guardians. Mortals were given the Rings to reset or maintain the balance. He took the device and inspected it.

Trevor mimed placing the Enhancer against the side of his head. "When you need to activate it, just place it against your temple and press the notch on the side." He waited while Jonah found the notch.

"Be careful." Trevor reached out to keep Jonah from actually pressing it. "You can activate the Enhancer without it being against your temple."

Jonah pulled his finger away.

"And never activate the Enhancer more than once on the same person," Trevor continued, "until the effect has worn off."

"What happens if I do?"

Trevor gulped and said, "You'll risk permanent brain damage."

Jonah held the device away, not sure if he wanted to have something that could damage his brain.

Mike wasn't afraid and lifted the Enhancer from Jonah's grip.

The young courier watched Mike. "It and the compass belonged to the last Deliverer. It was said only he could work both."

Mike almost dropped the Enhancer. "Jonah's the special one, not me."

Trevor's gaze turned calculating. "I know. Odd isn't it that you can also work the compass?"

Mike shoved the device into Jonah's hand like it was red hot. "What does that mean?"

For once, Trevor's expression seemed genuine and concerned. "I don't know. It's something we can ask the Elder when we cross over."

Trueblood frowned and pulled a small token from her tunic pocket. She held it up for all to see. Jonah thought it was one of Wick's pieces. "They've arrived," she said.

Omar motioned to Mabel. "Go and stall for as long as you can."

"I'll offer them some sweet tea." Mabel hurried from the room.

"Wick?" Omar nodded at a gym bag on the floor near Robert and Wick.

Jonah recognized it as the one the young mage used to carry his magical paraphernalia around. Wick knelt and unzipped his bag.

"What's this?" Trevor asked, frowning.

Omar ignored the question as he placed the compass and the Enhancer inside the bag. Wick zipped that closed and stood straight as Marcus stepped through the basement entrance. Jonah knew that guarded look on his godfather's face. Marcus wasn't alone.

A short, plump woman came through the door next. She bobbed on her feet as she took in everyone in the room. Marcus gestured to Trevor, and the woman wobbled to him.

"Let the healer check you out," a sharp voice commanded.

The last person to enter was a barrel-chested man with a deep tan complexion who was wearing a royal blue, knee-length tunic over his blue dress shirt and dark slacks. The Alliance Symbol was done in gold thread on the left tunic breast. The man's haircut matched his voice, military in style.

Marcus gestured to the man and said, "This is Mage Rubio, a member of the Alliance Council."

Mage Rubio noted everyone's position like a soldier scouting the location of the enemy before attacking. Once satisfied, he marched over to Trevor, who the healer had forced to sit.

Mike hovered nearby until Rubio turned his formidable gaze on Jonah's buddy. Mike paled and retreated to the sofa. While the healer poked and prodded Trevor, Rubio barked hushed questions at the boy.

At one point, the healer moved to lift Trevor's shirt, but the boy yanked it back into place. "You're not helping me," he shouted.

The healer stood back and frowned at him. Rubio stroked his chin before snapping his fingers at Rex. "Montgomery, take this young man to Alliance Headquarters."

"You can't do that," Jonah and Mike shouted at the same time. Lynn looked just has mutinous.

Marcus and Kevin maintained a resigned silence.

Rubio whirled to face the kids. He let his eyes linger on Jonah. "So much like your father, young man." He waved to Rex, who moved to obey.

"You can't take him," Mike insisted. He stepped right up to Rubio.

The mage's eyebrows rose. "I'm afraid we can."

Jonah turned to his godfather for help, but Marcus held up his hands. "The Council wants to question Trevor."

Even Kevin acted subdued in front of this new mage, although Jonah could feel the anger rolling off him.

"Montgomery," Rubio barked. Rex nodded, gripped Trevor's arm, and marched him out of the basement. Rubio turned on the spot, taking in the rest of the group. "Send them all home, Marcus. And join the rest of the Council at headquarters. It's gonna be a long night."

Rubio turned for the door and paused when he noted Mabel standing there. "Another time for the sweet tea, Mabel?" After a respectful nod, the mage slipped by Mabel and out of the basement.

Marcus clapped his hands to cut through the barrage of questions and shouts. "We don't have time for this." He met everyone's indignant gaze. "We will finish this mission."

"How?" Robert asked. "They jacked Trevor."

"And what about the mole?" Lynn added. "I bet that's how the Council found out you had Trevor."

Omar raised one of his precise eyebrows at Lynn's comment. "She's right, Marcus. Agent Ramsey will be on the alert for their return."

Jonah hadn't considered that angle. "Should we leave the gym bag here?"

"No," Marcus answered. "The Alliance has access to this place. It's better you keep it out of sight." He checked his watch. "Eleanor, can you and Kevin make sure everyone gets home?"

Mage Trueblood nodded. "Of course." She motioned for Robert, Wick, and Mike to join Lynn and Jonah.

Marcus surveyed the assembled group of young people. He drew in a deep breath, let it out, and said, "You've accomplished a lot today."

When Marcus paused, Omar took over. "What Marcus is trying to say is he's proud of you."

Jonah gulped, never expecting that from his godfather. "What'll happen to you?"

"Don't worry about us," Marcus answered. "We'll be back as soon as we can. Until then, be careful."

"Okay," Jonah replied for everyone. He didn't have Lynn's Sight, but deep inside, he knew things were going to get worse.

CHAPTER TWENTY-ONE
DISBANDED

"I don't like it," Jonah said, pausing in his manipulation of the compass.

Lynn nodded her agreement as she leaned against the breakfast bar. The warm morning sunlight making a counterpoint to her sour expression.

Kevin, along with Trueblood, stood in the middle of the Hightowers' family room. He frowned. "We were ordered onto other projects by the Council. We can't stay in Mount Vernon today."

Robert, who sat on the opposite side of the bar, dropped his spoon in his cereal bowl. "That's bull."

"It's the mole," Jonah insisted.

"We know that." Kevin looked just as angry as Jonah and his cousins. The young Fallen Reaper's hands were balled into fists. "The mole has fixed things to keep us away from you all."

"Then why do it?" Lynn raised an eyebrow.

"Because it's our job." Trueblood's serious tone cut through any further objections. "Marcus will sort it out and we'll be back."

Jonah thought the mage was missing the real point. "I'm worried about Ramsey."

"There's no reason for him to bother you. We have the courier." Trueblood crossed to the sofa and stared at the compass in Jonah's hands. "Even so, I think you should put that in your cousin's archive box." She motioned to Mike. "The Enhancer, too. For safekeeping."

While Jonah agreed placing the compass in the Seeker's box was a safe option, he also had doubts. In a pinch, the compass could transport everyone to safety, so he'd rather hold on to it. As for the Enhancer, Jonah noted Mike kept the device in his shirt pocket and didn't seem inclined to give it up.

Trueblood glanced at her watch and headed for the hallway and front door.

Kevin lingered. "If Ramsey does show up, little man, phase, no matter who's around. The Alliance can deal with the consequences."

"Kevin…" Trueblood warned from the hallway and stepped into view. "That's not wise."

"I don't care." Kevin turned to Lynn. "Keep your blades ready to use. The agent may have more of his goons with him."

Lynn nodded. Kevin waved and followed Trueblood out of the house.

Once they were gone, Lynn retrieved her blades from her room. When she returned, she waved to Jonah. "Let's go. We need to put the compass and mind booster in Robert's archive box."

Robert's cell phone rang. He answered and then held it away from his ear. Wick's voice rolled out of the speaker, sounding agitated.

"We're on the way." Robert hung up. "Wick says to get our butts to the teen center."

*

Wick waited in the teen center atrium, his face a mask of fury. "She has people in the attic." He pointed toward the second floor. "They're talking about taking over our clubhouse."

Lynn and Robert sprinted for the stairs at top speed without asking any questions.

"Who's in the attic?" Mike inquired, trailing behind Jonah and Wick.

The young mage growled before saying, "The director has county people measuring the space."

Mike reached into his pocket and pulled out his talisman. "Why didn't the token warn us?"

Wick grimaced. "I took it down so they wouldn't keep setting it off."

Robert and Lynn's longer legs allowed the twins to reach the attic first and they stormed inside. By the time Jonah and the others caught up, the twins had already barreled out and down the second-floor hallway to the administration section.

"Hey," a startled secretary called out, "you need an appointment!"

Jonah, Mike, and Wick stumbled into the main office just in time to see Robert and Lynn crashing through the director's open door. They rushed by the agitated secretary and crowded into the office behind the twins.

The director's office was large, but overly stuffed with paper, books, and other official documents that littered every available surface, including the large desk.

The director shot to her feet. "I beg your pardon! You can't barge into my office."

"And you can't take our attic space," Lynn countered.

The shorter woman arched her eyebrows. "The attic belongs to the county."

"You made a deal with us!" Robert yelled. "If we cleaned it out and I ran the website, you agreed to let us use the attic for our clubhouse."

"Things have changed." The short woman held up a hand. "As for the website and servers, you can administer those from the offices on this floor."

Robert and Lynn started yelling at the same time, causing the director to march around her desk and past the group before slamming her office door.

She whirled to face the twins. "First of all, no final decision has been made. The Director of Public Facilities, my supervisor, wants to know the square footage, just in case."

"We know why he's doing it." Robert's voice was a little calmer but still full of outrage. "Brandon's dad."

The director averted her gaze for a moment. Jonah caught the look of guilt on her face and his insides began to burn.

Jonah knew the only reason she hadn't thrown the twins out was because she liked Lynn. Jonah's cousin belonged to a group of the older girls who were working in a teen center mentoring program. They helped younger girls that were suffering from troubled home lives.

"You might as well know this now." The director stopped when someone knocked at the door. She took a moment to smooth her brow with her hands. "Come in."

A police officer stepped inside the room, causing Jonah to instantly fear the secretary might've called for help. But the officer smiled at them as he hooked his thumbs into his leather belt. Stocky, with obvious muscle underneath his uniform, he nodded his bald head at the stunned kids.

The director gestured to the man. "This is Lieutenant Cook. He's the resource officer assigned to the teen center."

"Why's he here?" Lynn asked, her voice cool.

Cook smiled and said, "I'll be working with the new youth group."

"What group?" Jonah countered suspiciously.

The director met their angry gazes. "We're disbanding the Practice Club and rolling it into a new club."

Once again, Robert and Lynn started yelling. Jonah joined them this time. "You can't do that!"

"It's already been decided. The police department is going to work with the restructured group," the director continued.

"All of you are welcomed to sign on," Lieutenant Cook added. "Just come to me or see the group's leader."

"Who's that?" Jonah asked.

The officer turned to the director. "I believe his name is Brandon Warner?"

The director nodded.

Jonah couldn't take any more; plus the office was growing very stuffy with so many people crammed inside. He slipped past Lieutenant Cook and into the fresher air of the reception area. He didn't realize Mike and Wick had followed him until he reached the second-floor railing and stopped.

Mike stood beside him. "What are we gonna do?"

"I don't know." Jonah smacked a hand on the metal railing. "Brandon! That weasel!"

"It was Brandon's dad," Wick said. "Marcus trumped him, so he attacked you guys. He's a punk, just like his son." Wick eyed Mike. "Where're you going?"

"I need to use the bathroom." Mike paused at the top of the staircase and pointed toward the east wing.

Wick frowned at him. "We need to stay together."

"I'll go with him," Jonah volunteered. He looked around and lowered his voice. "If anything happens, we'll jump to the creekside and make our way around to the front parking lot."

Wick hesitated before exhaling a breath and ruffling his short dreads. "Okay. But hurry back. Lynn's already in a foul mood."

"Right." Jonah followed Mike to the bathrooms in the east wing. While Mike went inside, Jonah leaned against the alcove wall and waited. His Death Sense spiked within seconds.

"Mr. Blackstone?" Ramsey stood behind Jonah with a cup of coffee in his hand. The man's sharp eyebrows were drawn together, giving his mocha-colored face even more of a hawkish look. "I need to talk with you."

"Actually," Jonah replied as he moved away from the bathroom alcove while taking out his phone, "I was about to leave." He swiftly sent a text to Mike, telling his friend to stay in the bathroom for now. Jonah reached the staircase and hesitated because Agent Harris was standing there.

Thinking he could lose Ramsey in the small library and then phase to safety, Jonah headed for the west wing. But as he started past the café, Ramsey edged in front of Jonah, forcing him to stop.

"This won't take long." The agent stepped into the café and flashed his badge to clear the nearer table. The kids grumbled as they gathered their things and shifted to another table in the back. Ramsey placed his coffee cup on the table and waved Jonah over.

With Agent Harris hovering in the background, Jonah was torn. He couldn't leave Mike all alone in the bathroom. He also couldn't run to the second floor to get help; at least, not with Harris blocking his way.

Jonah had to get rid of the agents. He took out his phone and texted Wick. That's when he realized he'd become the subject of Ramsey's full-on stare. The intensity of the man's attention sent another warning throb to Jonah's Death Sense.

He sauntered over, pulled out a chair and sat. "What do you want?"

Agent Ramsey signaled to Harris and then took the chair opposite Jonah. He slowly sipped his coffee, contemplating Jonah before leaning over the steaming cup. "Where is the courier, Mr. Blackstone?"

Jonah jumped when his phone buzzed in his pocket. It had to be Mike or Wick, no doubt, wondering what was happening. Jonah tried to act casually, shrugging as he peeked at his phone's screen. Drawing on the honest truth, since he had no clue where the Alliance held Trevor, he replied, "I don't know."

Out of habit, he filled his mind with the truth of his answer. *I don't know. I don't know.* Ramsey couldn't do a Reaper Stare, Jonah reasoned. Only Reapers and Fallen Reapers could manage to do that. And Ramsey wasn't a Fallen one. But the previous signal from his Death Sense made Jonah curious about the agent.

When Ramsey lowered his gaze and sipped his coffee, a look of disappointment was on his face. "It's understandable; the Alliance wouldn't tell a child that bit." He smiled when Jonah struggled to keep from reacting to the insult.

A commotion from above, drew Jonah's gaze toward the balcony. His heart sank because Agent Harris had cornered Wick and his cousins. The agent also seemed to have drawn the resource officer into what looked like a spirited discussion.

Ramsey's gaze shifted between Jonah and the second-floor argument. He smirked. "First, Deyanira came to this out-of-the-way town," the agent began while leaning closer, "now the traitorous courier comes here. Why is everyone so interested in a half-breed like you?" Ramsey's eyes narrowed as he studied Jonah. "Perhaps you can discover the location of the courier, and tell me? I'll leave this place if you do. Otherwise..."

Jonah narrowed his own eyes. "Otherwise what?"

"You'll lose much more than just your pathetic fighting club and the attic hideout."

Jonah heard the blatant threat in the man's voice, but his own anger peaked. He shot to his feet.

The move startled Agent Ramsey, who instantly reached for that hidden weapon underneath his jacket while simultaneously rising to his feet.

Jonah's Death Sense spiked as he prepared to phase to the bathroom, no longer caring if anyone saw him. He intended to grab Mike, get to the creekside, and hope the Alliance could sort everything out. He concentrated hard, and was about to make the mental nudge and phase when a nearby cell phone went off with a loud, obnoxious ring-tone.

Ramsey's gaze flickered to the closest table and then around the crowded café. The agent frowned while withdrawing his hand from inside his jacket. Jonah nearly sighed with relief to see it empty.

Ramsey scowled at him. "I'm watching you, Blackstone."

"Fine! You do that," Jonah spat back at the man. After briefly pausing to make eye contact with Wick, who was still stuck with Agent Harris on the second floor, Jonah exited the café. He and Mike would wait for Lynn and the others outside the teen center. There were too many enemies inside today.

As if proving his point, Brandon's snobbish laugh cut through the air just as Jonah stepped into the atrium. The bully and Antwan had four girls gathered around them. Brandon's eyes narrowed when he saw Jonah.

Before anything else could happen, Jonah veered into the east wing and straight to the bathrooms. He peeked around the alcove's corner and toward the atrium. Ramsey had left the café and was beckoning to Brandon and Antwan to approach him. After a brief conversation, Brandon pointed toward the alcove.

Jonah shrank out of sight and slipped into the boys' bathroom.

Mike jumped and waved his phone around. "What's going on?"

"Agent Ramsey's in the teen center. He knows the Alliance has Trevor and he threatened all of us."

Brandon's snide voice sounded from right outside the bathroom. "I saw the freak come this way."

When someone pushed on the door from the other side, Jonah grabbed Mike's arm and phased.

CHAPTER TWENTY-TWO
THE CHASE

Mike shivered, rubbing his arms as soon as they re-appeared at the creek side. He moved off along the bank. Jonah lurched into motion, following his friend until they reached the bend in the water's course.

Moss-covered stumps littered this area of the creek. Mike chose one, sat, and clasped his hands together. "He threatened us?"

"More than that," Jonah said. "Ramsey wanted to attack me." He surveyed the woods. Wick and the others had to be free of agent Harris by now, he decided, and motioned to Mike. "We should go–"

He paused because he sensed the tell-tale increase of pressure. Leaves crunched from the direction where they had first appeared in.

Jonah pulled Mike away from the stream side and into the trees where they both huddled, watching.

"Someone followed me."

Mike shook slightly. "Do you think it's Kevin?"

"No," Jonah whispered. "Kevin wouldn't know we're here."

"But who else could follow you?"

Jonah's first thought was Agent Ramsey. His fear was confirmed when he made out the agent's blue shirt and tan pants through the gaps in the trees.

Ramsey stepped into view, using his boot to shift aside the remains of an old fire. As Jonah watched, all the clues snapped into place. His initial suspicion that Ramsey wanted to pull a blade in the first encounter had been dead on. And the stare the Agent used in the café had been a true Reaper Stare. "He's a fallen one."

"Oh my God," Mike breathed in a horrified voice. "Jonah, this is bad."

"Tell me about it."

Mike punched Jonah's arm. "No, I mean we still have the compass and Enhancer. If he catches us with those…"

Jonah pushed aside his mounting panic and focused on his idea. "We have to phase."

"Ramsey'll follow you again," Mike said.

"I don't have a choice."

Mike nodded, looking grim. "I'm ready."

Ramsey moved along the creek's edge and in their direction, his attention on the ground. Jonah realized the agent was tracking them by their foot prints in the soft soil. Ramsey's gaze lifted to the tree line and settled on their hiding spot.

Now or never, Jonah told himself. He pictured his destination and phased.

When they reappeared, Jonah gritted his teeth until the dizziness passed. They stood atop his favorite grassy hillside, well outside the city limits of Mount Vernon. The distance and double phasing had taken a little out of Jonah and he regretted not bringing any candy. He leaned forward, resting his hands on his knees for a second before tugging Mike along behind him.

He hoped the extra distance would delay Agent Ramsey long enough for them to hide in the trees and make an escape. However, Agent Ramsey appeared a few seconds later.

"Halt!" Ramsey's order rolled down the hillside.

The command had the opposite effect on the boys. Jonah and Mike sprinted off through the nearby trees. Mike was careful to keep hold of Jonah's shirt, and that made it rough to get away. Plus, Jonah struggled with his mounting desperation in order to think about the next location to phase.

He certainly didn't want to lead the agent to his parents' hideaway. But he had to do something because Agent Ramsey drew closer with each second they remained on the hillside. Finally, a less than perfect option occurred to Jonah.

He hesitated before phasing and warned Mike, "Here we go."

Jonah had his hands up and ready to break his forward momentum when he reappeared in the cramped stairwell of the Oak Hill Mall parking garage. He succeeded in not smacking the wall, but Mike rammed into his back.

Jonah slumped against the cold concrete, the air knocked out of him. The disorientation was worse.

Mike was on point and pulled Jonah to his feet. "Come on, Jonah. You know he'll be here any second!" Mike hustled him up the stairs.

They burst through the stairwell doors, startling a mother and her three kids.

"This way." Mike wanted to go deeper into the parking structure.

Jonah had a better idea and yanked Mike in the opposite direction. "No. This way."

Adrenaline surged through Jonah as they ran across the pedestrian walkway that connected the parking garage to level three of the shopping mall. A stairwell door banged open behind them just as the boys entered the building.

Mike slowed his pace at once to a fast walk and glanced at Jonah. "Why are you so dizzy now? You weren't like that before."

Jonah wondered the same thing. When he had phased himself and Mike from his parents' hideaway, he barely felt any dizziness. And that had been two hundred miles.

"I think," he began, working through the problem, "it was the compass. It used my power, but maybe it also charged me." The more Jonah thought about it, the more it made sense. Plus, something else niggled at the back of his mind. He pushed that aside when he spotted what he needed.

"There!" Jonah pointed at a candy shop.

They swerved inside the brightly lit store, nearly knocking over a little kid picking candy from a bin. Jonah crouched behind a large display of jelly beans of all colors and flavors. Mike fumbled with the dispenser. His hands shook, but he managed to scoop jelly beans into a cellophane bag. Mike paused and drew out several to hand to Jonah, who glanced around before popping them in his mouth.

"Thanks," Jonah mumbled around the mouthful of beans.

"You're the only kid who has to eat candy." Mike cracked a smile and added, "Stay down."

Jonah watched the front doors as Mike went to the counter. He jerked when Agent Ramsey paused just outside. Then the agent turned to peer inside the candy store. Jonah kept his head down, hoping that no one would notice his strange behavior.

"Jonah…" Mike whispered and waved to him. He had hid behind a large woman looking at a display of lollipops when Ramsey appeared. "Come on." He peeked outside, the small bag of candy clutched in his right hand. "Ramsey just went inside a game store. Let's go."

Jonah felt exposed as he and Mike exited and retraced their path to the pedestrian bridge. They needed a place to hide and call for help. Before they could reach the exit, a security guard came out of those doors. The man glanced in their direction and reached for a radio on his belt. Jonah had the sinking feeling that the startled mom had called security or maybe the candy store owner had reported them. He didn't wait to find out which and changed direction, heading for the down escalators.

The boys received an unpleasant surprise when they spotted Agent Ramsey talking to another mall guard. The agent pointed in their direction. Knowing it was impossible to go unnoticed anymore, the boys sprinted down the escalator, apologizing to all the people they bumped and pushed along the way.

"What's the plan?" Mike panted just behind Jonah as they reached the bottom and hopped the next escalator down to the first floor. "You can't phase in public."

The statement made Jonah look up as they neared the bottom of the last escalator. The security guard hurried after them, but Agent Ramsey stood at the railing on the third floor, watching. Jonah knew that had they not been in public, Ramsey would have simply phased right on top of him and Mike.

Just as they turned for the main mall doors, a third guard jumped them. Jonah pushed Mike forward while he dropped to his knees to avoid the guard's outstretched arms. The man stumbled past and over. Jonah scrambled after Mike and out the front doors.

The situation became trickier as a black SUV screeched to a halt right in front of them. Mike faltered, but Jonah nudged his friend to the right.

"Go around, into the parking lot."

Jonah dodged to the left as a beefy guy in all black hopped out of the truck. The man only paused for a moment before moving toward him.

Jonah kicked the truck's door, sending it flying into the man's arms. Then he dodged around and into the parking lot. He expected to catch up to Mike, but the guy recovered quicker than expected and snagged the back of his shirt. Jonah twisted out of the man's grip and nearly froze.

The small white skull clipped to the man's lapel reflected the bright sunlight. *Grimnion.* Fear propelled Jonah in the opposite direction from Mike and down a different row of cars.

The goon kept right on Jonah as he dodged between vehicles.

"Let go," Mike called out.

Jonah phased without thinking about it. He appeared right behind another Grimnion, who held Mike by the arm. In his other hand was a scythe.

"Hey!" Jonah yelled.

The man spun around, slicing the air with the weapon. Jonah ducked under the swing and Mike used the distraction to stomp on the man's foot. Then he ran around one end of the car and Jonah went the other way. They met up on the opposite side and scurried between adjacent cars until they were at least two rows away.

Jonah dropped to the ground and waved Mike to follow as he rolled under a van. Mike bumped into him a second later, and they watched the black shoes of men crossing back and forth.

"Jonah, why didn't you phase us?"

"I have to be careful where we go."

Mike's eyes widened. "Oh. But won't he sense what you just did?"

At that moment Jonah noticed a different pair of shoes walking closer to their spot. Once again, something began to nag Jonah, but he didn't know what.

Mike elbowed him. "Jonah…"

"I see him."

The boys heard Agent Hunter's angry voice shouting over his radio. "I don't care about the mall security. Put a nullifying net over the entire parking lot. Do it now before Blackstone can phase."

The muffled thump of the nullifying poles hitting the surface of the heated parking lot and sinking into place reached their ears.

Mike's eyes were as wide as his own, Jonah imagined. Time was up. They were so close to each other, it was easier for Jonah to slide an arm across Mike's back. Just as Jonah phased, he felt the trap snapping into place over the parking lot. But it was too late to stop. The ripples from the phase already played over his and Mike's bodies.

The next second, he experienced a wrenching pull. It was so unexpected that Mike slipped free of Jonah's grip in the middle of the phase.

"No!"

CHAPTER TWENTY-THREE
REVELATIONS

Jonah's fear for his buddy overshadowed his own terror at being sucked back to the parking lot and Agent Ramsey. He focused on his destination, not knowing how or if he could get away from the trap's pull.

He strained, his muscles aching as he reached out, willing himself to go forward. His Reaper powers obeyed, moving him toward his destination. As he did so, he felt another presence, familiar and frightened. *Mike!* Jonah latched onto his buddy's soul.

"Come on!" He pressed all of his will into the struggle to free himself. Just when Jonah thought he'd split in half from the opposing forces, the real world returned and he slammed onto the smooth cold concrete surface of the parking garage ramp. Mike slumped beside him.

The shock of the close escape, combined with the change from the broiling hot pavement of the parking lot, caused Jonah to suck in a startled breath.

Mike groaned, rubbing his head. "I hate phasing."

A horn blared and tires screeched. Jonah glanced up in time to see a large SUV bearing down on them. He grabbed Mike and rolled to the side. The SUV drove over the exact spot where they had been.

Jonah helped Mike to his feet and they dodged between a row of cars. The change in air pressure came just as they ran into the nearest stairwell. Jonah's exhaustion increased, making his frustration more unbearable. When they reached the top level of the garage, he turned to Mike. "Ready?"

"Yes!"

This time, they reappeared at the ravine near the practice field. It was the only deserted place Jonah could think to go. He led the way along a fallen log which lay across the gap. The drop to the bottom of the ravine was maybe twenty feet.

Jonah thought it significant that neither he nor Mike even hesitated to run across the log in an attempt to reach the thicket of woods on the other side. Agent Ramsey appeared behind them, as Jonah expected, and then the agent did what Jonah didn't expect. Ramsey phased to a spot on the opposite site of the ravine, blocking their escape path.

Jonah stopped.

Mike bumped into him and then screamed at Ramsey. "We didn't do anything wrong."

Agent Ramsey didn't respond as he stalked toward them.

Jonah pushed Mike in the opposite direction, and they ran back the way they came. But Jonah already knew what the agent would do. But it was Agent Harris who appeared in front of them on that side of the ravine. And Harris brought along two Wraith-possessed goons.

Jonah's nagging warning became a cold reality. He had focused on Ramsey and forgot about his partner. With Ramsey a Fallen One, it only made sense that Harris would also be one.

The henchmen withdrew their weapons and started for the log. They planned to box Jonah and Mike between themselves and Agent Ramsey, who remained at the edge of the ravine

Ramsey smirked at Jonah. "Give up, young Blackstone."

"Use the compass," Mike whispered. "Remember what your godfather said about Deyanira not being able to follow us."

"He also said they weren't sure that's why Deyanira didn't follow."

Mike pointed at Ramsey. "It's time to test that."

Jonah didn't see any other options. He pulled the compass from his pocket but held it behind his back, hiding it from Ramsey's view. Mike caught on and activated the device.

As the first Grimnion stepped onto the log, Trevor appeared behind the goons. In one motion, he knocked the closer man over the edge and into the ravine.

"Trevor?" Jonah and Mike gaped at the boy.

Trevor grabbed the second Grimnion and hurled the man backward toward Agent Harris. But Harris dodged. At the same time, the agent pulled out two gleaming Reaper blades and attacked Trevor.

Jonah's heart rate spiked with fear for the boy, but Trevor was full of surprises. He too had blades. He blocked Harris's blows and scored a quick cut on the agent's left arm.

Ramsey's shout shocked Jonah and Mike out of their stupor. "No!" He activated his own blades and started across the ravine.

Jonah prepared to activate the compass just as a small object whistled up from the ravine below at high speed. His Death Sense spiked and he moved to push Mike aside. He was too late. The scythe struck Mike in the chest.

Mike collapsed forward with an explosive exhale of breath. The next moment, his entire upper body and head were engulfed in a brilliant light.

"Mike!" Jonah grabbed hold of his buddy. But he wasn't ready for the added weight and lost his own footing. Both boys tumbled off the log.

As they fell, Jonah only had seconds to concentrate and phase before they crashed into the broken limbs and branches below. He pictured the small section of grass near the center of the practice area and phased.

The softer earth cushioned the impact but, Jonah still let out a painful *oomph*. Mike flopped beside him and didn't move. The light engulfing his upper body and head was gone.

Jonah shook his friend by the shoulders. "Mike. Mike."

When Ramsey appeared, Jonah roared at the man in anger, dived for two practice batons the club kept nearby, and threw both weapons at the agent.

Ramsey knocked the batons aside and pointed a blade at Mike. "That was your fault, young Blackstone. How many more of your friends and family will have to die?"

Tears streamed down Jonah's face. His first impulse was to attack Ramsey again. A voice in his head said, *No. Get Mike's body away.* Jonah held up his compass in a shaking hand just as Trevor appeared.

The courier grabbed Jonah's hand and pressed it against the green activate button before Jonah could reach out for Mike.

"Wait!"

The compass activated and the clearing was gone in a second. He and Trevor reappeared at his parents' hideaway.

Jonah struggled in the courier's grip. "Let me go."

In answer, Trevor zapped Jonah in the neck with a small device.

Blinding pain shot into Jonah's head. His legs buckled and he dropped to his knees, cradling his head in his hands. The sharp pain from the jolt subsided, but his head was left buzzing.

"You bastard," Jonah managed through clenched teeth.

Trevor stood back, shocked. "I'm… I'm sorry. I thought you had Mike. I wouldn't have…" The boy swallowed. "It's too late."

"No it isn't. " Jonah lurched to his feet but when he tried to phase, his fuzzy mind refused to cooperate. He roared in anger at Trevor, "What did you do to me?"

Trevor moved away from Jonah's grasping hands. "You can't, Jonah. They'll catch you."

"But Mike," Jonah's jaw quivered. "He's dead."

"He's not dead," Trevor shot back.

Jonah sensed the raw despair in the courier and it shocked him.

Trevor took a deep breath to calm himself. "The Enhancer activated. I'm sure Mike's just unconscious from the shock of it."

Two conflicting emotions warred inside Jonah. He wanted to believe Mike would be fine. At the same time, Jonah hated Trevor for ruining his chance to get his best friend to safety. "I have to go back."

Trevor moved fast and pinned Jonah's arms behind his back. "I'm sorry, Jonah, but I can't let you do that."

"They'll hurt my friend."

"No they won't." Trevor shook him. "Listen to me. Ramsey will want to trade Mike for me. That's their way."

Jonah struggled but Trevor's grip was too strong, and his head still buzzed. "Whose way? Fallen Reapers?"

"No," Trevor answered, "something a lot worse. Hunters."

CHAPTER TWENTY-FOUR
RAMSEY'S DEMAND

Kevin's powerful upper cut struck Trevor below the chin. The boy landed on his butt and slid backward into Robert and Lynn's desks. The twins scrambled to keep their computer monitors from toppling onto the ground.

"You lying punk." Kevin stalked toward Trevor, his fist balled and ready to strike again.

"Hold on." Rex stepped between Kevin and Trevor. "Let the boy speak, then you can clobber him."

"You're not helping, Rex." Marcus frowned at Kevin until the young Fallen Reaper retreated to the sofa and sat beside Jonah.

"I understand your anger," Marcus continued, "And Jonah's."

"And ours," Lynn seconded from her spot behind the computer desks. She and Robert stared daggers at Trevor as Rex pulled the boy to his feet.

The thought of Rex helping the courier angered Jonah even more. He stabbed a finger at Trevor. "He let Agent Ramsey take Mike."

"He would have caught you–"Trevor began.

"Shut up!" Jonah didn't want to hear anything Trevor had to say. The last few hours had been the worst of Jonah's life as his terror over Mike's fate worsened.

Marcus stood in front of Jonah, blocking his view of Trevor. "We sent people to the clearing. Ramsey set up a nullifying trap and had four of his henchmen waiting."

Jonah hung his head low. He didn't want to see Trevor's decision as smart.

"Listen to your godfather," Rex urged. "They left Mike's candy bag in the open, right where you'd see it. They would have played your emotions to catch you."

"And," Marcus added, "Ramsey would possess the compass and Enhancer." He let out a breath. "The agents will offer to trade Mike, which means he'll keep your friend alive."

Kevin snorted and leaned against Jonah. "If anything happens to Mike, I'll take care of Ramsey and Trevor."

Jonah welcomed the comment but it didn't matter, not with his friend out there. And Trevor's genuine sorrow over Mike's situation also bothered Jonah. He wanted to hate Trevor, accuse the boy of not caring, but he couldn't.

When Jonah noticed his godfather watching his reaction, he covered by asking, "Why didn't you know about Ramsey and Harris?"

Marcus' eyebrows shot up and he exchanged a glance with Trueblood and Rex before answering. "This is our first time dealing with Hunters in the mortal world."

"But, what are they?" Lynn asked. She and Robert moved closer to Jonah and Kevin.

"They are former archivists who've been placed in the mortal realm for special assignments," Marcus explained. "Until they are activated, they lead normal mortal lives."

"So they're sleeper agents," Jonah said.

Marcus nodded. "In a way. A Hunter can stay undercover for years before he's activated."

All the talk of being activated reminded Jonah of Kevin's meditation. "If they have patterns like yours, that means they have to recharge or lose power?"

Marcus stroked his chin. "We energize our patterns on a frequent basis because we continually use our power. The Hunters go inactive for years, so their binding patterns retain their charge far longer."

Robert pointed at Trevor. "What about him?"

"I'm not a Hunter." The boy threw up his hands in a normal human gesture. "I crossed through the portal."

Kevin glared at him. "So what? That just means you're like Deyanira."

Trevor clutched the bottom of his shirt and twisted it in his hands. Jonah sat straighter, remembering the boy didn't want the healer to look at him. He nudged Kevin and pointed at Trevor's shirt.

Kevin's face went slack. "Do you have binding patterns?"

Trevor hesitated before answering. "The Elder put me through the trial." He winced.

According to Jonah's godfather, the patterns were a painful part of the falling process. Jonah couldn't miss the look of understanding passing between Rex, his godfather, and Kevin. For once, he felt outside a closed circle and understood why.

Unlike the others, Jonah was born to his powers. He didn't have nor need the patterns.

Kevin nodded to Trevor in sympathy, and the fire in the Fallen Reaper's attitude lessened as he crossed his arms. Jonah was about to ask Kevin if he was alright when something in Jonah's pocket spiked with heat.

It was like pressing a sun-heated coin on his bare arm. Jonah dug out Wick's talisman, recalling that after clearing the county people out of the attic space, Marcus had instructed Wick and Trueblood to restore the protections.

Jonah wasn't the only one to react. Lynn, Robert, and Trueblood did the same thing, each gaping at the coin.

Wick jumped up. "Someone's messing with the door."

Kevin pulled a blade and bounded down the stairs. The attic door opened and then closed with a soft thud. Kevin returned, holding a small white envelope in his hands. "I found this taped to the door." He handed it to Marcus. "I also saw Brandon running down the stairs to the atrium."

Wick ruffled his dreads while trying to peek at the note. "I bet Ramsey doesn't want to show his face right now, the jerk."

Marcus read the note once and then passed the piece of paper to Kevin. "Just as I said. Agent Ramsey wants to trade Mike in exchange for Trevor."

"How long do we have?" Trueblood asked.

"The meet is set for seven-thirty." Marcus glanced at his watch. "We have just over three hours to prepare. The exchange takes place at this location." He held up a picture that had been inside the folded message.

Kevin's jaw tightened. Rex grunted and Trueblood shook her head.

"What's special about that place?" Jonah asked. As far as he could see, it was a simple field of sparse wild grass and red clay.

Kevin handed the note to Wick and then told Jonah, "It's where I fell."

Jonah noted the older boy's haunted expression. "That place?"

"Yes." Kevin leaned against the back of the sofa next to Jonah again. He gazed at his large hands as he spoke. "The Alliance used that field a lot. Ramsey's letting us know that he's on to us."

Lynn took the picture and examined it. "Where is this?"

Kevin lifted his gaze to the photo. "North Georgia."

"It's not in Mount Vernon." Lynn furrowed her brow. "That's strange."

"Why?" Kevin slipped his hands in his pockets and shrugged. "You know distance isn't a problem for us."

"Yeah, I do." Lynn handed the photo to Robert and Wick, who huddled close to examine it. "It's almost like Ramsey wants to pull you away from here and..." Her eyes flickered to Jonah for a split second.

Rex nodded. "The little lady makes a good point. The mole did the same thing; why not try it again? Perhaps he wants Jonah after all."

"But that doesn't make sense," Jonah objected. "The mole ordered Ramsey to leave me alone."

"Then Ramsey is acting on his own, which makes it even more dangerous," Trueblood said.

"We can't give him Trevor." Jonah was shocked to hear himself defend the boy he wanted to punch a short while ago.

"Thanks, Jonah." Trevor gave him a tired smile. "You save Mike. He's more important than me."

Jonah wanted to object when a tiny light flared in mid-air, drawing his attention. He dismissed it as a lightning bug that had made its way into the attic. Then something larger zipped out of the pinpoint of light and expanded.

Everyone gasped except Kevin and the adults. The glittering shape formed into an undulating Alliance symbol, three interlocking circles with a pair of wings above. The symbol wasn't much bigger than a large butterfly. Adding to the effect, the symbol's wings flapped as it floated in the air.

Wick was ecstatic. "That is so freakin' cool!" He rushed over to peer at the beacon.

Marcus pulled Wick back as the beacon flared and faded away and a real vortex formed in the air.

Rubio exited the magical doorway. After a brief nod to Marcus, the intimidating mage turned to Trevor, held up his hand, and muttered, "Nishati," in his military voice. A beam of energy shot from his raised hand and enveloped Trevor. The boy let out an involuntary gasp.

"Hold out your arm," Rubio ordered. Trevor complied.

Lines appeared on Trevor's forearm and flared, leaving behind a sundial-type impression near the wrist.

Rubio drew in a deep breath. "That should help, for now."

Jonah grabbed Trevor's forearm to get a closer look at the tattoo. "You can't recharge his patterns with a spell, can you?"

Rubio chuckled. "That was for his mortal body." He rubbed his square chin while watching Trevor. "I'm guessing your patterns carried one charge?"

Trevor nodded.

Rubio crossed his hands behind his back. "Well, the Alliance would never think of giving you to Ramsey."

Jonah's relief over Trevor's fate only lasted for a millisecond. "What about Mike?" He had a growing sense of dread that worried him sick. The last time he experienced that had been…

All at once, Jonah's head split open with pain. His Death Sense was off the scale. Before he could stop himself, he bent forward and vomited on the floor. Everyone cleared a space out of reflex. But in seconds, Lynn and Kevin rushed forward to help him.

"It's Mike." Jonah paused to wipe his mouth. "Ramsey's hurting Mike!"

Trevor produced the device he had used to stun Jonah before. When Jonah saw it, he roared at the boy, "Stay away from me!"

Kevin whirled on Trevor and his face went slack when he saw the device. He grabbed Jonah's forearm. "Don't try to help Mike."

Marcus stepped forward. "Kevin's right. Ramsey may be laying a trap for you."

Jonah gave them a feeble nod. His head hurt too much to do anything else. Lynn pulled him to the sofa. She sat down and had Jonah stretch out with his head on her lap.

Robert was at their side with a bottle of water. Jonah took it, sat up and gulped it down. He gagged when his Death Sense spiked once more, then stopped.

Lynn forced him to lay back again and cradled his head in her hands. "It'll be alright."

When Jonah could trust his voice, he said, "He's not being hurt anymore."

Rubio stroked his big chin, eyeing Jonah. "So the boy can phase to someone's aid on instinct. Interesting."

Jonah's godfather's expression went stony. "That's something we shouldn't share with the whole council. Not with the mole around." Rubio looked ready to argue, but Marcus turned to Jonah. "Don't worry. We won't let Ramsey keep Mike." He paused as Rubio created another vortex. "I'm sorry, but we have an emergency meeting."

Rubio pulled Trevor in front of the vortex. "You won't be able to phase away again."

Trevor nodded, looking shocked and haunted, Jonah thought.

"We'll be back. Just stay safe," Marcus urged.

"What about the clubhouse?" Lynn gestured around the space.

Marcus's reaction intrigued Jonah. He glared at Rex as he said, "Ask him." With that, he stepped through the vortex with Trevor and Rubio.

Once the magical opening sealed itself, everyone turned on the Fallen Reaper.

Rex scratched the side of his big nose. His face had gone scarlet red with embarrassment. "Well, it seems the facilities manager's boat appeared several miles from his summer cottage and up a tree." Rex sucked in a breath. "He's taking his vacation early to sort it out. So no final decision on the attic for at least two weeks."

Wick, Lynn, and Robert whooped and clapped.

Jonah eyed Rex. "Marcus is pissed with you?"

"That's an understatement, buddy." Rex let out a low whistle. "But seriously, we'll get your friend back. Don't worry."

The last thing Jonah could do was not worry, considering his best friend was being tortured by a deranged GBI agent. One way or another, he knew he had to rescue Mike.

CHAPTER TWENTY-FIVE
BATTLE PLANS

The late afternoon turned into early evening before Rubio returned with additional Alliance personnel. They commandeered the clubhouse conference table and sitting area, and a hornet's nest of activity ensued.

Jonah and his cousins were left alone and out of the action. They debated among themselves whether the people traveled back and forth from Alliance HQ, the trade-off spot, or both. At one point Lynn followed Kevin to the conference table as plans for the trade were discussed.

Fifteen minutes in, Lynn slipped away and waved for Jonah, Robert, and Wick to follow her to the attic stairs. Jonah wanted to stay in the clubhouse.

Lynn twisted his ear and whispered, "Come on, hero."

Only when Kevin joined their group did Jonah relent and follow his cousin. Lynn didn't explain until they entered one of the smaller game rooms on the first floor.

Kevin stationed himself near the entrance to keep other kids from interfering. Robert and Wick took two of the chairs around the game table. Lynn forced Jonah into the third and took the fourth chair, opposite him.

"What's happening, Lynn?" Jonah raised an impatient eyebrow at his cousin.

Lynn waited for Kevin's nod before answering. "They're gonna use Trevor as a decoy."

"That's not gonna work," Jonah blurted out.

Lynn waved him silent. "He'll have extra protections and a lot of Alliance members ready to go. They want Ramsey to believe the Alliance is serious about the trade."

"But," Jonah stammered, "what about Mike?"

"They don't expect Ramsey to actually release Mike, which is why the Alliance plans to rescue him. It'll happen at the same time the fake trade is taking place."

Jonah couldn't believe what he was hearing. He glanced at Kevin for confirmation.

The young Fallen Reaper leaned against the doorframe and gave Jonah a sad nod. "Rubio's gonna lead that attack. He's pretty good in a fight."

Jonah couldn't relax, not with the tension he sensed in Lynn and Kevin. "What's worrying you, Lynn? Do you sense something?"

"No, but," she paused to swallow, "they got the location from a human agent they caught. And it's outside of Mount Vernon."

"You still think it's suspicious that the locations are always far from here?"

"Yes, I do." Lynn's tone left no doubt.

Kevin abandoned his perch in the doorway in order to kneel beside Jonah's chair. "Marcus said the same thing, but he was overruled. That's why he wants you to stay at the Guest House."

Jonah appreciated Kevin's idea, never truly considering that he was in any danger.

Kevin tapped Jonah's knee with his fist. "We'll all go. Robert, Lynn, and Wick."

Wick perked up at that news.

Robert smiled. "At least you'd have the video games to keep your mind off things, little cousin."

When Jonah continued to frown, Kevin leaned back. "What's the problem?"

Jonah threw up his hands, angry that the others didn't get it. "Kevin, if Mike isn't where they think, he'll still be in danger. We have to do something."

Kevin let out a breath. "Listen…"

Jonah leapt to his feet. "Lynn, you agree with me, don't you? If Ramsey's leading everyone out of Mount Vernon, then… then I bet Mike's here somewhere."

Lynn toyed with one of her braids. She did it whenever she was seriously considering an idea. Jonah silently urged his cousin to agree.

She leaned forward, her hands resting on the game table. "My intuition says Jonah's right. God forbid."

Kevin closed his eyes. "Where?"

Jonah traded a glance with Lynn. "The Crossroads?"

"No go," Kevin countered. "After you told us about the dream-walk, and seeing as Ramsey's using Wraiths, Marcus had the place checked out. We saw signs the agents had been there, but now it's empty."

A couple of younger kids appeared in the doorway, chess box in hand. Kevin caught their eye. "Use the next room." The kids gulped and hurried off. Kevin turned back to the others. "Lynn's on the right track. Ramsey and Harris needed a place empty of people and Wraiths."

Robert snapped his fingers. "I know where they could be. The old mill."

"Cool idea, Bobby," Wick agreed. "It's only a mile away from the Crossroads and it's been abandoned for over a decade."

"Huh, guys." Jonah waved his arms around. "Won't Ramsey have his own people there?"

"I'm sure he will." Lynn stood and turned to Kevin. "Are we gonna do this?"

Kevin's shoulders slumped. "You guys are trying to get me fired."

"You can claim it was all part of Rubio's plan," Wick laughed and plopped his boots on the table. "In fact, you can say he created the diversion just for you." He high-fived Robert.

Kevin scowled at the boys.

Jonah crossed his arms and stuck out his chin. "I'm saving my friend."

"We'll need protection." Lynn kicked Wick's boots off the table. "You got more shields, young mage?"

Wick exchanged an excited glance with Robert. "You bet I do. I've been working on a couple of them since, well," he looked at Jonah, "since Jonah gave me that power boost last summer."

Lynn crossed her arms. "Why didn't I know you worked on this?"

"You spent all your time working on your boyfriend," Robert said and wiggled his eyebrows at her.

When Lynn dipped her chin and narrowed her eyes, Robert hurried to explain. "Wick used Jonah's power boost to experiment with a couple of special shield bracelets."

Kevin's earlier scowl transformed into one of intense anticipation. "How powerful are they?"

Wick raised his eyebrows. "Really, really powerful."

Kevin shook his head in wonder. "Why aren't you guys working for the Alliance?"

"I told Trueblood a lot of stuff."

Lynn scoffed at Wick. "I bet you never told her about the bracelets."

"Well, not exactly …"

Lynn yanked one of Wick's short dreads. "I thought so."

Kevin glanced at his watch. "We better go. I'll have to actually take all of you to the Guest House."

"We'll be able to leave, right?" Lynn asked. "What about Mabel?"

"No problem." When Lynn raised a skeptical eyebrow, Kevin held up his hands. "She's in Washington for the day."

Lynn smirked. "For someone who didn't want to do this, you sound like you had a plan already in place."

Kevin hooked a thumb at Jonah. "Things always go sideways when he's involved."

Jonah punched the boy's arm and regretted it. Kevin's bicep was hard as steel.

"One of these days…" Kevin flexed his muscles.

"You guys can fight later." Lynn wrapped an arm around her brother's neck. "Robert needs to get the bracelet from the Seeker's box."

The group was in luck. Rex was the only Alliance member still in the attic when they returned. Jonah breathed easier. The big Fallen Reaper was cool, and not as suspicious of them as his godfather or Trueblood.

Robert conferred with Wick in front of the old file cabinet where he kept the archive box. Lynn went to the old editor's desk and rummaged around in a drawer. She pulled out a county map and handed it to Kevin. When Lynn noticed Jonah just standing there, she nodded toward the clubhouse section where Rex sat in an armchair, an opened report on his lap.

Jonah got his cousin's meaning and crossed to the sofa, wondering how to distract the Fallen Reaper. He needn't have worried.

Rex looked up from his report to smile at him. "How're you doing?"

Jonah shrugged and sat. It occurred to him that he didn't need to hide his growing worry from the Fallen Reaper. It was real and he let it show.

Sure enough, Rex sensed his mood because he laid the report on the steamer trunk and leaned closer. "Don't worry about your buddy. We'll find him and bring him home."

"I know." Jonah's doubt about their little plan surfaced and for a moment, he almost came clean.

Rex shook his shaggy head. "It's no need to feel guilty about what happened. I'm sure Mike won't blame you."

Jonah nodded and took a deep breath to calm his raw emotions. Rex remained focused on him until a loud click caught the man's attention. Jonah recognized that sound. It was the locks on Robert's archive box. Rex started to turn around and would have caught Robert handing the bracelet to Wick if not for the sudden change in air pressure.

The Fallen Reaper's attention shifted at once to the attic window instead, where Marcus and Trueblood appeared. He jumped to his feet to greet his colleagues.

Marcus paused to note everyone in the attic. Wick had shifted his body to hide the archive box from view. Jonah held his breath, waiting as his godfather started a quiet conversation with Rex and Trueblood.

As soon as that happened, Wick used the opportunity to snatch the bracelet from Robert and slip it in a pocket of his fatigue pants. Robert closed the box and put it back in the lowest drawer. That done, he and Wick sat at the card table and pretended to pour over one of their books on the supernatural.

Marcus disengaged from his conversation and stood back as Trueblood produced a vortex and left. By then Jonah and the others huddled in a group. "Innocent thoughts," he mouthed to everyone.

Marcus noticed and furrowed his brow before focusing on Jonah. "You've been to the Guest House before, so it should be easy. Back porch."

Jonah nodded. Lynn placed an arm around his shoulders. Kevin gripped Robert and Wick by the forearms.

Marcus glanced at his watch. "You better go."

Kevin phased first. Jonah followed a second later, and the attic disappeared.

Once they arrived at the Alliance Guest House, Kevin eyed Jonah. "How do you feel?"

Jonah took a moment to assess his strength. "Not bad." That was true. The journey didn't produce any dizziness.

"Good. That means you're building your phasing muscles."

Lynn shook Jonah's head with her hand. "That's about the only muscle he's working out."

Jonah ignored her quip, instead choosing to focus on Kevin's unexpected compliment.

Kevin motioned to everyone. "Wait here." He disappeared inside the house for about ten minutes. When he returned, he cracked a smile. "Making sure nobody's here and to get these." He held up a pair of binoculars. "I thought we could use them."

"Thanks." Lynn took them.

Kevin handed a set of keys to Wick. "It's all yours, young mage."

Wick flashed a lopsided grin while handing Kevin the shield bracelet.

Once Kevin slipped it around his wrist, Robert and Wick moved aside and waved.

Kevin gripped Jonah and Lynn's arms. "If this doesn't work, I'm out of a job. After Marcus kills me." He phased them away.

CHAPTER TWENTY-SIX
THE OLD MILL

Modern GPS, and a good Internet connection, allowed Kevin and Lynn to pull decent satellite images before leaving the attic. They'd chosen half a dozen pictures of a distribution building across from their goal: the old Iron Works mill. Jonah was impressed with the amount of work the two managed while he had distracted Rex.

But he also experienced a pang of guilt over fooling Rex and hoped the Fallen Reaper wouldn't get in trouble. If not for that worry, and the impending danger to Mike, Jonah would have found the whole operation cool.

Lynn held the binoculars to her eyes, gazing at the decrepit mill from their hiding place behind a stack of wooden pallets. "Why can't the bad guys ever set up shop in a luxury hotel?" She lowered the binoculars and frowned. "Last summer it was a creepy plantation house, and now this."

Kevin laughed. "You wouldn't believe some of the places I've had to go to."

Jonah found that bit of information interesting. He didn't know if Kevin meant his time with the Alliance or his time as a Reaper.

Lynn peered through the binoculars again. "I don't see anyone. We could be wrong, unless they used the river to approach the building."

"Let me borrow those." Kevin held out his hand. His attention seemed to be focused on the treetops to the right of the mill. The top of a rusted bridge rose above the trees where the highway crossed the river.

Lynn slapped the binoculars in Kevin's hand. "What's up?"

"I'm gonna see if you're right." Kevin phased without warning, drawing a startled breath from Lynn.

"You guys do that on purpose." She pinched Jonah's arm.

"Hey!" Jonah rubbed the painful spot. He jumped when Kevin returned less than two minutes later.

"They have boats docked at the old pier behind the mill," Kevin announced, causing Lynn to gape at him.

Her gaze shifted to the distant bridge. "You phased way up there?"

"Yep. Don't worry. I went to the top of the center pylon. None of the people in the cars passing below could have seen me." Kevin grinned. "What's the plan, Lynn?"

"You go in first."

He nodded while gazing across the lonely highway.

Jonah didn't understand. "That's the plan? He goes in first? What about the people inside?"

Lynn nodded. "Exactly. Kevin'll draw away any Grimnions inside."

"They'll hurt Mike if he tries that."

"I don't think so." Lynn crossed her arms. "My bet is they'll focus on catching Kevin."

"They'd have to hit me first." Kevin flexed his hands. "I'm fast."

Jonah gulped. "Maybe... maybe we should find another way."

Lynn tapped Jonah on the forehead. "This is the best plan. Kevin leads the Grimnions on a goose chase around the old mill."

Kevin held up his right wrist. "I use Wick's shield bracelet to hold off the bad guys."

"Jonah and I free Mike and get to safety." Lynn patted the compass Jonah wore clipped to a chain and under his shirt.

He caught on. "Oh, that's right. I can use the compass to take us to the hideaway. And Ramsey can't follow." Jonah began to like the simple plan more than he had at first.

"Kevin can get away once we're clear." Lynn held her chin high, waiting to see what the Fallen Reaper would say about the plan.

Kevin fingered the shield bracelet around his right wrist while gazing across the highway. For a second, Jonah feared he would suggest they tell the other Alliance members anyway.

A moment later, Kevin nodded. "Let's do it."

Lynn bumped fists with him. "I'm ready."

Kevin gripped Lynn and Jonah by an arm and phased.

They reappeared right outside a set of large wooden double doors that were painted a grayish-green color. Rusted metal bars ran horizontal at the top and bottom, and someone had cut through a large chain and left it on the ground for anyone to see.

Kevin grabbed the edge of the door and paused to give Jonah a playful shove on the head. "Find Mike and get out. Don't worry about me." He held up the wrist with the bracelet. "Okay?"

Jonah gulped and nodded. The seriousness of the whole thing left him feeling queasy. He took a deep breath to quell his stomach and prepared to do his part.

Kevin pulled the door open just enough to slip inside. Lynn and Jonah waited for several tense seconds. All at once, shouts and snapping sounds of what Jonah thought were stun weapons rolled from inside. His heart spasmed with worry over Kevin.

Lynn activated her blades and motioned with the right one for Jonah to follow.

He paused right inside the front doors in shock. Kevin zipped around the inside of the mill, with at least five guards trying to zap him. The Fallen Reaper mixed blinding-fast sprints across the floor with micro phases. At one point, he appeared right by a guard and knocked the man into a wall with one blow.

Kevin phased away right before the other guards fired on him. Jonah's mouth hung open in awe.

Deafening booms of discharges hitting the rusted metal walls rattled the entire building. Jonah's admiration for

Kevin's bravery and skill went up a notch. He would have stood there and ruined their own part of the plan except for Lynn, who kept her head.

She yanked Jonah behind a large piece of chipped concrete and out of sight. "Stay focused."

Jonah's face heated with embarrassment. "Sorry."

The building had been stripped of equipment. The only things remaining were reinforced foundations where the machines had been. The central part had a ceiling over four stories high. With most of the window panes busted out, Jonah thought the place looked like a weird cathedral.

Lynn indicated a walkway on the right with stairs leading up to an administrative level. The glass panes of the old offices were broken out and the metal walls rusted and dented. Lynn pointed one blade at that level and the other blade toward a stairway leading to a sub level. "Up or down?"

Jonah closed his eyes, thinking back to his escape with Mike from Agent Ramsey. When the Grimnion had grabbed Mike, Jonah felt his buddy's terror and had phased to him. Recalling the sensation, he reached out with his power. In response he received a vague sense of fear and confusion.

Jonah focused and pointed at the stair to the sub level. "The basement."

Kevin phased to the top floor of the office section, almost directly above their position. At once, the stun blast impacted the railings and walls around him. The Fallen Reaper activated Wick's shield to block most of it.

As soon as the blasts faded, Kevin dropped the shield and his arms blurred into motion as he shouted the deflection spell and batted aside several shots with his blades before phasing.

"Whoa," Jonah breathed.

Lynn's eyes were just as wide as his. "He wasn't kidding about being fast."

She recovered quicker than Jonah and waited for the sounds of battle to move far away before darting to the stairs. Jonah followed. He didn't know if Kevin sensed them or not, but the Fallen Reaper had all the guards occupied on the opposite side of the mill.

Jonah wished he could phase right to Mike, but that was a sure way to activate Ramsey's trap. They needed to check the situation below if they wanted to get Mike and escape. Forcing himself to stick to the plan, Jonah descended the steps and paused at the bottom to listen.

He closed his eyes and reached out with his Reaper side. He sensed Mike's soul straight ahead, but not Ramsey's. Either the agent wasn't here or he'd found a way to mask his soul. A serious case of doubt assailed Jonah at that thought.

Screwing up his nerves, he inched forward. The sunlight only reached this level through metal grates in the main floor. The effect created intense pools of light among the shadows.

Jonah heard something move up ahead, a soft scraping sound and low mumbling, just beyond a patch of light at the end of the corridor. Lynn pressed a small LED flashlight into his hand. Jonah lit it and moved forward. Within a few steps, his foot came down on something soft. Jonah shined the light at the floor and leapt back, heart racing because Agent Harris' lifeless face stared back at him.

Any other person would have been repulsed or scared at the sight. Jonah was, but he was also half Reaper. It was that side of himself that surged forward to touch the body while cushioning his mortal self from the initial shock.

There was little blood, except for the two large spots seeping through the fabric of the man's shirt. At the center of both spots was a large cut. The surprised expression remained frozen on Harris' face.

Jonah stood there, unmoving, until Lynn drew close.

She nudged him in the back. "Jonah, what's going on…" Her voice trailed off into a hiss of disgust. "He's been stabbed by blades."

Of course, Jonah said to himself. Ramsey must have killed his partner. But why?

Jonah squinted up into the brilliant sunlight just beyond Harris' body. That section of space appeared to be directly underneath a vertical shaft. Light poured in from windows far above and reflected off the pale, chipped walls.

The sound came again. Muttering, Jonah realized. Nonsense jumbles of words, rushed together. Jonah's eyes adjusted enough to make out a small shape in the relative darkness. That shape moved and Mike's face came into view. The sunlight made his eyes and his already light complexion glow.

Jonah dropped the flashlight, leapt over Harris and ran toward his buddy, forgetting any possible trap. Lynn covered his back, her blades held ready as she continually scanned the patches of darkness.

Mike's rocking back and forth stopped with a sudden jerk and his vacant expression cleared. "He's waiting for you to come and get me, Jonah. Go back!"

Jonah ignored the warning as he knelt beside his buddy. When he reached out, Mike recoiled. For the first time, Jonah realized that Mike's eyes did glow. It was obvious when his friend leaned back into the shadows.

"Mike, your eyes are glowing," Jonah said in a hushed voice.

"Really?" Mike's normal inquisitive tone asserted itself. He glanced up and over Jonah's head. "He's watching."

Jonah whirled, and that's when he noticed the tiny glint of light on a camera lens. He had to appreciate the agent's creativity. He couldn't sense Ramsey's soul because there was no soul present to sense. The agent was watching remotely, via camera.

Mike began to rock back and forth, shocking Jonah. Words tumbled out of his mouth. They were equations, calculations, and locations in English and occasionally in a dialect Jonah didn't recognize.

The sight horrified Jonah, but he reached out for his buddy again.

The motion focused Mike and he yelled, "Don't touch me. You'll get stuck here!" Mike shifted his leg so Jonah could see the strange lock around the ankle. "It'll keep you from…"

"That's enough!"

Agent Ramsey appeared on the other side of the bright sunlight. He stepped forward and clapped his hands. "I was beginning to think you wouldn't take the bait, Mr. Blackstone."

Jonah's wishful fantasy that they would succeed in getting Mike without facing Ramsey vanished. He and the others had known this was a trap and that Ramsey never intended to take Trevor. But they couldn't have anticipated the low rumble of arriving vehicles that filtered down to their level. No doubt more of Ramsey's men had arrived, Jonah decided, experiencing renewed fear for Kevin.

The Fallen Reaper had Wick's bracelet, but even with that, Kevin wouldn't be able to hold out forever. And he also wouldn't go anywhere until he knew Jonah and the others were safe.

Agent Ramsey's false smile morphed into a pure sneer. "Well, half-breed? Are you prepared to surrender or see your friends and family die?"

Jonah's breaths hitched in his lung as the awful weight of responsibility descended on him. Coming up with a plan and carrying it through were two different things. If this didn't work, Jonah would have to face another friend or family member being tortured or worse. He couldn't do that. Not again.

He rose to his feet. "I thought you wanted the courier?"

"His real value is that he sought you out." Ramsey pointed at Jonah. "I want to know why."

Mike whispered, pleading, "Don't let him get to you. Don't try to save me."

Jonah shifted until he pressed against Lynn. He readied himself to phase. "What'll the Grand Oracle say?"

Ramsey narrowed his eyes. Jonah couldn't tell if the man was going to yell or attack. The agent shook himself and plastered a sneer on his face. "That courier's out of time. With the portals closed, he's stuck here. Have you ever seen what happens to a supernatural who can't cross back?"

Jonah begin to see that the man was more than dangerous; he was sick. Despite the mole's order, this Hunter killed his own partner and gave up a chance to capture Trevor.

It's always about me.

Lynn met Jonah's sad gaze. "It's okay, Jonah."

Ramsey cackled like a madman. "No it isn't. My allies have arrived. That Fallen Reaper upstairs is capable, but even he can't win against the odds. Perhaps I can hurt him in order to convince you to submit." Ramsey cocked his head to the side. "Well young Blackstone, what will you do?"

Jonah didn't respond. Instead, he slipped a finger through a loop on Lynn's jeans. She nodded, the barest fraction, but enough to let him know she was ready.

Leaving Mike behind hurt Jonah like nothing else. He didn't want to, but he needed the agent to follow. It was the best option to save his friend. Jonah prepared himself and had to look away from Mike in order to nudge himself and phase.

CHAPTER TWENTY-SEVEN
HUNTER'S TRAP

Jonah and Lynn reappeared on the top floor, in the mill's old office section. He heard Agent Ramsey's laugh carry through the building.

Jonah tapped his cousin's hand. "Lynn-"

"I got it." She darted down the stairs to the level below.

Ramsey appeared on the landing. "I'm disappointed, Jonah Blackstone."

Jonah tried to ignore the taunt as he focused on the next location, this time the main floor. What he saw almost ruined his desperate idea. More of the agent's men had swarmed inside and converged on Kevin.

The idea of going for help himself entered Jonah's mind as he changed his destination and reappeared on a catwalk high above the mill's floor. He could get to Marcus and the others, but Jonah was afraid Ramsey could escape before the Alliance returned. Desperation began to mount and he forced himself to stay with the plan.

"Really, child." Ramsey scoffed as soon as he appeared on the catwalk. "Haven't we done this dance before? You can't escape me. Unless…"

Jonah didn't waste time listening to the rest of Ramsey's words. He began running and phased at the same time. He reappeared in the office section, already in a full sprint. He had just reached the stairs at the far end of that level when Agent Ramsey appeared behind him.

Ramsey lunged. Jonah dodged and leapt down the entire row of steps to avoid the agent's grasp. He slammed onto the lower landing harder than expected, but fear propelled him as he leapt down the next set of steps to the ground floor.

Agent Ramsey leaned over the railing and called after him, "I don't care if your cousin saves the boy. You are the trophy, Jonah Blackstone."

Jonah phased to the third level landing again. Only then did he realize the mistake. He'd settled into a pattern. Ramsey appeared right next to him and swung with a blurred punch. The power of the blow to Jonah's shoulder sent him sliding across the metal floor and smacking against the guardrail.

Ramsey blurred into motion and stopped right over him. "I'm going to enjoy cutting every bit of useful information out of you." He grabbed Jonah by the front of his shirt and hissed, "Now, I take you to my master."

Shoving Jonah against the stone wall, Ramsey turned him roughly around, and twisted his right arm back. The agent whispered right in Jonah's ear, "You and your cousin are nothing more than common criminals."

An explosion erupted from below, followed by several anguished grunts. The force of it rattled the ground. Jonah saw the flash of light reflected off the grimy walls, but couldn't see anything else.

The commotion drew Ramsey's attention. He dragged Jonah along with him to the railing to look over. Jonah twisted around in time to witness the fading effects of a blue wave of magical energy. At the center, Kevin knelt on hands and knees, breathing hard. Around him was a wide circle of downed Grimnions.

More rushed in and began using stun prods to shock Kevin into submission. Ramsey laughed so hard, his entire body shook. The movement caused pain to ripple up Jonah's twisted arm.

"The Fallen Reaper has fallen. Next we'll round up your cousin and that strange boy. Perhaps I'll make you watch as I kill them, hmm?"

Ramsey produced another pair of the strange cuffs and snapped them open. At that moment, Jonah felt the change in the air. It was different from someone phasing, which produced a slight pressure from displaced air. This was more of a pulling sensation, the same kind created by a vortex.

When the agent paused, Jonah thought he also sensed the coming vortex until vibrations rattled the metal floor. Something large bounded up the stairs. Within seconds, a huge Grim Hound sailed through the air, right at Ramsey. The beast succeeded in knocking the startled agent away from Jonah.

The cuffs clattered to the ground. With the pressure gone, Jonah whirled around and stared in awe as the Grim Hound snapped and ripped at the agent's arms. Ramsey phased before the beast could tear him apart. The Grim Hound let out a snarl of frustration and bounded down the steps. Jonah wondered if the hound could sense the trail a person left behind when they phased.

He peeked over the railing, hoping to see the beast tearing into Ramsey. Instead, he gaped in surprise as at least a dozen men in black pants and tunics streamed out of the supernatural gateway. The new arrivals engaged Ramsey's guards.

Jonah thought this development was the most welcoming sight at the moment. If not for the red skulls on the left breast, which seemed to be unnaturally bright, the two groups were indistinguishable.

As the men clashed, Jonah caught sight of Kevin on the far side of the mill floor. The young Fallen Reaper knocked out the guard covering him and phased away. When he didn't reappear inside the mill, Jonah knew Kevin went for help.

A sound to his right drew his attention. Jonah prepared himself to phase and only relaxed when Lynn reached the landing with Mike in tow.

The railing began to vibrate. Jonah backed away just as two of Ramsey's men vaulted over. They came at him, both slicing the air with handheld scythes.

"Jonah!" Lynn tossed him a blade just in time. He activated it and held off the first deadly swings from his attacker.

Lynn released Mike, whirled like a pro, and met the second goon. He scored a vicious slash across Lynn's right forearm.

She muffled her scream, ducked under his follow-up swing, and kicked him in the midsection. The man hit the railing and tumbled over.

Jonah blocked another slice from his attacker and dived to avoid two swings. He rolled to his feet and maneuvered himself around so the Grimnion's back was to Lynn. Only then did he noticed her cradling her injured arm.

Before Jonah could think of another move, the large Grim Hound roared up the stairs again, ignoring Lynn and Mike.

Jonah's attacker sensed the danger and tried to turn, too late. The Hound managed to sink its teeth into his back and lift the man off the ground. With a violent twist of its large head, the Grim Hound snapped the henchman's back.

Mike's already pale face went paler as the beast dropped the dead man to the ground. Lynn looked equally as horrified. The Grim Hound snapped its massive jaws at them but didn't attack.

Jonah registered what bothered him from the moment he saw the beast. The Grim Hound had saved his life, like it had been commanded to do that. "Why'd you help me?"

The Grim Hound gazed at him with its red-in-red pupils. It opened its mouth, displaying the double row of sharp teeth only to let out a mournful growl.

Jonah stepped closer, not sensing menace, just curiosity. He understood in that moment. This was the same Grim Hound that had come to Morningside Drive. He had dreamt he was in the creature's head. *But how could it be the same one?*

Emily, one of his godfather's team members, had killed that Grim Hound by cutting off its head in the fight at Deyanira's chamber. Jonah concentrated on the beast. It stirred, keeping the eye contact and cocking its head sideways as if recognizing him.

Jonah was sure it was the same Grim Hound. Apparently chopping off its head just destroyed the physical body and sent the supernatural creature back across to the Afterworld. Probably until someone summoned it again, Jonah concluded. If that was true, then how did you kill a Grim Hound? He'd have to ask Marcus about this, if they survived.

He thought of reaching out to touch the beast, but the Grim Hound's snout lifted up into the air, sniffing, and then it whirled and thundered down the stairs.

Lynn overcame her shock first and pointed at Jonah while favoring her bleeding arm. "Get us out of here, hero."

Mike, who had moved closer to help Lynn, gasped and pointed below. "Look!"

Lynn and Jonah rushed to the railing.

Deyanira stood in front of her vortex in the personae of Neera. Today she wore a flowing black dress with sleeves that flared along the ends. Her red hair was curly and it cascaded to her shoulders.

She surveyed the continued fighting like a warrior queen. A stray shot from one of Ramsey's men zipped her way. Deyanira waved her hand and the shot flared against a protective barrier.

Meanwhile, the Grim Hound bounded across the plant floor and to her side. It made several strange growls, audible over the noise of the fighting.

Deyanira's gaze shifted at once up to the third floor landing, where Jonah stood. His knees began to shake, but his Death Sense was quiet. She meant him no harm.

"Jonah, do you think she sent the Grim Hound to help you?" Mike's quiet question shocked him.

At that moment, Agent Ramsey appeared in the midst of the fighting below, blades out and ready to engage Deyanira. It was if the sight of the KIN had pushed all other thoughts out of the man's deranged head.

Deyanira pointed a slender finger at Ramsey. "Where's the courier?"

"That's none of your business, witch."

"Hasn't anyone told you the Blackstone child is more trouble than he's worth?"

Jonah bristled at her comment at the same moment his Death Sense spiked.

Ramsey signaled, and stun blasts arched up from the floor and toward Jonah's position. He, Lynn, and Mike stumbled back, but the discharges exploded against a protective shield that shouldn't have been there.

Deyanira laughed. "I should have known."

When Ramsey risked a glance toward the third floor landing, Deyanira used his momentary distraction to attack.

She whirled her hands, conjuring two balls of green supernatural fire. The sudden flare of light blinded Jonah for a second.

Agent Ramsey weaved his blades in swiping motions as he shouted, "Kulinda!"

The balls of supernatural fire shattered into flaming fragments that drifted harmlessly to either side.

Jonah gawked at the display of power until someone nudged him in the back. Kevin stood right behind him with Marcus, Rubio, and Trueblood.

"Get Jonah and the others out of here." Marcus's voice and face shook with repressed anger and worry.

The adults positioned themselves at the railing, blocking Jonah's view of the battle. Despite wanting to object, Jonah also knew it was dangerous to disobey his godfather at this moment. He yanked the compass out of his shirt and waited as Mike and Lynn locked arms with him.

At the last minute, Kevin noticed what Jonah was doing. "Don't use the compass." He blurred into motion and gripped Jonah's arm a second before the compass activated and the mill disappeared.

CHAPTER TWENTY-EIGHT
THE LECTURE

Mike reached for Lynn's bloody arm as soon as they reached at the hideaway. "You're hurt."

Lynn jerked the arm away with a grunt of pain. "I'm fine," she managed through clenched teeth. She nodded toward Jonah. "Take my blades. I need to sit."

He pulled back the adjacent bushes to reveal the brick stairs to the hideaway. Lynn consented to Mike's help in order to remain on her feet. They maneuvered past Jonah and through the gap in the bushes.

"Hold up." Kevin blocked Jonah's way. "Why'd you use the compass?"

"That was the plan." Jonah grabbed Lynn's discarded blades.

Kevin scowled. "That was before things changed. We should have phased back to the clubhouse."

"I didn't know. Besides, it's better to be safe, right?" Jonah squeezed around the older boy and hurried to catch Mike and Lynn.

Kevin grumbled and followed to the courtyard above. "Has Marcus been here before?"

Lynn opened her mouth to say something at the same time her strength gave out. She collapsed on the edge of the closest bench. Mike hovered over her until she shook her head.

Mike recoiled. "I just wanted to help."

"I know, Mike. Thanks, but I'm fine." She waved him off.

Mike shoved his hands in his pockets as he plopped on the second bench beside Jonah.

Kevin stormed over to Lynn. "I don't care what you say to Mike. You're not okay." He ripped the bottom half of his shirt, leaving his abdomen exposed, and knelt in front of Lynn. "Hold still." Ignoring her protests, he wrapped Lynn's arm with the shirt and tied it with practiced motions.

Once he finished, Kevin whirled to look at Jonah. "She needs a doctor."

"No." Lynn shook her head. "I'm staying until this is over."

Kevin ripped off the remains of his shirt in frustration. "You're as bad as Jonah."

"Hey, we were in this together, remember?" Jonah's flare of irritation with Kevin subsided when he saw the way the boy balled the ruined shirt in his hands. He was nervous, and Jonah could guess why. They both knew Marcus well enough to dread the coming storm.

Meanwhile, Mike sucked in a breath and reached for Jonah's face. "You're hurt too."

Jonah wiped the dried blood off his mouth and wiggled his sore nose. "Ramsey threw me around."

"He's insane," Mike agreed while knocking dirt out of Jonah's picky hair.

Lynn watched with a pained smirk on her face. Jonah's own face warmed.

Mike didn't seem to care as he continued the inspection. When he finished, Jonah turned the tables. "Did he hurt you?"

"No." Mike hugged himself, rocking back and forth.

For a moment, Jonah feared his friend would start muttering to himself again. But Mike seemed over that now. "What about your ankle?"

Mike glanced down at his leg. "It's fine."

Jonah didn't believe his buddy. He could see two dark cuts on the right side of Mike's shirt. Both were stained red.

Jonah touched the shirt. "Don't lie to me."

Mike covered the cuts with his hand, keeping Jonah from prodding the spot. "He wanted to know how you got away and why he couldn't follow."

Jonah's insides froze. "Did you tell him about the compass?"

"I don't think so." Mike hugged himself again. "When the pain got too bad, I blacked out. But when I came around, Ramsey had a spooked look on his face." Mike winced. "He only did it twice."

Lynn cradled her arm, head cocked to the side. "I bet it was the eyes. They were glowing back in the mill."

"They were?" Mike touched his face. "What about now?"

Jonah peered at his buddy's eyes. "No. They're not anymore." He pointed at Mike's scorched left-side shirt pocket.

Mike reached inside the pocket and pulled out the Enhancer. "Oh no."

The device was blackened and ruined.

Jonah nodded, recalling Trevor's claim. "The Grimnion's scythe hit it. You took a jolt from the Enhancer."

"That's why my eyes were glowing?" Mike waved his hand in front of his own eyes, blinking. "I doubt it was supposed to work that way."

Kevin watched the entire exchange with a sour look on his face. "Are you three finished? Can we go now?"

The Fallen Reaper cursed under his breath when his cell phone rang. Kevin yanked it open while spearing Jonah with an irritated glare. "We're at the hideaway. Lynn's hurt."

Marcus, Trueblood, and Rex appeared in the courtyard before Kevin could even put away the phone. Jonah's godfather motioned at once to Lynn.

Rex hurried over. "I'll get you to a hospital." Lynn started to object, but that was cut short by a grimace of pain. "We have a plan in motion for this type of thing," Rex explained, helping her to her feet before they phased away.

Trueblood led Mike to the vacated bench and spoke to him in a quiet tone.

Marcus stood over Jonah like a storm cloud. "What am I going to do with you? Your actions were totally reckless! I know I'm not your father but…" He trailed off as he raised his balled fists and let out a frustrated growl.

"Mike's my best friend," Jonah began.

"Of course he is, but I'm supposed to protect you as best I can. You should have trusted me. Frankly Jonah, I think it shows a lack of respect."

Marcus turned on Kevin. "And you're a full member of the Alliance and should have known better." He took a deep breath. "The Council's waiting for you at Headquarters." Marcus handed Kevin a talisman. "I advise putting on a shirt."

Kevin's eyes widened in embarrassment. He met Jonah's worried gaze briefly, then nodded to Marcus and phased.

With Kevin gone, Marcus signaled Trueblood. She rose and motioned for Mike to stand beside her. "You should get home to your family."

Mike hesitated. "What about Jonah?"

"He'll be fine."

The look of doubt on Mike's face got to Jonah. "Go on. I'll catch up later."

Mike hugged himself and waited while Trueblood opened a vortex. He waved to Jonah as the mage urged him into the opening.

Marcus didn't say anything for several quiet moments after the vortex closed. When he spoke, his voice was calmer, but still tinged with anger. "You want to be treated like an adult, Jonah? You want to be treated as part of the team? Well, team members check in and let the rest know what's going on. We share information so we can all be prepared to help."

"I know about teamwork." It was dangerous to argue with his godfather, but Jonah couldn't stop himself. "You didn't tell the Alliance about Trevor."

Marcus reared back, surprised. "I had good reasons for it."

"So did we."

"Jonah…"

"You were impressed with us yesterday."

Marcus covered his face with his hands. He lowered them after a moment to reveal a tired expression. "I won't lie. I was impressed with you and the others." He raised his hand and ticked off his points. "But in this case, you failed to see the benefit of marshaling all resources to your advantage or accurately using the knowledge you have. That's a lack of experience. You and Lynn will make good leaders one day, if you two can learn that."

Jonah crossed his arms, considering his godfather's words.

"I know you have skills and can fight," Marcus continued. "Even so, you could have been overwhelmed and without backup. If we had known about the plan-"

"You would have said no." Jonah shrank away from the fury radiating off his godfather.

"You, young man, were lucky." Marcus's chest heaved up and down. "Perhaps luckier than most, but lucky nonetheless." He pointed to where Lynn had been sitting.

Jonah was shocked at the blood-stained piece of shirt Kevin had left behind. A pit formed in his stomach.

"Lynn can't heal herself. You're going to get your cousins and friends in trouble one day and not be able to handle it." Marcus leaned over Jonah. "Do you understand me?"

"Yes, sir. I understand."

Marcus stood tall. "You have your father in you, that's for sure. He would go off and do things on his own." Marcus stopped to take deep breaths. "This whole affair has everyone acting strange. Rex messes with a mortal, you go off half-cocked, and Kevin risks his job."

The barb about his father stung Jonah. "I wasn't alone."

"That makes it even more dangerous. You owe it to those who follow you to make sure you've done everything you can to protect them from harm." He leaned down to force Jonah to look at him, the first time he'd done that in a while. "I thought after last year, we had an understanding."

Jonah's stomach turned itself into knots because of the disappointment on his godfather's face.

When he didn't keep yelling, Jonah began to see that his godfather was unsure what to do next. He glanced around, searching for something else to talk about. "My dad told you about this hideaway? Is that how you could phase here?"

"Actually, I've been here before. In fact," Marcus gestured around him, "I became a member of the Alliance Council about where you're sitting."

His words pushed through Jonah's embarrassment from being fussed at, and a flood of memories opened. Jonah saw the moment to which Marcus referred. He had witnessed it the previous summer when the Protector's Ring took him to the Afterworld.

"My dad gave you his badge, and made you take his place on the Alliance Council." Jonah's voice caught and he stopped. He could read the unspoken question on Marcus' face. "I went to the Afterworld last summer. The Deliverer showed me records of my parents. I saw that moment."

Marcus swallowed and stared at his feet for several quiet moments. "Jonah, the Afterworld archivists can only store the records of mortals, in their first life. The lives of the Fallen Ones aren't recorded. It's one reason our kind is forbidden."

"Then how did I see those memories?"

"It was the Deliverer. He was here."

Jonah's eyes widened with understanding. "His spirit was in the Protector's Ring. But what about the mortals in the Alliance? Can their memories be accessed when they die?"

"No, they can't," Marcus answered. "When a mortal dies and moves on, their soul is intact and their memories go along with them. All the Archivists do is record the birth, type and means of death, and other dry facts about the life. They never have access to more personal memories unless a person chooses to share."

Marcus rubbed his hands together in a nervous motion. "That being said, there're rumors of a way for an individual's memories to be viewed without permission. It was whispered by those in the Afterworld that the Grim Reaper trapped and imprisoned certain souls. Through use of ancient magic, he's able to siphon off their memories and view them."

Jonah shivered despite the summer temperatures. "Couldn't he do that with any soul?"

Marcus shook his head. "Even the Rulers of the Afterworld have to follow some rules. The vast majority of mortal souls are beyond being tampered with. But in select cases, he can ensnare the soul if he personally kills the individual. It's a violation."

The more Marcus explained, the more Jonah wanted to be anywhere other than the darkening hideaway. This was downright creepy. The only up side was that his godfather didn't sound angry anymore.

Marcus peered at Jonah in the gathering gloom. "I think we've talked enough about this." He raised a questioning eyebrow. Jonah nodded. "If our story is to be told, it'll be written by someone else."

Jonah's godfather drew nearer and opened his long coat to reveal the golden Alliance badge clipped to an inside pocket. He unhooked it and held the badge in his palm.

Jonah's hand shook, as much from the recent excitement as from nervousness, as he gripped the badge. At once, a tingle of familiarity shot up his arm. "Wow."

Marcus nodded. "Your father owned that for many years. Being who you are, I'm not surprised you can sense his lingering touch on it." He looked off. "I considered having the Alliance make me a new one."

"Why?" The thought of his godfather discarding something that his dad entrusted to him made Jonah angry.

Marcus held up his hands. "You don't understand. I wanted to give the badge to you, Jonah, when you came of age."

The indignation leaked out of Jonah, replaced by a little shame. "I'm sorry." As soon as Jonah said it, the tense, raw concern over his friends and the crazy agent flowed out. A tear rolled down his face. "I'm sorry Lynn's hurt and Kevin's in trouble and..." Jonah let the rest go unsaid. Otherwise, he wouldn't be able to stop crying.

Marcus sat beside him on the bench and patted Jonah on the shoulder. "You're special. You're Reaper and human."

Jonah wiped his watery eyes to look into his godfather's face. "You mean a half-breed?"

Marcus frowned. "No, I mean in one being. As you grow older, more people will follow you. Most won't understand, and some will even fear." Marcus did something he rarely did: he allowed his own emotions to show.

Jonah sensed utter belief in his godfather. It was humbling. "You think I'm a hero."

"I know it. That's a powerful thing for a young man to accept and experience." Marcus tightened his grip on Jonah's shoulder. "Until then, I have to watch over and protect you. So do me a huge favor and stop making it so damn difficult."

The edge had returned to his godfather's voice. Once Marcus released the iron grip, Jonah leaned forward, resting his elbows on his knees, and gazing at his dad's Council badge.

He considered Trevor's sacrifice, coming here while knowing he might never get back. Jonah's throat tightened when he recalled his mom's last words to him. She and his dad did everything out of love for him.

Everything Marcus told him clicked into place and rocked Jonah. So much depended on what he did with his power.

His bottom lip trembled with the weight of that knowledge. "I'm sorry." He meant it with every bone in his body. Speaking those two simple words made him feel hollowed out.

Marcus sat straighter. "The fact that you said that means everything." He placed a hand over the badge. "Now is as good a time as any to have the replacement made." He lifted the badge from Jonah's slack grip. "I should hold on to this one for now."

Jonah didn't want to part with it, but he trusted Marcus to keep his word. After all, his godfather truly believed in his destiny.

CHAPTER TWENTY-NINE
LYNN'S ROOM

The hum of different, overlapping voices greeted Jonah when he and Marcus returned to the clubhouse. All the conversations came to an abrupt halt as Robert, Wick, and the Alliance members focused on Jonah.

He gulped, suspecting everyone was talking about him. He pushed that aside, realizing someone was missing. "Where's Mike?"

Rex chuckled and ruffled his untidy blond hair. "He put up a fuss, but I took him home. That kid has a lot of spunk."

Good, Jonah thought and then he met Robert's worried gaze. "What about Lynn?"

"She's at the hospital, getting stitches." Robert looked miserable.

Marcus gestured to Rex. "You should take Jonah and Robert home. I don't want them riding their bikes this evening. I'll escort Wick."

Rex nodded and motioned the boys to move closer.

But Jonah refused to budge. "Wait a minute. What happened after we left the mill?"

Marcus leaned against the back of the sofa. "Agent Ramsey ran off after a brief fight with Deyanira. We think he went through the portal and to the Afterworld."

"Chicken." Rex smacked his beefy fists together in disgust. "Big talk when it comes to hurting kids." He glanced at Robert and Wick. "No offense."

Jonah's eyes widened. "He'll tell the Grand Oracle about me."

"Probably," Marcus agreed. "But remember, he doesn't know anything about the back door. And he didn't get the compass."

"He'll be lucky to keep his head." Rex chuckled at the very idea.

Marcus frowned at his fellow Alliance member. "Take them home, Rex."

"I already called home." Robert waved his phone.

"Still..." Marcus stood.

"What else happened?" Jonah speared his godfather with a steady gaze. When Marcus looked as if he would refuse to answer, Jonah added, "You told me to come to you."

Marcus frowned. "You know that's not what I meant." He paused, noting everyone's curious expressions. "We had a little talk with Deyanira."

Robert and Wick were as shocked as Jonah.

He had a sick feeling what the sorceress asked. "She wanted Trevor and you told her no."

Marcus subjected Jonah to a Reaper Stare. "She says you owe her one. You care to explain?"

"I don't know why she helped us." That was true. Jonah didn't know why her Grim Hound saved his life. Twice.

Rex ignored the silent battle between Jonah and his godfather. "We suspect Deyanira was in a right state with the mole. Nothing like a little in-fighting with the enemies."

Jonah shifted his focus to Rex to prevent his godfather from looking him in the eye any longer. "But how do you know that?"

"Deyanira didn't know about the courier when you came across her." Marcus blinked, ending his Reaper Stare. "She's the Grim Reaper's main minion in the mortal world yet wasn't aware of what was happening, so…"

Jonah loved the conclusion. "She was out of the loop."

Marcus nodded. When Jonah and the others started to ask more questions, he held up a hand. "That's enough for tonight."

"But what'll we tell my mom and dad?" Robert asked.

Jonah perked up when he heard the question and nodded his head in agreement.

"We told your father that Lynn injured herself while exploring the old mill." Marcus fixed his gaze on Jonah and Robert. "And we're making sure there's no evidence of what really happened." He lifted his chin to look at Rex. "Take them home."

*

No one in the Hightower house was interested in sleeping, least of all Lynn. Aunt Imma alternated between talking with Uncle James and checking on her. Robert played Jonah in a lackluster video game. His thoughts clearly fixated on his sister's injury.

When Aunt Imma returned to the living room for the fifth time, complaining about Lynn not resting, Robert had enough. He threw the game controller aside and went to hover in his sister's doorway. Jonah joined him.

Lynn's room was generally off limits to the boys. So Jonah found it interesting whenever he got a peek inside. The soft touches were a surprise, like a small stuffed teddy on a shelf. But Lynn didn't go in for pinks and lavenders. Her room was in softer shades of red and orange.

Numerous posters were on the walls, a mix of music groups, athletic stars, and entertainers. And of course, Lynn had a shelf full of her sports trophies as well as academic awards. She lay propped up in bed, her bandage-wrapped arm cradled on a soft pillow.

Lynn motioned them both inside. Robert sat on the edge of the bed while Jonah leaned in the doorway. Her face was drained of color and her eyes closed to mere slits.

She was tired, Jonah decided, despite her refusal to rest. That got to him. "I'm sorry you're hurt."

Lynn waved away the apology. "What happened?"

Jonah wanted to tell her, but Robert was faster. "Mike went home and Deyanira said Jonah owed her a favor. Can you believed that?"

When Robert paused for a breath, Jonah added, "Oh, Kevin was called back to HQ to talk with the Council. He's in trouble."

Lynn blinked several times, forcing her drooping eyes to remain open. "They should give Kevin a medal."

Robert snorted.

But Lynn wasn't laughing. She watched Jonah with a tired, yet shrewd expression. "I wonder why she helped you, considering the pain she caused before?"

Jonah shrugged but began to seriously consider the possibility.

Robert laughed again. "Please, Lynn. She didn't help Jonah. Marcus said she was just pissed about being left out of the action."

"Not true, brother." Lynn lowered her voice when they heard a creak from the hallway.

Uncle James stepped into view and peeked inside Lynn's room. "Just checking."

"I'm fine, Dad." Lynn gave him a tired smile.

Uncle James motioned to Jonah and Robert. "You boys don't stay too long. She needs to rest. And that's an order."

As soon as he left, Lynn's face turned serious again. "As I was saying, Deyanira sent her Grim Hound to help Jonah."

Robert's jaw dropped. "No way."

"Yes. Weird, isn't it? I can almost believe she likes Jonah."

"Our little cousin, huh?"

"Funny, Lynn," Jonah frowned.

A little fire creeped into Lynn's face and posture. "You don't think she sees that as a favor?"

"No." The answer was immediate because Jonah didn't want to accept the truth. "Well, maybe."

"That's a scary thought." Robert shivered.

"Well, we can deal with that later." Lynn nudged her brother. "Did you two talk to Mike? I want to know why Ramsey killed his partner."

"Mike told me and Wick. The agents got in a big fight." Robert pointed at Jonah. "About him. Harris wanted to make the trade and take Trevor to the mole. Ramsey thought Jonah was more important and would help him get back his old position in the Afterworld."

"They fought and Ramsey killed him?" Jonah could imagine the deranged agent doing that.

"Yep." Robert cringed. "And Mike saw all that."

Lynn rotated her head on the overstuffed pillows to look at Jonah. "I'm sorry to say it, but everything revolves around you, Jonah."

"Tell me about it," he scowled, not liking his friend and family suffering because of him. His godfather's words made him feel even worse. "Marcus shouted that at me after you left the hideaway."

Lynn's eyes opened with interest and Robert turned on the bed to face him. Jonah didn't see any way to avoid telling his cousins about the lecture. He did omit the more embarrassing parts of the encounter.

"Ouch, little cousin." Robert leaned back on the bed, careful not to crush Lynn's leg.

"He's right, Jonah. I can sense that." Lynn nodded and settled into the pillows.

Robert grinned at his sister even though her eyes were closed. "You mean like your feeling that you, Jonah, and Kevin should rescue Mike?"

Lynn suddenly sat forward and shoved the side of her brother's head with enough strength to almost push him off the bed. "I was right, smart butt."

"You were lucky that Deyanira showed up. What if..." Robert's smug expression morphed into awe. "You didn't see that, did you?"

"No, but I knew it would work out, somehow." Lynn rubbed her forehead. "My intuition's gotten stronger since Jonah came here."

Robert made a cross with his index fingers. "You two are spooky."

Lynn bumped him with her leg. "Says the boy who can pick thoughts out of people's heads."

"I can't pick any thought, they have to concentrate and... I draw... it. Okay, I'm a freak, too."

"Say that a little louder." Lynn glared at her brother. "I don't think Mom and Dad heard you." She reached for his head and Robert batted her hand away.

Lynn closed her eyes and settled back. Jonah thought she was asleep until she spoke in a soft, drowsy voice. "You, me, Jonah, Kevin, Wick, and Mike are all important. I can just tell." She yawned. "And Trevor. Don't forget Trevor."

When she lapsed into silence and didn't move, Robert reached over her to pluck the empty water glass off the bedside table. "That took long enough."

Jonah smiled. "I'm gonna tell her you said that."

Robert shrugged as he turned out Lynn's light and ushered Jonah into the hallway. Once he closed the door, Robert headed to the kitchen to talk with his parents.

Jonah yawned again and decided to turn in. The exhaustion made his legs feel like rubber. Although he meant to stretch out on his bed, he collapsed on it in a wave of drowsiness. He didn't even care about undressing. Instead, he rolled onto his back, trying to think about everything that happened, but his mind refused to focus or cooperate.

Bowing to the inevitable, Jonah gave up and welcomed the buzz in his head until he fell asleep.

*

Cold.

That was the sensation Jonah experienced in his sleep. Then his eyes opened and he understood why. He stood in a dismal environment, overlooking an expanse of frozen tundra. Overhead, the bleak grey of an overcast sky added to the general gloominess. He turned on the spot, knowing he was in a dream-walk again.

Frigid cold began seeping through his socks, forcing Jonah to dance around on the spot. He stood on a solid piece of twisting rock that jutted out of the icy ground below like a tree root. He'd never seen anything like it. Other formations dotted the landscape, but this one was the largest. About twenty feet from Jonah, a portion of the rock had been sheered off, making a large, irregular platform.

Jonah shivered and blocked his face from a sudden spray of ice crystals carried on the wind. All the while, he tried to keep his feet in motion. It didn't help. The icy bits stung his exposed skin as he hugged himself, trying to keep warm. This was weird. In all the other dream-walks, he was more like a ghost, having the ability to float through walls but never feeling anything.

Why could he feel everything now? Before he could puzzle it out, he felt the change in air pressure behind him. Fear propelled Jonah as he scampered along the rough rock surface, ignoring the sharp jabs to his soles, and found a shallow crevice in which to hide.

He rose onto his knees to peek over the rim just as a short person appeared on the makeshift platform of the outcropping. Jonah squinted through the increased wind blasts to make out the features.

The newcomer was clothed in a reaper's long coat, black gloves and hat, and he wore a face mask. The eyes were the only part of the face visible.

Could this be a meeting place, Jonah wondered. As if in answer, he sensed the change in pressure again. Deyanira phased into view in her full Reaper form. Her hair was all but gone except for a lone straggly red braid on the back. The ritualistic scars that marked her as one of the KIN were visible. And her blood red robes bellowed behind in the wind as she stalked toward the waiting figure.

Jonah's knees quivered as the reality of his precarious situation became obvious. If Deyanira was in true form that meant he was in the Afterworld, the domain of the Undead. All the other dream-walks occurred in places on the mortal side. A ghost in the Afterworld was just another spirit. Not only could he feel things, this also meant he wasn't invisible, either.

Jonah went still because Deyanira had proved before that she could sense him if he moved. Well, this time she could also see him just fine. He prayed that wouldn't happen.

The short man jabbed a finger at the her. "You stupid witch!"

Deyanira's hands blurred as she conjured supernatural fire and flung it at the man.

He was ready, producing two Reaper blades. "Kulinda!" He batted the fire aside.

"Have a care, mole." Deyanira shot lightning at the man.

He used a shield to block the attack.

Deyanira laughed.

That angered the man even more. "Why'd you save the boy?"

"I didn't save him." Deyanira pointed a slender finger at the mole. "I taught you a lesson."

"What lesson was that, witch?"

Deyanira raised her hands, energy playing around her fingertips. "You call me witch one more time and I'll kill you."

"The Grim Reaper won't like that." The mole thumped his chest with a gloved fist. "I'm valuable to him."

"You're a fool." Deyanira lowered her hands. "The idiocy of using Hunters should be evident to you by now. There's a reason they were banished to the mortal realm. They're all unstable."

"I had Ramsey under control." The short man began pacing back and forth, forcing Deyanira to turn and keep the distance between them. "If you hadn't interfered, we'd have the boy and the courier."

"As I said, you're a complete fool. Ramsey didn't care about the courier. He wanted the Blackstone child." Deyanira tapped the side of her bald, scarred head. "Think, mole. Why would he do that unless he wanted to impress his master?"

The short man stopped his constant movement. "Impossible. Ramsey hated the Grand Oracle for banishing him…"

"He's never abandoned the desire to return home in glory. What better achievement than to bring his master the boy who commanded a Protector's Ring?"

"But the courier—"

"He'll die in the mortal world soon enough. If the rebellion against the Grand Oracle continues, so much the better for my master. But at least the Alliance will have lost its Afterworld connection. That was your mission, nothing more."

The mole pointed a blade at Deyanira. "Don't lecture me. You failed the Grim Reaper last summer. There are others within the KIN who are on the rise."

Deyanira conjured more flame. "Who? The Rasmussen siblings? Eh? And you decided to go around me and work with them?" She launched the fire at the ground around the man's feet.

Caught by surprise, the mole yelled and stumbled back.

"Pathetic," Deyanira scoffed. "I warned the master you weren't a good choice to send into the midst of the Alliance."

She raised her hand and the mole prepared to defend himself with his blades. "Tell me," Deyanira continued, "where's Ramsey now?"

"I-I don't know," the mole admitted. "The Alliance thinks he crossed over."

"The Alliance thinks," Deyanira mocked the man. "Ramsey didn't cross through the portal."

"Well, I didn't know that. The Council is letting Marcus keep details secret. I'm being exposed here."

Deyanira threw back her head and laughed. Her red ponytail swayed with her amusement. "That's your own fault." She sobered. "I suggest you find a way to get the details before you're no longer useful to us."

"But..."

"Ramsey used you, mole. He's still in the mortal realm and his goal remains young Blackstone." Deyanira whirled and phased from the platform.

Jonah let out a relieved breath when he awoke in his own bedroom. He'd have to warn Marcus about Ramsey.

CHAPTER THIRTY
KEVIN'S STORY

Not again.

Lynn and Aunt Imma's raised voices awakened Jonah from a hard but sound morning sleep, the kind of slumber you slip into after staying awake most of the previous night.

Throwing off his covers, Jonah tried to rub the sleep out of his eyes as he entered the family room. Lynn sat on the sofa, her bad arm propped up by a couple of cushions. Her uninjured arm was raised in agitation as she argued with her mother.

"I don't have to sit around."

"Yes you do." Aunt Imma placed a bowl of chopped fruit on a cushion. "The doctor said you had to be careful not to pull out the stitches. That means taking it easy."

Lynn had to gulp down a mouthful of fruit in order to yell at her mom, who had gone back into the kitchen. "But I'll go crazy just sitting around the house."

"Robert and Jonah can keep you company."

"Mom!" Robert dropped his spoon in his cereal. He sat at the kitchen table, wearing his normal morning cut-offs and oversized t-shirt. "That's like a punishment for me."

Aunt Imma turned from the stove with her spatula raised, temporarily abandoning the scrambled eggs she was cooking. "Robert Hightower, you'll help your sister."

By then, Jonah had ducked into the family room. "Aunt Imma, I had plans with Mike this morning."

Aunt Imma shook her head as she slid Robert's eggs onto a plate. "Jonah, your cousin is hurt."

"Mom, I'll stay home until noon." Lynn caught Jonah's eyes and nodded. "I have research to do for Dad, anyway. Don't make Robert and Jonah stay. That's punishment for me."

"Oh, Lynn." Aunt Imma noticed Jonah's sad expression and gave in. "Fine. I'll call in to work. I can be a few hours late."

Lynn couldn't hide her dismay.

Jonah grinned as he hurried off to shower and dress.

Lynn stopped him just as he reached the back door. "Hey, we're having a Practice Club meeting late this afternoon. Rico's gonna come by and get me once mom goes to work."

"Okay. I'll let Mike know." Jonah slipped outside.

*

The Littletons lived in a cul-de-sac at the opposite end of Morningside Drive. Their split-level home was painted robin's egg blue and always reminded Jonah of a beautiful blue sky. It was one reason he had painted a wall in his room the same color.

Punctual Mike stood at the top of their sloping, U-shaped driveway with his bike in hand.

"How're you feeling?" Jonah asked as he brought his bike to a stop.

"Fine." Mike glanced back at his house. "You think someone from the Alliance watched the house all night?"

Jonah hadn't considered that before. "I doubt it." He debated mentioning Deyanira's revelations from the dream-walk until he caught the relief on Mike's face. "You weren't scared last night?"

"No." Mike toyed with the gear shifter on his bike. When he caught Jonah watching, he stopped. "Why'd you and Marcus take so long to come back?"

Jonah hesitated at the change of topic. "He fussed at me."

"I knew it. That was a dangerous thing you guys did."

"You wish we didn't?"

"Of course not." Mike hopped on his own bike and started down the street. When Jonah caught up, he asked, "So, what did your godfather say?"

Jonah repeated the details of Marcus's lecture as they rode to the teen center. He included the parts he had skipped over with Lynn and Robert, grateful for a best friend who would keep these personal details private.

He began to rethink that, considering Mike apparently didn't feel the same way, not if he kept parts of his own life secret. As they paused at a stop sign, Jonah decided to broach the subject.

That's when he sensed the change in air pressure. An involuntary spike of fear shot through Jonah. He chided himself. It couldn't be Ramsey because his Death Sense didn't twinge. Whoever the person, they must be a member of the Alliance.

Mike noticed. "Something wrong?"

Jonah shook his head, reasoning that his godfather had acted on the news about Ramsey remaining in the mortal world. "Let's see what's up at the clubhouse."

*

Despite the chance of losing the attic, Jonah had never seen the space busier. Rex talked with yet another group of Alliance people near the attic window.

Jonah began to think their attic clubhouse was a weird sort of tourist attraction for the Alliance personnel. *Come and see where the boy who used the Protector's Ring hangs out! Just fifteen bucks.* He grinned, causing Mike to give him an inquisitive glance.

As he turned away, Jonah noticed Trueblood standing across the old card table from Wick and Robert, who must have arrived just before them. The Seeker's box was open, and Wick held his second bracelet in his hands. He was in the process of giving it to Trueblood.

Jonah hurried to them. "Why're you taking Wick's bracelet? It wasn't his fault we used the other one to rescue

Mike. Don't blame him." He knew something was off when everyone stared at him in confusion.

Rex let out a hearty chortle in the background.

Trueblood's mouth tweaked with a suppressed smile.

Wick flashed Jonah a lopsided grin. "It's not about that. Trueblood and Rubio are impressed and want to examine it at HQ."

"Yeah, little cousin." Robert worked to hide his own grin. "They asked to borrow it."

"Oh." Jonah's building anger cooled in seconds, leaving him embarrassed. "Sorry."

Trueblood lifted the bracelet from Wick's hands and let out an appreciative sound. "This is very powerful. No wonder Kevin was able to hold out against Ramsey's people." She inclined her head toward Wick. "We'll take good care of this, young mage. You have our oath."

Wick stood tall and returned the respectful acknowledgement with a nod.

Ever mindful of her schedule, Trueblood checked her watch, moved to the attic window, and produced a vortex. With a final nod to Jonah, she entered the opening, leaving Rex and the others behind.

Seeing the vortex, and feeling its magical pull reminded Jonah of his ride to the center. "Rex, who followed us this morning?"

The big Fallen Reaper clapped his beefy hands. "Oh, that was Kevin. We needed to be more careful now that we know Ramsey didn't cross over."

"Ramsey?" Mike's eyes bugged out and he shoved Jonah. "You didn't tell me Ramsey was around and that someone followed us."

"Sorry." Jonah described the dream-walk to Mike. By the time he finished, Mike couldn't hide his anxiety.

"Don't worry, fella." Rex gestured to himself and the other Alliance people. "We won't let you and Jonah out of our sight."

Mike nodded.

"Where's Kevin?" Jonah asked.

Rex rubbed his square chin, thinking. "I reckon he's downstairs now that you're in the clubhouse."

"I'll be back." Jonah started for the attic stairs.

"Where're you going?" Rex asked.

"Down to talk with Kevin."

"I'm going too." Mike hurried to follow.

It was easy to find Kevin when they reached the atrium. He sat in the café, gazing out the windows, an island of calm in the general bedlam of the kid-filled café. In fact, Kevin was so still, Jonah began to worry. He and Mike approached the table but glanced at each other, neither wanting to be the first to interrupt.

Without warning, Kevin's eyes shifted to them. "You two geeks are weird."

Jonah cracked a smile at the Fallen Reaper's teasing tone. "You're the one staring into space." He pulled out a chair next to Kevin and sat down.

Mike took the one opposite the older boy, watching him with an avid expression.

Kevin went back to staring out the rear windows of the café. "I wasn't staring into space. I was listening."

Jonah gawked at the chattering kids all around them. "To what?"

"Conversations."

Jonah grinned. "Eavesdropping?"

Kevin sighed and threw up his hands. "No. I'm training my ears to separate streams of sounds."

Mike leaned over the table. "Do you have enhanced hearing?"

"Yeah."

"Cool! Is it like Superman? He had to train himself to isolate sounds."

Kevin glanced at the ceiling and shook his head in mock misery. "Well, not exactly."

"But similar, right?" Mike nodded in a thoughtful way.

Kevin shrugged. "It comes in handy on assignments."

"Oh. You're training for the Alliance." Mike stood. "We can leave you alone."

"Jonah would never do something that thoughtful." Kevin crossed his arms on the table and leaned forward, giving Jonah his full attention. "What's the problem, little man?"

Jonah hesitated, wondering if he should ask about the meeting with the Council.

Kevin guessed what was on his mind and frowned. "Yes, I got in trouble. Mandara, he's the lead Fallen Reaper, tore me a new one, after complimenting me."

"He did? Oh." Jonah could sympathize.

Kevin frowned and lowered his voice to a rich baritone. "I admire initiative and bravery, Mr. Brown. We need that in the Alliance."

Goosebumps ran up Jonah's arms. He hadn't heard this Mandara character before, nor could he guess if Kevin's impression of the man was accurate or not. What pained Jonah, and produced the goosebumps, was that Kevin's imitation sounded so much like Jonah's dad.

Mike dropped into his seat and tapped the table to get Kevin's attention. "That's a good thing, right?"

"No, it isn't." Kevin sighed. "You two don't understand Council politics yet."

"Politics?" The word snapped Jonah out of his moment of reverie.

"There are factions on the Council." Kevin placed his right hand flat against the table. "Mandara, Rubio, and others are part of a faction called the Hardliners. They believe we should fight the KIN and these Hunters." He placed his left hand on the table next, far apart from the right. "Marcus and the others are considered Moderates. They think we should be cautious. In the middle are the Centrist members, keeping the peace."

Mike's expression was serious as he held up three fingers. "Moderates, Centrists, and Hardliners. Got it."

Kevin shifted his gaze to Jonah. "Then there's you."

Jonah's eyes widened. "What do you mean?"

"Anytime you use your powers, the Hardliners like it. I bet they toast each other in private." Kevin scowled.

Jonah didn't know how to respond.

Mike hugged himself and began to rock back and forth. "You mean they want Jonah to be a weapon." His voice was flat and sure, like he had figured that out.

Kevin swallowed, watching Mike. "Yeah, exactly. Are you alright?" Mike glanced down at his crossed arms and stopped his rocking. Kevin gave him one last worried look before turning to Jonah. "You're not a weapon for anyone. Marcus has been saying it, too."

Jonah was dumbfounded by that news. He never knew about Alliance politics. But to find out Council members wanted him to do more worried Jonah. He also began to piece together why Kevin got in trouble. "You told Mandara that?"

Kevin nodded. "He expected me to support their position. I'm not Marcus's apprentice anymore, and I helped you rescue Mike. But when I disagreed with him, suddenly I was too close to you and Lynn and acting like a kid instead of an adult. And he decided someone older should watch over you for a while."

"Who?" A sinking feeling developed in Jonah's stomach. Marcus would be too easy a choice.

Kevin shook his head. "Don't know, but the Council can assign anyone they want to monitor you."

"I don't want anybody else," Jonah said, pounding the table. "I want you."

Kevin's eyebrows shot up. He leaned forward to play with Jonah's shield bracelet. "Well, when this assignment's done, I'm gone. Rex jokes they'll send me to Siberia."

Kevin tried to be flippant but Jonah heard and sensed the anger inside him. "That's not funny." Jonah let his raw emotion flow. It angered him that Kevin accepted the unfair situation, but what could he do?

Mike started rocking again. "It's not fair. You saved my life. I wonder if the mole is behind this." His eyes had gone unfocused, like he was referring to his own internal source of information.

"I told you. If I hadn't argued, Mandara would have been cool with everything. And I can't see the mole getting him to do anything. Mandara's too bullheaded." Kevin gazed directly into Jonah's eyes. "And I don't care what they think. You're not a weapon."

The sincerity rolling off the older boy staggered Jonah. It was even stronger than Marcus's belief from the previous evening.

Jonah swallowed. "Thanks."

"I know you don't get it yet. But you will, and soon." Kevin stood. "By the way, the Council agreed to have you open the back door into the Afterworld. Trevor's going home."

Mike's expression changed from slightly vacant to concerned. "How's Trevor?"

Kevin shrugged. "Fine, the last time I checked."

"We should open that door to the Afterworld as soon as possible."

"I'll make sure to tell the Council." Kevin grinned at Mike. "Relax. We're making the arrangements for everyone to stay at the Guest House during the mission." Kevin held out his fist. Jonah and Mike bumped it with their own. "See you two later."

With that, he strolled out and nodded to the Alliance guy hovering at the café entrance. More than a few of the girls watched him leave. Jonah envied Kevin. The boy was tall and carried himself with a confidence Jonah only wished he had.

CHAPTER THIRTY-ONE
THE AWAY TEAM

Jonah and Mike arrived for the emergency meeting of the Practice Club to find other kids already there. Anthony unloaded a cooler from his father's truck. Rodney helped him place it near the center of the field, on the grass plot. Lorraine hovered near, ready to drop bottled water and juices into the container.

"Whatsup, guys?" Anthony waved as he said goodbye to his dad.

Mike joined the others and helped stock the cooler. Jonah nodded in greeting but walked to the edge of the clearing. It wasn't that he didn't like the other kids. They'd been cool after his ruined birthday party.

It was the plot of grass. Seeing it caused a spasm of regret. He couldn't shake the image of Mike's unconscious body laying right where Ramsey had knocked him out. He didn't want to relive his own terror that his best friend had died.

And he had to add Kevin's situation to the worry load. In a way, Trevor had been perceptive about the feeling of being suffocated. Whenever Jonah grew anxious over things and was around a lot of people, their souls pressed on him. He gazed into the Georgia pines, listening to the sound of the others talking and laughing.

Eventually Mike came over and pressed a bottle of cranberry juice into Jonah's hand and then quietly sipped from his own while watching the surrounding trees. His buddy's willingness to hang with him, even when moody, got to Jonah.

He'd never said anything to Mike about recent events nor asked how he was really doing. Jonah opened the bottle and took a sip of juice before saying, "I'm sorry I left you behind with Ramsey."

Mike's eyes widened. "It's okay, Jonah. I don't blame you."

"Yeah, it was that Trevor. If he hadn't–"

Mike lowered his bottle. "I'm not mad at Trevor either."

"Why not?"

"He was right. And if you'd gone back, Ramsey would have taken you to the Afterworld. Even Deyanira admitted it." Mike poked Jonah's arm. "You see that, right?"

"Yeah, I guess, but…"

"I feel sorry for Trevor." Mike hugged himself, worry etching his face.

Jonah gagged on his own sip of juice. "He lied to us about having powers."

"I know." Mike shrugged. "He's put his life on the line, just like we did."

Jonah didn't know what to say to his friend. In the end, he didn't have the right to be angry in Mike's place. So he tried a different angle. "You and Lynn were hurt. I wouldn't blame you if you stayed behind and don't cross over."

"No. I'm going." The steel in Mike's voice surprised Jonah. "I helped you figure out the riddle and I used the compass."

Jonah leaned away at Mike's determined tone.

Mike continued, his voice raising. "And Trevor's brave." When Jonah couldn't hide his frown, Mike grew testy and shouted. "Has your Death Sense ever gone off around him? Well?"

"No." Jonah hated to admit that, but it was true. "And keep it down. The others are looking at us."

"Well then." Mike squeezed his empty bottle between his hands, looking defiant. "Trevor's one of the good guys."

Jonah watched his best friend's angry expression while recalling Mike's comments back in the bookstore. "You like Trevor, don't you."

Mike crossed his arms, staring down at a rock he rolled beneath his right foot. "Yes, I do."

"Oh." Jonah blinked, not expecting Mike to be that honest. "Does he even like you back?"

Mike nodded and his jaw tightened. "We're alright?"

"Yeah." Jonah glanced behind them to make sure the others weren't trying to eavesdrop. "How can you know that about Trevor?"

Mike glanced at Jonah. "He called me."

"When?"

"Last night. He called to apologize for what happened. And, we–talked for a long time."

Jonah couldn't believe it. "How did he get a phone?"

"I didn't ask." Mike looked away. "The important thing is he called."

For a wild moment, Jonah imagined the slippery courier phasing down to Mike's room for a face-to-face talk last night. But that shouldn't have been possible. Rubio said Trevor wouldn't be able to phase from HQ again. But the guilty look on Mike's face said otherwise.

Jonah's eye's widened. "Mike?" When his buddy blushed, Jonah knew that Trevor had indeed found a way to visit. "How did he…"

"I don't know and don't care." Mike blushed even more.

Oh my God. Jonah experienced equal parts shock and envy. "What did you two do?" As soon as he asked, a wicked grin spread across Jonah's face.

Mike glared at him. "We *talked*!"

"Yeah, right." Jonah laughed and shoved his buddy. "How long did he stay and *talk*?"

Mike pulled a scandalized expression just as Lynn entered the clearing, arm in a sling and Rico hovering over her. Mike hurried over to talk with them, leaving Jonah alone with burning, unanswered questions.

He didn't have time to revisit the conversation because Practice Club members arrived in steady groups until the entire roster was present. Vincent, the leader for this year, began the meeting. Everyone had heard rumors about the Club's situation, but Lynn's detailed recounting of her conversation with the director shocked and angered the group.

"Yo!" Vincent's tough voice cut through the clamor Lynn's news produced. Everyone quieted in seconds, waiting. "Let Brandon and his friends meet at the Teen Center." He pointed at the ground at his feet. "We'll meet here." He pumped his fists in the air.

Everyone cheered. That soon gave way to chants of, "Boycott. Boycott. Boycott!" During the chanting that followed, Jonah glanced around the assembled crowd, noting the invited friends of members, including Wick's girlfriend Tamara.

Watching her holding Wick's hand and chanting along with the others brought his discussion with Mike to the forefront and the truly nagging aspect of it all. In the midst of everything happening, even Mike had found someone. Once again, Robert's quip from a few days ago stung Jonah. He was the odd boy out. Would he ever find anyone?

Kevin stepped into view at the entrance to the clearing, causing a stir. Jonah forgot that most of the club members had never met Kevin. Lynn was on point and whispered to Vincent.

Rico strode over to greet the Fallen Reaper. He turned to the Club. "Hey everyone. This is Kevin, and he's cool."

After exchanging greetings with Vincent, Kevin made his way to Jonah's side while drawing curious looks from several club members.

"What's up?" Jonah asked the older boy.

"Everything's set for ATL." Kevin lowered his voice to a whisper. "What's happening here? I heard the chanting. You gonna have a protest march?"

"Not really." Jonah smiled, glad to have Kevin standing beside him. As the gathering ended, he and Jonah trailed behind the rest of the club members, taking their time walking toward the nearby school.

Kevin used the opportunity to give him all the details of the plan. Along the way, Jonah came to realize he liked listening to Kevin talk. The boy was so sure of himself, even after getting in trouble. Jonah wished he could always be as confident.

By the time they reached the building's gravel parking lot, most of the other kids were gone, either on foot, bikes, or in cars. Mike stood near the main road, waiting for Jonah.

Kevin stopped, shoved his hands in his pockets, and hunched his shoulders. "I have to get back to HQ."

"Oh." Jonah didn't want him to leave. When Kevin was around, he didn't feel like the odd person.

"Well, see you soon, little–" Kevin stopped when Jonah glared at him. "I need something to call you."

"How about my name?"

"Nah." Kevin stroked his chin. "I could use geek boy or hero."

Jonah glared at him. "Those belong to Lynn."

Kevin grinned. "How about the Deliverer or the One?" He snapped his fingers and treated Jonah to a mock bow. "Or Son of Isaiah."

"No way."

"Well, I guess it's little man." Kevin started for the woods behind the school.

"I hate that name." Jonah watched the older boy's retreating back, mindful of his own fervent wish for more muscles. "I'm gonna grow."

"I'll believe that when I see it." Kevin turned, his teasing grin giving way to an earnest expression. "Besides, you'll always be my little man." With that, Kevin stepped into the shadows of the tree line and phased.

The thrill Jonah experienced at Kevin's words lightened his footsteps as he rolled his bike to Mike, who was waiting.

"What did he say to you?" Mike peered into Jonah's face.

Jonah blinked. "Ah, the arrangements for the Guest House are ready."

"No." Mike shook his head. "That's not it."

"Why'd you think that?" When Mike grinned, Jonah grew irritated. "What?"

"You were smiling all the way over here and your expression was all dreamy."

This time, it was Jonah's turn to be embarrassed.

*

From the moment Jonah's group arrived at the Guest House, he and Mike were shuffled away from the others and made to endure several meetings in the library. Eventually they were released in order to prepare for departure. The boys headed straight to the bat cave.

"Trevor!" Mike shouted, hurrying to the courier's side. "How're you doing?"

"Weak." He offered Mike a tired smile. "It's good we're finally going. I'm running out of time."

Mike nodded his head in sympathy. His hands twitched as if he wanted to reach for Trevor. "Can't Rubio help?"

"He's done all he can. I have to cross over or..."

Mike shuddered.

Jonah was about to say he was sorry when Kevin entered the basement carrying a bundle of light grey tunics and pants. He tossed a pair to Jonah, Trevor, and Mike. "Get changed. We're leaving in a few minutes."

Trevor laughed at Jonah and Mike's confused expressions. "I suggested we should put on something so we blended in when we arrive in the Afterworld."

Jonah thought everyone made a strange sight after donning the baggy clothing. In the Afterworld, it might look normal but here, they were like extras in a fantasy movie.

Kevin handed Jonah and Mike standard survival backpacks.

Jonah held his up, a questioning look on his face.

Kevin took the pack and held it so Jonah could slide into it. "The doorway is on this side and we don't know the weather conditions or terrain. So we have the packs, just in case."

Jonah nodded. It made perfect sense. Plus, he might also need it on the other side.

Trevor fussed over Mike, making sure he was ready to go while carrying on a whispered conversation. Jonah was convinced the two boys had done more than just talk. He frowned, feeling envious because he didn't have anyone to fuss over him like that. Well, except Aunt Imma. She didn't count.

Kevin cleared his throat to get Trevor and Mike's attention, then he led their group upstairs, through the den and kitchen, and outside to the large patio. Several more adults were present, including Rubio, Marcus, Trueblood, and Rex. All four of them were dressed in similar grey tunics and pants.

Jonah's attention was drawn to a large octagonal metal platform at the center of the patio. All the furniture had been moved aside to make room. He guessed the platform was about seven to ten feet in diameter.

A waist-high pole with a small hole near the top edge was attached to one end of the platform. Jonah pointed at the strange sight. "What's that?"

The Alliance adults grew quiet and waited as Marcus strode over to them. "We have a theory about the compass." He indicated the pole. "We think that if you attach the compass to a device, the entire piece can be moved."

Mike gasped. "Oh. That's a good idea."

"Maybe." Jonah frowned. "But why use it?"

Rubio's usual military tone carried a trace of humor today. "Because, young man, it's a little more dignified than everyone holding on to you."

Trevor and Mike stepped onto the platform in unison and began inspecting the short pole. Jonah hesitated when Lynn, Robert, and Wick exited the house.

Lynn didn't have her sling but held her arm close to her side and wore a solemn expression as she walked to Kevin. She activated a blade with her left hand and held it toward him, point first. Kevin nodded in understanding, activated his own, tapped the blades once, and then held still, blade against blade.

Everyone grew quiet, watching.

Lynn didn't seem to notice or care. "Keep Mike and Jonah safe."

Kevin nodded. "I promise."

Jonah was close enough to see the goose bumps race up Lynn's arms. Golden lines flickered in the air and settled onto the crossed blades as well as Lynn's and Kevin's forearms.

Wick pressed closer, reaching out to touch the blades, but stopping before doing so. "Very cool!"

Rubio let out an impressed grunt.

Lynn deactivated her blade and motioned Jonah and Mike to join them. Mike tried to bring Trevor along, but the boy held back, shaking his head. Lynn huffed, reached over, and pulled Jonah and Mike into a hug. Robert and Wick piled on, careful of Lynn's injured arm, and patted everyone on the back. After a long moment, which moved Jonah to his very core, they parted.

Lynn playfully nudged Mike with a fist. "Alex would be proud of his little brother."

Mike's face suffused with color at the compliment.

Lynn took both deactivated blades and held them out for Jonah. "Bring them back or else…"

Jonah didn't know what to say, so he accepted the cylinders in silence and nodded.

Rubio clapped his hands and motioned everyone onto the strange platform. Then the mage pointed to the pole. "Compass there please, Mr. Blackstone."

Jonah nodded and snapped the compass into place. The device pulsed with power when Jonah opened the true face and entered the code, creating a slight tug on his ability.

Rubio was the last to mount the platform. In all, eight people were part of what Jonah realized was a first group. *It's our own away team*, he thought, wishing he could whisper it to Mike and get a laugh. A second team of Alliance personnel waited at the edge of the patio.

"We're ready." Rubio nodded.

The reality of the situation finally registered. Jonah knew where they were going, but not until now did he truly face the prospect of crossing over. What would they find at the final location? Things had been so busy, he hadn't had a chance to consider it. Well, Jonah told himself, he'd find out in a few seconds.

After sucking in a breath, he activated the compass.

CHAPTER THIRTY-TWO
UNEARTHLY EARTH

The group reappeared inside a pitch black cavern. The only illumination was six large symbols at their feet. The air was close and bone dry. Jonah sucked in a startled breath at the lack of moisture.

"Keep still for a second." Marcus gripped Jonah's arm. "Let your bodies get used to it."

Jonah took shallow breaths, willing himself to relax.

Rubio and Trueblood ignited balls of blue flames in their palms and proceeded to drop them around the edge of the platform.

"Rex." Rubio's bark echoed off the walls, giving an idea of the cavern's size.

"Oh yeah." Rex sounded embarrassed.

The sudden change of air pressure let Jonah know the Fallen Reaper had phased away.

Marcus guided Jonah and Mike off the platform. Trevor stuck close to them as the group waited. Rex reappeared on the platform with two more Alliance guys in tow. They carried a large plastic container and a couple of flashlights.

In quick motions, the men opened the container and pulled out small, battery-powered LED lights. They moved around the cavern, activating and placing the lights against the wall. The extra illumination from the LEDs reflected off a smooth ceiling above, spilling soft, amber light into the space. The result was a cozy feeling.

Mike knelt down to touch the six large symbols etched in the cavern's version of a platform. There wasn't a designation stone here; each symbol was its own stone.

"Whoa." Mike traced the design in the air with his finger. "Jonah, it's three interlocking circles and wings."

Jonah knelt beside Mike to look at the cavern's dusty floor. "It's the Alliance symbol." Something about this version of the symbol, the circles, was familiar. He tapped his forehead, trying to remember, and then he had it. They were like the calendar circles he'd seen in photos his parents took of an excavation.

Jonah glanced at his godfather. "My mom and dad would have loved this place."

Marcus nodded and held out the compass.

Jonah rose to his feet, pulling a puzzled expression. "You won't need it anymore?"

"Now that we've been here, we can phase back and forth." He nodded at the compass, and Jonah took it.

As if proving Marcus's point, Rex phased into the cavern again, this time carrying a large trunk. He unpacked a compact table. As soon as it was unfolded, he unrolled a laminated map on the tabletop.

A mortal member of the crew affixed an LED to a portable light stand and pointed it at the table.

Marcus moved closer. "Let's see where we are." He allowed Jonah and Mike to scoot in front of him, since he could look over their heads.

Rex used a marker to draw a dot on the world map, in the Southern US. He drew a second dot in the area of the Eastern Sahara. In fact, the area was a vast desert near the borders of Libya and Sudan.

Laying a yardstick between the points, Rex drew a connecting line. That done, he started a second line, this time from a location in France, but it also ended on the same dot in the desert.

The nearest labeled regions were Gilf Kebir and Jebel Uwainat. The names seemed familiar to Jonah.

"I know those names." Mike tapped his finger on the map in excitement. "They're in the Eastern Sahara Desert."

Kevin snorted. "That's obvious."

"I know that, Kevin. I mean that's the most remote place on Earth." Mike leaned over the map to trace his finger along the outlines of the area. "I have a book about it."

Rex drew a circle around the area. "Well, we're hundreds of kilometers from those locations." He grinned at Mike. "You know your stuff, young man."

"That would explain the outside." Rubio paused to smack dust off his gloves. He had returned to the cavern through an opening Jonah hadn't noticed. A strong flinty smell accompanied the mage as he stepped closer to the table.

Mike jerked upright, staring at the mage. "What's outside?"

Rubio vibrated with suppressed enthusiasm. He placed his hands flat on the map. "Prepare yourself. The sight is something, even at night."

He led the way across the chamber and to the opening. Jonah glanced into the dim exit to see an ancient set of steps carved into the rock.

Regular flares had been spaced along the pathway. Jonah's sense of wonder increased as he followed his godfather out of the cavern. They ascended the steps toward a black opening. The closer he got, the more pinpoints of light Jonah saw.

Mike gasped, staring ahead. "Jonah. Those are–" His words caught in his throat as they exited the cavern and stars exploded into view above.

The starscape extended from horizon to horizon and was so bright and clear, Jonah imagined he could reach out and touch them. Even more interesting was the sudden cold wind that nipped at his face.

He huddled in his thin grey clothing and tried to find the horizon. It was easy to see because the stars abruptly ended in a thin line. There were no obstructions of the sky, just open desert.

Lifting his gaze overhead, Jonah's breath caught in his own chest because the stars began to move. The entire sky rotated like a time-lapse video. The effect was so jarring that Jonah almost lost his balance.

Kevin steadied him. "You okay?"

Jonah nodded, afraid to speak and break the spell, or whatever was happening. He tore his gaze from the rotating sky and focused on the ground. Ghostly images of people moved around on the leveled stretch of desert near the base where Jonah's group stood.

The people wore loose-fitting clothing and their skin was jet black. He could tell because they had lamps stationed all around the area, revealing a series of angular stones arranged in circular patterns.

That's it! The large circles were ancient calendar circles. A long succession of people used the stones, large and small to chart the stars in the sky.

The overwhelming sense of an immense span of time and history flowed over Jonah. This place had been a center of astronomical observations for thousands of years.

He marveled at what must be a weird sort of waking-dream. He'd always seen things happening in the present. He'd never seen things from the past. Certainly he'd never seen things happening over millennia.

A sense of connection to something greater awed Jonah. He was outside of his body, space and time, a traveler over the eons. The past and the future were just beyond his perception, but if he pushed, Jonah was sure those vistas would open to him. Is this what it meant to be a Deliverer?

Kevin's hold on Jonah's upper arm tightened a bit. "Jonah?"

The concern in the boy's voice grounded Jonah. He blinked, dispelling the vision. "This place is really old."

Mike gazed at him in the darkness. "It makes sense that the last Deliverer chose this site. Even today, satellites don't pass over and it's been ignored by explorers."

Jonah nodded. "I get that. But the place, it's…" He couldn't put it into words. The weight of history still pressed on his senses, his soul.

Marcus motioned toward the entrance. "Let's go down. We're here for a reason."

If Jonah thought returning to the cavern would help to dispel the pressure of history and time, he was wrong. The sensation grew more pronounced, and Jonah realized the source. "There's power in this place."

Marcus faltered and turned to him. "Power?"

Jonah sucked in a breath. "Yes. It's getting stronger the closer we get to the cavern."

He was right. The power was almost alive now, and it focused on him. Fear gripped him and he sought out that safe place within himself. The haven opened and enveloped his mind. At the same time, the intrusive pressure turned questioning in nature.

Calmer now, Jonah assessed the nature of the power and understood. "This place wants to know something."

Everyone in the cavern stopped whatever they were doing and watched Jonah. He noted some awed expressions as well as suspicious ones.

Marcus dropped his voice to a whisper. "What does the cavern require?"

"It wants to know if I'm a Deliverer."

Marcus nodded. "Answer it."

Jonah wondered how to do that before deciding to answer the same way the cavern asked. He had to use his mind. *Yes. I am a Deliverer. Yes.*

In response, a rush of power seeped through the earth and into his feet and legs. "Whoa." Jonah sucked in a breath. The sensation was almost a violation of his body.

Rubio raised his right hand, palm toward Jonah. "I can sense the power. It's entering you."

Jonah pointed at the large Alliance symbol. Ghostly workmen floated in and out of his vision, carving the original design on the floor. "It's coming from below."

"A seal, perhaps?" Rubio looked skeptical.

Jonah agreed, but there was no obvious seal here. That's when faint lines appeared on the ground, elongating, spreading and connecting until they outlined shapes in the stone. The overall design was circular and the segments fit together like... like...

"Do you see them? The lines?" Jonah asked the group.

No one else seemed to have the same perspective, except Mike, who pointed at the ground. "I see them, Jonah."

The lines flared in Jonah's augmented vision and the name for the design came to him. "They're cover-stones." He raised his hand and concentrated. *Come on, show the others.* After a few tense moments, light flared along the lines and everyone gasped.

When the light abated, clear edges to the stones were revealed.

"I'll be." Rex's mouth hung open.

Rubio signaled to the mortal members of the group. They started to pry the stones loose with spades. With Kevin, Rex, and Marcus helping, the group was able to lift the heavy cover-stones away, one at a time, uncovering a smooth surface below.

"Stand back." Jonah raised his hand and concentrated, the power singing to him now and urging him on. A click sounded and the flat surface moved aside to reveal a golden seal.

An awed silence spread through the cavern.

Finally Rex said, "That's a seal."

Rubio frowned at him.

"Hey, someone had to say it. That's how it's done in the movies." Rex's smart comment broke the shocked tension. The big Fallen Reaper winked at Jonah. "I'd say you have the only key to open that, buddy."

Yeah, Jonah thought. At the very center of the seal was a round depression. It was like the one in the doorway to the underground chamber where his parents had died. At once, a sense of foreboding assailed Jonah and he wanted to step away.

Mike leaned against him. "Jonah, you have to do it."

"I know." He swallowed then stepped over the edge and onto the seal.

The metal was hard and solid beneath his feet as he moved to the center to place the compass in the depression. It fit perfectly, but nothing happened.

Mike knelt at the edge of the seal and whispered, "Maybe you have to rotate it."

Jonah lowered himself to his knees and tried turning the compass to the left. It wouldn't budge. But when he tried turning it right, it easily rotated ninety degrees, made a solid click and then came loose into his grip.

Jonah stumbled back as a brilliant shaft of light erupted out of the opening where the compass had been. The entire seal bucked, heaving Jonah onto the cavern floor. The seal began to fold in on itself. A huge opening appeared, and a circular set of steps. The first ten were visible, but the rest were shrouded in shadows.

Mike pointed. "Oh my God."

Trevor and Kevin huddled in behind Jonah and Mike. The adults begun to whisper among themselves.

Jonah called out to them, "You want to check it out first, just in case?"

Rubio looked ready to do just that.

Marcus shook his head. "With that seal in place, I think it's safe. After all, you're the Deliverer." His godfather smiled. "And the cavern responded to you."

Kevin snorted. "That's lawyer double-talk for 'You go first.'"

Jonah exchanged an excited glance with Mike and Trevor. "Let's see what's down there."

CHAPTER THIRTY-THREE
THE BACK DOOR

Despite Marcus's comment, Kevin made it clear he had no intention of letting Jonah go first. He activated a blade and motioned Jonah to stay behind him as he took the initial tentative step onto the circular stairway.

Jonah was all too glad to let the Fallen Reaper lead, especially when blue flames roared to life, illuminating the entire length of the stairwell. A collective intake of breath went around the gathered people.

Kevin waved for Jonah, Mike, and Trevor to follow, and he began the descent. Jonah discovered the steps were shallow, forcing him to focus on what he was doing. There weren't any safety railings either. One slip and he'd tumble the entire way down.

The pale blue light reflected off the shiny obsidian of the steps and the curved wall. Unlike the worn, earthen steps leading up to the desert, these appeared smooth and well-maintained. Jonah couldn't shake the feeling that this place had awakened from a long sleep, one that had preserved whatever they would find below.

Mike huddled close behind, occasionally bumping into Jonah as they followed Kevin down and down. He whispered, "Wow. The lights are beautiful."

Jonah agreed, enjoying the cooler air inside the stairway. The change was comfortable after the bone dry cavern above.

When they finally reached the bottom, a row of purplish-blue flames erupted to life along the walls, illuminating a circular room. At the center was a crystal pedestal topped with a flat pinecone-shaped piece of smooth metal.

Kevin stopped beside the glowing pedestal, waving his hand over the device but never touching it.

Trevor gestured at it. "That has to be it."

Mimicking Kevin, Jonah stretched out his hand above the blank metal surface. The entire pinecone-shaped slab began to glow brighter.

The tremor rippling along the floor was the first warning. Then the far wall parted to expose a portal, larger and older than any Jonah had seen. This one had been made into the rock wall itself. The symbols around the opening were carved into the stone, much like the Alliance symbol in the cavern they had left behind

Jonah also noticed a depression had formed on the flat top surface of the pedestal.

Kevin nudged Jonah. "I think it likes you."

Mike huddled close, the pale light reflected in his wide pupils. "You gonna do it?"

In answer, Jonah placed the compass in the depression and held his breath. Like with the seal above, nothing happened. So he tried to turn it like he had before.

Still, nothing happened.

On a hunch, he tried to remove the compass, and it came away into his palm.

Jonah inserted the device two more times without any results or indications that the compass would activate anything. He became aware of the expectant silence of the others, and his face warmed with embarrassment.

After a fourth try, he took the compass in his hand. "It's not working." He turned to Trevor. "Are you sure about this?"

"Yes. It has to work." Trevor's voice shook and beads of sweat dripped off his forehead.

Jonah sympathized with the courier. If he couldn't open the doorway, Trevor would be stuck here to die.

Kevin tapped his arm. "You were able to open the seal. Why not this?"

Jonah thought he could read the unspoken truth on Kevin's face. Some hero he was turning out to be. He was the Deliverer, yet he couldn't open the doorway.

"Maybe you're doing it wrong." Mike brushed his finger along the edge of the depression. When the surface brightened even more, Mike snatched his hand away. He appeared unhurt, just stunned.

Mike's action reminded Jonah of the incident at his parents' hideaway, and a light went off in his mind. He stared at the compass as awareness dawned on him. All this time, he assumed it was about him, the Deliverer. But this was a *Seeker's* compass. And just as he wasn't a Protector nor meant to wear the ring, maybe he wasn't the one to own the compass either.

Shame hit Jonah like a punch to the stomach as he gazed at Mike. Jonah had assured Mike he was important to the group. But deep down, he saw his buddy as the weak link, the one without the power and in need of being protected.

But Wick had said everyone had a purpose. They just needed to find it.

Jonah gulped, ignoring the curious stares of the others. "I'm sorry, Mike. I really am."

"Sorry for what?"

Jonah held the compass out to his buddy. "You're the one who's supposed to use the compass, not me."

Trevor moved to stand right beside Mike, his face displaying awe. "You're a Seeker?"

Mike's gaze shifted back and forth between Trevor and Jonah, like a caged animal. "Are you sure, Jonah?"

"Yeah." The truth of the situation settled on him, and he smiled at Mike. "It's your purpose."

An ecstatic grin covered Mike's face as he cupped the compass in both hands, holding it high like a treasure. If Jonah wasn't mistaken, the device glowed in Mike's hands. When he faced the pedestal and lowered the compass into the niche, the entire structure began to hum with power.

Jonah's Death Sense spiked at the same time one of the Alliance men standing by the entrance screamed out in pain. A spray of blood splattered the wall as the man collapsed to the ground, dead.

A blurred shape roared into the chamber and toward the pedestal. Marcus and Kevin moved at once to intercept, their own bodies blurring.

The attacker stopped right beside Mike. It was Ramsey, and he grabbed Mike to use as a shield between Kevin and Marcus. The Fallen Reapers halted their blurred response, blades activated and ready to strike.

Kevin growled at Ramsey and moved forward, but Marcus pulled him back.

Rex yanked Jonah away from the agent.

But Jonah struggled in the big man's grip, terrified that his buddy was in Ramsey's clutches again. "Leave Mike alone. You can take me instead."

"Jonah!" Marcus shot him a warning glance.

Agent Ramsey tightened his hold on Mike's neck. "I don't want to take you, half-breed. I want to see what this boy can do with the compass."

"Liar."

Ramsey raised an eyebrow as he adjusted his grip. He nudged Mike. "I see the value of this boy now. He could be a true Seeker, the only one who can open the inner compass."

Marcus moved to block the agent's direct sight of Jonah. "How did you follow us?"

"Yeah." Jonah peeked around his godfather. "We used the compass. You can't trace that." But as Jonah said it, he recalled the agent's earlier use of modern technology rather than magic. That meant some kind of tracking device and… "The mole."

Ramsey grinned, looking smug. "Everyone was so worried about the supernatural that you didn't stop to consider everyday technology."

Jonah turned to his godfather, whose face had gone slack. Marcus began to pat his pants and then his grey tunic. His jaw slackened when he pulled out the new Alliance badge.

"That's right, traitor." Ramsey laughed.

Marcus's hand shook as he turned the badge over, found the embedded tracker, and yanked the tiny device free. He smashed it in his other hand and then threw it aside while glaring at Agent Ramsey.

"Now, move aside." Ramsey shook Mike for emphasis. "Let's see what the boy can do."

Marcus waved everyone back.

Jonah didn't like where this was going and yanked on his godfather's arm. "Don't let him do it."

"It's okay, Jonah," Mike said, sounding stronger than Jonah would have expected. "I wanna see if you're right about me." Mike shrugged in Ramsey's grip and the rogue agent relaxed enough for Mike to move to the pedestal.

He rested his slender hand atop the compass, fingers spread apart. For a moment, nothing happened. Then Mike gasped and his eyes began to glow a soft amber. The entire compass strobed with golden light, flashing patterns around the cavern walls.

Jonah shook his head because the patterns weren't on the walls. They had coalesced in mid-air, like a holographic image. He watched, mesmerized as a glowing, semi-transparent code floated before them. This one was composed of strange symbols that weren't on the compass.

It had to be the code into the Afterworld hideout, Jonah realized. He worried about Ramsey seeing it.

"Decrypt the code, boy," Ramsey ordered.

Rubio stepped forward. "Don't do it, young man."

"He has no choice." Marcus glared at his fellow Council member.

Mike manipulated the compass face while never taking his eyes off the code. It shifted into more recognizable symbols. Mike reached out and touched the decrypted code. Six symbols around the ancient portal flared with light, surprising everyone. The center portion of the rock face began to waver. When the turbulence stabilized, a scene appeared.

The cavern on the other side was so real, it was like looking out a window. Jonah took in the details of the room. It was similar to the cavern they were in, but much brighter with natural light. And there was an identical pedestal at the location. Jonah thought of the two caverns like terminals on either end of a secret route to and from the Afterworld.

Rubio shook his head in disgust, watching Ramsey study every detail of the room, no doubt so he could phase there later.

The agent nudged Mike. "Now, open the inner compass."

Mike pulled his hands from the compass and crossed his arms. He raised his chin in defiance.

Ramsey glared at him and activated a blade. He pressed it against Mike's chest, in the same spot he'd cut the boy before.

Marcus waved at the agent. "Don't hurt him. Mike, do it."

Rubio puffed out his chest in anger. "Marcus, we can't let that agent see that information."

Marcus whirled on the mage. "You want Ramsey to kill the boy?"

Rubio hesitated a fraction too long for Jonah. Eventually, the mage shook his head. But Jonah began to have a new, lower appreciation for Alliance Council politics. He didn't like what he saw.

Marcus raised his hands in a pleading gesture. "Mike, I appreciate your willingness to be brave, but I won't stand by and see you hurt." Marcus motioned to the compass.

Mike rested his hands on the device again. He closed his eyes and this time, a tidal wave of glowing, semi-transparent codes, numbers, and circles whirled through the air.

The much-larger display settled into a half-sphere above and in front of the pedestal.

"Amazing." Ramsey laughed in awe. "Those are designation codes for all the lost archives. They contain hidden knowledge that could change the balance of power."

Mike reached out and touched a close circle of seven glowing symbols. They revolved around each other in a cluster. As soon as his finger touched one of the codes, it enlarged at the same time six different symbols on the stone portal flared with light.

The vista shown was a forested area with strange colored trees and vegetation. Ramsey tensed when Mike pressed another code, but he didn't object. The scene shifted to a frozen, desolate tundra that elicited a startled moan from Marcus.

Rex swore under his breath. "I'll be. Never thought I see that place again."

Jonah recognized it as the same location of his last dream-walk.

The agent whispered to Mike, who selected another code. The view inside the portal changed to a scene of a bright, sunlit room with white walls, display shelves, numerous windows, and clear skylights overhead. The place was pristine and orderly, like a museum.

Marcus blinked in stunned silence. "Mike, choose another code."

"I don't think so." Ramsey ripped the compass from the niche in the pedestal while pulling Mike with him toward the portal.

Kevin, who had been watching the man all along, rushed forward in a blur of motion. Ramsey activated a shield and a blue distortion blossomed around the agent and Mike. Kevin hit the protective bubble and bounced sideways into the pedestal.

Ramsey dropped his shield and lunged for the opening. He would have made it through except Trevor shot forward and wrested Mike free of the agent's grasp. The courier paused for a split second to make sure Mike was okay before he plowed into Ramsey. He and the agent sailed through the opening and into the Afterworld.

When they hit the pristine floor on the other side, they slid along it for a few feet. Trevor grabbed the compass and tried to pry it from Ramsey's hands. The agent delivered two punches to Trevor's chest, sending the boy to the ground.

"Trevor!" Mike screamed.

The sight of the device in the agent's grasp angered Jonah. He sprinted for the opening. Someone shouted his name, but it was distorted as the chamber around him blurred.

Just before he crossed the portal's opening, something tugged on his tunic and yanked him back into real time. But his momentum couldn't be stopped and he tumbled through the opening and onto the marble floor of the pristine room.

Mike fell beside him.

Jonah rolled over just in time to see Trevor and Ramsey grappling with each other at the opposite end of the center aisle. Trevor tried to use the small stun device on Ramsey, but the man knocked it aside and the device skittered down a side aisle.

Jonah scrambled to his feet and rushed forward to help. His hands were mere inches from Ramsey when the slippery agent noticed and phased himself and Trevor from the chamber, leaving Jonah grasping empty air.

He collapsed to his knees and smacked a palm on the floor in frustration. "No!"

Mike joined him, looking stunned. "They're gone. With the compass."

Jonah whirled around. Instead of the open portal and his friends on the other side, he faced a blank, off-white wall. He gripped Mike's arm, thought about the chamber they had left behind, and tried to phase. A sudden, sharp headache made him gasp.

He couldn't phase out of this place. The awful realization settled on him. They were stranded in the Afterworld without the compass nor anyway to get home.

CHAPTER THIRTY-FOUR
THE REPOSITORY

"I'm sorry, Mike." Jonah continued to stare in dismay at the blank wall.

Mike elbowed him. "It wasn't your fault. We all wanted the compass."

"Yeah," Jonah answered, picturing the chamber in his mind. He tried to imagine the distance, but he couldn't. The chamber was on the mortal side, yet he did sense a faint power.

When he raised his hand, Mike stirred. "What are you doing?"

"I think I can sense the power in the chamber."

Mike placed his own hand on Jonah's shoulder. The effect was immediate and they sucked in identical breaths.

Jonah could clearly see the chamber in his mind's eye now. In fact, he could picture Rubio, Trueblood, Marcus, and Kevin. All stared in his direction, wide-eyed and shouting to them, almost as if they could see him and Mike.

That's odd. Was this another waking-dream, Jonah wondered. That's when Kevin darted forward, straight at them.

"Hey!" Jonah leapt backward on instinct, pushing Mike along just as Kevin walked through the wall. Unlike Jonah, Kevin remained on his feet and halted his forward momentum before he bowled over them.

"Leave it to you two geeks to jump right into the belly of the beast," Kevin scoffed.

Trueblood and Marcus stepped through the wall next. Like Kevin, they remained on their feet, and with more dignity.

Mike darted around Kevin and up to Marcus. "We're sorry."

Marcus raised a hand to calm him. "I understand."

Jonah joined his friend, looking for any clue that his godfather was actually furious with him. But he sensed a guarded curiosity from Marcus and relaxed. "How did you cross over?"

"I feared the portal had closed behind you and Mike," Marcus said. "Rubio used a series of spells to augment the fading power in the pedestal. His quick thinking kept the gate open. The problem was he couldn't open it enough to allow us through." He gestured to Trueblood, and she stepped forward.

"That's when it opened on its own and we saw both of you standing here." Trueblood turned and pressed her hand against the wall, frowning. "It's like you were helping Rubio reopen the doorway. We were able to cross over, but he had to remain behind to keep the connection open."

Jonah traded an awed look with Mike. "We were concentrating on the chamber, together."

Trueblood nodded. "It seems that worked. Perhaps the power from the pedestal was still connected to you?"

Jonah didn't know, but even if that was the case, the possibility seemed useless now. He frowned. "You're stuck here."

Marcus inspected the room with a tense expression on his face. "What happened? I suspect Ramsey and Trevor phased away."

Jonah nodded then snapped his fingers. "Hey! You can track them, right?" He glanced between Kevin and his godfather, feeling a surge of hope at that idea.

Kevin shrugged. "We could, but that would be a bad move."

"Why?" Jonah's face warmed at Kevin's rejection.

Marcus broke off his silent surveyal of the room. "Because you can be sure Ramsey phased to a secured location."

Mike paled at that answer. "You mean, Trevor's in trouble?"

"I'm afraid he is." Marcus frowned. "By now, the Grand Oracle has the compass and the courier."

"That's our worst nightmare." Kevin smacked his hand on a nearby shelf, causing the entire thing to rattle.

He whirled and walked down the center aisle, causing Jonah to wonder at the boy's increasing agitation.

Mike wore a stricken look on his own face. "We have to save Trevor and get the compass back."

"He's right." Jonah tore his gaze away from Kevin, who stopped near a window, head bowed. "And we have to get to the other location before Ramsey."

Marcus shook his head. "I wouldn't worry about that. It'll be protected against phasing, and Ramsey can't use the compass."

Mike nodded, but Jonah frowned. "Wait, my parents were able to use the compass. Maybe Ramsey can do it too."

"Jonah, you and Mike have proven the compass is special. I suspect your parents were never able to use it."

"What do you mean?"

"Your parents were good archeologists, but how did they find the Protector's Ring, the compass, and the Enhancer, all devices that had been missing for over two thousand years?" Marcus raised a questioning eyebrow. "I'm starting to believe they had help."

Jonah thought his godfather made a good point. But that didn't answer the pressing question. "Who would help them?"

"Perhaps this Elder we were supposed to meet."

Mike brightened at the thought. "Then Ramsey won't be able to get into the other location. Good."

"Exactly. That's our first piece of good news." Marcus turned to continue surveying the room.

Jonah decided to do something more than worry over Kevin's mood shift and copy his godfather. He took a deep breath and forced himself to notice the room for the first time. "What is this place?"

"A repository," Marcus stated in a sure tone.

When his godfather didn't offer more information, Jonah continued looking around. The space was a large oval with eight free-standing shelving units, four to each side of a center walkway. Each unit had numerous translucent displays, ten rows of ten cases each, or a hundred on each side.

The portion of the room near the wall where they had crossed over was open, with a large clear-top desk and sleek chair to the side. The space on the opposite end of the room had two slender benches built along the curving wall. The space between the benches was empty, or so Jonah thought. He had to stare at the wall a long time before he detected the outline of a door.

For no other reason than the presence of that door, Jonah decided that was the front of the repository. He would have asked Kevin about it, but he balked when he saw the frown on the boy's face.

Trueblood crossed to the window Kevin stood in front of and gave his forearm a gentle squeeze. "There won't be any Grim Guards here."

Kevin swallowed hard. "Just never expected to be back here... you know?"

Trueblood nodded. "We read the report."

Jonah exchanged a glance with Marcus when he heard that. "What report?"

"Kevin's report of his fall." Marcus watched the younger Fallen Reaper. "That's a story for later." Marcus lowered his voice. "So don't ask about it. Okay?"

Jonah gulped. "Yes sir."

Mike, gazing through one of the other large windows, beckoned to Jonah. "Come see this."

Jonah raced over and gawked at the spectacular view. They were so high that wispy clouds obscured a portion of the vista. But the flow of tear-drop ships, among other vehicles, could be seen through the gaps.

Pressing his face against the glass, Jonah peered into the clouds, and sucked in a breath. "Mike, do you see the lights through the haze? I think they're windows, like in an office building."

Mike darted between the display shelves and to an opposite window. "It's the same over here. I think it surrounds this tower."

The clouds cleared away as if blown on a sudden wind, giving Jonah an unobstructed view of a mammoth entry gate, far off in the outer wall of buildings. An entire glistening city was housed inside the larger outer building, reminding him of an immense fort.

"It's the Central Archive complex, gentlemen." Marcus stood behind Jonah, gazing out the window with a neutral expression. "You're standing near the apex of the Central Spire."

Jonah's jaw dropped. "You mean the Grand Oracle's somewhere in this building?"

Marcus nodded. "He has a suite of offices at the apex."

"And a killer view, no doubt." Kevin's voice was taut with suppressed emotion. "We should leave."

Marcus inclined his head. "I agree, but–"

Mike sucked in a quick, shocked breath, and Trueblood and Kevin were at his side in a flash.

Jonah followed his godfather to see what had startled Mike. He stood in front of a section where every case contained a single small carafe-shaped bottle. Each bottle was the same size, no more than six inches in height, and decorated in wild and mesmerizing colors and patterns.

The shapes seemed to be cut into the bottles themselves, allowing shimmering light to flare through the designs.

Marcus let out a low hiss of disgust.

"What do you think those are?" Jonah glanced up at his godfather.

Mike gestured at the small name tags with each bottle and said, "Those are names. For a second, I could decipher them."

Marcus spoked through a clenched jaw. "Reach out, with your Reaper side, Jonah."

Jonah closed his eyes and did as his godfather suggested. In an instant, he confirmed Mike's comment. "Those are human souls."

His insides burned. This proved the legend his godfather had mentioned at the hideaway.

"Those were the Grand Oracle's enemies," Marcus said. "All people important enough for him to kill in person."

That statement caused a ripple of pain to shoot through Jonah. *Like my parents.* The Grim Reaper had murdered them in person. A horrible thought occurred to Jonah. Did the evil being have his own morbid trophy case?

Mike backed away.

Marcus took a deep breath as he pointed toward a skylight. "Kevin? Can you phase outside the glass?"

"Don't," Jonah said.

Marcus frowned at him. "Why not?"

"I already tried it."

"Just as I remembered." Marcus lowered his gaze from the skylight. "The walls of the Spire are proofed against that sort of thing. Unless you break the glass and disrupt the pattern."

"Then we break it." Kevin balled his hands into fists.

Marcus shook his head. "It'll be protected and take a lot of force to punch through."

Trueblood raised an eyebrow. "Then we have no choice but to go through the front door."

Marcus shifted his gaze to the front. "I'm afraid so. Trevor's being held inside the Spire anyway."

A reddish light began to flash around the room along with an irritating buzzing, startling everyone. Mike grimaced as he covered his ears.

Jonah did the same, but it didn't help. "What's happening?"

Marcus seemed unaffected by the sound. "I think the Grand Oracle discovered how Ramsey returned to this place."

The distinct noise of approaching feet came from outside the room. Trueblood moved into the open area. Kevin went and stood at her side, blades drawn.

Marcus activated his own blades and stepped in front of Jonah and Mike. "When the door opens, blast them with a spell, Trueblood. We'll punch our way through and find a transport alcove."

Kevin and Trueblood nodded. Jonah had no clue what a transport alcove was, but he suspected it would get them away from anyone chasing. He didn't have any time to speculate because the door whooshed open to reveal grey-robed men with royal blue sashes. They were shocked to see Trueblood and Kevin.

In those crucial seconds, Trueblood hit the guards with a spell, knocking the front line backward into their companions. Kevin charged in and began fighting before the men could recover.

"Stay right behind me," Marcus ordered and followed Trueblood and Kevin out of the room and into the wide corridor beyond.

Jonah discovered he couldn't stay right behind because his godfather had to whirl and cut his way through the determined guards. Jonah activated Lynn's blades and stuck close to Mike as they tried to stay out of harm's way. When that proved futile, Jonah focused on defending Mike and himself.

More grey-robed men rushed in from their left, the direction they were trying to go. Kevin moved to counter, but there were too many. A few got around him and charged for the boys. Jonah waited until the last moment and instead of using the blades, he ducked and flipped the first attacker.

Mike dodged another, allowing Kevin to rush over and strike the man down.

Marcus and Trueblood had been separated from Jonah during the fight. They were attempting to fight their way back when a crystal partition dropped into place, blocking their way. Marcus hit and sliced at it with his blades, but only his muffled yells could get through.

Jonah sensed a powerful presence at the same moment Marcus's eyes widened. A regal man in a flowing grey robe approached from a side corridor, a full complement of guards with him.

The cowl of the newcomer's robe was folded back, revealing long, silver hair. He was very old, with deep lines etched into his thin cheeks. The corners of his mouth curved into a frown. His nose was long and pointed, and his dark grey eyes darted back and forth as he took in Jonah and the others.

Kevin let out a growl of anger, planted himself in front of Jonah and Mike, and whispered, "That's the Grand Oracle."

CHAPTER THIRTY-FIVE
JAILBREAK

The Grand Oracle's physical appearance may not have been as awful as the Grim Reaper's, but the evil intent around the being was just as strong and overpowering to Jonah. This ruler of the Afterworld sneered at Kevin in total arrogance and took his time to point out Marcus and Trueblood, still on the other side of the barrier. "Bring me those rebels. Now."

Jonah watched in mounting horror as Trueblood pulled Marcus away and down a side corridor just moments before the barrier opened, allowing the guards to swarm after them.

"Now, young Reaper." The Grand Oracle raised a boney hand and Jonah immediately clutched at his own throat. "If you don't want me to kill this one, drop your blades."

Kevin cursed and threw his weapons to the ground in disgust. Two guards rushed in to clamp him in semi-transparent stun-cuffs. All the while, Jonah continued struggling to breathe as the pressure increased to an unbearable point.

The Grand Oracle raised his hand and Jonah's feet left the ground. "Trying to rescue the courier scum?" The powerful being closed his hand and the pressure worsened, causing Jonah to gasp in agony. "You will tell me everything."

Jonah let out a strangled whimper and thought he'd pass out, but the Grand Oracle released him and let him drop to the ground. "They want to see the courier. Let them see their friend." The Grand Oracle strode past Jonah, who lay gasping for breath, and through the open door of his repository.

The guards rushed to Jonah. They were rough as they slapped stun-cuffs on his wrists and pulled him to his feet.

After placing cuffs on Mike, the boys were hustled down a side hallway. They arrived at a small rectangular alcove that didn't look wide enough to accommodate Jonah's group. The guards didn't hesitate to shove him inside and then press in behind. Jonah had no clue why until the familiar sensation played along his body and they phased.

The group reappeared in an identical, yet much darker, alcove. Jonah realized they had used a transport alcove and immediately thought of his godfather and Trueblood, and hoped they got away.

In addition to the low lighting, the place, with walls and floor of a deep, polished grey stone, had a sterile look to it. Jonah and Mike's sneakers made pitiful squeaking sounds as they stumbled along under the steel grip of the guards. Kevin's boots, on the other hand, were as quiet as the older boy himself.

After a short hallway, they turned a corner toward a checkpoint. Two powerful Guardians stood vigil on either side of a crystalline door. The hoods of their robes were drawn forward, hiding the faces in shadows.

Kevin went rigid beside Jonah, his jaw tight. "Just like Grim Guards. All they need are the scythes."

One checkpoint Guardian snapped to attention and pressed his hand to a glowing pad situated at chest height in the grey wall. The door whooshed upward to reveal a long, dark corridor with muted lighting.

Cell blocks lined the bleak corridor. As they stumbled forward, prodded in the backs by painful jabs, Jonah tried to glimpse what was behind the doors. All he saw were blurred darkened shapes through the opaque crystal.

A third of the way down, the guards yanked them to a standstill and opened a door on their right. After removing the stun-cuffs, the guards shoved the trio inside. Jonah bumped against the back wall before he could stop himself. Mike fell rather hard on a wafer-thin blue floor mat.

Kevin remained on his feet and whirled around, almost in a blur. The guards were ready, weapons raised.

One guard laughed at Kevin. "Filthy Reaper."

"I'm not a Reaper anymore." Kevin huffed out his words.

"That makes you even more pathetic." With that, the guard activated the cell door.

"They don't care for Reapers, I guess." Mike propped himself against the cell wall, watching Kevin.

"Not really." Kevin swore under his breath while circling his spot. "The Grand Oracle and Grim Reaper don't trust each other, and their people are even worse."

A muffled voice called out from an adjacent cell. "Mike? Is that you?"

"Trevor?" Mike scrambled toward the cell door.

Kevin gripped Mike's arm and stopped him. "Don't touch it. It'll shock you unconscious."

Mike gaped at the door. "Sorry." He moved to the wall and leaned his head against it. "Trevor, it's me."

"I guess Jonah and Kevin are with you?" Trevor's voice sounded clearer.

Jonah scanned the wall and spotted the slender vent near the floor.

Mike also spotted it because he sank to his knees against the wall. "We came after you, but Ramsey phased away. You okay?"

"I'm getting better." Trevor paused. "At least I'm in the Afterworld now."

Kevin snorted. "That's gonna do you a lot of good."

"What?" Jonah was shocked at the bitterness in Kevin's tone.

"He means," Trevor called out, "they're gonna interrogate and kill us."

Mike smacked his hand against the cell wall. "Don't say that, Trevor."

"It's the truth, Mike. I'm sorry."

Trevor sounded so sure and fatalistic to Jonah. He glanced at Kevin who, nodded in confirmation.

"You don't understand," Mike continued. "There's a chance Marcus and Trueblood can help us."

Trevor didn't respond immediately. When he did, Jonah thought his voice sounded guarded. "Explain."

Mike nodded and turned on Kevin. "Why did Ramsey call Marcus a traitor?"

Kevin blinked in surprise before furrowing his brow. "Duh! All Fallen Ones are traitors to them."

Mike shook his head. "But he didn't call you a traitor, just Marcus." Mike's light brown eyes sparkled with determination. "Marcus was a Archivist or a Guardian, wasn't he? Otherwise, Ramsey would have called him Reaper, like the guard just called you."

Kevin worked his jaw, refusing to answer.

Jonah realized where Mike's questions pointed and he rose to his feet and gripped the older boy's forearm. "Is Mike right?" Kevin gave him a hesitant nod, sending Jonah's mind racing back through everything he had assumed about Marcus. "But I always thought my godfather was a Reaper. He..."

Kevin let out a huff and threw his arms up. "None of that matters right now."

"I think it does." Mike lifted his chin, looking vindicated. "Marcus will know this building, and he'll find a way to free us."

"If Marcus knows his way around, he could find our operatives." Trevor sounded confident now.

Kevin gave Mike a skeptical look. "How do you two figure that?"

Mike's expression was sure. "It's a high probability."

Jonah cracked a smile despite the situation. "You're not gonna quote the probability like Spock, are you?"

The smile that touched Mike's face reassured Jonah. "No."

When Mike averted his gaze, Jonah knew his buddy was gonna do exactly that. The mind boost and touching the compass had changed his friend in more ways than Jonah expected. It was cool, but Jonah also worried about the long-term effects on his buddy.

Trevor called from the adjacent cell, "I trust Mike. Jonah's godfather must have been a rebel before he fell. That means he knows some of the safe…"

"Don't." Kevin smacked his hand against the wall, blocking out the rest of what Trevor said. "The walls could have ears. So everyone just settle down and wait."

Kevin gestured for Jonah to sit down on one of the two mats and then joined him.

Mike leaned his head against the cell wall and started talking to Trevor in hushed tones.

Kevin grunted, watching the quiet conversation.

Jonah searched for something to say in order to keep the worry out of his mind. He really wanted to ask Kevin about the day the young Reaper fell, but he promised Marcus he would not do so. As he also watched Mike, Jonah wondered what his buddy and Trevor chatted about. They seemed to have no problems at all.

So, why did he and Kevin have such a hard time? Throwing caution to the wind, Jonah nudged the older boy in the side. "You think Trevor told Mike everything? You know, how he died the first time." Jonah regretted mentioning that personal subject when Kevin tensed. "I'm sorry. I didn't mean–"

Kevin glanced at him. "I doubt it. First Death is personal for a reason." Kevin's voice sounded hollow and a bit angry as he went back to watching Mike's conversation. After a long moment, he let out a breath. "Everyone didn't die doing something… noble." Kevin tapped his fist against the floor.

Sensing the boy's pain, Jonah said, "I'm sorry."

"Stop apologizing." Kevin sucked in a breath and met Jonah's gaze again. "I might tell you someday."

"Really? I mean, you don't have to."

Kevin bumped Jonah's leg with his fist and then let it rest there. "Who else am I gonna tell?" He shook his head and looked away.

Jonah understood in that moment that Kevin didn't have any friends. How could he, Jonah decided. He was a Fallen One and surrounded by adults. No wonder the boy liked to hang out with Jonah's cousins and friends.

And me. Even now, Kevin continued to playfully tap Jonah's knee with the back of his fist. And Jonah recalled the boy's parting comment after the Practice Club meeting.

Jonah pushed aside the shyness, not wanting to waste this chance. "You volunteered to watch over me, didn't you?"

Kevin shrugged. "Yeah, so?"

"You like being around… us." Jonah tripped over saying *me*. "We're your age and you can be yourself."

That caused Kevin to laugh. "I can be myself around the Alliance people, Jonah."

"No you can't. They're all older than you." Kevin started to shrug again and Jonah shoved the boy. "If the Alliance thought you were too close to our ages, why'd they let you come to Mount Vernon in the first place?"

Kevin's jaw worked for a moment. "That's a long story."

"We're connected." Jonah's voice cracked on the last word despite his intent to sound sure of himself. "I know it."

Kevin had been slouching against the wall. He pulled himself into a more upright position and leaned close to Jonah. "Does it bother you?"

"What? Being connected?"

"No." Kevin nodded toward Mike.

Jonah's eyes widened. "Mike's my buddy. I don't care who he dates."

Kevin laughed. "That's not what I mean. Mike's the one who took the mind boost and opened the doorway. He's the center of attention, not you."

Jonah glared at Kevin, knowing the boy hadn't meant that at all or had been vague on purpose, testing him. Either way, it irritated him. "I don't like being the center of attention."

"Yeah, but you are. Well, at least most of the time." Kevin laughed again.

Jonah decided to let that go and stay on topic. "I wasn't lying about the other thing. Mike's still my friend."

Kevin huffed, causing Jonah to wonder about the older boy's true feelings on the subject. He nudged Kevin's hand and asked, "Does it bother you?"

"Seriously? With all the things I've seen and we know." Kevin waved off the notion. "I'm cool."

Before Jonah could press Kevin more, the Fallen Reaper held up his hand and cocked his head to the side, listening. "Someone's coming." Kevin snapped his fingers to get Mike's attention. "You can talk to your boyfriend later."

Mike's oatmeal face went dark red. He cast an accusatory glare at Jonah.

Jonah held up his hands. "I didn't say anything."

"Quiet." Kevin motioned Mike to the back wall with Jonah. Once they were in place, Kevin positioned himself in front of the cell door, hands at his sides.

The quiet footsteps stopped right outside. A second later, the lock clicked and the door hissed open.

Marcus and Trueblood stood outside the cell with two guards, though not the same guards who had put the boys in the cell.

Jonah scrambled to his feet and ran to greet his godfather.

Marcus didn't even try to hide his relieved grin. "We thought you might need rescuing."

Jonah nodded and then pointed at the cell wall. "Trevor's in the next cell."

"We know."

At that moment, Trevor stepped into view. Mike gasped and moved past Jonah to see his friend. The courier had several cuts, a swollen black eye, and other bruises on his face as well as dark blood stains on his grey tunic.

"I thought they didn't …" Mike couldn't finish.

"This?" Trevor winced as he motioned at himself. "The Guardians were having a little fun with the traitor, that's all."

One of the new guards passed over a bundle that turned out to be tunics like the ones Jonah and the others already wore, except these had hoods.

Kevin glared at the man as he took one. "Why do we have to wear these?"

"You need to blend in." The guard motioned for them to change. Once they were done, the man turned to Trevor and said in a respectful tone, "Courier, we should leave now. Our diversion won't last forever."

The guards waited for Trevor's decision, impressing Jonah with the deference they showed the boy.

Trevor slipped on his tunic and then helped Mike. He gazed into Mike's eyes when he finished. "If anyone deserves to wear these garments, it's you."

Jonah resisted snorting, thinking the boy was trying to score points.

Trevor gave Mike a respectful nod and then turned to the guards. "He's a true Seeker. The first in over two thousand years."

The guards gazed at Mike in wonder and then executed respectful bows to him.

Trevor nodded. "Lead the way."

Mike grabbed Trevor's wrist. "Where?"

"To get your Seeker's compass."

CHAPTER THIRTY-SIX
HERETICS, HALF-BREED, MORTALS

The reality of the jail break began to settle over Jonah, putting his nerves on edge. He couldn't resist worrying they would be caught at every turn. However, they were able to reach the transport alcove without trouble.

The entire group was too large to fit inside. Marcus joined one of the guards, Trevor, and Mike on the platform. The guard pressed the appropriate button and the group disappeared.

The remaining guard presented Jonah and Kevin with their confiscated blades before stepping onto the platform.

"Thanks." Jonah nodded.

Kevin took his blades and motioned Jonah into the alcove. He and Trueblood positioned themselves so that Jonah was behind them and with the alcove wall at his back.

A second later, bright sunlight hit Jonah's eyes, forcing him to shield his face. The source of the illumination was a set of large windows just across the hallway. Marcus stood there, little more than a dark silhouette, looking out the window.

The striking image reminded Jonah that his godfather had been Archivist or Guardian. He wondered what emotions Marcus experienced now.

Trevor and Mike waited a few feet away. When Jonah and his group stepped from the alcove, Trevor made a hand signal to the guard. The man took the lead position and they started down the hallway.

Kevin remained at Jonah's side, and that reassured him as their group ventured further into the Spire. After negotiating the fourth hallway without trouble, Jonah grew impatient. "Where are we going?"

Marcus glanced back. "The Grand Oracle is moving his entire repository to a more secure location underground. We plan to intercept it and take the compass."

"Oh. Okay." Jonah could think of only one way to do that. "Are we gonna attack?"

"No." The lead guard spoke while keeping his attention on the way ahead. "You'll pose as low-level Inquirers who've come to inspect and record the items. It's part of my responsibilities to escort new Inquirers around the Spire, after all." The man paused at the next junction and tapped the blue sash that he'd slipped on. "I'm part of the Spire Guardian Corps."

Two grey-robed Archivists approached their group. The men bowed to them as they passed. When they were out of earshot, Trevor turned to Jonah. "You have to understand. Once we do this, my friends will be exposed." He motioned and the group continued on.

Jonah followed Trevor, growing more uncomfortable but keeping his thoughts to himself.

The lead guard glanced back and spoke in a quiet voice that wouldn't carry far in the hallway. "Do you understand, young one? We can never go back. Our ranks will be forfeited and we'll forever be traitors and heretics."

"That is until the Rulers of the Afterworld are overthrown." Trevor balled his right hand into a fist. "That's the whole point of the Rebellion."

Marcus spoke into the uncomfortable silence that enveloped the group. "I appreciate how difficult it must be for you. Accepting that everything you've prepared for is finally upon you is hard."

Glancing at Marcus, Trevor asked, "Is that how you felt, before you fell?"

Marcus stroked his own chin, thinking about his answer. "Yes. I was fearful."

Trevor bowed his head, deep in thought. But he spoke in a hushed voice. "When Jonah used the ring, the Elder knew he was the Deliverer. The rebellion couldn't hide behind cryptic comments and prophecies anymore."

The courier sucked in a deep breath and continued. "Our own fears and doubts had to be put aside in order to make the hard decisions." He paused by a window and peered out, forcing the others to stop.

Jonah saw a strange otherness come over the boy's features, the same thing that happened to Kevin at odd moments.

Mike slipped a hand into Trevor's. The courier glanced down at their clasped hands and smiled to Mike before turning to the others. "The Elder planned for nearly two thousand years. Today, we're required to take action." He gave Mike's hand a squeeze, collected himself, and started forward again.

Despite Trevor sounding surer of himself, Jonah could sense the increased apprehension in their group. He also thought the courier's little speech sounded too final.

The lead guard signaled for the group to halt while he inched forward to peer around the next corner. "The way is clear, Courier." The man wore a grim expression. "The halls are too quiet for my liking."

Trevor nodded. "What about the door?"

"Nothing. The security must be inside the chamber."

Trevor's own face was a somber mask now. He inclined his head to the rear guard. "I'll meet you and the others at the rally point."

Marcus gasped. "The rally point?"

"You've been there?"

Marcus pulled a frown. "Yes and we can't phase there. It's protected against that."

"Of course." The guard smiled. "You'll need a ship." He bowed to Trevor. "May the Deliverer quicken your steps, Courier."

Trevor raised his right hand, palm forward. "Deliverer's speed to you."

Jonah marveled at the formal parting, thinking it cool, but it also filled him with misgivings. He couldn't quicken anyone's steps, no matter how much they invoked his name. They made him out to be something special. Like he was godlike.

The lead guard stood tall and gathered all the dignity his soon-to-be-forfeited rank provided him. The change in the man was amazing to witness and spoke of all he would lose within the next few minutes.

The further display of faith for their cause and the willingness to sacrifice their lives touched Jonah. A snatch of conversation between Marcus and Uncle James came back to him. Uncle James, while researching a book he wanted to write about the Civil Rights struggle, had engaged Marcus in a deep discussion.

The reason was obvious. Marcus displayed detailed knowledge about the historic era. Jonah suspected his godfather's first life had occurred back then. The discussion with Uncle James turned to the issue of an event versus a movement. Jonah recalled his godfather's total conviction when he described the difference.

An event, according to Marcus, was just that, a moment in time. But a movement was about sacrifice. Jonah stared at the backs of the Spire Guardian and Trevor. They represented a movement and were willing to sacrifice everything for the cause. They'd been at it for a long time, waiting for…

Me. Jonah swallowed past the sudden lump in his throat.

Kevin leaned against him. "You okay?"

Jonah nodded, afraid to say anything.

"Follow me and keep your hoods up." The Guardian strode around the corner as if he owned the place.

Jonah and the others did as he said and followed. When they reached the closed door, Trevor patted Mike's forearm and motioned him back. But Mike refused to leave his side.

Marcus gripped Mike by the arm and forced him to stand beside Jonah. "Trevor needs to be free to act. You and Jonah stay between us, got it?"

Mike's resistance wilted and his face reddened at Marcus's sharp tone. "Yes, sir."

Once Trevor nodded they were ready, the guard pressed his palm against the glowing panel beside the door. It hissed open.

Stacks of the square crystal containers from the Grand Oracle's repository had been loaded onto flat hover dollies and left in the middle of the space. There were other containers around the outer wall, all labeled and numbered. Other than that, the bay was empty.

A warning pricked Jonah's Death Sense as he searched the dollies, looking for the compass.

Mike tapped his arm. "It's on the second dolly."

"How do you know?"

Kevin hissed for them to keep quiet.

Trevor threw back his hood and scanned the deserted space. "This is odd."

"It's a trap," Marcus agreed. "We can't go back now." He gazed at the boxes. "I wonder if the compass is even here."

"It is." Mike rushed to the second dolly and opened a small container that reminded Jonah of Robert's Seeker's archive box. Mike reached inside and withdrew the compass.

Jonah's Death Sense spiked at the same time the door to the bay opened.

Everyone turned in that direction. The Grand Oracle marched through the door with confident, unhurried strides. At least twenty Spire Guardians fanned out behind him. The worst part for Jonah was Ramsey's smug smile as the man walked just behind and to the side of the Grand Oracle.

Shadows streaked across the floor, drawing Jonah's gaze toward the skylights. Four tear-drop ships hovered outside, weapons visible on the otherwise sleek hulls.

"It seems you were right, Hunter Ramsey." The Grand Oracle's voice was like sharp steel. It filled the space even though he didn't shout.

The dangerous being came to a stop and his Guardians fanned out in a semi-circle, blades drawn. The Grand Oracle's slate blue eyes narrowed as he peered at each member of Jonah's group.

"Heretics. Mortals." The Grand Oracle's gaze stopped on Jonah. "And the half-breed."

Jonah's stomach churned. The man's use of the term was a thousand times worst than Ramsey's.

Trevor activated his blades and stepped in front of Jonah's group. Kevin was only a second behind. When Marcus moved to join them, Ramsey detached himself from the Guardian's group and moved off to the side and activated his blades. Marcus adjusted his own position in order to block any attempt by Ramsey to get at Jonah.

A Spire Guardian with golden thread bordering his blue sash, tried to plant himself between Kevin, Trevor, and his Master.

The Grand Oracle barked at the man. "Move aside, Captain. Leave the traitors to me." The Grand Oracle had his own blades, ancient looking with a dull silver color and Angel script covering every inch.

As the Guardian Captain moved aside, the Grand Oracle raised his weapons in acknowledgement of Trevor and Kevin.

Trevor blurred into motion and attacked. The Grand Oracle wasn't flashy, but his movements were quick for an ancient-looking man. He blocked every tactic Trevor tried. When Kevin ran forward to help, the Grand Oracle raised one hand and shot a spell that smacked into Kevin's raised blades. The blocking spell that Jonah had seen others use had no effect and Kevin was knocked aside.

Ramsey blurred into his attack, but Marcus was ready. He and Ramsey whirled and fought in the common cadence of blurred motion and sudden stops that characterized the Fallen fighting style.

The rebel Guardian and Trueblood worked in a tandem, holding back the other Spire Guardians. Jonah pulled out Lynn's blades and motioned Mike back against the dollies.

Trueblood almost lost her concentration when she saw him step forward. "Jonah…"

"I can fight." As if to test Jonah's point, a Guardian slipped between the mage's barrage of supernatural fire and spells.

Jonah slipped into defensive moves, blocking every thrust and swipe of the Guardian's blades. He couldn't be sure, but the man seemed surprised that he was so capable.

That shock proved the guard's undoing because Trueblood nailed him with a spell.

The man dropped to the ground and didn't move. Jonah whirled, blades ready to hold off any others. He wasn't prepared to see the Grand Oracle grab Trevor by the wrist and whirl the boy across the floor. Kevin regained his feet and charged the Grand Oracle while doing a better job of blocking spells with swipes of his blades.

Jonah thought his friend would actually succeed in reaching the Grand Oracle until the man lifted Kevin off the ground without touching him. Jonah winced in sympathy as Kevin struggled in the obviously painful grip.

"Guardians!" Trevor yelled.

Four of the enemy Spire Guardians reversed sides and attacked their own people. Using the momentary confusion to his advantage, the rebel Guardian in Jonah's group pulled two silver orbs from his tunic and heaved them into the air. The devices continued upward and attached to the ceiling high above.

Meanwhile, Trevor rushed the Grand Oracle, forcing the man to release Kevin and defend himself. At the same time, the silver orbs exploded overhead, sending huge sections of the bay ceiling crashing to the ground. Trevor blurred into motion and snatched Kevin to the side as the debris rained down on the Grand Oracle and a couple of his Guardians.

Ramsey lost his focus. "Master!"

Marcus scored two cuts across the man's chest before the agent phased to the opposite side of the pile of rubble and out of reach.

The debris pile moved and heaved upward to reveal the Grand Oracle. He was untouched and protected behind a powerful shield. He showed no concern for the broken bodies of his dead Spire Guardians in the rubble.

With a roar of anger, the Grand Oracle pushed his shield outward, sending the debris flying in every direction. A huge chunk headed straight for Jonah and Mike. The boys dived in different directions to avoid it. Trueblood used a charm at the last minute to turn the chunk of metal into a brittle material.

It impacted between Jonah and Mike and produced a cloud of fine dust. Mike staggered out of the cloud, clutching the compass.

The Grand Oracle noticed. "Never!" He shot a bolt of supernatural lightning at Mike.

Trevor shouted and charged forward, a blade in one hand and another silver orb in the other. He tried to deflect the lightning with the blade, but the volley was too powerful. The lightning struck the right side of Trevor's chest and heaved the boy up and across the floor.

He landed a few feet away from Kevin and Marcus. The silver orb tumbled free of Trevor's slack grip as the boy convulsed with painful spasms. Mike shouted and darted toward him.

Jonah did the same but his body blurred into motion and the next second, he knelt over the courier. He choked at the sight of the large burn mark on the boy's chest.

Trevor gripped Jonah's arm. "Where's Mike?" His voice was full of pain and his breathing labored.

Mike crowded in beside Jonah. "I'm here."

Trevor's gaze shifted. "I couldn't let you die. You have to… survive. Seeker."

"No, no, no." Mike repeated the word in a hushed voice.

The Grand Oracle watched with a sneer on his face. "Your Master, the so-called Elder, was foolish to trust in one so young." He raised his hands, gathering power to strike again. "You'll discover what happens to those who oppose the Rulers of the Afterworld."

CHAPTER THIRTY-SEVEN
SACRIFICE

Energy coursed around the Grand Oracle's fingertips as the powerful creature prepared to fry Jonah and his group. Trevor fastened onto his wrist and Jonah sucked in a startled breath as the shield bracelet activated, launching a blue distortion into existence around him and the others.

The Grand Oracle sneered. "That pathetic shield won't protect you heretics." He lit up the barrier with an impressive volley of supernatural lightning. The protective bubble held, despite several cracks that suddenly appeared. The force of the attack shook Jonah's arm.

Trevor pulled Jonah almost to the floor, forcing him to twist his body just to keep his left arm up and the shield activated

"The Elder..." Trevor's words were almost too low to hear and garbled because of the blood dripping from the corner of his mouth. "Get... to... him."

"I don't know where he is." Jonah faltered just as the world around them went crimson.

The Grand Oracle changed from lightning to red flames. The cracks in the shield widened even further under the new assault and the pressure shook Jonah's left arm even more mercilessly.

Trevor worked his mouth. "Take my power and knowledge."

Jonah tried to pull free. "I can't."

"What are you saying?" Mike looked appalled.

"It's the only way." Trevor pressed Jonah's right hand against his burned tunic, just above his heart. "Take it, Jonah."

"What about your soul?"

Trevor released his grip and fumbled with an intact portion of his tunic. His trembling hand pulled out one of the ornate, little bottles. "Hold it in here and take it to the Elder." When Jonah leaned back, cold steel entered Trevor's voice. "Do… it." The boy gestured to the silver orb bomb. It wobbled on the floor outside the shield, instantly forgotten by the Grand Oracle.

Trevor shook Jonah. "You don't have much time."

Jonah knew he didn't have any choice. His arm vibrated so much that his teeth began to clack together.

Trueblood pressed her hand over his, adding her own power to the shield. "Hurry, Jonah."

It was rare for the mage to use his first name and only highlighted her seriousness.

The heat of the assault had already warmed the inside of the shield, making their breaths ragged, and now threatened to suffocate them. If the shield did fail, the Grand Oracle would surely roast them all.

Jonah exchanged a frightened look with his godfather, then with Mike.

"Don't do it," Mike urged, his voice full of shock and hurt.

Jonah closed his eyes. Wetness touched his cheeks, but he ignored the tears and dug his hands into the fabric of Trevor's tunic, calling on his power.

At once, his Reaper half responded and Trevor's power and remaining life force flowed into his hands. Mike continued to yell behind him, but a sudden silence in the room caused Jonah to open his eyes.

The Grand Oracle looked appalled. His Guardians backed away, undisguised fear etched on each of their faces. The sight of them spurred Jonah on and he pulled every ounce of power from Trevor. Even near death, the boy retained a tremendous amount of energy.

Strength surged into Jonah and his mind opened up to a shocking truth as he touched the boy's soul. He could obtain knowledge from a person as well! At the same time, knowing that sickened Jonah; because it made him little better than the Grand Oracle.

The last of Trevor's life force flowed into Jonah and a golden light erupted around the boy's body, forcing Jonah to cover his eyes. The light felt warm and gentle against his skin. He peeked between his fingers and watched, becoming entranced as the glowing light collapsed on itself until all that remained was a brilliant pinpoint of soul energy.

Everyone watched the soul as it began to rise into the air. Jonah reached out a hand and the soul stopped and bobbed closer to him. He held out the bottle. Like a moth drawn to a flame, the soul jerked into motion and flowed into the container. The sigils carved into the sides flared with rich, golden light. Jonah replaced the stopper, mentally noting how warm the bottle was to the touch, along with its steady heartbeat.

After slipping the soul bottle into a pocket, Jonah stood.

The Grand Oracle's mouth twisted in disgust. "You're an abomination!"

Several of his Guardians dropped their blades to the ground in horror. Some began to mutter in shocked voices, "The Deliverer."

When a Guardian tried to flee, The Grand Oracle enveloped the man with a volley of lightning. Whirling on another who had also dropped his blades, he killed that guard on the spot with another bolt of lightning.

"The boy is not a god and therefore, he can't be a Deliverer." The Grand Oracle glared at his own men. "I'll prove it by killing him."

The dangerous being fired lightning, but Jonah reactivated the shield and used his augmented powers to strengthen it. He also sent the barrier surging forward. The Grand Oracle crossed his arms while muttering a spell. The barrier passed harmlessly over him, knocking his remaining Spire Guardians against the back wall, where they slumped to the floor, dazed.

The Grand Oracle retaliated with red flames. Jonah called on the wind, summoning it through the broken skylights to produce a blast. He succeeded in stopping the flames only a few feet away from his group. Gritting his teeth, he managed to push them back for a moment, but the flames still advanced.

"Jonah…" Marcus whispered.

"I know." Jonah never expected to hold out, even with the extra power. "Kevin."

He flicked his chin up. Kevin glanced that way and nodded. He gripped Jonah and Mike by their tunics. Marcus did the same for Trueblood, their helpful Guardian, and a surviving rebel.

The flames inched ever closer, coming to within a foot, where they began to blister Jonah's face. He shifted, using a gust of wind to push the flames into the remaining overhead skylights. Shards of crystal rained down. The blast of redirected fire caught one of the hovering crafts in the side. The ship spun away, trailing smoke as it slipped out of sight.

Jonah sucked in a breath, ignoring the chaos and clamor. "Now!"

The ripples played along his arms as Kevin phased them out of the chamber. They reappeared on top of one of the remaining armored craft that hovered outside the Central Spire. Marcus, Trueblood, and the rebel Guardians reappeared atop a second craft.

The movement alerted the pilot below Jonah, and the craft shifted into a tight spiral, moving away from the tower. The ships were large, but the hulls were curved and sleek, making it hard to stay in place. Mike yelped, lost his footing, and slipped. Kevin grabbed his arm and hauled him back.

"Sorry." Mike scrambled wrapped his arms around Jonah's arm.

Jonah was torn between his terror of sliding loose and dropping to his death, and the sheer wonder of the spectacular view of the Central Archives complex spinning below him. Mike let out a startled breath and clutched Jonah's arm even tighter.

The pilot's maneuver saved their lives because seconds later, a huge explosion blew a large hole in the Central Spire. Even so, the craft bucked hard when the pilot strove to establish more distance from the bellowing plume of smoke and debris.

Jonah lost his own grip and tumbled free, Mike with him. Kevin pushed off and grabbed both boys by the arm and phasing them safely to the huge public square far below.

Since phasing happened in a split second, they appeared in the square before the falling bits of Spire could even reach the ground. Jonah and the others stared in horror as debris smashed all around them, injuring several innocent people and creating panic and bedlam.

When Marcus appeared with Trueblood, the mage had the presence of mind to zap a huge chunk of wall with a spell before it slammed onto a huddled crowd of people. The spell transformed the debris into a powdery dust that merely coated the hapless bystanders. *At least they weren't killed*, Jonah thought.

Amid the screams of pain and shock, many people were pointing skyward at the huge plume of smoke now streaming from the windows of the upper section of the Central Spire.

Mike nudged Jonah. "Do you think the Grand Oracle is…?"

"Let's move," Marcus cut in. He motioned toward the nearer of two immense, curved colonnades.

Jonah was struck by how similar this space was to the pictures he once saw of St. Peter's Square. The colonnades all featured walls with three huge mosaics. He gasped because they were also very similar to the vistas they observed in the Deliverer's portal.

He opened his mouth to ask about the mosaics just as flashes of weaponry fire from a dogfight high overhead drew everyone's attention. One heavy-duty tear-ship fired on the others and led them away.

Kevin cheered. "Way to go!" He herded Jonah and Mike under the cover of the colonnade.

"What?" Jonah asked before registering that Marcus didn't bring the rebel Spire Guardians when he phased. He gazed at the retreating crafts. "They stole one of the ships?"

"Yep. A diversion," Kevin said, pushing through the bewildered crowd. "They'll try to come back and get us."

Jonah was about to point out that wasn't likely when Spire Guardians charged them from both directions, shoving people out of their way.

Marcus pointed at a large, two-tier craft with an open-air, upper deck. It was crowded with frantic people, each one trying to escape the chaos.

Jonah's godfather phased Trueblood and himself to the top deck of the vehicle as it rose into the air. Jonah,

Mike, and Kevin followed. The upper deck was truly open. It didn't have seats, just guardrails around the sides and a central, waist-high rail to lean against.

The archivists on board were startled at their appearance, but soon cleared a space around Jonah's group. Ramsey's arrival, however, produced a stampede of citizens to the lower deck. The agent's grey robes were burnt away in places and the side of his face was dripping blood. Ramsey ignored the people streaming past him as he zeroed in on Jonah with slices of his blades. Jonah was able to dodge them easily until he lost his footing and landed on his butt in a sprawl.

Ramsey attempted to skewer him with a blade, but Kevin leapt over Jonah and stopped the agent. With his own blade locked against Ramsey's, Kevin twisted his weapon and succeeded in disarming the man. It thudded onto the vehicle's hull. Before Ramsey could regain his weapon, Kevin kicked the man in the chest and sent him tumbling over the railing.

Two more Guardians were engaging Marcus. He whirled and sliced at one. When he ducked a swing from the second, Trueblood hit the man dead center with a blast of green flame. The Guardian fell over the edge, his arms pinwheeling as he plummeted helplessly to the ground.

Marcus took down the remaining attacker with a cut across the man's chest. A third Guardian appeared right behind Mike and grabbed him in a bear hug. Mike crouched in a defensive move and flipped the surprised attacker over his head.

Jonah shouted, "Sakoto!" Calling on the wind was easier for him in this situation. All he had to do was augment the existing slipstream. The result was a hard blast that sent the last Guardian off the back of their craft.

Marcus winked at Jonah. "Good move, but we need to get clear and find our own ship. I don't think the rebels are coming back for us. Mike, do you remember any codes we can use?"

Mike nodded and yanked the compass free of a pocket just as another Guardian appeared almost on top of him. The attacker grabbed hold of Mike before Marcus or Kevin could react. The sudden action smashed Mike against the railing and knocked the compass free of his hand, sending the device over the side of the vehicle.

Trueblood raised her hand. "Duck!" Mike stomped on the Guardian's foot and slipped free. Trueblood nailed the man in the face with a stunning spell.

Jonah shot forward to grip Mike by the tunic and pull him away from the railing just as the stunned attacker tumbled over and out of sight.

Mike broke free of Jonah and hurried to the railing to look over the side. After a moment he dropped to his knees and exclaimed, "The compass is gone!"

CHAPTER THIRTY-EIGHT
SEEKER'S COMPASS

Jonah searched the Central Complex square below, but it was in vain, and he wanted to scream. The compass was gone. All their fighting and Trevor's sacrifice had been for nothing.

Marcus tapped his arm. "Watch, Jonah." He indicated Trueblood with a tilt of his chin.

The mage had her right hand extended as she muttered a spell. Her long ponytail whipped behind her in the wind. Marcus shook Jonah and pointed.

He blinked with surprise when something grew larger and began to approach their vehicle at a fast rate. He jumped to his feet when he realized it was the compass. Zooming past him and Mike, it landed on Trueblood's outstretched hand.

The mage handed it to Mike.

He took the compass, gazing into her face with awe. "Thanks."

"You're welcome."

Jonah's Death Sense, which had remained on constant throbbing warning, spiked when several heavy-duty ships set off in pursuit. They emerged from an opening high up in the outer wall. *A hangar bay*, Jonah thought. The knowledge from Trevor's mind produced images of the location in his head. *Ships! Just what we need.*

Jonah turned to his godfather. "Marcus–" The vehicle bucked beneath Jonah and slowed.

Mike had to clutch the compass with both hands so he didn't drop the device over the edge again.

Jonah's godfather reached out to steady Mike. "They must have ordered this craft to stop."

"Easier to shoot us." Kevin pointed toward the approaching craft. Pinpoints of light flashed on the lower hulls of the ships as they fired.

"Are you serous?" Jonah had his answer when the enemy shots peppered the top of the craft. Trueblood threw up a shield to protect them, but the muffled cries from below meant the rest of the passengers weren't so lucky. The enemy ships zoomed overhead and began to circle around like vultures.

The mage's normal solemn voice was tinged with fury when she rasped, "Those beasts! They'll kill everyone on board just to get us."

Jonah shared her outrage because he felt responsible. He was, after all, the target of all their shots. "We need to get off this thing."

"Unfortunately," Marcus said, his voice taut with anger, "most of the places I know are either shielded against phasing, or full of innocents." His jaw tightened, watching the ships approaching. "I won't endanger anymore people."

"I have an idea," Kevin and Jonah shouted at the same time. But Kevin was faster and gripped Jonah and Mike by their arms and phased before the ships could fire again. They appeared atop a curved building very near the base of the Central Spire. Marcus and Trueblood materialized beside them.

The vehicle they escaped from took a few more hits, but the attackers flew by, their crafts growing larger in size as they zeroed in on Jonah's group. He didn't know how the enemy pilots managed to guess where they were.

Then, a different craft, circling high overhead, zoomed downward and began firing at them. *A spotter*, Jonah decided as the rooftop exploded around them.

Kevin sprinted across the roof, keeping his grasp on Jonah and Mike. He phased again, just as the initial two attackers drew close enough to add their fire to the onslaught that was wreaking destruction on the building. Marcus matched his moves.

They reappeared on the adjacent rooftop. It was one of six rows of curved buildings, *that were similar to the Pentagon's ring corridors*, Jonah thought. He didn't have any time for more sightseeing because they had to keep phasing to avoid enemy fire. Judging from the increasing damage to the buildings, the shooters didn't seem to care about the people inside there, either.

Perhaps Marcus came to the same conclusion because he called out to Jonah, "We need to use the compass."

Jonah didn't agree. For one thing, every time they tried, they had to phase again just to avoid the barrage of fire and explosions. Plus, he had a plan.

As if proving his point, Kevin growled in frustration and phase three more times in quick succession, and had to hop across five of the buildings. The enemy crafts broke off to circle around for another attack run.

Jonah knew they only had seconds to put his idea into motion. He shouted to his godfather, "I know where to get a ship! Follow me." He grabbed a handful of Mike's tunic and phased.

He and Mike reappeared in a hangar bay full of the teardrop ships. Kevin, Marcus, and Trueblood also appeared within a second. The startled pilots and bay crew could only gape with astonishment at them.

Jonah knew the Guardians would follow once someone reported their location. He didn't waste any time and ducked under the nearest ships. Sure enough, he felt the telltale shift in air pressure as their pursuers instantly appeared in the bay.

"Where are you going?" Kevin's voice was curious as he followed close behind.

"Where do you think? The Guardian said we needed a ship." Jonah continued the mad dash under three more crafts before he stopped to clamber up the ladder of an open one.

Kevin grabbed the back of Jonah's tunic to stop him. "Yeah, but that's too small. And how did you know to come here?"

"I got some of Trevor's memories when I touched his soul."

Marcus frowned while Kevin looked unnerved.

Trueblood didn't say anything as she produced a shield to protect them from enemy fire.

Mike's face paled, but he remained focused and pointed to a bulkier craft off to the right. "Try that one."

Jonah maneuvered to the ship Mike selected. Unlike the sleek, tear-shaped ships, this craft had an oblong, flat-topped cargo hull, complete with side hatch. Kevin opened it like he'd done it a hundred times before and waved Jonah and Mike inside first.

The ship's cockpit contained only two seats while the forward cargo section had four facing seats. Rushing to the front, Jonah dropped into what he assumed was the pilot seat. Mike came in beside him, breathing hard and looking paler than normal.

Kevin crowded in behind. "Jonah, you don't know how to fly."

"No, but Mike does."

"That's a single-prop," Mike sputtered, sitting forward, "not something like this."

"Relax." Jonah cracked a smile at his friends. He felt unusually confident despite their situation. "Trevor knew how to fly."

As Mike and Kevin gawked at him, Jonah immersed himself in the strange new knowledge, allowing the information to guide his hands. He pressed a certain spot on the clear glass panel and the whole thing lit up with blinking, multicolored displays.

Touching a different glowing readout resulted in the ship sealing itself. Something thunked against the outside and clattered to the ground.

"It's the Guardians, trying to get in," Marcus said. "Stay focused, Jonah. We are safe, but don't dawdle."

More Guardians pounded on the hull, but Jonah followed his godfather's calm instructions. He concentrated, placing his hands over the touch-sensitive controls as he delved into Trevor's memories again. *That's it*, Jonah said to himself, activating the ship. It lifted off the deck, accompanied by startled yells and heavy thuds as the shocked people slid off the hull.

Pressing another control, Jonah sent the craft forward while activating its simple gun. In a way, it reminded him of one of the video games he often played with Robert. Jonah fingered the control, getting the feel of it while peering at the targeting display now splashed across the lower left of the viewport.

Two of the attack ships lumbered into view just outside the hangar bay doors.

Mike pressed himself back into his seat. "Jonah?"

"I see them." He targeted the engine of the enemy on the left and fired. Their own ship rumbled at the release of the brilliant orbs of plasma fire. Jonah's aim was true and the craft took a direct hit to its engine. The craft jerked sideways, opening the gap between the ships. Jonah angled skillfully between the attackers and out of the open hangar bay door.

Kevin gripped the backs of both chairs to keep from tumbling into the rear section. Jonah didn't have time to see if Marcus and Trueblood were strapped in.

His heart pounded like crazy in his chest. If he stopped to consider he shouldn't have known how to do that, they would surely have been in trouble. His hands shook, which was unfortunate owing to the sensitivity of the controls. The ship responded by almost flipping over in mid-air.

"Sorry about that." Jonah forced himself to relax as he sent the ship straight up, pressing everyone further into their seats. Distant thuds sounded, followed by a violent bucking.

Mike crossed his arms while scanning the console readouts.

Jonah began to wonder if his buddy could actually read the screens. "Mike?"

Mike shook his head, keeping his attention fastened on the controls.

Jonah turned to the front viewport, or rather, the portion of the hull that became transparent when the ship sealed itself. The craft was slipping through the wispy clouds toward, what Jonah assumed was, an opening at the top of the complex. He could see bright sky and clouds. In fact, he wondered why more ships weren't coming in and going out this way instead of using the massive entryway below.

"Jonah?" Kevin tapped him on the top of his head. "You can't get out that way because..."

Within seconds, projectiles impacted the invisible barrier above.

"There's a shield, smart guy."

"I didn't know."

Kevin shoved his head. "I thought you had Trevor's memories."

Jonah ignored the barb as he took the ship into a wrenching sideways turn. Mike gripped his armrests, and Kevin hung onto the seat for dear life.

The ship came around, and Jonah dived down along the central tower. When the hostile fire began to ping against the ship again, he leveled out, barreling toward the entryway. That wouldn't work either. Even from this distance, he could make out the rows of heavier ships waiting, and virtually blocking the exit.

"I understand the controls," Mike said. He tapped the console. A smaller window blossomed on the forward view screen, and Mike and Jonah sucked in simultaneous breaths. "He's alive and waiting."

The Grand Oracle stood on a floating platform, the ranks of Guardians behind him. His robes were frayed and blackened from the explosion and his silver-grey hair stuck like spikes out around his head. As they watched, he raised both hands and the air around him began to distort. Pinpoints of amber light appeared on the gun ports of the surrounding vessels.

Jonah pressed his eyes closed, shifting through Trevor's knowledge for a way to escape. "I know the location of the rally point."

Marcus crowded forward to see outside. "Jonah, I know the location too, but we can't get through the Grand Oracle's blockade."

"Yes, we can." Jonah smiled up at his godfather. "The rally point has a code. The Elder showed Trevor before he crossed over."

Mike held up the compass. "Tell me the code." He didn't look at Jonah and his voice sounded tight and tense.

Jonah nodded and did as Mike asked.

Kevin snorted. "You think the compass can move the whole ship?"

"Yes I do," Mike acknowledged. "Just like it moved that platform. But we need to attach it to something."

Kevin activated his blade and plunged it into a thin air vent. He twisted the blade to widen the opening. Then he took the compass from Mike and wedged it into the space. "There you go."

Mike frowned. "That's crude."

Kevin shrugged. "Sue me."

Mike manipulated the compass dials. His eyes began to glow as a display appeared around the compass. The 3D versions of the symbols in Trevor's address were highlighted. The green *activate* button on the compass pulsed in readiness.

Marcus sighed a relieved breath. "Let's get out of here."

Mike stiffened in his seat and pointed at a readout that began flashing red. "Something's coming up behind us, and fast."

A second later, a dull thud vibrated the hull and their momentum dropped. It was so sudden that Kevin flew forward, crashing against the console. Marcus and Trueblood let out simultaneous, muffled cries. It was like someone was yanking them from behind.

Jonah glanced at his friend. "Mike, what's happening?"

Mike stared at the readouts in disbelief. "Someone hooked onto this ship."

"Look!" Kevin pointed out the hull as he heaved himself off the console.

The air distorted around the Grand Oracle as the man weaved a huge spell, something Jonah hadn't seen so far.

Trueblood's voice was still calm, but tinged with concern. "You should get us out of here, Jonah. That's a powerful spell he's conjuring."

A huge distortion wave rushed toward their craft when the Grand Oracle released the spell. The many ships arrayed behind him expelled volleys of energy from their weapon ports. As the supernatural firestorm sped toward him, Jonah reached for the *activate* button.

The spell traveled faster than Jonah could anticipate, appearing around them in less than a second. The ship bucked so hard that Jonah banged his head against his side of the hull. Mike let out a startled grunt before landing on the side of Jonah's seat.

Kevin slid to the deck while Marcus and Trueblood were thrown into the back of the craft. The vibrations and jerking were horrifying, but Mike managed to pull himself into his chair while staring out the front. His mouth hung open in horror.

Jonah braced himself to keep from being flung into the hull again. He dived forward and jabbed the green activate button just as the maelstrom of destruction engulfed their ship.

CHAPTER THIRTY-NINE
RAMSEY'S LAST RIDE

The ship continued to buck and gyrate around Jonah and the others. A horrific grinding sound of something being torn loose came from below their feet. To their right, a control panel sparked and exploded. Mike yelped, being the closest to the damage.

Jonah waved the resulting vapors away to glance out the front. Roiling fire and super-heated currents continued to obscure the view for several more terrified moments. Just as he began to worry, an azure sky appeared and the warm rays of the sun touched his face.

Jonah sighed in relief as he checked their location. The Central Archives complex and the Grand Oracle had been replaced by a semi-forested area and a meandering river below. Jonah leaned back in the pilot's chair.

It was only now that an incessant beeping attracted his attention. The display around the compass flashed what was clearly a warning signal. With his head still dizzy from the heavy bump against the hull, Jonah couldn't concentrate enough to understand what it meant.

Mike, leaning far to his left to avoid the sparking hull panel, began working the controls. Jonah turned around in his seat to find Kevin and Marcus helping Trueblood to stand. She favored her left foot, so Marcus held on as they moved to the back seats.

Kevin must have also heard the beeping because he returned to the cockpit and leaned over the back of Mike's seat. "What's wrong?"

"That ship came through with us and it's…"

A screeching sound drowned out the rest of Mike's comment. An accompanying heavy vibration began at the back of their ship and continued to the front. That's when a smaller tear ship tumbled by, trailing smoke and fire. And it was still attached to their ship by a burning cable.

Jonah glanced at Kevin. "Can't you phase outside to the hull and cut the cable?"

"It's too late for that. Hold on." Kevin gripped the back of Mike's seat. The cable reached its maximum length and yanked their ship hard to the right before snapping. The smaller Guardian craft tumbled end over end and exploded in a sudden ball of expanding gas and fire.

"Oh my God." Jonah couldn't believe his eyes.

Beads of sweat broke out on Mike's forehead as he worked at the controls. Their own craft continued to buck and wobble despite his efforts.

"One of the engines was damaged." The certainty in Mike's voice and manipulations of the controls impressed Jonah. Whatever Mike did worked because the vibrations in the hull finally subsided. "I'm pulling back on the power to compensate. That should level us off. I think."

With the mind boost from the Enhancer, Jonah realized it was quicker for Mike to read the display than it was for him to call up Trevor's memories. Plus, Mike had taken flying lessons and Jonah imagined that all ships had certain things in common after all .

Mike brought the ship around so it was facing where they had come from. He set it into a swaying hover so Jonah and everyone else could watch the remains of the guardian ship dissipate and its debris float away on the wind.

Jonah settled into his seat again, rubbing his bruised head. "Thanks." Mike nodded without taking his eyes off the controls.

Although the annoying beeping had stopped, other lights still blinked. Jonah pointed at a large yellow one. "What's that?"

"Oh." Mike touched a control and the alarm stopped blinking. "We overshot the rally point." He met Jonah's gaze. "Should we head back?"

"No." Marcus came forward again. "Jonah, did Trevor know the location of the hidden base?"

Jonah closed his eyes, calling up Trevor's memories. "Yeah, but we need to change course a little." He told Mike the numbers that appeared in his head.

Mike frowned at him while entering the coordinates. "We should take it slow." He glanced at Marcus, who nodded. Mike sent their ship forward at a reduced speed. Finished with that detail, he leaned back in his seat and held out his left hand. "Give him to me."

Jonah needed a second to remember the soul bottle in his tunic pocket. With all their banging around, he was afraid the bottle might have been damaged. But when Jonah pulled the bottle from his pocket, it seemed fine. He handed over Trevor's spirit.

Mike pressed the bottle against his chest and closed his eyes. The spirit within flared brighter at the contact.

Jonah had the sudden feeling he was invading a private moment. So he turned to Kevin, who also averted his gaze to look out the front viewport.

Jonah tapped Kevin's hand. "Why not have the rally point at the hidden base?"

Kevin snorted. "That's too dangerous. What if the enemy discovered the location?"

Marcus nodded in agreement. "It's safer to have the rally point at a distance. That way the rebels have a checkpoint where they can clear anyone arriving. From there, they run people to the hidden base in ships. Only the pilots know the actual location."

"Oh." Jonah stared out the front viewport, thinking. "Hey. Wouldn't someone have seen us fly over?"

"Yes. That's why I told you to continue on." Marcus frowned. "I'm surprised they haven't–"

A dull thunk stopped Jonah's godfather in mid-sentence. The sound came from the rear compartment, followed by the screeching of metal. A warning light on the console began wailing.

Trueblood called out, "Marcus."

Jonah's godfather hurried into the back. Kevin followed, staring up at a blade sticking through the upper hull.

"What the…" Kevin muttered.

"It's a Guardian." Marcus drew his blades.

Jonah knew the real deal. "It's Ramsey." He hit Mike's armrest to get his attention. "Stop us."

Mike slipped Trevor's spirit bottle in a pocket and touched the ship's controls. The craft jerked and its forward momentum slowed to a bouncing hover. Something tumbled along the upper hull until two blades punctured the metal again, just behind the cockpit.

Jonah unstrapped himself and yanked the compass free of the air vent. He pulled out one of Lynn's blades and phased.

Despite the lack of forward movement, air buffeted Jonah's face as he appeared atop the bulky craft. Ramsey's burnt tunic flapped in the strong breeze. The agent pulled his blades from the hull and stood straight.

His face morphed into a rictus grin. "So, half-breed. You choose to face me instead of hiding behind the adults."

The frightful sight of Ramsey filled Jonah with rage instead of fear, and he charged the agent. Ramsey swung at him but Jonah expected that, blocked the man, and ducked under the blow.

The result was that Ramsey had his back to Kevin and Marcus, who had just phased outside the craft.

"Jonah, what are you doing?" Marcus called.

Jonah charged Ramsey again and shouted, "Sakoto!" The wind whipped at the man's feet and unbalanced him enough that Jonah tackled him. He had prepared for this moment. He was going to take Ramsey far away from the people he cared about. With that decision firmly in mind, he pressed the compass's activate button.

The next moment, Jonah and Ramsey reappeared at the rally point's destination platform, nestled inside a partial sandstone enclosure. The open side overlooked the base camp below.

Jonah had to focus on the immediate. He tried to dodge, but Ramsey's foot blurred into motion and caught him in the stomach.

Pain flared along Jonah's side as he flipped through the air and hit the ground outside the enclosure. He rolled to his feet to confront Ramsey, who was relentless and fast. Jonah called on his training and blocked most of the blows. That seemed to anger Ramsey, and he mixed in small phases, attacking from all sides and scoring more cuts and hits.

The cunning agent reappeared in a crouch to nick Jonah across the back of the leg. Jonah screamed and went down to one knee. He whirled, striking out with a blade, but Ramsey did another micro-phase. When he appeared behind Jonah, he lashed out with a boot to the back.

Jonah tumbled forward, losing a blade. He heaved and coughed up blood that splattered onto the light-colored stones beneath him. Ramsey attacked again before Jonah could regain his feet, scoring a stab to the left arm and numerous hits. The barrage ended with a power punch to the abdomen.

Jonah flew backward and landed in a heap, his remaining blade skittering across the stones and out of reach. The pain was unbearable, but Jonah was desperate now. In a last-ditch effort to escape, he clutched at the compass.

"No you don't, young Blackstone. You're not gonna use that compass." Ramsey lurched forward and yanked it away. A demented grin split the man's mangled face. "I will kill you and prove that you're not special. The entire Afterworld will know that Jonah Blackstone was not a Deliverer. He was just a pathetic half-breed."

Struggling to his knees, Jonah had to admit he didn't have any power left and he was physically done. And Lynn's blades were too far away. Despair threatened to overwhelm him, but he pushed it to the side. He'd successfully used the compass to keep the deranged agent away from the others. That's all that mattered now.

Ramsey nodded as if sensing Jonah's thoughts. "Yes, you're gonna die, young Blackstone. Don't worry; I'll take your broken body to your friends. And with me will be the full might of the Grand Oracle. This rally point and the hidden base will become smoking craters and all your friends here in the Afterworld will burn."

Ramsey loomed over Jonah, blade poised to strike. "When I return to the mortal world, I'll take care of the rest of your mortal family."

Jonah knew the man wasn't bragging. As the pain and mental anguish roared back with an oppressive zeal, something happened. Jonah's Reaper side surged forward and engulfed him in that calm inner space. Once that happened, the answer to his problem became clear.

He remained outwardly subdued as Ramsey stood behind him and grabbed a fistful of his hair. Bending Jonah's head back, the agent grinned in his face. "What are you gonna do, half-breed?"

Ramsey raised his blade, poised to drive it into Jonah's chest and through the heart.

But Jonah wasn't afraid. He was the Deliverer. His steady gaze met Ramsey's and in a moment of pure spite, Jonah mustered his best Obi-Wan voice. "If you strike me down, Darth, I shall become more powerful than you could possibly imagine."

Ramsey's confident stance faltered for the first time. "You are an abomination. Even a fool fears his own death." He scowled and brought his blade down, but it never connected.

Jonah had summoned his will and clamped his hands on Ramsey's blade-bearing hand to stop it. At first, the man tried to apply his full weight to drive the blade downward, but Jonah's Reaper powers surged forward, preventing that.

As soon as the Hunter's power begin to leak away, Ramsey understood the true danger and tried to release Jonah. "No. Impossible!"

Jonah held on, using the man's own power to strengthen himself. The blade slipped from Ramsey's hand and clattered on the stones. Jonah used the moment to flip Ramsey over and onto his back. Then he straddled the agent, pressed both hands against the man's chest, and began to suck every ounce of energy from him.

When Jonah spoke, the words that came to him weren't totally his own. They were the Deliverer's, as if the being spoke through him.

"You, the Grim Reaper, and the Grand Oracle have corrupted everything. It will end!" His last words shook the ground.

Ramsey gripped Jonah's hands, trying to pull free. But he was helpless as he aged before Jonah's eyes. "No!"

Ramsey's patterns, visible beneath the rips in the robe, vanished as the man aged twenty years. His normal chocolate complexion turned waxen in a few seconds. Jonah continued to pull until the spark of life that was the agent's soul began to flow toward his hands. His Reaper side wanted to take it.

A shadow zipped across the ground and stopped right overhead. Jonah dimly acknowledged that Mike had figured out where the compass had taken them. He remained focused on Ramsey even when Kevin and Marcus appeared on the platform and charged out of the partial enclosure.

The Fallen Reapers skidded to a halt half a dozen feet away, frozen in surprise.

"Jonah, stop!" Marcus inched closer but didn't move close enough to touch the boy. "You're not a killer like Ramsey."

Jonah didn't care. The Grim Reaper killed his parents. The mole had sent this dangerous man into Mount Vernon to threaten his friends. Lynn had been hurt, Mike tortured, and Trevor killed by the Grand Oracle.

"Agent Ramsey must go back and answer for his crimes," Marcus persisted.

"No." Jonah's voice was choked with rage and pain. "No."

Kevin knelt down to look Jonah in the eye. "What would Lynn say?"

The absurdity of the question momentarily broke through Jonah's fury. He glanced at the young Fallen Reaper.

Kevin returned the gaze. "Little man." He opened his emotions to Jonah and allowed his true feelings to show. His desire to protect Jonah, even from himself, surged forward.

Jonah's rage receded in the face of their mutual bond. When he met his godfather's worried gaze, all the things that Marcus had said to him at the hideaway registered. How would he use the incredible power he possessed?

The blinding hatred lifted and Jonah could think straight again. He resisted the urging of his Reaper nature and pulled his hands away from Ramsey's body.

Aside from sucking in a gagging breath, Ramsey didn't move. For a moment, Jonah feared he may have killed the man anyway. Then the agent's chest rose and fell, and Jonah relaxed. Ramsey wasn't dead, but he was totally mortal now.

CHAPTER FORTY
RALLY POINT

"Guardian vessel, identify yourself!" The challenging young female voice broke through the ship's speakers.

The rebels had noted their entry and the explosion of Ramsey's ship. No less than three armored rebel crafts had taken up positions around their own.

Mike watched the rebels dart around, seamlessly swapping positions and keeping the larger craft pinned in place. "Wow, they know how to fly."

That was as much as Jonah saw before he winced and huddled back on a bench in the rear section of the stolen craft, nursing his bruises and cuts. Trueblood offered to perform the Nistashi spell on him as soon as he boarded the craft, but he refused.

His healing process had been jump-started by taking Ramsey's power, but the man had inflicted serious damage. Kevin speculated it would take Jonah a couple of days of sleep to fully heal.

Ramsey lay on the floor against the back wall, cuffed and still unconscious. Kevin doubled-checked the restraints and then paused to set Lynn's retrieved blades beside Jonah. He hurried to the cockpit to drop into Jonah's vacant seat.

Jonah started to follow when Marcus got up, but his godfather gave him a look that was first furious and then sympathetic. "You should relax and let your body heal. I'll handle this."

"I'm okay." Jonah thought his voice sounded tired. He ached all over and smelled of dirt and otherworldly vegetation from his fight with Ramsey. Marcus crossed his arms and didn't move.

The warning blared from the speaker again. "Guardian vessel, identify yourself or we will open fire."

Realizing it was a losing battle, Jonah obliged his godfather and settled down.

Marcus nodded and hurried to the cockpit. He partially blocked Jonah's view as he leaned between the forward chairs. "Can I speak to them?"

The top of Mike's head, visible above the back of the co-pilot's chair, bobbed in affirmation. "Yes."

Jonah imagined his friend adjusting a set of controls.

Eventually, Marcus nodded and cleared his throat. "This is Marcus Armstrong, member of the Alliance Council. We've just escaped from the Central Archives."

The sound of a hushed conversation issued from the hidden speakers before the original voice returned. "Is the courier with you?"

Marcus exchanged a troubled glance with Kevin before saying, "I'm afraid I have sad news to deliver. The courier is dead."

A semi-transparent window opened, taking up the entire forward-view glass and showing the angry visage of an attractive young female rebel pilot. Her almond-shaped eyes narrowed, taking in Marcus and the group. "What happened?"

"The Grand Oracle killed him." Kevin's answer produced more shocked outburst from someone off-screen. "We have his soul."

The pilot's eyes widened, but she recovered quickly. "Give it to us."

Marcus shook his head. "I'm here as a representation of the Alliance Council and at invitation from your Elder. Do we have permission to proceed to your base? We will only hand over the courier's soul to the Elder. That was his final request."

The pilot turned in her seat, whispering to someone else again.

Jonah feared they would demand the courier's soul bottle anyway and then shoot them out of the sky.

Perhaps Mike sensed the same thing because he raised the spirit bottle into view. The pilot sat straighter in her seat. At the same time the person off-screen, a red-haired man, squeezed into view. The look of sadness in the man's eyes got to Jonah. It was clear he must have known Trevor.

Marcus gripped the back of Mike's seat. "This young man is a true Seeker." Marcus motioned toward the back of the craft. "And we have the Deliverer with us. Both young men befriended the courier and fought beside him. They share your loss."

The pilot's eyes snapped to Marcus. Now that she wasn't glaring at them, Jonah could see her eyes were a deep aquamarine and complimented her golden skin tone.

She shifted her gaze to the red-haired man, waiting for his decision. When he nodded, she turned back to Marcus. "Follow us. May the Deliverer quicken your journey."

The connection was cut. Mike tucked the bottle away and touched the ship's controls. It shuddered and begin to move, following the lead rebel ship.

Jonah relaxed as much as he could, but he also worried about the rebels' reaction when they reached the base. Would their awe wear off and the anger return? Trevor had touched a lot of lives, judging from the reactions. In a way, Jonah regretted ever doubting the boy.

Maybe he could ask Mike about Trevor when they returned home. That seemed so far away, even now. Jonah shifted his gaze out to the cockpit and the viewport. A squat mountain on the far side of a high plateau grew larger. Jonah called on the fading vestiges of Trevor's memories. *That's it.*

A wide rectangular opening near the top of the mountain turned out to be a hangar bay.

Kevin glanced at Mike. "Can you land us?"

"No problem." Despite the sluggish controls and the constant rattles from the craft, Mike guided the damaged ship through the bay opening and landed with a soft thunk.

Kevin patted the back of Mike's seat. "Not bad for a geek."

Mike shrugged and everyone left the craft to meet the rebels. Jonah consented to a helping hand from Kevin while Marcus helped Trueblood, but in short order, Jonah and Mike were standing side by side in front of the assembled crowd.

Guardians, Archivists, and other Afterworld citizens had gathered in the rebel hangar to greet them.

The red-haired man from the rebel ship stepped forward with the young female pilot in tow. Jonah was surprised to see the man wore the uniform of Spire Guardian. "Where's the courier's soul bottle?" he demanded. A few of the gawking people seconded the man's question.

Jonah nudged Mike to pull out the soul bottle. When he refused, Jonah whispered, "It was Trevor's last wish."

Mike's face paled. He took the bottle from his pocket but passed it to Jonah and crossed his arms, hugging himself.

The rebel Guardian reached out and touched the bottle but didn't take it. "I was there when the Grim Guards attacked the meeting. I… I trained young Trevor." The man sucked in a breath to steady himself. Then he gazed at Jonah. "Truly, you are the Deliverer." He gave Jonah a respectful bow.

"Trevor," Jonah gulped, "I mean, the courier told me to bring his soul to the Elder."

The rebel Guardian straightened. "It is right that his soul ascend to the final plane." He motioned to a double door behind him. "The Elder awaits you."

"Marcus." Trueblood pointed to her injured ankle. "I'll never make the walk."

The female pilot raised her hand and motioned to someone near the back of the crowd. A woman in a plain white tunic moved through the people and over to Trueblood. From her way of inspecting the mage's ankle, Jonah guessed the woman must be a doctor or Healer.

She beckoned over a couple of men to help Trueblood to a side room.

When she saw Jonah's bloodied tunic, she paused. "You should come for treatment."

"No." Jonah didn't mean to yell but his voice rattled the hangar. People backed away, frightened. *Most won't understand and some will even fear you.* Jonah sucked in a deep breath to calm himself, but his voice still echoed with the words of past Deliverers when he spoke. "I have to see the Elder."

No one objected this time and the rebel Guardian and pilot led Jonah's group from the hangar. The Guardian remained stoic, but the young pilot's movements took on a reverent aura the further into the heart of the mountain the journeyed. She would glance back at Jonah and then hurriedly turn forward again. He didn't like it. The rebels already used his name as a parting blessing. What else could there be?

Soon, Jonah and his group stood before a large door made of smooth, dark stone. The pilot pushed the door open. She and the Guardian bowed, and motioned for everyone else to proceed.

Kevin peeked. "Wow." He entered with Mike right behind him.

Jonah paused at the opening to face the young pilot. "You aren't coming?"

The pilot met his gaze for a split second before averting her eyes. "We may not view his true face." She cast a quick glance at the Guardian for confirmation and then bowed again.

Marcus guided Jonah through the door. His breath caught because the cavern was beautiful. The floor was a deep emerald green, and glossy. But his feet didn't slip as he moved forward.

Toward the center of the space, seven pillars rose from the floor to the ceiling. Each had semi-transparent sides with multiple glowing white objects swirling around the interiors. The light from the objects hit the royal blue and violet patterns on the pillars and created ever-moving shapes on the walls.

"Awesome." Jonah's voice was hushed, as seemed proper in this place. The pillars reminded him of large soul bottles. Going on that idea, he let his Reaper side surge forward. "These are souls."

Marcus stopped in his tracks. "Are you sure?"

Jonah held his hand toward the nearest of the strange containers. Not only were these souls, they were powerful. "Yeah. I can feel them."

Kevin's hand hovered near his blades. "Remember the bottles in the Grand Oracle's place? I bet these are trapped souls."

As if in response to Kevin's words, the souls swirled around faster, emitting brighter light.

A deep baritone voice rolled from the shadows. "They are not trapped souls." The source, a tall, barrel-chested man, stepped into view. He wore bellowing robes of pale gold and matching sandals on his feet. The sash around his middle was emerald green like the floor. His snow white beard stood out in stark contrast to his ebony skin. And to Jonah's amazement, the man wore glasses.

The image of a wizened grandfather popped into Jonah's mind. As this being strode toward them in a dignified manner, the increased illumination from the swirling lights reflected off his bald head.

"These are ancient souls who've volunteered to stay behind and offer guidance to our resistance. I meditate and commune in harmony with them." He frowned at Kevin. "The soul bottles you witnessed are the Rulers of the Afterworld's perversion of the communing ritual."

Marcus had placed himself between the newcomer, Jonah, and Mike. He inclined his head to the man. "Prime Archivist. Or should I say Elder?"

The man took his time before nodding. "My real name is Prime Archivist Aristobulus, High Master of the remote Rocky Plateau Archives."

"That's a big title," Kevin whispered to Jonah as he crossed his arms, watching the man.

Jonah heard the awe in Kevin's quip and shared it.

"I never had the pleasure of meeting you, Elder, before my fall." Marcus moved aside to reveal Jonah and Mike. "This is Jonah Blackstone."

The Elder nodded, eager. "Yes, the Deliverer." His eyes shifted to Mike. "And you?"

"He's a Seeker."

Aristobulus pushed his glasses up on his nose and inspected Mike. "That is a remarkable honor, young man. There hasn't been a true Seeker in over two thousand years." He stood tall and patted his chest. "In fact, the last one was me."

Mike gawked at the man. "You're a Seeker?"

"Oh, not anymore. I worked with the last Deliverer toward the end. When he finished his work, my ability to open the inner compass faded." He held out a hand to Mike, but Jonah pulled the compass from his own pocket.

The Elder took it and caressed the device like a beloved possession. "The ability is temporary and bestowed on the one who's to help the Deliverer. I retained enough power to help your parents."

Marcus grunted.

Jonah gaped at the Elder. "You put the codes in the compass, didn't you?"

"Yes. I was able to enter the primary or surface level codes but not touch the inner compass."

Mike stirred. "And you helped Jonah's parents find the Protector's Ring and the Enhancer?"

The Elder bowed like he was happy that someone acknowledged that feat.

Jonah glanced at his godfather, who wore a pained expression. "Did you know my dad worked with the Elder?"

"No I didn't." Marcus worked his jaw. "It explains a lot and leads to many more questions."

Jonah blinked at his godfather's sudden anger. Strangely enough, he thought about Marcus and his dad and the final days of his parents. Marcus had accused his dad of not sharing information because his dad had worked with the Elder in secret.

All at once, Jonah had that perfect moment when an unpleasant but forgotten memory snaps into place. *The Elder.* He'd also been the one his father called for back in the chamber before Deyanira attacked. Jonah was sure of it, and had been ever since Trevor called the man Elder. Only now did he make the connection.

He activated one of Lynn's blades and waved it at the Prime Archivist while shouting, "You let my parents die!"

CHAPTER FORTY-ONE
THE ELDER

Kevin, the first to overcome his initial shock, grabbed Jonah around the waist.

Jonah continued to yell. "It's his fault."

Marcus stared at his godson, confused. "Jonah?"

"No! You don't get it." Jonah struggled in Kevin's grip. "My parents called for him the night they died." He pointed a blade at the Prime Archivist. "Didn't they? You're the Elder my dad called. But you didn't show up and the Grim Reaper killed them!"

Marcus turned on the man. "Is that true?"

"Yeah, it is!" Jonah shouted.

The Prime Archivist held up his hands and shocked Jonah when he nodded in agreement. "The young man is not totally wrong. I did not come when his father called."

"Why not?" Kevin asked, releasing Jonah.

"I couldn't return to that place. It had been compromised and I had already crossed to the Afterworld. Isaiah knew that, as well as the risks in rebelling against the Grim Reaper."

"You let them die," Jonah shouted.

"I could not have helped, young man. The Grim Reaper is more powerful than I am. Only the Grand Oracle could stand against him and they have common cause, for now."

Jonah's hands shook with anger and the fresh reminder of his loss. Marcus squeezed his shoulder.

Mike turned on the Prime Archivist. "Why couldn't you come back and help Jonah's parents?"

"I had to protect my identity and the rebellion on this side." The Prime Seeker exchanged a worried glance with Marcus. "I am sorry."

Marcus grimaced like he had a bad taste in his mouth. "I can't say I agreed with the secrecy, but I understand." He turned Jonah so they faced each other. "It's the reason we have the Alliance, Jonah. Our fight is in the mortal world. Your father understood that."

Jonah wanted to hate the Elder, and he did feel anger toward him. But even Marcus accused his father of doing things on his own. Jonah opened himself to a Reaper stare and then subjected the Elder to it. The man vibrated sincerity and conviction. But underneath, Jonah sensed falsehood.

Mike must have seen it too because he stirred and pointed at the man. "You're not the leader."

"He's right," Jonah joined in. "You're not the Elder, are you?" The anger threatened to return. Was this man covering for the one who could have helped his parents?

A tense silence filled the chamber until the Elder let out a long breath. In response, the seven containers glowed brighter and in the midst of the brilliance, short silhouettes appeared. After the light show faded, seven diminutive figures remained. The souls had taken on human forms.

As one, they stepped through the container walls and floated toward the group. Jonah tensed as the apparitions zeroed in on him and Mike. Each soul had aged skin and wizened features. The tallest was still shorter than Jonah.

At first glance, he mistook the dark skin tone and hanging garments for those of African Pygmies. But another name popped into Jonah's mind. His parents once told him about a short people called the Twa. *Yes*, Jonah thought. *An ancient, wise, and diminutive people.*

There were seven Elder Souls in all; four female and three male. Four, two female and two males, surrounded Jonah while the remaining three converged on Mike.

When the Elder soul in front of Jonah spoke, it was with a blending of multiple voices. "We are the Elders." Their combined voices were similar to a well-tuned choir speaking in unison, but each voice carried a different note of a chord. "As you can see, we could not cross to your realm to help your parents. We are sorry for their loss."

Jonah gulped, not needing his Reaper stare to sense the truthfulness emanating from these souls.

"You are a Deliverer," the Elder intoned. It touched Jonah's chest with an ethereal hand. He stilled himself for the coldness associated with a Wraith's touch. In this instant, the contact was warm and calming.

Jonah's lingering pain from his injuries disappeared as well as his anger, sense of betrayal, and loss. He drew in a

startled breath, feeling whole and energized. "Thank you."
The Elder nodded.

A female Elder pointed to Mike. "He is indeed a true
Seeker. He'll be able to consecrate new designation stones,
if he believes in his power."

Mike stiffened when the woman pressed her palm to
his chest. But after a moment, he relaxed, allowing the
three beings to crowd around and touch him. The tableau
reminded Jonah of a blessing ceremony, or the laying-on-
of-hands from his aunt's church.

"He is in great pain over the loss of our courier." The
female Elder withdrew her hands. "We also share your pain,
young one, but the courier's soul will move on to its final
plane of existence." She spread her short arms, indicating
the cavern. "This is all an illusion. The true existence is
out there, when you ascend. Therefore, we celebrate the
courier's ascension."

Marcus motioned to Jonah. "Give them Trevor's soul."

Jonah withdrew the spirit bottle while thinking about
the Elder's words. They touched something deep inside
him. He gazed at the pillars. "You aren't trapped. You can
come and go, to the other plane?"

The Elder's eyes brightened like two pinpoint stars. The
effect was a thousand times more powerful than a Reaper
Stare. Jonah knew his very soul was exposed to the being.
"You are perceptive. The energy pattern, or spirit of the
Deliverer, truly rests on you."

Aristobulus lifted the offered container from Jonah's
hands. "Come."

Jonah assumed the invitation for him and the others because the Elders had already floated away between the seven pillars. They converged on the round fountain at the center of the cavern.

The Prime Archivist spoke in a voice like a teacher. "Spirits are energy patterns, young one. Have you ever wondered about geniuses in art, music, science, or political movements who seem to appear in every age? They are honored with the spirit energies of those disciplines, eternal patterns that appear when needed."

The pool of dark liquid in the fountain began to glow at the wave of the Prime Archivist's hand. "Deliverer and Seeker are names given to the energy patterns that come whenever the need arises and anoint the chosen vessels for a given time. You and your friend have those powers."

The Prime Archivist turned to Mike and frowned. "Your pain is the deepest. Would you prefer the honors?"

Mike took the place of honor beside the Prime Archivist. "What do I do?"

"Hold it above the pool." Aristobulus waved a hand over the water. "This is the well of souls, a natural pathway to the next plane."

Following the directions, Mike held Trevor's spirit bottle over the glowing liquid. The Elders joined hands and sang a peaceful hymn. The words were ancient and unknown, but the voices mixed in beautiful harmonies and touched Jonah's soul with peace and hope.

Mike's breath hitched in his chest and tears rolled down his cheek. When the Elders reached the climax of the hymn the bottle bucked in Mike's hand and Trevor's soul emerged. It hovered in front of Mike, who reached out and brushed his fingers against it. For a moment, the soul brightened.

A glistening shaft of light appeared, extending from the waters to the ceiling. Trevor's soul zipped around Jonah and the others one time and then zoomed up and into the light. After a short interval, the light winked out, plunging the pool into dimness again.

Jonah hooked an arm around Mike's trembling shoulders.

Mike shook his head. "I'm okay." He met Jonah's worried gaze. "Trevor said goodbye."

"It is done," the Elder souls intoned. They separated, each re-entering their crystalline container and giving up the human forms.

The Prime Archivist turned to Marcus. "I believe we have details to cover before you return to the mortal realm?"

Marcus inclined his head. "Yes, we do."

As he and the Prime Archivist walked away, deep in discussion, Jonah and Mike moved to one of the low benches lining the wall. The seats were wide and had thin cushions on them.

Mike perched on the edge of one, and Jonah joined him. Kevin hovered nearby, but far enough away to give them privacy. Jonah thought of asking Mike if he was really okay but was afraid of the answer.

After a long silence, Mike spoke. "I always knew what you were, but… to see you take someone's soul was…" He hugged himself while staring at his feet.

"Trevor asked me to do it. And I didn't take his soul."

"I know." Mike glanced at Jonah. "You almost lost control with Ramsey. I don't blame you."

"You think I'm an abomination?" Jonah didn't bother to hide his growing anger at the situation.

"I didn't say that." Mike pitched his voice lower. "I saw how afraid Marcus and Kevin were of you."

"Yeah, so did I." The thought pained Jonah. Not only had he frightened the rebels, he had also frightened Kevin and his own godfather. In a way, the Grand Oracle and the Grim Reaper were also afraid of him. Why else would they want him dead? "I scare everyone." Jonah's voice quivered.

He raised his hands, staring at them while recalling the sensation of pulling power from Ramsey. Is this what it means to have the spirit energy of the Deliverer inside of you?

Mike nudged Jonah's arm. "I'm not afraid of you."

The sincerity of Mike's words touched Jonah and helped to dispel his dark mood. "We're gonna be cool?"

Mike took a long time to answer. "Yeah. I need time to get over losing Trevor."

When Mike offered him a weak smile, Jonah's belief they would be cool with each other increased. He needed that. He didn't want to be alone with this heaviness of history and purpose. He suspected Mike didn't either.

Kevin stirred and moved closer to the boys, drawing Jonah's attention. He also noticed Marcus approached along with the Prime Archivist, who also held a thick book.

Mike blinked in surprise when the man offered him the book. He took it and ran his hands over the leather cover. "The Deliverer's Tales?"

The Prime Archivist smiled and patted the cover of the book. "I was there when the last Deliverer finished this." He turned to Jonah. "You're the new Deliverer and will need this book. Your friend is your Seeker and will translate it for you."

Kevin peered at the cover. "What will it tell them?"

The Prime Archivist met their combined gazes. "How to defeat the Rulers of the Afterworld."

CHAPTER FORTY-TWO
PARTING TOKEN

"What we need is our own portal." Kevin's statement ground the meeting with the rebels to a halt. He and Marcus stood in the rebel's staging area, in the midst of an argument with them about the risk of a journey to the Afterworld's pedestal room.

The problem was that the location of the chamber was close to the Grim Reaper's realm, and that worried many of the rebels. With no other option for returning Jonah's group home, Marcus wanted his godson to step in as the Deliverer and command the rebels to do it.

Jonah had resisted, not wanting to risk any more lives, nor encounter Deyanira again. That's when Kevin intervened.

The young Fallen Reaper shrugged. "Even if we secured the pedestal location on this side, Mike and Jonah are the only ones who can activate the ancient portals. We can't snatch them away to the desert cave whenever we need them." He glanced at Marcus. "Can we?"

Mike raised his hand. "I don't mind."

Marcus smiled at him. "Kevin's right. Having our own portal would allow us to connect directly to the portal you have here."

Mike wilted at that announcement. Since receiving the book, his attitude about the whole Seeker thing had changed.

"This presents us with an additional problem," Marcus concluded, stroking his chin.

Jonah leaned close. "So you don't want me to order them to do it?"

Marcus frowned at him, but Jonah didn't mind because he had a solution and the idea was simple as well as deserving. Plus, it would avoid going near the Grim Reaper's domain, at least for now.

He stood and everyone went quiet. The rebel Guardians sat straighter, waiting for his words. He gulped, reminded that they saw the Deliver almost as a religious figure. "Do you have something to stick the compass to a surface?"

After staring blankly at Jonah for half a second, the rebel pilot who had challenged their group earlier snapped her fingers and exited the staging chamber. She returned a minute later and handed Jonah a putty-like material.

"We use this to attach things to rocky surfaces. Will that work?"

"Perfect." Jonah hefted the malleable material in his hand.

Marcus raised an eyebrow. "What are you planning?"

Jonah grinned at his godfather. "I know where we can get a portal."

As soon as Jonah's group stepped through Deyanira's portal, Trueblood erected a protective shield.

Deyanira and several of her Grimnions hurried into the amphitheater moments after the group arrived. Her eyes widened in disbelief. The shock only lasted a second before the sorceress recovered and attacked with lightning and fire.

Trueblood didn't break a sweat as she fed power to her shield.

Jonah slapped the putty to the side of the portal and turned to Mike. "Do your thing."

Mike pressed the compass into the material. The code for the Deliverer's cavern was already entered. As Mike pressed the green activate button, Jonah turned and waved to an outraged Deyanira. The amphitheater disappeared before the evil Reaper's last barrage of spells could engulf them.

Jonah's group created a commotion when they appeared inside the Deliverer's cavern. Rubio, who had been in the process of entering the opening to the lower chamber, stopped in mid-motion, slack-jawed.

Jonah couldn't resist patting the side of the portal and saying, "Special delivery, from Deyanira."

Along with the portal, a bound and gagged Ramsey returned with the group.

Rubio grunted in surprise as he moved closer to inspect the agent. "I think the GBI will have a time identifying Ramsey. He's aged so much."

Trueblood crossed her arms, scrutinizing Marcus. "Interesting. I didn't realize the binding patterns slowed down the aging process."

Marcus frowned at her. "I told you. The trauma of *losing* his power had more to do with the aging."

Trueblood wore a rare smile on her face. "Rex confessed to me a year ago."

Marcus refused to meet her gaze, but he smirked. "The first person to mention this to Omar will get the worst assignments for a year."

Everyone laughed as the other Alliance people converged on the away team, the name Jonah and Mike had started calling the group.

*

The Alliance Council decided not to parade Jonah and the others around HQ. Marcus said Jonah's Afterworld dream-walk had convinced the group of the mole's existence. Until the Alliance could discover the mole's identity, they opted to send select personnel to the Guest House and question the group.

Kevin, Jonah, and Mike were shuffled from endless meetings and debriefings about the adventure. First, Rubio reviewed and recorded their individual narratives for the Alliance Council. Then various department representatives concerned with different aspects of the supernatural world asked their own questions.

After all that, Jonah had to tell his cousins and Wick all about the trip. Lynn grumbled because she missed out. Wick displayed equal parts wow and envy at not being present to witness mage Trueblood in action. Robert professed his simple relief at his little cousin returning unharmed.

Despite their denials, Jonah suspected his cousins and Wick had spent the bulk of their time playing video games while he risked his life in the Afterworld. He didn't mind because he wanted to get his own time on the deluxe gaming systems before heading home.

That's exactly what Jonah did. He was into his fourth round, blasting through enemy fighters on the screen and beating his cousin Robert when Kevin and Mike entered the basement. Mike slumped into a big armchair, looking tired. Jonah understood because Mike had to endure a series of separate tests to determined any lingering symptoms from the Enhancer's mind boost.

Jonah set his game controller down. "How're you doing, Mike?"

"Fine." Mike screwed up his face despite his answer. "My mind is still going ninety miles an hour." He tapped his forehead. "Maybe the Elders or the compass did something to me."

Jonah nodded. "Don't forget the mind boost."

"How can I? It's weird. I... I started watching the Spanish channel."

"So..."

"I don't understand Spanish, but I followed the show." Mike looked perplexed. "When a commercial came on and I saw the text in Spanish, I realized what was happening."

"Wow, Mike. That's great." Jonah winced at the forced cheerfulness in his own voice.

"It's not." Mike frowned.

"We're all different. That's what you said," Jonah smiled.

Kevin snorted at the comment and sat on the couch beside Jonah.

Lynn, who reclined on a facing sofa with her brother, nudged Kevin's foot with her own. "Well, are they done with Jonah and Mike?"

Jonah sat up straighter, wanting to hear the answer.

Kevin shrugged. "Yeah, they are. Marcus is on his way here."

They didn't have to wait long before Marcus descended the steps. The tall Fallen Reaper paused, looking around the basement.

Mike gasped and pointed at a thick brown paper package in Marcus's hand. "The Deliverer's Tales?"

Marcus nodded and held out the bundle. "Yes."

Mike ripped off the packaging and let out a sigh as his fingers moved across the ancient cover. "We thought you were going to keep it?"

"It's coded and only you can translate it."

"Thank you, Mr. Armstrong." Mike opened the book and started reading. Robert and Wick huddled close to peek at the ancient book over Mike's shoulder.

Marcus wore a bemused expression on his face before announcing, "We promised your parents a fun yet educational tour of Monarch Associate's internship program. We should do that to keep up appearances."

Jonah couldn't believe he'd forgotten about the cover reason for coming to Atlanta. "When?"

"We'll get started tomorrow. Tonight, just relax and have fun. Pizzas are on me, although Mabel complained about wanting to cook everyone a decent meal."

Jonah's godfather remained true to his word. And the group relaxed, enjoyed pizza, movies, games, and just general silliness. Lynn spent increasing amounts of time on the phone to Rico. Wick did the same with Tamara.

Jonah wasn't the only one to notice. Mike did also, and that would inevitably lead to one of his bouts of quiet time. Each time, Robert would warn Jonah to give Mike space.

The next morning, the group visited the Monarch Associates building in northern Atlanta. They attended a genuine presentation on the internship program, given by people Jonah suspected didn't know about the Alliance.

After a flurry of phone calls home for permission to stay a few extra days, Marcus let the kids decide the attractions in and around Atlanta they wanted to see. Jonah enjoyed the outings so much, the trip to the Afterworld began to recede in his thoughts. Even Mike overcame his reoccurring periods of sullenness and started joking around.

All too soon, the time came for Jonah and his crew to head home to Mount Vernon. A quiet excitement filled the air as everyone gathered their bags on the morning of the departure.

Lynn stopped in his doorway, her bag slung over a shoulder. "You may be the Deliverer, but we're not waiting for you to drag around."

Jonah stuck out his tongue at his cousin.

She held up a fist. "I'm ready to get back to the blog."

"You mean Rico?" Despite taunting his cousin, mention of the clubhouse brought up an unpleasant worry for Jonah. "Do you think they're gonna take the attic from us?"

Lynn shook her head. "Marcus didn't tell you?"

"Tell me what?"

"When he replaced our computers last summer, Monarch Associates made an additional donation of computers to the center. In exchange, the director signed a agreement to lease us the attic. Unless they give us a location of equal size, we get to keep the space."

Jonah let out a relieved laugh. "That's cool. I bet her supervisor wasn't happy."

"He wasn't. Someone from Monarch went down there with the signed agreement. It's why Marcus was angry with Rex. We were always in the clear." Lynn pointed at Jonah's bag. "Get moving or I'll have Rico give you laps around the practice field when we get home."

"Ha, ha." Jonah zipped his own bag closed and left his room.

Mike, Wick, and his cousins were already there, along with Kevin. Jonah noticed at once that the Fallen Reaper wasn't smiling. Kevin also didn't have a travel bag. A horn honked from outside. Lynn peered out the open door and motioned the others to follow.

When Jonah reached the door, he didn't head outside. Instead, he sat his own bag down.

Kevin gave him a sideway glance. "Your ride is here."

"You aren't coming back with us." He didn't phrase it as a question because he knew what Kevin would say.

"Nah. I'm off on another assignment."

"After all we did? Can't you get the Council to let you stay?"

"When you and Mike proved how special you were, Mandara became more of a pain about his people watching you."

Jonah kicked his bag in frustration. "I want you to stay."

"You can't get everything you want, Jonah."

"Why not?" Jonah looked into Kevin's serious face. "I'm the Deliverer. Mike's the Seeker. They need us. I can tell the Council you have to stay or–"

Kevin whirled on Jonah, shocking him. "Or what? You'll start making demands? That's not the way to act." The older boy's control slipped as his raw emotion spilled out. "You think I want to leave?" He snatched up Jonah's bag and crushed it in his grip while taking a deep breath.

"You were right, okay? I don't have any friends and…" Kevin faltered, staring out at the other kids around the van. "I can be myself with you."

Jonah was stunned by the boy's honesty and the knowledge that Kevin was just as angry about the separation. The difference was that Kevin as an Alliance member, had a job to do. "I'm sorry."

Kevin leaned against him. "I'll be back in a few months. I promise."

The goose bumps raced up and down Jonah's arms. The same effect appeared on Kevin's darker skin.

The boy slapped a hand over his forehead. "I need to stop making promises around you."

Jonah latched onto the comment in hopes of stalling the inevitable. "Why?"

"You'll learn one day."

Jonah crossed his arms. "Tell me now."

"Nope, little man."

Kevin hefted Jonah's carry bag in one hand and used his other to push Jonah outside and down the front steps to the van. He stowed Jonah's bag in the back and closed the rear door.

Jonah waited by the passenger sliding door. When Kevin came around, they touched fists.

Kevin smirked. "I'd tell you to behave yourself, but I know that won't happen."

"Funny." After a second goodbye wave, Jonah climbed inside the van.

Robert, Lynn, and Wick took the first two rows of seats. Mike had climbed in the very back, reading the Deliverer's Tales. Jonah joined his friend and stared out the side window at Kevin as the shuttle pulled away from the Guest House.

While his cousins and Wick begin to talk about what they planned for the rest of the summer, Jonah remained quiet. Once again, the deep certainty Kevin would keep his promise returned. Concentrating on the sensation helped to beat back the sadness Jonah experienced over their parting.

Fifteen minutes into the trip home, Mike snapped the old book closed and rested it on his lap. He pulled out his phone, fiddled with it for a few minutes, and then showed Jonah the screen. His buddy had pulled up the list of summer movies.

"We missed a lot." Mike scrolled through the information on his phone's screen. "Let's catch up when we get back."

Jonah grinned and in no time, they dived into all the reviews and info about the latest sci-fi, fantasy, and action releases. Maybe they did have the eternal spirits of the Deliverer and Seeker resting on their shoulders. But right then, they were like any other teenage sci-fi geeks planning the rest of their summer.

The shuttle reached Mount Vernon before either Mike or Jonah realized it. The first stop was Wick's house. Tamara waited for the young mage at the driveway.

Next was the Littleton's. Mike's spirits seemed better to Jonah as he got out at his home.

"Call me." Mike waved his cell phone before heading inside.

The Hightowers' home was the last stop. Rico leaned against his tricked-out car as the shuttle pulled to a stop. Jonah laughed because Aunt Imma hated that car.

Robert retrieved his bag and headed inside after a wave to Rico. Lynn wasted no time pulling their bags out of the back, hurrying to Rico and hugging him.

Ignoring them, Jonah reached for his own bag, only to discover something clipped to it. He turned the bag around and found his dad's Alliance badge fastened to the bag's strap. A note was also attached. Jonah ripped that loose and read it.

I got this from Marcus. Be good.

K.

Jonah smiled at Kevin's thoughtful gesture as he unhooked the gleaming badge and slipped it in a pocket. It was odd, but in a way, his dad's old Alliance badge represented as much to Jonah as the either Protector's Ring or Seeker's Compass.

John Darr is a native of the state of Georgia. As a graduate of Columbus State University with a B.A. in Communications, and with work on his M.F.A. degree at Howard University in Washington, D.C., John has over twenty years of experience as a writer, screenwriter, independent filmmaker, and educational television producer. He loves long walks in picturesque locales, playing tennis, and helping others realize their creative dreams. John currently resides in Arlington, VA. Visit him online at www.johndarrbooks.com.

www.ingramcontent.com/pod-product-compliance
Lightning Source LLC
Chambersburg PA
CBHW032134110726
47902CB00003B/573